Award-winning *USA TODAY* bestselling author **Yvonne Lindsay** has always preferred the stories in her head to the real world. Married to her blind-date sweetheart and with two adult children, she spends her days crafting the stories of her heart. In her spare time she can be found with her nose firmly in someone else's book.

A *USA TODAY* bestselling author, **Robin Covington** loves to explore the theme of fooling around and falling in love in her books. When she's not writing, she's collecting tasty man candy, indulging in a little comic book geek love, hoarding red nail polish and stalking Chris Evans. Robin is a 2016 RITA® Award nominee, and her books have won the National Readers' Choice and Golden Leaf Awards and finalled for the RT Reviewers' Choice Award, the Booksellers' Best Award and the Award of Excellence. She lives in Maryland with her hilarious husband, her two brilliant children (they get it from her, of course!), and her beloved fur babies, Dutch and Dixie Joan Wilder. Drop her a line at robin@robincovngtonromance.com —she always writes back.

D1142634

SEDUCING THE LOST HEIR

YVONNE LINDSAY

TAKING ON THE BILLIONAIRE

ROBIN COVINGTON

MILLS & BOON

First Published in Great Britain 2020
by Mills & Boon, an imprint of HarperCollinsPublishers,
1 London Bridge Street, London, SE1 9GF

Seducing the Lost Heir © 2020 Dolce Vita Trust
Taking on the Billionaire © 2020 Robin Ray Coll

ISBN: 978-0-263-28012-8

1220

MIX
Paper from
responsible sources
FSC™ C007454

This book is produced from independently certified FSC™ paper to ensure responsible forest management.

For more information visit: www.harpercollins.co.uk/green

Printed and bound in Spain
by CPI, Barcelona

SEDUCING THE LOST HEIR

YVONNE LINDSAY

This book is dedicated to all the amazing people (including some of my own family) who had to stay on the front lines and put themselves at risk during the pandemic. I salute and thank you all!

One

She'd only had two glasses of champagne, but she was already beginning to feel a little buzzed. Definitely time to stop drinking alcohol. Honor Gould had learned the hard way, by watching her mom, what happened when buzzed turned to drunk and drunk turned to dangerous and stupid decisions.

The noise in the downtown Seattle hotel bar had reached deafening levels as conference delegates poured in. It never failed to amaze her to see so many people who could be totally professional in their day-to-day business get so messy when they let their hair down. She rarely let go of her rigid self-control, and certainly never among strangers. No, Honor had a plan, and getting a little too drunk or a little too loud was not anywhere on her list of things to do.

One of her fellow conference delegates passed her a fresh glass of champagne. Honor shook her head.

"No, thanks, I've had enough," she said firmly.

"Aw, come on. It's not every year you get to celebrate

being commercial interior designer of the year," the guy protested, pushing the flute of sparkling golden liquid back in her direction.

To shut him up, Honor accepted the glass and lifted it in a toast, but the glass never made it to her lips.

"Thank you," she said with a smile that masked her irritation.

"That's more like it," he said. Then, to her relief, he turned his attention to a new group of people coming into the bar, their raucous laughter filling the air.

Honor moved away from the crowd to find a quieter spot at the end of the bar. From here she could do her usual observations before heading up to the room she'd booked to ensure she'd be fresh for the early session she was presenting tomorrow morning before going into work. She doubted the session would be particularly well attended, given that many of her fellow conference goers would likely need to sleep in after tonight. But that didn't bother her. She was mostly interested in adding the presentation to her résumé. After dragging herself up from the gutters her mother had been satisfied dwelling in, Honor was on a trajectory to success and wealth of the kind she'd perpetually dreamed as a little girl. The award at the dinner tonight, her presentation at this prestigious conference—they were all tiny steps along the way to reaching her goals. To security. Comfort. Choices.

She put the untouched champagne flute on the bar behind her and ordered a sparkling mineral water from one of the bar staff, who were run off their feet with the steady influx of patrons. She'd drink her water and head back up to her room. No one would notice she was missing, and it would give her an opportunity to go over her notes for tomorrow again.

Honor had just received her drink and raised the glass to her lips for a sip when she felt a frisson of awareness send a trickle of heat down her spine. She turned slightly, her gaze instantly arrested by the arrival of a newcomer to the bar.

Keaton? He was here? Had he come to surprise her?

She couldn't believe her eyes. Her fiancé was not a man of spontaneous actions. When she'd told him she'd be at the hotel for the conference for two days, he'd merely nodded and continued with his work. When she'd invited him to attend the awards dinner as her plus-one, he'd mentioned some business dinner he couldn't get out of. And yet, here he was, heading past the bar toward a small table set against a wall.

He was a handsome man. A real head-turner. But Keaton always acted as if he was completely unaware of his appeal to others, and today was no exception. He looked tired. Shattered, in fact. He lowered his tall frame into a chair and looked up with a smile at the waitress who instantly approached him. Interesting that in a room packed full of patrons and potential tips, she made a beeline for Keaton, Honor thought with an ironic smile. She realized she was using the thumb of her left hand to twirl her engagement ring back and forth, like she always did when she was slightly anxious about something, and forced herself to stop.

There was an air of something different about him tonight that she couldn't quite put her finger on, but then she got it. He was dressed far too casually. Keaton Richmond was the kind of man who never dressed down—not even for a picnic. Not that they'd made a habit of casual al fresco dining, she conceded. But the leather jacket draped over his shoulders looked well worn and soft, as if he'd owned it for years. She didn't remember seeing it on him ever before, but then again, as they didn't live together, it wasn't as if she was privy to everything he had in his wardrobe.

He lifted his head and scanned the room, his eyes skimming past her before doubling back to give her another look.

She smiled at him. He didn't smile back initially, but then his lips curved into a half smile that sent a bolt of longing straight to her core. She straightened and was about to move toward him, but he turned his head and continued to survey the room before focusing his attention to the bar snacks menu standing on his table.

So, he was playing a game now, was he? Pretending he didn't even know her. Honor didn't know whether to be annoyed or intrigued. Maybe he'd actually listened the last time they'd had a discussion about where their relationship was heading. Goodness knew they hadn't had sex in months and, even then, it had been an outlet rather than an expression of devotion. She'd begun to wonder if all her hopes and dreams for her future were on the road to being dashed.

Keaton had been noncommittal when she'd suggested they spice things up in the bedroom, maybe even move in together before the wedding, for which they had yet to set a date. This limbo they'd allowed themselves to fall into had begun to niggle at her in ways it shouldn't have. She and Keaton had worked together at his family's firm since she'd joined it five years ago, and they'd begun to date two years ago. They'd gotten engaged eighteen months later.

It had hardly been the romance of the century, but then again, Honor had told herself she was never looking for romance. Look at where that had gotten her mom. No, when she'd won her role at Richmond Developments, she'd set her sights on the top of their corporate ladder, and if marrying the CEO's son would get her there faster, then she was prepared to do even that to reach her goal. Besides, it wasn't as if she didn't like or respect Keaton. They just needed to rekindle the spark now and then.

But games weren't his style.

So why was he playing one now?

It intrigued her on a level that made her want to play along and see exactly where this was headed. The waitress brought a tall lager over to Keaton's table. Again, he surprised her. She'd never known Keaton to drink beer. Not even on a hot summer's day. She continued to observe him as he lifted the frosted glass to his lips and tipped it up, taking long, steady gulps. She watched the muscles of his throat work as he swallowed, saw the moisture glistening on his lips as he set the glass down again. Felt the visceral tug of desire that pulled hard inside her as he licked his lips. He looked up again. Caught her eye.

He looked surprised to find her still staring at him, and he gave her that half smile again. Honor felt her nipples tighten into hard nubs that rubbed against the lace of her demi-cup bra. Wow. She couldn't remember when she'd felt this uncontrollably drawn to him. It was time to stop playing games and time to act. Honor reached into her clutch and extracted one of the two room key cards she'd been given at check-in and palmed it in her hand.

The woman sashayed across the room; there was no other way to describe it. She was dressed in a formfitting black cocktail dress with very interesting cutouts at the waist that fit as if it had been made for her. Logan watched as she determinedly made her way through the crowd. Several people tried to draw her into conversation, but she smoothly turned each attempt aside, her focus solely on him.

He'd had no sleep on the twelve-plus-hour flight that had left his home city of Auckland, New Zealand, at nine last night. On arrival in Los Angeles, he'd caught a connecting flight up to Seattle. Severely jet-lagged and trying desperately to adjust to a time zone that was twenty hours behind his own, he'd forced himself to go for a walk and stay awake on arrival. Now all he craved was a cold beer, a light meal and bed. He wasn't looking for polite conversation or company, but it looked as though company was coming, whether he wanted it or not.

And, he had to admit, she was a darn fine-looking woman. Her blond hair was long and thick and swept over one shoulder, the ends of it just reaching her breasts. Breasts he could see a glimpse of through the keyhole at the front of her dress. The garment was sophisticated and sexy. Even so, he'd bet it would look better off. Like on the floor of his hotel room.

Logan shook his head. *Nope, nope, nope.* He wasn't here for any of that. He was here to find his identity, however lame that sounded. Hell, he was a grown, thirty-four-year-old man. If he didn't know who he was by now, he was probably making a mess of his life. But he'd been confident he knew exactly who he was—right up until he'd found that box tucked away in the back of his late mom's wardrobe when he was clearing her house for sale. Everyone joked about finding skeletons in a closet after someone had passed away. He hadn't expected to be the skeleton.

A sense of frustration beat at the back of his mind. He'd spent his whole life calling Alison Parker Mom. But, as it turned out, she wasn't his mother. And now he was here in the United States to find the people who were his real parents and hoping like hell they'd accept him.

In his moment of reverie, the stunning creature in the killer black dress had drawn up closer to him. He felt her presence before he became fully aware of her intentions. Her hand caught his chin and tilted his face up to hers and then, quite shockingly, she kissed him.

At first Logan didn't respond—in fact, his overtired brain was in such a state of disbelief he couldn't even react, but then instinct won over. The silky softness of her lips on his sent every nerve in his body into screaming overload. His eyes slid closed, and he focused solely on the sensation of her mouth on his. On the feel of her tantalizing lips, and then on the thrilling texture of her tongue as she licked the seam of his mouth. All sound around them faded into nothing. All he could hear was the pounding of his blood through his veins as his heart rate went into double time. All he could smell was the sultry, spicy hint of her fragrance.

And then it was over. She was moving away. His eyes flicked open. He went to speak, but she put one forefinger against his lips.

"Don't say a word, lover. Room 6035. Meet me upstairs in ten minutes."

With that, she pressed a key card into his palm and walked away. He watched in stunned amazement as she continued out into the foyer and toward the elevator bank. Logan's fingers closed tight around the key card. There was no way in hell he was going to follow her upstairs. No way. Therein lay trouble for certain. He'd be drugged, have organs stolen and wake up in a bath packed with ice.

Or he'd have the best freaking night of his entire life.

The sliders and fries he'd ordered arrived, together with a second beer. He eyed them both before rapidly consuming the sliders and leaving the beer. No more alcohol for him. He needed a clear head. He flicked a glance at his watch. Ten minutes was up. He could still feel her lips on his own. Before he even realized he had reached a decision, Logan left a handful of bills on the table and was on his feet and walking toward the elevators.

He got out on the sixth floor and walked down the corridor, hesitating a moment outside room 6035. Then he raised the key card to the reader at the door. The light went green, and he stepped inside. The room was dimly lit, but he had no difficulty finding the enticing creature who'd kissed him senseless in the bar and then made him break with every ounce of common sense he'd ever possessed. What was he doing, coming to a stranger's hotel room like this?

The woman still wore her dress but had slipped off the killer heels.

"I'm glad you came," she said, walking toward him.

She wound her arms around his neck and reached up to kiss him. Again, that intoxicating blend of her fragrance wafted gently around him, seducing his senses into believing that coming here was a very, very good idea. Logan felt his entire body go up in flames. He wanted her like he'd wanted nothing else. Regret, doubt, confusion—those were all emotions for other people to worry about. Not him. Not now. Not here.

He slid his arms around her waist and pulled her in closer. He didn't feel the need to speak, had no desire to break the spell. He deepened the kiss, letting his tongue slide between her lips and experiencing the stimulating taste that was uniquely this woman. She splayed her hands through his short-cropped hair, her nails gently raking his scalp and sending tiny electric jolts through his entire body.

And then her hands were at his shoulders, sliding his leather jacket off and tugging at his shirt. He moved his hands to assist her and broke contact with her lips for only as long as it took him to tear the shirt up over his head and away from his overheated flesh. When their lips met again, he could feel the texture of her dress against his bare skin, but it wasn't enough. His hands slid around her back and up to the neckline of her dress, feeling for the zipper. Success! He caught the tab between a thumb and forefinger and slowly, slowly pulled it down.

Logan wrenched his mouth from hers and stepped away, not wanting to miss a moment of this reveal. At first the woman looked coy, as if she had suddenly grown shy, but then as he watched she lifted her hands to her shoulders and shrugged the top of her dress loose before letting it slide down her body. His breath caught in his throat at the sight of her. Honey-gold skin gleamed in the low light of the hotel room. Her breasts swelled and spilled over the half cups of her black bra, and a matching pair of briefs slung high on her hips, making her legs look as if they went on forever.

He swallowed against the sudden dryness in his mouth and stepped forward. He started to reach for her, his hands hesitating only an inch or so from her body. He could feel the heat pouring off her, a heat matched by his own body.

"May I?" he asked.

She smiled and ducked her head in a faint nod. It was all the encouragement he needed. He cupped her breasts through the lacy bra and thumbed the hard peaks of her nipples. A tiny gasp fell from the mystery woman's lips, and he captured it in another kiss. He couldn't seem to get enough of her. He eased the straps of her bra off her shoulders and pulled down one cup. Her nipple was a taut bud, and he pinched it lightly between his forefinger and his thumb. He felt the tremor that rippled through her.

"Is that okay?" he asked, his voice little more than a growl.

"More," she begged him.

He repeated the movement, then lowered his head to capture that deep rose-pink nub of flesh with his lips. Again, she shook and sighed. He laved her nipple with his tongue before nipping it lightly.

"More," she demanded now, her hands holding his head to her as if she couldn't bear for him to stop.

And nor could he. Everything about her called to him. Her scent, her taste, her husky pleas that were driving him mad. This all felt like some crazy dream, but he knew he didn't want to wake up. Reality would come back to bite him soon enough. For now, he'd take what he'd been freely offered. And he'd give in return.

Logan backed her against the bed and eased her onto the mattress. He stood between her legs and unbuckled his belt before kicking off his shoes and sliding down his jeans and socks. He didn't trust himself to remove his briefs just yet. Right now he felt as though he was primed and ready to blow. Her slightest touch would be his undoing, and there was no way he was wasting this opportunity. First of all, he was going to make absolutely certain that his mystery woman was with him all the way.

He hooked his fingers in the sides of her panties and slid them down her long, glorious legs. A neat triangle of dark blond hair nestled at the apex of her thighs; he hadn't seen anything quite as sexy in a very long time. Logan lowered himself over her body and reached under her to unsnap the fastening on her bra before easing the confection of lace away from her skin.

"Has anyone ever told you just how exquisitely beautiful you are?" he asked, skimming his hand lightly over the peaks of her breasts before cupping their full weight and squeezing gently.

"Only you," she said on a hoarse whisper, her eyelids fluttering closed as he began to kiss her breasts.

She was writhing beneath him, her hips straining against his. It was all he could do not to unleash his arousal and take her right then, but he was determined to do this right. To ensure she found her pleasure before he even considered taking his. He kissed a warm, wet trail down over her rib cage and to the center of her stomach before drawing a moist line to her belly button with his tongue. He swirled the tip of his tongue in the neat indentation before continuing lower.

He knelt on the floor beside the bed and leaned into her. His nostrils flared on the heated musky scent of her sex, and a pulse of demand bolted through him. He'd never been as completely aware of another human being as he was of this woman. He gently cupped the heated core of her body and felt her push against his palm, striving for more pressure.

"Impatient?" he asked softly.

He took his hand away and blew a stream of air over her mound and lower still. Her skin there glistened with moisture, and the waves of heat that poured off her almost scorched his fingertips as he let them drift around her entrance.

"You're torturing me," she moaned as he dipped one finger inside her.

"But it's a nice kind of torture, right?"

She clenched tight around him, and for a second all Logan could think about was what that tension would feel like around his penis. But it wasn't his time yet. First, he had to have her trembling with satiation and then he would lift her back up to the heights of physical pleasure all over again. He pressed his nose against her mound and inhaled her deeply, feeling her in every part of him. Then, using his tongue, he began to tease at her clitoris. At first it was just small darts of pressure, but then he began to swirl his tongue around the tight bead of nerve endings. Her breathing grew more rapid, and he looked up at her. Her head was pressed back against the mattress, and a light sheen of perspiration made her chest glisten. A rosy flush was spreading there and her nipples had drawn even more impossibly tight than they'd been before.

Logan eased another finger inside her, stroking her inside and driving her toward what he hoped would be her ultimate satisfaction. He never stopped with the movements of his tongue and then, when he felt she was on the verge of breaking apart, he closed his mouth around her clit and drew on it hard. She fractured beneath him. Her inner muscles squeezed his fingers in a rhythmic pulse that drove him wild. He waited until her body went lax before he moved.

"I didn't know you had that in you," she said in a voice laden with satisfaction.

"Oh, I've got more."

He reached for his trousers, slipped his wallet from his

pocket and dragged a condom out. It might be a cliché, but it always paid to be prepared. He quickly slid off his briefs and covered his length with the condom before standing, hooking her knees with his hands and scooting her to the edge of the bed.

"You still okay?" he said.

He'd stop here and now if she said no. It would likely be the toughest thing he'd ever done in his life, but he'd do it.

"Never better," she answered. "Do it. Do me."

He smiled as he positioned himself at her entrance. She was slick with her recent orgasm, and he was inside her in one easy glide. Logan squeezed his eyes shut and held on to the last remnants of his control as he felt her body adjust around him.

"What are you waiting for?" she asked, giving him a squeeze with her internal muscles.

"This," he said as he withdrew and surged back into her again.

At that point everything blurred; there was nothing else in the world except her body and his, joined in the most intimate way a man and woman could be joined. He pumped into her, and she met his every thrust with one of her own. Her breath came in gasps and her hands clutched the bedding beneath her. Logan forced his eyes open, forced himself to look at her, to imprint her image—like this, beneath him, as lost in him as he was lost in her.

He saw that flush creep over her chest again and knew she was close to coming. He had to see her into that sea of pleasure before he could let go. The pulse started deep inside her body, growing stronger with every surge until she peaked, and with it, he reached his climax, too. Again and again, his pleasure rocketed through him. Deep, intense and fiercely satisfying on a primal level.

Logan lowered himself onto her and rolled them both onto their sides. He was still inside her, could still feel her body and his, hearts beating to their perfect rhythm as their pleasure began to ebb and reality began to take its place. The woman raised one hand to his face, tracing his features and looking deep into his eyes.

"I didn't know we could be like this," she said. "That was—no, *you*—were perfect."

"We were perfect," he agreed.

He kissed her then, long and deep and slow. This wasn't the kind of thing he'd ever done before, but they'd both been willing partners and together they'd found a perfection not many had the pleasure of reaching on their first time together.

First and last, he reminded himself. He withdrew from her body and they lay there, their hearts and breathing returning to a normal tempo. He needed to clean up, so he rose from the bed and went through to the bathroom. When he returned, he noticed immediately that she had pulled the covers over herself and fallen fast asleep. While his instincts urged him to join her there, he saw the dismissal in her actions.

She'd had an itch, and he'd scratched it. No harm. No foul.

Logan reached for his clothing and quickly dressed. Leaving her key card on the bedside table, he switched off the light before letting himself out of the room.

He'd never see her again, but he'd never forget her, or this night, for as long as he lived.

Two

Honor woke early the next morning and stretched out in the bed. She reached across for Keaton and was disappointed, but not at all surprised, not to find him there. A large grin spread across her face. Last night had surpassed all her expectations. Even now her body tingled from the pleasure he'd given her.

When she'd suggested spicing things up in their relationship, she'd never expected him to take the suggestion to heart. Oh, sure, she knew he'd heard her when she'd somewhat nervously broached the subject a week or so ago, but when he'd barely even acknowledged her, she had shelved the request in the back of her mind. Keaton was, well, Keaton. Calm, sometimes pedantic and always controlled. Even last night he had remained controlled, but the role play had definitely been something new. Sex between them had always been perfunctory at best. Not to mention infrequent. In fact, she'd begun to fear he was considering breaking off their engagement. Pretending to be a stranger had been a brilliant idea. The way he'd explored her body had been as if it had all been entirely new to him. He'd even put on a bit of a barely discernable foreign accent in the few words they'd exchanged.

She brushed one hand across her breasts, remembering how his touch had felt. How the roughness of his beard had so deliciously abraded her skin. Keaton usually shaved twice a day and never went out with stubble, even though it had looked so darn sexy on him last night. She wondered if she'd be able to convince him to let himself go a little more often. To relax that incredibly strict control he had on himself. Maybe next time, she could play the stranger.

Honor giggled out loud as she considered various situations where she could fulfill the fantasy. The idea of Keaton taking charge and making her an offer she couldn't refuse, as she'd done with him last night, held massive appeal. She squirmed a little against the sheets, regretful that he wasn't here. She had been the recipient of all his attention last night, and she'd unashamedly been the taker. Next time she would show him, using the full extent of her imagination, just how grateful she was that he'd made the effort.

She turned her head and looked at the digital bedside clock. She'd have to get a move on if she was going to make her presentation this morning. She rose from the bed and went through to the bathroom, a new smile pulling at her lips as she spied the empty condom packet in the trash. Honor turned on the shower faucet and stepped under the spray without waiting for it to warm up. Right now, she needed to focus on the conference. Then, later today, she'd be back at work. Back to normal. Back to Keaton.

Anticipation thrummed through her veins. Hopefully last night was the beginning of something new and exciting for them. Her concerns that Keaton had become disengaged from her emotionally had been valid, she was sure of it. But whatever had caused the distance between them no longer seemed to be an issue.

If her worst fears had been realized and he'd broken off their engagement, she had no doubt she would have been expected to leave Richmond Developments. It wouldn't matter how many years she'd worked there. Douglas and Nancy Richmond were fiercely loyal to their children, Keaton and Kristin. Everything they did, they did for them, and it was well-known that Keaton, as the eldest, would assume his father's role as CEO when Douglas retired in two years' time. And it was Honor's hope that she would ascend the ranks to be his second in charge.

Childhood poverty had driven Honor's ambition. Watching her parents tear each other apart with their infidelity and then watching her mother's subsequent spiral into despair and guilt after Honor's dad had walked out for the last time had made Honor determined to never fall into that trap. It was why she had accepted Keaton's proposal. He was steady. There'd be no rapidly flaring emotions that escalated into nasty and vicious arguments. Theirs would be a marriage built on having the same dreams and goals for the future. On living life on a continuous trajectory to success and security.

She'd told herself she was happy with all of that. That it was exactly what she'd wanted all along. But with Keaton reluctant to set a date for the wedding, she'd begun to know fear, and with that fear had come the dreaded sense of insecurity she'd known all too well as a child.

Honor stepped out of the shower and dried herself and reached into her toiletry bag for the solitaire engagement ring Keaton had placed on her finger six months ago. Even his proposal had been one of stolid, pragmatic discussion. Afterward, they'd gone out together to shop for the ring, again, an exercise in restraint, for although he hadn't placed a limit on the price of the ring, he'd eyed it more as an investment piece than a declaration of undying love. She wore the large princess-cut diamond set in platinum with pride. To her it was another example of just how far she'd come.

The ring stuck a little as she pushed it over her knuckle, but with a little coaxing it was back where it belonged. She didn't know what had made her take it off last night after she'd given her room key to Keaton. Somehow it just felt as if it fit the fantasy.

All in all, last night augured well for their future together, she thought as she quickly applied her makeup, brushed her hair into a French knot and slipped into the trouser suit she'd brought to wear today. The severe cut of the cream jacket, teamed with matching tailored trousers, gave her an edge of sophistication blended with a no-nonsense air of business. The beige camisole she wore beneath it had just a hint of antique lace at the neckline to soften the sharp edges. She gave herself one last look in the mirror and nodded. Yes, she'd do.

In the elevator down to the conference, Honor slipped out her phone and keyed a message to Keaton.

I miss you already. Can't wait to see you again. Xx

There was a smile on her face as she pressed Send and put the phone back in her pocket. She didn't expect Keaton to respond. But after last night, it might have been nice to think he would. Before she went into the conference room where she'd be presenting her seminar today, she checked her phone. Nothing. She shouldn't feel disappointed, she told herself as she hooked up her laptop to the system and loaded her PowerPoint display, but it didn't stop her checking her phone once again before the first of the attendees began to wander into the room.

Nothing. Pushing back the biting sense of letdown, Honor focused her thoughts on her notes and began her presentation. She'd have time enough to tell Keaton how much she'd appreciated his actions last night when she got back into the office later today.

Logan rolled over in his bed and stared at the ceiling. Jet lag was an utter bitch. Even though he'd tried to force his body to adjust to the different time zone, he still felt as though he'd need to sleep for a week before he'd feel half-way normal again. But then again, maybe normal was an aberration.

"Too early to be philosophical, mate," he told himself out loud and forced himself from the bed and into the bathroom.

Last night certainly hadn't been normal—not in any way, shape or form. In some respects, he felt a little disappointed in himself. He'd never used another person purely for pleasure before. Not like that. Not without at least getting to know and understand the other person a little better. Hell, he didn't even know his late-night lover's name, even though he knew exactly what drove her into a frenzy—knew exactly where to touch her to make her forget the world and feel pleasure so deeply the edges between where he'd ended and she'd begun had blurred into insignificance.

Would he bump into her again tonight, he wondered? Or this morning, in the lobby downstairs? He studied his reflection in the mirror and shook his head. Man, he looked rough. His beard was growing in, and he needed to attend to that straightaway. He didn't want to bump into anyone looking this disreputable.

After showering, shaving and dressing, Logan headed out to find some breakfast. He had a couple of hours, at best, to get himself adjusted to the time zone and to consider how he was going to accomplish what he'd come here for. Hell, eat breakfast? His gut twisted into a knot and suddenly that was the furthest thing from his mind. Facing his birth mom and dad would be the hardest thing he'd done in his life, knowing they were the people who should have raised him. The people who should have shared each milestone in his life.

Would they understand how, like them, he'd always been drawn to architecture, even as a kid? Would they value his ideals in his work and how he'd built a multimillion-dollar business gutting old buildings and rebuilding them from the inside to create eco-friendly living and work spaces all through Australasia? Would he fit into the family that he'd been born into but never known his entire life?

He had no doubt they'd want proof he was who he said he was. Logan wasn't stupid. He'd done his research. He knew Richmond Developments was on the cutting edge of property development here in the Pacific Northwest. It seemed to Logan that they were in the same kind of business. Except where his parents' company bought old buildings in prime locations, razed them and built new, he preferred to pay homage to the historical character of his projects, preserving and repurposing special features while at the same time bringing them into the twenty-first century. No, his family would likely not immediately welcome him with open arms. Maybe since they were in the same business, they'd think he had ulterior motives. They'd be cautious, and rightly so. They'd need tests done, but eventually his link to them would be proven. And then what?

He wondered, and not for the first time, if he'd have followed his path if he'd been brought up here instead of in New Zealand. Had Alison Parker had any idea of what she was doing when she'd stolen him from his crib in the nursery at the hospital and taken him to raise as her own? She couldn't have been in a rational state of mind—he understood that. She'd given birth to a stillborn son the same day Logan and his twin brother were born. The loss had unhinged her. After her death a couple of months ago, he'd read her old diaries in a growing state of shock.

It had been clear, even to him, that she must have been suffering some kind of psychosis after the loss of her own child. Replacing her dead baby with one of two living children born to someone else had made perfect sense to her at the time. As she'd written in her diary, why should they have two healthy babies when her own had died? Surely it was only fair that they each have one? As twisted as it was, he could see how her grief-stricken mind had justified her actions that day.

And she'd done her best by Logan. When her husband had died on a black ops mission, she'd left the United States to return to her home country of New Zealand, where she'd raised Logan as a typical Kiwi kid. Surfing in the summer, skiing in the winter, he'd grown up with the best of everything she and her parents could provide, and if anyone asked why he looked different from his cousins, with his dark blond hair, fair skin and pale gray eyes, it was explained that he resembled his father. He was family and had always felt accepted as such.

But even so, Logan had always felt a lingering sense of disconnection, too, as if he didn't quite belong. And after finding that box with his mom's old diaries and his original baby ID bracelet with his real name on it together with the one of her dead son, he'd finally understood why. He hadn't told anyone back at home the real reason for his trip to America. They all thought he was here to expand Parker Construction's business interests. And maybe, if everything went well, he would.

The time to make his way to the Richmond Developments headquarters came around all too quickly. After his walk, Logan returned to the hotel to gather his briefcase and went downstairs to summon a cab. At Richmond Tower, Logan checked his appearance in the shiny reflective walls of the elevator and approved the professional look he'd gone for to strike just the right note. In his briefcase were scanned copies of Alison's diaries and the baby bracelets. He'd arranged this meeting with his birth father on the pretext of discussing a business opportunity with him. And it wasn't a complete lie. Logan strongly believed that Richmond Developments was missing a very important niche in the market. The world was looking to repurpose more and more, and conserving old buildings and their histories was the wave of the future. People needed something to be grounded in—as he well knew.

The elevator doors slid open onto a plush reception area. The two women at the front desk both looked up and smiled at him. But behind the smiles, there was confusion, also. The younger of the two stood up.

"Mr. Richmond?"

"I'm Logan Parker to see Mr. Douglas Richmond," Logan said firmly.

"You're Mr. Parker," she said in a confused tone of voice.

The other receptionist tugged on her arm and muttered something, and the younger woman forced a smile to her face. "I'll put a call through."

Logan had discovered he had a twin and that his twin worked here in the family business. He'd hoped that by coming here and meeting his family in their place of work that it would dilute what could be a somewhat fraught reunion. What he hadn't really stopped to consider was the interest there might be in his twin's mirror image suddenly turning up unexpectedly.

"A Mr. Parker is here to see Mr. Richmond," she said discreetly. "Yes, sir. I'll bring him through myself."

She rose from her chair and walked up to Logan. "Please come with me, Mr. Parker."

He followed her down a long corridor, past an openplan office area where people were industriously busy at their workstations. When the receptionist reached a set of large wooden double doors, she knocked before swinging them both open.

"Mr. Parker to see you, sir," she announced before turning back to Logan. "Go on in." She gestured for him to go inside.

"Thank you."

Logan stepped through the doorway and felt as if he'd entered the lion's den. He squared his shoulders. Whatever happened next would determine the course for the rest of his life.

Three

An older man rose from his executive chair behind a large mahogany desk. Despite his tan, his face paled visibly.

"Keaton? What are you doing?"

"No, sir, I'm Logan Parker."

The older man's face paled visibly.

"Who the hell are you?" he demanded, obviously defaulting to anger.

"As I said, I'm Logan Parker. Although you may remember me by another name," Logan said firmly as he stepped forward and offered his hand.

"Another name? Explain yourself."

"I was born Kane Douglas Richmond," Logan said as calmly as he was able.

"That can't be. Our son disappeared more than thirty years ago. Isn't that right, Nancy?"

When he first walked in, Logan hadn't seen the woman standing by the floor-to-ceiling windows of the large corner office. He turned to face her and heard her sharply indrawn breath.

"Kane? Douglas, could it be…?"

Her knees buckled slightly as she looked at him, and she put a hand out to the chair beside her to steady herself. Tears began to roll down her face and she shook as she reached out a hand.

"Kane. Oh my goodness. Douglas, it's him. It's our baby boy come back to us after all these years."

Douglas Richmond moved quickly from behind his desk and guided his wife into a chair before turning to face Logan.

"What's the meaning of this? Who are you?" he demanded again.

"Sir, I'm sorry. I probably should have told you who I was ahead of our meeting, but I wasn't sure you'd see me if I claimed to be the son who was stolen from you decades ago."

"And that's what you're claiming?"

"Douglas, can't you see it? He's identical to Keaton," Nancy said, reaching up and grasping hold of her husband's hand. "It has to be Kane. Our firstborn."

But Douglas Richmond was determined not to be convinced. "I understood you requested this meeting to discuss business. What do you really want from us?"

"Yes, I did," Logan admitted. "And that's something I'd still like to talk over with you. But first, I would like to show you these. I can understand that you're both shocked—I was, too, when I discovered my true identity."

Logan placed his briefcase on a chair and opened it. He took out the diary copies and the ID bracelets from the hospital and placed them on his father's desk.

"These belonged to the woman who raised me. Please, look at them at your leisure. If you prefer, I can leave them with you now and return at a later time."

It was clear his father and mother were completely shell-shocked by his arrival. To be totally honest, he was, too. Looking at his dad was like entering a time machine—one that projected him thirty years ahead. And his mom, too. He had her coloring—the exact same shade of pale gray eyes. Despite their obvious distress at his sudden appearance in their lives, he could feel a tenuous connection with them already. One born of recognition, of blood. Even so, perhaps it was a good time to leave. To let them absorb the information he'd brought with him.

"I can see my arrival here has unsettled you both. Let me give you some time." He dropped his business card on the diaries. "You can reach me on my mobile number. I'll wait at my hotel for your call."

He turned toward the door.

"No, don't go!" Nancy cried out and struggled to her feet.

She came across the carpeted floor, stopped directly in front of him and reached her hands up to his face, cupping his cheeks.

"Nancy, you can't be sure it's him," Douglas said cautiously.

"Don't you dare tell me I don't know my own son," she said fiercely, never taking her eyes off Logan for a second. "This is my boy. You grew within my body. I birthed you, held you, nursed you and then you were stolen from me. But now you're returned to us, and our family is once again complete."

Logan didn't know what to do or say, but his silence didn't deter Nancy.

"Douglas, call in Keaton and Kristin. They need to meet him. They need to see their brother."

To Logan's surprise, his father did just that. He placed two calls in quick succession requesting that his two other children come immediately to his office.

"Take a seat, young man. I'm sure we won't have to wait long," Douglas said gruffly before resuming his seat behind the desk. He didn't take his eyes off Logan for a minute.

Logan sat and remained still. Nancy had taken the chair next to him. Both his parents kept staring at him, his mother with a look of sheer wonder on her face, his father with disbelief. It couldn't have been more than two minutes before there was a peremptory knock at the door and another man walked in. Logan rose and turned to face the newcomer.

"What the hell is going on?" his mirror image asked with a look of shock on his face.

Logan stared at his twin brother. His identical twin. It was uncanny staring at another person who was the spitting image of yourself. They even had the same haircut.

"Keaton, meet your brother, Kane, or, as he's known, Logan Parker," Nancy said in a slightly unsteady voice.

"I don't know who this impostor is, but I don't have a brother," Keaton said firmly.

Logan felt the words as though they were a physical blow. All his life he'd wanted siblings. Now that he'd discovered he had two, it had become all the more important to him that they believe he was who he said he was—their long-lost brother.

"If it's any consolation," Logan said, "until very recently I had no idea you existed, either."

There was a commotion at the door, and a young woman came in. Probably his sister, judging by her resemblance to Nancy.

"What's going on? Who's this?" she said before coming to an abrupt halt as she saw her brother standing there with his double.

"Kristin, this is your brother," Nancy said. "Your other brother."

"He can't be. My other brother is dead."

"I can assure you, I'm very much alive," Logan replied.

"How can that be possible?" Kristin said, turning on her mom. "You told me when I was little that he was dead."

"What your mother said was that your brother was gone. The rest was your own interpretation," Douglas said gruffly. "Obviously there is a strong resemblance—"

"Resemblances mean nothing," Keaton said insistently and took a step closer to Logan. "I don't know who the heck you are, but you have a nerve coming here and trying to pull this off. How much money do you want?"

Logan snorted. "Money? I have plenty of money. What I don't have, and what I've been cheated of my entire life, is my family."

"So, you thought you'd appropriate ours?" Kristin said snidely.

Logan reached for the hospital ID tag he'd put on his father's desk. "If I was an impostor, would I have this?"

Kristin took one of the tiny bracelets. "Anyone could fake this."

Logan firmed his lips into a straight line. This wasn't turning into the warm family reunion he'd hoped for.

"Look, I'll do whatever it takes to prove I am who I believe I am." Logan stared back at Keaton. "Just tell me where and when I need to be at the lab for the DNA test, and I'll be there."

"You're very confident of your claim," Keaton said.

"I'm not in the habit of lying or misleading people," Logan answered firmly. "Look, until my mother—at least, the woman who raised me—died recently, I always believed that she and her late husband were my parents, even though I didn't look much like either of them. Mum met her husband when he was stationed at Antarctica with the joint forces support force. She was a New Zealand nurse stationed there, too. She followed him to the US and they married here. It was only after she passed away that I found these." He gestured to the diary copies on the desk. "And the ID bracelets."

"To the best of my knowledge, Alison Parker learned her husband had been killed on deployment and went into labor with her own son. He was still-born. I can only surmise that her grief, doubled, drove her over the edge. She states in her diary that while the nursing staff were doing a shift changeover, there was an emergency in another room and the nursery was left unattended for a brief time. She entered the nursery from the maternity ward where she'd just been discharged and simply lifted me from my crib, hid me in her overnight bag and took me home.

"She later traveled from Seattle to Los Angeles and applied for a passport for me in her dead child's name at the New Zealand consulate. The military helped with her return to New Zealand on compassionate grounds. And, because she was known to have been pregnant, no one thought anything of the fact that she had a baby with her. She'd come to the US on her New Zealand passport, which was in her maiden name. I can only assume that any attempt to trace her was thrown off by that."

Nancy stiffened in her chair. "That definitely explains it. Remember, Douglas, the hospital staff and police virtually ripped the hospital apart looking for Kane. They investigated everyone who'd been in the hospital during the time he was born and there was one woman they'd had difficulty tracing but they'd excluded her from the investigation because when they found her on security tapes she wasn't carrying a baby, only a bag." She swallowed a sob back. "And you were in that bag."

Before anyone could say anything else, there was another knock at the office door.

"I'm sorry I'm late, everyone. I just got back into wor—"

All eyes turned to the woman who'd just come into the office. A woman Logan recognized instantly. His late-night lover. But she wasn't the warm, sexy creature who'd approached and kissed him then invited him up to her room. Instead, she was a cool, remote corporate type—wearing an enormous diamond on the ring finger of her left hand.

And, as she looked from his brother to him, he saw the exact moment that she realized exactly whom she'd propositioned last night.

"Keaton? What's going on?"

Logan watched as she crossed the office to stand at his brother's side.

"That's what we'd all like to know. This guy claims to be my twin brother."

Honor fought the urge to flee. This couldn't be happening. There couldn't be two Keatons, and the longer she stood here the more strongly the truth reverberated through her. She'd slept with a stranger. Sure, he'd looked like her fiancé, but no matter which way she looked at it, she'd cheated on Keaton. And not just cheated, but cheated on him with *his brother.*

The bitter taste of bile flooded her mouth and she swallowed it back. This couldn't be happening. Fidelity was her line in the sand. She'd seen exactly what unfaithfulness could do to a family and she'd vowed, always, to be faithful. And yet somehow, she'd made the most monumental mistake of her entire life.

Douglas reached across the desk and grabbed one of the duplicate diaries stacked there.

"I suppose I'd better read these. In the meantime, Nancy, could you look into how we can have DNA testing expedited?"

"Yes, dear, I'll check on it right away." She started toward the door but paused and turned back to Logan.

Honor watched as her future mother-in-law took the hand of the man with whom Honor had committed her biggest mistake. The man who, with only a few words, could destroy her carefully, painstakingly constructed future. Under the bright office lights, a myriad of diamonds glinted on Nancy's fingers, each one a gift from her husband and a testament to his love for her. Honor began to worry at her own diamond ring with her thumb. How on earth was she going to work through this?

Nancy leaned closer to the newcomer and said, "Don't worry, my son. It'll work out. I know in my heart you're telling the truth. A mother always knows."

Honor watched as Nancy went through the door to her connecting office. It had always amazed Honor that Nancy and Douglas believed in working closely together even after all this time. It had added to her sense of security knowing that even with all life had thrown at them thirty-four years ago with their firstborn being kidnapped, her future in-laws continued to stand strong together. It was what she'd always hoped for, for herself and Keaton. And, while she wasn't on his management level yet, she was working steadily toward it. When Douglas and Nancy retired, she and Keaton would be the power couple here at Richmond Developments. And when that happened, she'd be living her dream.

But only if the truth of what she did last night was never revealed.

Something stabbed sharply in her chest. How could she keep what she'd done a secret? Even knowing it would destroy her relationship with Keaton and likely see her have to find another position elsewhere, she knew, deep down, that she ought to come clean. And what of the stranger? Would he keep their one night of illicit passion secret, or was he the kind of man who'd use their secret to gain leverage with the Richmond family?

Right now, she had no way of knowing what kind of person he was. Obviously, she knew he was a talented and generous lover, but what was he like as a man? He'd accepted her offer to come up to her room without a backward glance. Having sex with a complete and utter stranger didn't really do much to recommend him, but then again, she'd been complicit in that. Forget that she thought she'd been making love with the man she'd pledged to marry. As Keaton's fiancée, she should have known all along that this man was not the same person.

But didn't you see the differences and choose to ignore them? a little voice that sounded horribly like her mother's asked from the back of her mind. *You think you're so squeaky clean, but you're no different from me after all.*

Honor clamped down on the thought immediately. Maybe she was all wrong here. Maybe it had been Keaton at the hotel last night. After all, she'd invited him to come along, had told him how important it was to her to be nominated for the award she'd won. And he'd known she wanted to spice things up between them. Even though she knew she was grasping at straws, she turned to him.

"Keaton, can I ask you something?" she murmured in his ear.

"Sure." He looked at her and his direct, pale gray eyes felt as if they were boring into the recesses of her soul—as if he could see the truth of her actions last night.

She forced a smile and leaned in to ask, "Where were you last night?"

"I told you, I had a business dinner," he said. "I'm sorry I couldn't be there for you to celebrate your win. Congratulations, by the way. We can do dinner tonight, and you can tell me all about it. Let's get through this mess first."

Honor looked past Keaton's shoulder at her secret lover, who was staring straight back at her. A shiver rippled through her. Fear? Or was it something else?

"Honor?" Keaton prompted.

"Yes," she said, gathering her wits about her. What had

he just said to her? Oh yes. "That would be lovely. I'll look forward to it."

Douglas spoke again. "Kristin, could you get Stella to bring in some strong, hot coffee for us? I think we all need something bracing."

"Whiskey might be more in order," she grumbled before stepping out of the office.

"Keaton, you haven't introduced your fiancée to Mr. Parker yet," Douglas said.

Honor saw the stranger's head jerk a little, as if he'd just received an electric shock. He looked from her to Keaton and back again. Confusion and what had to be a million questions vied for supremacy in his eyes. She couldn't hold his gaze. Couldn't face the damnation she knew she'd see there if she looked at him for too long. Beside her, Keaton stiffened before making the introduction.

"Honor, this, apparently, is my long-lost twin brother, Kane, also known as Logan Parker. Parker, please meet my fiancée, Honor Gould."

Logan stepped forward and offered Honor his hand. "Pleased to meet you, Ms. Gould."

Honor slowly let go of the breath she'd been holding. She'd half expected him to admit that he'd already met her, but it appeared he was happy to pretend he hadn't. Hadn't met her, hadn't kissed her, hadn't touched her body so intimately that she was in danger of flaring into a plume of smoke at the sheer memory of what he'd done to her, with her.

But she could see the questions in his eyes, and she knew she'd have to face them down—sooner rather than later. Her mind working overtime, she admitted to herself it would need to be sooner. She couldn't risk him disclosing to Keaton what they'd done. At least with the way Keaton had been bristling around Logan, they were hardly likely to be sharing close conversation any time soon. She took his hand, schooling herself to remain calm, but she hadn't anticipated the electricity that sizzled through her palm at his touch.

"And you too, Mr. Parker," she finally managed to say through stiff lips. "Your arrival here is quite a surprise."

As if that wasn't the biggest understatement of her life.

"I can imagine," Logan Parker replied.

Was that a twinkle in his eye? Did he find this situation funny? A bolt of anger shot through her. How dare he? He had to realize that she'd made an innocent mistake, even if what had transpired next had been anything but innocent. She had to get him on his own to clarify this situation and ensure that he would keep what they'd done strictly between them.

But could she trust him?

Four

The next hour passed painfully slowly. Somehow Nancy used the Richmond influence to have a private lab technician come directly to the office. The man swabbed Douglas and Nancy, then Keaton and Logan. It seemed that when big money talked, people moved and moved fast.

After the technician had left, Honor excused herself.

"I'm sorry, I have an off-site client meeting in half an hour. I really need to get going. I hope you'll excuse me."

Nancy looked up and smiled. "Of course, Honor. I was thinking we should have a family dinner back at the house tonight. Take the opportunity to get to know Logan a little better."

"Oh, I'm sorry, Keaton and I have other plans for tonight." She looked across to her fiancé. "Unless you want to—"

"Yes, Mom, we do. Neither of us will be able to make it. Perhaps some other time," Keaton added, overriding the suggestion Honor was clearly about to make that they change their plans.

Logan had no doubt that Keaton was hoping "some other time" would never happen. Hostility poured off his brother in waves. He could understand it. For thirty-four years, Keaton had been the much-loved only son of his parents. Now he had competition. Kristin appeared to be aloof, too. She hadn't exhibited any of the curiosity he knew he himself would have displayed in the same situation. He might have sought his family and found them, but along the way he'd also discovered a whole pile of doubt.

Obviously, a family like the Richmonds would need to be careful. They'd built an empire on very tight-knit foundations. It only made sense that they'd close ranks to protect it. But there'd been no doubting the recognition and joy on Nancy's face. Douglas, too, seemed less reticent than his children when it came to Logan.

He sat back in his chair. It would take time to prove it, but he had every confidence he had as much right to be here as any of them.

And then there was the conundrum of the intriguing Honor Gould. Logan watched her talking to his brother by the windows that looked out over the water. It was obvious that she'd been shocked to discover she'd slept with the wrong twin, but what did that say about her relationship with Keaton? Surely she must have seen that while they might look the same, their similarities ended with that. From what Logan could tell, his brother was a very tightly reined-in person emotionally. Was he equally as tightly reined in when it came to intimacy?

He didn't like what the thought of his brother and Honor being intimate did to him—and especially didn't like the powerful surge of possessiveness that swept through him. Logan shook his head slightly. Whatever, it was none of his business. If Honor wanted to pretend they'd never met before, he was good with that. At least for now. But he still felt the pull of attraction between them, and he had no doubt that would become very uncomfortable before long. He hadn't missed the engagement ring on her finger this morning, either. The ring that definitely hadn't been there when he'd gone to her room last night.

Man, last night. He fought back the groan of desire that threatened to pour out of him. Yeah, that would go down well right now—*not*. He had to keep his mind off Honor Gould, but it was going to be damn hard when she was right here in the room. Didn't she mention she had some off-site visit she needed to be at? And yet, all of a sudden she didn't appear to be in a hurry to leave after all. She was still standing and talking with Keaton, whispering and gesturing and occasionally looking Logan's way. But then, thank goodness, she began to move toward the door.

There was no kiss or hug between her and Keaton as she departed. *Interesting.* They might be engaged, but there didn't appear to be any real closeness between them. In fact, Logan was willing to wager that he had been closer to Honor last night than his brother had been in a very long time.

Stop it, he told himself. *You're grasping at straws. Competing with a brother you never knew you had until a couple of months ago over the woman he's engaged to.* As if that wasn't the most cynical thing of all. He didn't know Honor—not what made her tick, what her favorite breakfast was, what music she enjoyed, the books she liked. Nor did he know his brother. Maybe beneath that stuffed-shirt, cold exterior, Keaton was indeed a warm-blooded male.

Logan caught his brother's eye and gave him a half smile of acknowledgment, but Keaton's expression didn't change. In fact, he turned away and with a muttered excuse to his father departed soon after Honor. Which left Kristin and his parents.

He decided it was time to get to know his sister a little better.

"So, Kristin—or do I call you Krissie?"

"Kristin. I loathe being called Krissie." Her response was succinct and laced with animosity.

"Right, duly noted. When I did a little research into the company before coming here, I saw that you're chief financial officer and heavily involved in the leasing side of the business—"

"You researched us? Kind of creepy, don't you think?"

"And you haven't googled me since you learned of my existence?"

He was taking a punt, but he suspected she had. If not when he'd seen her pull her phone out of her pocket while the lab tech was here, then definitely when she'd left the office to request the coffee.

She had the grace to look shamefaced. "I might have."

"Were you being creepy, or merely looking to be informed about who you were dealing with?"

"Touché," Douglas commented with a chuckle. "He has you there, Kristin."

She looked annoyed, and Logan attempted to put out the fire of discontent that was building in her eyes.

"I get it. I hate walking into any situation with my eyes shut. And, yes, I admit that I probably should have had my lawyers approach the family with my claim." He shook his head. "Not that I'm making any claim. I just wanted to find my family. My real family. The people I have a connection with that goes beyond today. The woman who brought me up loved me, and her family loved me as if I was their own, but I always knew I was different. Can you imagine what that was like?"

He watched Kristin's gaze soften and heard the muffled sound of compassion that came from Nancy. He waited a couple of beats, letting his words sink in.

"So you can understand my need to find out what I could when I discovered the diaries. I don't expect you all to include me in your lives. But obviously I would like it if we could have some crossover, whether that be on a personal or business level."

"Business? You were serious about that? Or was that just the ruse you used to get in to see Mom and Dad this morning?"

"It's no ruse. If you looked me up online, you'll know I'm an experienced architect and I specialize in the repurposing and renovation of old buildings."

"Well, if you looked us up online, you'll know we specialize in pulling old buildings down."

He laughed at the belligerence in his sister's tone and found a growing respect for her. She didn't back down. He liked that.

"And that's where I think you're missing an opportunity."

"Tell me more," Douglas said, leaning forward and resting his elbows on his desk.

The next several hours passed in a blur of conversation as they discussed the pros and cons of their respective businesses. Toward the end of the afternoon, Douglas leaned back in his chair and smiled.

"If you are who you say you are and you hadn't been taken from us, I wonder where Richmond Developments would be now."

"Oh, come on, Dad. We don't even know for certain that he's your son," Kristin said, obviously not ready to let go of her reluctance to accept Logan as her brother.

"Kristin, I think the sooner you come to terms with the fact our family dynamic may be about to change, the better."

"Well, it's hardly going to change for me, is it? After all, you only ever wanted Keaton, as your eldest living son, at the helm when you retire. So is that going to be Logan now?"

Logan looked from his birth father to his sister in shock. He certainly hadn't expected that. Nor, to be honest, did he want it. At the very least, he had no right to intrude on Keaton's position both as Douglas's son and within the company hierarchy.

"You know my wishes," Douglas said severely. "And I'll thank you not to try and cause trouble."

"Dad, stop treating me like I'm five years old."

"Then stop behaving like you are."

Kristin looked at her father, hurt clear on her features. "I think I'll go back to my office now."

And without saying another word, she left.

"I'm sorry you had to witness that," Douglas said with a wry twist to his mouth. "Kristin tends to let her emotions get the better of her."

"Now, Doug, that's not entirely fair. You bait her," Nancy objected.

"And she needs to learn that sometimes you have to lead with your head, not your heart."

Logan watched the interplay between his parents. Would Nancy continue to stand up to Douglas? No, it was clear she was about to concede the point.

"Looks like it's just the three of us left," Nancy commented. "Shall we head back to the house early? Logan, perhaps you'd like to stay with us until you find a place of your own?"

"I have my room at the hotel," Logan remonstrated. "I'm happy to stay there for now. Besides, I plan on returning to New Zealand, not settling down here."

"No," Nancy cried out. "I haven't had you for the past thirty-four years. You can't go back so soon."

"Well, I'm not going back immediately, but eventually. I do have a company to run."

"Possibly two," Douglas said enigmatically before rising from his chair. "But for now, you'll at least come home for dinner, won't you?"

Logan looked from his father to his mother. "Yes, I'd like that. Thank you."

He still had so many questions he wanted to ask. So many answers he sought. He might as well continue the conversation tonight, even if his siblings weren't going to be there. *Or Honor*, the voice at the back of his mind pointed out. He quashed the thought before it could take flight. For now, he would have to be satisfied with what he had right here in front of him. After all, hadn't that been his goal in coming here all along?

But no matter what he told himself, his body remembered his brother's fiancée with an ache that wouldn't go away.

Honor was on tenterhooks, waiting for Keaton to arrive at her apartment. She double-checked the table setting, lit the tall candles in their holders and tweaked the blooms she'd picked up from Pike Place Market on the way home from work and arranged in the crystal bowl she'd found in a thrift shop a few months back.

Everything looked perfect. On the surface, at least. But she couldn't quite shake the feeling that life as she knew it was about to change irrevocably. It terrified her. One aberration could rip apart her carefully planned life and destroy any chance of the future she had worked so hard for all her life.

She heard the door buzz. Keaton must have arrived. He was the only person on her "do not announce" list she'd left with the concierge downstairs. She flew across the room, pulled open the door and embraced Keaton.

"I have missed you so much," she said on a rush of air.

He extracted himself from her embrace. "Honor, we were together this morning."

"But not just the two of us. I feel like we never have time for each other anymore." At the quizzical expression on his face, she realized she was probably saying too much, too soon. "I'm sorry. It's been a heck of a day. Come inside and sit down. Can I get you a drink?"

"Sure. I'll open this for us, shall I?" Keaton showed her the bottle of merlot he'd brought and went through to the living room.

Honor glanced at the wine label and grimaced slightly as she saw it was imported from New Zealand. Seemed there was an awful lot coming from New Zealand right now.

"Something smells good."

"Lasagna," she answered. "The merlot will be perfect with it."

She got two glasses from the kitchen and brought them through to the living room. Keaton opened the bottle and poured them each a glass. He handed her one, and she snuggled in beside him on the couch.

"Don't you wish we could do this every night after work?" she probed.

He'd never responded to her suggestion that they move in together. Instead he'd been evasive and turned their discussion back to an issue they'd been having with a bulk supplier for one of their commercial developers at the time. Honor loved Keaton, she really did, and admired his work ethic like nothing else, but his ability to avoid answering a straight question with a straight answer drove her slightly crazy.

"I can see where it will have its benefits," he agreed before dropping a kiss onto the tip of her nose.

She pulled a face. "That's no way to say a proper hello to the woman you're going to marry," she said before reaching up to turn his face to hers and kissing him.

She put everything she had into the kiss. All her guilt about last night, all her hope that she hadn't destroyed the now-tenuous link between herself and Keaton. He didn't respond at first, and she wondered if she'd pushed him too hard. Keaton was the kind of man who liked to initiate things. It had never really bothered her that much. But now, it lit a wick on her anger.

Why didn't he want to take her and ravish her? They'd been apart for a few days while she'd been at the conference and then they'd had the upheaval of Logan Parker turning up. Surely he should be turning to her for comfort. Wasn't that what couples did in times of stress and strife? But even as she kissed him, she felt his restraint. Sure, he went through the motions, but where was the passion?

Had it ever been there?

She hated that she was now second-guessing herself about a relationship she was prepared to stake her future on. Or at least she had been until she'd realized she'd slept with the wrong brother. No! She couldn't think like that. She had honestly believed that she'd been with Keaton, hadn't she? She'd honestly believed that her staid, upright, workaholic fiancé had dressed in clothing she hadn't recognized and spoken in a different accent to indulge in role play and put a bit of fun in their relationship.

Honor pulled away from Keaton and took a sip of her wine. Her hand shook a little as she raised the glass to her mouth. Not because of how he'd kissed her, but because she'd realized that she *had* noticed things were off about Logan Parker and that she'd chosen to ignore them, even though common sense told her that Keaton would never have done that.

And now she'd been unfaithful to him. It was more than she could contemplate. For all that she'd set herself on a pedestal so much higher than her mother, she was cut from the same cloth. The right thing to do would be to admit her awful mistake to Keaton, return his ring and step down from her position at Richmond Developments. But if she did that, she'd lose everything.

Keaton sighed, and she looked up at him in concern. He never sighed. Never expressed weakness. Ever.

"Are you okay? It's been a heck of a day, right?" she asked him.

"That's one way of putting it. Do you think he's genuine?"

"Who? Logan?"

"I didn't have any other brothers come back from the dead today, so, yeah, Logan."

She hesitated. She'd thought him real enough last night. "Actually, yes, I do think he's genuine. Why did you think he was dead?"

Keaton shook his head slowly. "I don't really know. I guess that the few times I can ever remember Mom and Dad talking about him, they called him their lost son. As a child I assumed that meant he was dead. And because losing him had caused them so much obvious pain, I never asked them any more questions about him. They only ever had the one photo of the both of us from when we were born, before he was abducted."

"Do they still have the photo?"

"Yeah, Mom keeps it in their bedroom, on her dresser, so she can see it every day. I used to think it was morbid, but I guess she never lost hope that he'd come home one day."

"And now he has."

"We don't know that for sure," Keaton said defensively, then sighed again. "But, yeah, I guess the writing is on the wall. You know, I feel like I've spent my entire life trying to make up for my brother's absence. Trying to be better than just one son for my parents. Working my ass off so that they didn't miss him so much and believing I could fill every gap left behind because he wasn't there. Seems I was wrong about that."

"Oh, Keaton. That's not true. Your parents adore you. They know how hard you work, and they appreciate everything you do. Everything you are. How could they not?"

He gave her a sad half smile, one so similar to Logan's that she felt a piercing shaft of compassion mixed with pain and regret puncture her heart. Poor Keaton. She'd never stopped to consider how he saw overachievement as the only possible option. After all, she was very similar herself. They had goals and they went for them. And, underneath it all, he was still that man looking for approval and acceptance from his parents.

The realization was shocking.

And now his position was on the verge of being usurped by his own twin. She could totally understand how unsettling that must be for him. And she knew equally as well that she had to do everything in her power to put her dreadful mistake behind her and ensure that he never knew what she'd done. It would crush him. Oh, sure, he wouldn't show it. He'd carry on working and being the incredible man he was. But now she understood that on the inside he'd be bleeding as if he'd swallowed razor blades.

A timer went off in the kitchen, and she rose to her feet.

"Dinner's ready," she managed to say without any trace of the turmoil she was feeling in her voice. "Come on up to the table."

Keaton followed her to the kitchen instead. "Can I help with anything?"

"Thanks, you can take the salad through. Oh, and bring the wine to the table. I think we're going to need it tonight, don't you?"

He smiled at her again, this time with a little more warmth behind it. "Good thinking."

They talked business during dinner, discussing how her site visit had gone today and doing more risk assessment on the upcoming stage of the project. It was only when they were clearing the table together and stacking the dishwasher that Honor began to steer their conversation back to a more personal subject.

"Keaton, I've been thinking," she started.

"Hmm?"

"Let's set a date for the wedding. A real date. Something soon. We don't need a big fuss. We both work too hard to plan anything too elaborate. I'd be happy with a ceremony at your parents' place, in the ballroom overlooking the lake. Wouldn't you?"

"Do you mean summer next year?"

She drew in a deep breath. "If we apply for a license tomorrow, we could make it sooner than that—maybe late January or early February. We can keep the numbers down, cater finger food rather than an ostentatious sit-down meal with a bunch of people we barely know. What do you think?"

"Sounds like you've been giving it some serious thought."

He was hedging, and it made frustration ripple through her. Wasn't he keen to consolidate their relationship? Didn't he want to take their future plans to the next level at all?

"Of course I've been giving it serious thought," she retorted sharply. "We need to set a date, Keaton. We've been sitting on the fence about it for far too long."

He grimaced. "January is too soon." When she started to protest, he put up a hand. "No, hear me out. We both have far too much going on at work right now to even think about a wedding next month. Besides, it wouldn't be fair to Mom. You know how much she enjoys planning things in advance. For her the anticipation is everything."

Honor felt his words like a blow. His mother's happiness was more important than hers? She scratched the thought from her mind even as it formed. Nancy was a warm and loving woman who had welcomed Honor into their family without as much as a second thought. It was churlish to think he was putting Nancy before her, even if it did feel like that.

"Don't you want to be married?" she couldn't help asking.

"Yes, *I do*." He grinned at the words. "See, I'm even practicing for the big day."

She couldn't help but give him a smile in return. Not often, but sometimes, he could be a total goof, and that tugged at her heart so hard. But even so, there was still no sign of his committing to a date for their wedding.

Keaton continued, "Look, why don't we sleep on it?"

He stepped up close, put his arms around her and bent to kiss her. But at the last minute, Honor turned her face away. To soften the rejection, she nuzzled into the side of his neck. She couldn't help it. She didn't want half-hearted from him anymore. She wanted it all. She wanted heart-stopping love. She wanted breath-taking passion. If they kissed now, she knew they would both be merely going through the motions. And if they made love? Well, she couldn't even allow her thoughts to go there. Not with the memory of Logan imprinted on her mind. She was every kind of awful bitch and she deserved all kinds of hell for this. But right now, she couldn't do it.

Honor pulled free of him.

"It's late," she said with genuine regret in her voice.

"You want me to go?" Keaton sounded surprised.

"I'm sorry. I'm tired, and I think that tonight I'd prefer to be alone."

Keaton's lips firmed into a straight line. It was about the only way he ever expressed displeasure or irritation.

"I don't think I'll ever understand you, Honor. One minute you're pressing for a wedding date and the next you're literally pushing me away? Is this some payback because I wouldn't agree to getting married next month?"

"No! Of course not. I'm sorry. I shouldn't have pushed you on that. I know you're dealing with a lot right now. But I am tired. I'll see you in the office tomorrow, okay?"

"Yeah, sure."

Keaton turned, but she could see he was annoyed with her. She'd be annoyed, too, if he'd done the same thing.

"Keaton?" she called as he walked toward the front door.

He stopped and turned.

"Yes?"

Suddenly she felt unbearably vulnerable. She'd crossed a line last night, and there might never be any turning back. Maybe she should have slept with Keaton tonight, but for some reason she felt as if that would be an even larger insult to him than turning him down.

"We're going to be okay, aren't we?"

His eyes met hers, and she caught her breath in the growing silence between them.

"Sure."

And then he was gone.

Five

She barely slept, and when she went into work early the next morning, Honor was irritated to find there was someone already in her office. In fact, the unwelcome guest was sitting at a desk that hadn't been there yesterday and her couches had been moved out. She frowned as she entered then felt her stomach plummet to her feet as she recognized Logan Parker.

How did she know so instantly it was him, she wondered, when only the day before yesterday she'd thought he was Keaton? Was it the way he held his head, the set of his shoulders? On first glance, he could have been his twin, but Honor knew on a far more primal level that this was not her fiancé.

"What are you doing in my office?" she asked as she stepped through the doorway.

He lifted his head and met her furious gaze. "Our office," he said calmly, then turned his attention back to his computer screen.

"You can't be serious," she seethed.

"Look, it wasn't my choice. Apparently the office Douglas wanted me to use is undergoing a refit, so this won't be forever."

"And he couldn't find you anywhere else?"

Logan gestured to the open plan area beyond her fishbowl of an office. Every available space was taken up by her design team.

"Take it up with the boss if you have an issue."

"I most definitely will," she huffed as she slung her coat on the stand in the corner of the room and went to her desk.

She sat down and booted up her computer, but she couldn't help but be vitally aware of the man sitting just across from her. In the end she gave up any pretense of trying to work.

"Care to tell me exactly why you're here?"

Logan closed his laptop screen and looked up at her. "Douglas spent a lot of time explaining the company structure to me yesterday. He's intrigued by what I do in New Zealand and wants me to consult on possibly incorporating some of my firm's ideas into Richmond Developments. As you're the head of the design team, he felt we would have a lot to discuss."

"And you didn't tell him anything?"

"Anything? What's to tell? I hardly know you or what you do."

He looked at her then, his light gray eyes boring into hers. She shivered, but the reaction had nothing to do with the temperature in the office and everything to do with the vivid memory of those very same eyes pinned on her as he'd entered her body.

"Exactly," she said, feeling more flustered than she cared to admit.

"You and Keaton have a nice dinner last night?"

He asked the question casually, but she saw the muscle

working at the side of his jaw. He definitely wasn't as casual about this as he was projecting, she thought with a sting of satisfaction.

"We had a truly wonderful evening together," she lied. Not for a moment was she going to admit that the evening had been awkward and discouraging. "And you? Was dinner with Douglas and Nancy what you hoped for?"

"Hoped for?" He quirked a brow.

"The return of the long-lost son. You know."

She almost instantly regretted her words. None of this was his fault, and yet she seemed bound and determined to paint him as the villain in the situation.

"It was a nice evening," he replied noncommittally. "They have a lovely home."

"It's where Keaton and Kristin grew up. Must have felt strange being there and knowing you were left out of that," she said, more softly this time.

"Yeah, but I wasn't exactly deprived in my childhood. I had a roof over my head and the love of my extended family. My mother and my grandparents gave me everything they thought I needed."

An awkward silence fell between them for a moment. Honor felt compelled to break it.

"So, what exactly are you working on?"

"Douglas gave me the specs of the block of buildings Richmond Developments bought last month."

"The waterfront block?"

"Yeah."

This was like squeezing blood out of a stone. "And?"

"I'm studying the plans, the layout of the land, historical engineering reports."

"He already has plans drawn for that project. Why is he getting you to look at it?"

"He's open to repurposing the existing structure versus demolition and a new build."

"You do know that the demo team is already booked for later this month."

"Which obviously doesn't give me a lot of time for a counterproposal."

He gave her a pointed look, as if to say, *kindly shut up and let me get on with it*. She felt the hot sting of a blush suffuse her cheeks.

"Don't you think that might end up being a waste of time?"

He shrugged, and the movement was oddly sexy. "Maybe, maybe not. I've got no stakc in this, so I have nothing to lose. But I do think that Douglas might be surprised at how potentially lucrative this could be for the company."

Logan made a decision. He was sick of this dancing around the very large elephant in the room, and Honor's passive-aggressive demeanor was really ticking him off. He wasn't the bad guy here, and it was about time she accepted that.

"That's a pretty big diamond you're wearing on your finger," he said, gesturing toward her left hand.

She paled visibly, and he saw her start to worry at her ring with the thumb of her left hand.

"Care to explain where that was two nights ago?"

Twin spots of high color appeared on her wan cheeks.

"I, uh…when I got back to my room, I took it off," she eventually admitted.

"I'm guessing you thought I was him," he said.

Logan's voice was flat and devoid of emotion, but inside his guts were churning. Knowing he'd slept with his brother's fiancée made him feel ill and had plagued him from the minute he'd been formally introduced to her yesterday. Keaton hadn't exactly been the most welcoming, and the last thing he wanted to do was give his brother any further reasons to hate him.

"I did. We, um, things have been a bit…" Her voice trailed off for a moment. "We've both been very busy with work. To be totally honest with you, we, um, hadn't been together in a while, and I thought he'd come to the hotel to surprise me and to inject a bit of fun back into our relationship."

Logan stood there, not saying a word, just watching her as she squirmed beneath his gaze. He'd spent much of yesterday furiously angry. Not that he'd shown it, but he'd alternately been irate at her then equally incensed with himself. Before that night, he'd never indulged in a one-night stand, ever. If he'd simply handed her key in to reception, as he ought to have done, none of this would have happened and he wouldn't be here, in their shared office, his senses tormented by the scent of her and his body plagued by the memory of what it felt like to make love to her. But if she hadn't approached him in the first place…?

How could she not have told the difference between them?

"Together? As in intimate together?" he probed.

She nodded.

"And you didn't think my accent odd?"

"To be honest, until you were in my room I barely listened to a word you said, and even after that I didn't stop to think beyond the fact that you were probably just in character, as it were."

"In character?" He shook his head. "So what now?"

"What do you mean, what now?"

"What happens next? Are you going to tell him?"

He saw the muscles in the slender column of her throat work as she swallowed hard.

"I… I don't know. I honestly thought you were him. In my own mind, I was having sex with my fiancé, not some random stranger in a bar. Believe me when I say I never do that kind of thing."

"Nor I," Logan admitted before sinking back into his chair. "So where to, from here? Do we just pretend it never happened?"

"That would be my preference," she said in a stilted voice.

He looked at her and couldn't help but remember how silky soft her skin was, or how responsive she'd been to his touch. He was getting hard just thinking about it, which was a really stupid thing to do. Thinking was dangerous, and touching her again—hell, that would be hazardous on a whole different level. He wondered how the hell he was going to stand being cooped up in the same office with her during work hours, and, no doubt, have to continue seeing her with his brother.

It was no less punishment than he deserved.

"Okay, so we never met before yesterday morning in Douglas's office."

Her features brightened with hope. "You can do that? Forget we—"

"I can. I have to. We both have to. I don't think you quite understand what I have at risk here. When I discovered who I was my sense of self was completely yanked out from under me. Have you got any idea what that was like?"

She looked at him, her eyes never leaving his face for a second. He saw the compassion there. But he didn't want compassion from Honor Gould. No, he wanted everything he couldn't have with her, but if he could begin anew with some form of understanding between them, then maybe they could get through this.

He continued. "She'd kept all the newspaper clippings about my abduction. Can you imagine that? Now that I've uncovered the truth about who I am, I don't want to destroy my only chance with the family I've just discovered. So, in answer to your question, yes, I can do that. I can forget, or at least pretend to, that our night together ever happened."

"I'm so sorry, Logan." She shook her head and lowered her gaze, but not before he saw the abject shame that filled her eyes. "I've honestly only been thinking about what this whole awful situation means to me. I never stopped to think how it impacted you as well."

"Then we're agreed?"

She got up from her chair and walked over to him. "Yes, we are. Care to shake on it?"

He accepted the hand she offered but was unprepared for the instant physical awareness that tingled through him at her touch. This was going to be so much harder than anything he'd ever done before. But he had to succeed, because if he didn't, he stood to lose everything he'd ever wanted his whole life. He let go of her hand quickly, before he could do something stupid like tug her forward into his arms and kiss her again like his body was urging him to do.

Douglas Richmond breezed into their office, and Logan fought to keep his expression calm when, right now, he felt like a kid caught with his hand in the cookie jar. He glanced at Honor, who looked similarly afflicted, and they moved apart as if they'd been caught doing so much more than innocently shaking hands.

"Ah, good to see the two of you getting along. Sorry I didn't get to discuss the new office setup with you before you got in this morning, Honor. But since I want the two of you to work closely together, it made sense. Any objections?" Douglas stared at her as if challenging her to argue.

To Logan's surprise, she held her own.

"Actually, I would have preferred notice, but I'm prepared to accommodate Mr. Parker for as long as he's here."

Douglas laughed. "As long as he's here? We've waited thirty-four years for our family to be complete. If Logan's claim is validated, the last thing Nancy and I would want is for him to go racing back to the far reaches of the Southern

Hemisphere again. I hope I can rely on you to make him feel welcome, Honor. You know how important family is to us."

Logan observed how she stiffened. This was likely her worst nightmare. Not only having to face up to her mistake, but having to work closely with him every day would put them both under a great deal of strain.

And temptation.

"Of course you can rely on me, Douglas. You know that. I'd do anything for this family."

"*Our* family," Douglas corrected gently. "You're a part of us, too, Honor. Logan has some very exciting ideas for Richmond Developments going forward. I want you to include him in your day-to-day activities so he can get a feel for how we operate. And, now, I suggest that the two of you come with me to the waterfront site so Logan can take a look at the buildings and layout there."

Logan nodded. "If you don't mind, I'd like to stop by my hotel room and get my camera so I can get some high-resolution images."

"Of course. Honor? You're free?"

Logan had the distinct impression that even if she wasn't, Douglas expected her to drop everything and join them.

"Let me check my calendar," she said and went through the motions of checking on her computer before nodding. "I can make myself available now, but I need to be back here by midday for another meeting."

"Good, good," Douglas said, clasping his hands and rubbing his palms together. "I'll meet you down in the parking garage in ten."

And without waiting another moment, he was gone.

Logan turned to Honor. "Is he always like that?"

"Always expecting everyone to fall in line? Yeah, pretty much."

"It's an imposition having me in here, isn't it?"

"It's not my place to say. I'm merely on the staff here."

"But you're engaged to my brother," he couldn't help adding. "Douglas said you're family."

"Yes, I am. And I'd be grateful if you'd continue to be mindful of that. I know you don't want to lose your new family, but I, too, have a lot at stake here."

"Noted," Logan said abruptly.

They left the office together and headed for the elevators. On the ride down, Honor looked as though she was mulling something over. After a few seconds, she spat it out.

"Did Douglas talk to Keaton about this new direction for Richmond Developments?"

"Not last night. As you'll recall, you two had a prior engagement. So, too, did Kristin."

Honor shifted a little on her feet. "Don't you think he should be apprised of this new development? After all, he is the vice president of the company. You might be the bright, shiny new toy for Douglas and Nancy, but Keaton's been here doing the heavy lifting since he graduated from college."

"I came to Seattle with a business idea and the hope that I could find acceptance within a family I had the right to know all my life but was cheated of." Logan defended himself, surprised by her sudden onslaught. "I'm not here to step on anybody's toes."

"It may pay to remind Douglas of that. He tends to get an idea in his head and run with it, at the expense of everything and everyone else."

"Thanks for the heads-up. I'll raise it with him as soon as I get the opportunity."

The elevator doors slid open and they walked out together, their footsteps synchronized as if they did this every day. Was Honor this in tune with his brother, Logan wondered before slamming the door on that line of thought.

"We wait here," she directed him when she came to a halt. "The limousine will be here shortly."

"Limousine? Douglas doesn't drive?"

"Douglas doesn't do anything himself that he can pay someone else to do for him," she said.

"I've always preferred to do things myself where I can. I find it keeps me sharper."

She looked at him with a surprised expression. "We have that in common."

"I suspect we have a great deal more than that in common," he commented.

And just like that, the heat level between them rose dangerously.

Six

"Don't. Just don't go there," she admonished. The elevator doors pinged open behind them just as a long black vehicle drove into the underground parking lot. "Ah, here's the car and here's Douglas, right on cue."

Logan had the distinct impression she was about to add the words *thank goodness*. He stepped forward and opened the door for Honor and his father and slid onto the wide bench seat next to her after they'd settled in the car. Honor shifted just a little farther away from him, making her point perfectly clear. Douglas, thankfully, appeared to be oblivious.

After stopping briefly at Logan's hotel so he could retrieve his camera, they drove about half an hour to an old waterfront development surrounded by a combination of low-rise business and apartment blocks. Logan alighted from the car and began taking random shots of the surroundings before focusing on the actual development site. Caged by temporary fencing, the collection of brick buildings looked derelict and unloved, but he could already see the warmth in the bricks and the shapes of the window openings that with new frames and glass would be like windows into the buildings' souls.

Oblivious to Honor and Douglas, he began to walk around the site, taking hundreds of photos. When he paused a moment, he saw his father watching him with a smile on his face.

"You're passionate about your work, aren't you, Logan? I can see it on your face and how you lose yourself in what you're doing."

Logan nodded. "Places like this need to be preserved wherever possible—that's what I'm passionate about. Finding the most cost-effective way to hold on to the past, while making sure the buildings can withstand the demands of the future in the most ecologically friendly way, is the challenge. Tell me more about the site. When was it built, and what was its main purpose?"

Douglas went into a detailed history about how the site had primarily consisted of warehouses for the past century and a half. Logan found himself nodding and making mental notes as they walked through the ground floor of one of the buildings. His hands itched to make drawings and concept designs. First, he'd do it all on paper, old-school. Then he'd load the necessary specs into his computer and use his design software. Obviously the architectural design team back at the office would need to consult on his suggestions, to make sure everything fit in with all planning requirements, but his mind was spinning in a million different directions with an expanding dream for the space. And if he could present his dream to Douglas and see him take Richmond Developments on a new trajectory, well, that would make everything all the sweeter.

He knew he'd taken a big risk in coming here, both from

a professional and personal point of view, but when he'd looked at the big picture, he'd known that finding his birth family was more important than anything he'd ever done. Back home, he had an incredible team of managers and staff running his company. He was in the position where he could have as little or as much input as he wanted, which had made this the perfect time to step away and pursue his new goal of discovering his blood kin.

As they spent some time in each of the buildings, Logan sensed Honor's impatience to return to the office. He could have spent the entire day here; in fact, he probably would sometime in the next week or so, but for now he needed to ensure he stayed on the right side of Honor Gould.

"I think I have everything I need for now. Thanks for taking the time out of your day, both of you, and for bringing me out here," Logan said as he put his camera back in its case and slung the strap over his shoulder.

"It's interesting watching you work," Douglas commented as they walked back to the car. "You approach everything with an artist's eye, I think, rather than from a practical point of view."

"I like to think I come at it from both angles, but I guess you're right. If you can't see the beauty in a thing before you start, why would you continue with it?"

Douglas barked a laugh. "A bit like when you meet the woman of your dreams, right?"

Logan's mouth twisted into a smile. "Something like that. Say, Honor, were you already working up color palettes for the new buildings Richmond Developments had planned to build here?"

"Of course. I've had a team on this project full-time for a month. The apartment specs were established even before that."

She sounded ticked off. As if her team's hard work may all have been for nothing.

"I'd like to see them if you're free this afternoon."

"I'm not."

The sharpness of her tone earned her an odd look from her future father-in-law.

"Perhaps tomorrow morning, then," Logan suggested.

"I'll have my assistant show you the concepts when we get back to the office."

Ah, so she was going to be like that. He'd obviously encroached on her work territory and maybe she also needed to reduce her contact with him. He watched her as she walked toward the limousine, ahead of him and Douglas. She ducked into the back of the car, and he saw she'd chosen the seat with her back to the driver.

"She's a fine-looking woman, Honor," Douglas commented as they neared the car. "But sometimes I think she and Keaton are too similar for theirs to be a truly happy marriage."

Logan was surprised at his father's observation. "How so?"

"They're each so intent on climbing the corporate ladder at Richmond Developments, I think they've forgotten to take time to let their relationship grow. I feel like they're still stuck in that dating phase and that they haven't moved past it. Nancy keeps telling me not to worry, but I can't help feeling those two are just going through the motions. Life, happiness—they're worth more than that."

Logan didn't know how to respond, but he didn't have to as Douglas was now occupied with climbing into the car. He took the seat Honor had occupied on the way to the site, while Logan now sat directly opposite Honor. He could see from the moment their knees brushed—the barest touch, but one he perversely engineered before he slid back farther into his seat—that she regretted being forced to stare at him, or past him, for the duration of the journey back to the office.

* * *

Honor couldn't wait to get to her meeting and away from the all-too-tempting presence of Logan Parker. Honestly, watching him at the project site should have been an exercise in complete and utter boredom. Instead, she found herself studying the expression on his face as he eyed the buildings and took photos and wondering what on earth was going through his mind. Sometimes his thoughts were as clear as glass, as excitement lit his pale gray eyes and animated his expression. Other times he was more pensive. And then there were the times he'd looked at her—whether by accident or design.

Each time their gazes had locked, she'd felt it like a physical touch and her body had responded in kind. Now, back at the office, she couldn't wait to put some distance between them. He was altogether too unnerving—and, she reminded herself, he was not Keaton.

She'd been unable to sleep last night after Keaton had left, tied up in knots at refusing him, yet at the same time still craving his twin in ways that shocked her. She'd never thought herself to be particularly motivated by sex, but after the night at the hotel… *No!* She had to put that out of her mind. What she'd done was reprehensible and, deep down, she knew she couldn't be intimate with Keaton while this awful secret stood between them.

Logan had agreed to keep things quiet, but could she trust him with what was inarguably the biggest and most destructive secret of her entire life? This went way past the occasional childhood shoplifting at the grocery store when her mom hadn't had enough money to buy a loaf of bread or a carton of milk. And, besides, she'd always suspected the store owner had turned a blind eye when hunger had forced her to steal. A compassionate man, he'd known that her mom was oftentimes incapable of looking after her daughter.

Honor blinked and had to drag her thoughts back to the present when she realized Douglas was talking to her as they entered the elevator from the parking garage at Richmond Tower.

"I'm sorry, my mind was already at my next meeting," she lied.

"That's what I like about you, Honor. Always thinking ahead," Douglas said with a smug smile. "What I was saying is that you need to include Logan in your meeting. It's with the new eco–wall covering company, isn't it?"

"It is, but I was going to get Steve to go through color palettes with Logan this afternoon."

Douglas made a dismissive gesture with his hand. "Logan has more important things to do than study color palettes. I want him up to speed with everything as quickly as possible, and the only way to do that is to be on the ground with eyes and ears open."

Honor gritted her teeth. "Logan did request to see the color concepts this afternoon," she reminded Douglas.

"Yes, I did and, to be honest, I'm still a bit slammed with jet lag so I'd appreciate the opportunity to spend some time in the office and keep absorbing ideas for the new project. I can spend all day tomorrow with Honor instead."

All day tomorrow? She shuddered at the thought. It was going to be impossible for her to get through her work with him shadowing her every move and thought.

"Fine," she said in a tone that left no one in any doubt that it was anything but. "Now, if you gentlemen will excuse me, I have a meeting to get to."

She left the two of them behind her as she made a sharp turn and headed to the conference room she'd booked for the afternoon. She was so annoyed and distracted that she was almost at the door before she realized she'd left her notes and her computer behind in her office. No, she corrected herself, not her office anymore—hers and Logan's.

Honor's hands clenched into tight fists at her sides as she did an about-face and strode swiftly to retrieve the materials she needed. When she got there, she didn't immediately see Logan until she was almost on top of him, and they both moved to the same side in a failed attempt to avoid a full-on crash.

She flung up her hands as their bodies connected, her palms pressed hard against the firmness of his chest. Instant awareness coursed through her as she remembered what it had felt like to touch him, skin to skin. Logan caught her upper arms to steady her and she instantly took a step back, breaking the unwanted contact as quickly as she could.

"I'm sorry," she said a little too breathlessly. "I wasn't looking where I was going."

"It's okay. Steve mentioned you'd need these for your meeting, so I was bringing them along for you."

"Thank you," she said stiffly, taking her laptop case from him. She quickly checked that all the papers were tucked in with her laptop, which of course they were, because Steve was nothing if not efficient. "Right, well, this will take me the balance of the day, so I'll see you tomorrow."

Without waiting for him to respond, she turned on her heel and stalked away. Damn him for being here. Damn him for even existing, she thought fiercely. Despite all her best intentions, she appeared to be incapable of being in the same space as Logan Parker without her entire body going up in metaphorical flames. What the heck was wrong with her? She had a fiancé already. A man who in every way resembled the one she was walking away from as if her life depended on it.

Every way? a little voice asked at the back of her mind.

Her stomach tightened into a knot as she forced herself to acknowledge the point of difference in the two men. Yes, she loved Keaton and she had promised to marry him. He was handsome and clever and, on occasion, showed wit that hugely appealed to her. But he didn't set her on fire the way Logan Parker did. Why not?

Honor fussed with her engagement ring all the way to the meeting room, and even when she got there she struggled to get her thoughts under control. It wasn't until her supplier and their team arrived for the meeting that she managed to switch off the clamor in her mind and focus on what she needed to do. One day she and Keaton would run Richmond Developments together as husband and wife. As Douglas and Nancy did now. They were of a like mind. They had the same dreams and visions for their joint future. This was the road to ensure lifetime security. She needed to remember that.

Logan was working on his laptop when Kristin came to the door of the office.

"Oh, you're here," she said. "I was looking for Honor."

"She's tied up in a supplier meeting all afternoon. Do you want to leave her a message?"

"No, I'll get hold of her later." Kristin made no pretense of hiding her nosiness as she tried to see what he had up on his screen. "Aren't those pictures of the new development site?" she asked.

"Yeah, we went there today. I'm working on a plan to persuade your father to save most of the buildings."

"Seriously? You know we don't do that kind of thing here. It's not cost-effective."

Logan shrugged. "Well, we'll see."

"Trust me, I know about these things. I don't run the finance department just for fun. There's no way you can recover the costs of repurposing those buildings as quickly as we would with a new build, if at all."

She walked all the way into the office and stood there,

arms crossed, feet planted shoulder width apart and looking as combative as she'd been yesterday.

"Sometimes it's not just about making money," Logan commented.

She laughed. "Are you sure you're related to us?"

He couldn't help it. He laughed out loud. "Yeah, I'm sure. Hey, do you know if the DNA results are back yet?"

"I don't think even Dad's money can rush those kinds of results. I'm pretty sure it'll be another few days, but even so, he's starting to sound like he doesn't need the proof."

"Do you?"

She uncrossed her arms and sank into the chair opposite his desk. "You look like my brother, but you don't sound like him."

"And yet, I know, in here—" he tapped his chest "—I'm your brother. How's that for weird?"

She frowned a little before responding. "So what happens if you are who you think you are? Are you staying here in Seattle? Forging a role for yourself at Richmond Developments?"

"It's still fluid for now," Logan admitted. "I have a strong team running my business back home, but there's always a need for a hand at the tiller. It was my brainchild, after all, and I'd hate to see anything change or slip while I was here."

"Ever considered a career in politics? That's a nonanswer if ever I heard one."

He cracked a half smile. "True. I owe you better than that if we're siblings, don't I?" He sighed and leaned back in his chair. "To be honest, I'd like to think I could forge a place here as long as I don't step on any toes. I know you and Keaton have both worked in the family firm since you left college and probably even before that."

Kristin nodded. "And?"

"And I don't want to be that newcomer who walks all

over you to get what he wants. That said, I should have been a part of this family and Richmond Developments all along. I want my place in *my* family."

Kristin nodded again. "I get that. But until the test results come back, you're in limbo, aren't you? What's the arrangement back in New Zealand? Are you on leave for a set period or have you appointed an interim CEO in your absence?"

"At this stage, I'm on leave for three months."

Kristin tipped her head to one side and looked at him seriously. "This is really important to you, isn't it? It's not just a matter of finding your birth family. It's more a matter of finding your entire identity."

Logan felt some of the tension he hadn't even realized he was holding in his body ease just a little. "That's exactly it. I had to give it my best shot. I figured that within three months I could prove my link to this family and discover whether or not I fit here. If I don't, well, I will always have my other family and my work back in New Zealand. I don't plan to abandon either."

Kristin nodded slightly, then her expression became curious. "Just how are your family back home handling your trip here?"

Logan twirled a pen in his fingers as he considered his answer. "Some of them are worried about what this will bring down on my late mother's name, especially with her having abducted me. But most of my cousins understand why this is so important to me. I'm not turning my back on them. I will always love and respect them. My grandmother is still living, and she gave me her blessing. We still consider each other family. End of story."

"We don't have any living grandparents," Kristin said bluntly. "They died before I was born, and Keaton was too small to remember them. Do you think your grandmother would accept us, too?"

Logan grinned widely. "She'd welcome you with open arms. If you're connected to me, you're absolutely connected to her, too. As well as all my cousins and, trust me, there are a lot of them."

"Mom and Dad were both only children, so we don't have cousins here. I think I'd like to be part of a larger extended family."

"Looks like we both stand to benefit if the results come back positive," Logan said.

Watching the expression on Kristin's face soften as they talked about his background gave him an insight into his sister that he wasn't expecting. She was a powerhouse here at Richmond Developments, but inside she was still a person who cherished family ties. She was looking for a place to belong, just as he was. He began to feel a glimmer of hope that she was on the path to accepting him and his place within the family.

"Those are great shots. What type of camera did you use? It wasn't your phone camera, was it?" Kristin asked, abruptly changing the subject as she turned to look at his computer screen. Clearly the time for family communion was over.

"No." He reached down beside the desk, took his camera from its case and handed it over to her. "I use this when I'm on a job, but I usually have it with me when I'm out and about, too. I don't want to miss anything that could be a source of inspiration."

Kristin lit up when she saw the camera, and he was intrigued to find they had a love of photography in common.

"Oh hell," Kristin said after a few more minutes of discussion. "I'm supposed to be elsewhere. We'll need to continue this later."

Logan stood as she did and held out his hand. Kristin hesitated a moment before taking it.

"Thank you," he said.

"For what?"

"For talking to me like I'm not the enemy. I'm not, you know."

She gave a short nod. "Yeah, well, I'm not the one you have to convince."

Seven

It became eminently clear at a dinner at his parents' house the following Sunday just whom he did need to convince—Keaton. His twin was as distrustful as he'd been on day one, and there was absolutely no sign of any acceptance or friendship coming from his direction. In fact, he appeared more openly hostile than before.

Honor, too, had become even more standoffish. But he knew she was aware of exactly where he was throughout the course of the entire evening, and he knew that because he was equally, painfully aware of her. Neither Honor nor Keaton had said more than a word or two to him all evening, nor to each other, to be honest. But it looked as though that was going to change any moment now, Logan realized, as he watched his brother stride toward him with a look of determination painted clearly on his face.

"Keaton, good to see you. Our paths haven't exactly crossed the past few days, and I'd like to catch up when you're free," Logan said as an opening gambit. He certainly wasn't expecting what came next.

"Stay away from my fiancée," Keaton said in a low voice.

"I beg your pardon?"

"I said, stay away from Honor. I've seen the way you look at her, and she doesn't need the pressure of having to ward off unwanted attention. Be a gentleman, Parker. Hands off."

Logan squared his shoulders and stared his brother down.

"Hands off? That would imply I'm trying to be hands on."

Had someone mentioned seeing the two of them at the hotel the other night? Was everything about to blow up in Logan's face? Surely his parents wouldn't be so welcoming if they knew what he and Honor had done. His gaze flicked past Keaton's shoulder to where Honor sat chatting with Kristin.

"Even now you can't stop looking at her. It's making both of us uncomfortable. Stop it," Keaton said firmly.

"I'm sorry," Logan began, deciding to take a placatory line rather than engaging in the full-on confrontation his alpha side wanted.

Keaton was right. He had been unable to keep his gaze off Honor tonight. She looked, as always, stunningly beautiful, but there was an air of fragility about her that hadn't been there the night he'd met her. It called on every one of his instincts to protect her and make her world right so the confident woman he'd met could come forth again. But it wasn't his place to offer her that protection, and he kept having to remind himself of that.

"She's a beautiful and clever woman, Keaton, and I'm sorry if I've made either of you uncomfortable," Logan continued. "Unfortunately, your father has put us in her office together. I can ask to be moved, if that would make you, and Honor, more at ease."

"Look, I can accept that Dad, for whatever idiotic reason that's currently taken his normally rational mind hostage, thinks that the two of you need to work together. Just keep it business, okay? Even now you're staring at her as if she's a triple-decker burger and you haven't eaten for a week."

"Triple-decker burger?" Logan couldn't help it—he burst out laughing.

Keaton had the grace to grin back at him. "What can I say? I'm hungry. Mom's idea of dinner is not really suited to people with a genuine appetite."

"Want to head out for a triple decker once this is over? It would give us a chance to talk, just the two of us."

Logan knew that if an olive branch was to be extended, it had to come from him. He was the outsider here and if he wasn't prepared to do what was necessary to make his brother happy, then he didn't deserve to be here, either. But should his brother's happiness come at his own expense? He clamped down on the thought before it could bloom into anything else.

Keaton was shaking his head. "Sorry, I have an early start in the morning. Business meeting in San Antonio, then on to Houston and up to Dallas over the next few days, so I'm heading home soon."

"Maybe another time, then."

"Sure. When I get back. We'll sort something out."

Keaton started to turn away, but Logan stopped him.

"Keaton?"

"Yeah?"

"Don't worry about me with Honor. I respect the fact that she's your fiancée, and I won't do anything to upset her."

Keaton stared at him hard, as if to gauge whether he was telling the truth, and for a moment it was unsettling looking so directly into a living mirror of himself. Whatever Keaton saw reflected back in Logan's eyes must have satisfied him, because he nodded and offered his brother his hand. The two men shook and then Keaton went to make his apologies to his parents before leaving. Honor, too, made her excuses and joined him.

As Logan watched them leave, he couldn't help but wonder if he'd end up being proved a liar. His desire for Honor had not abated. Not when she'd sniped at him in the office. Not when she'd all but ignored him on a site visit. Not when she'd studiously avoided him at this family dinner. Was her bad temper because she continued to fight her own attraction for him, or was it that he made her uncomfortable like his brother had said?

Whatever it was, the knowledge that Honor was with Keaton should have been enough to quell any feelings he had for her. The very thought of his brother's hands on her was enough to send a murderous rage through his mind the likes of which he'd never experienced before. And that, in itself, was more than enough warning that he needed to get some level of control on his feelings. No, better than control. He needed to rid himself of them altogether.

Honor Gould was strictly out of bounds.

As Keaton drove her home, Honor mulled over the fact that he was going to be away for several days. While he was around, she could tell herself that the magnetic pull she felt from Logan Parker was nothing to worry about. But with him gone? She gave herself a hard mental shake as they pulled into the parking garage at her apartment building. She was made of sterner stuff than her mother. She was far more driven to succeed and far more motivated. She was not going to let Logan Parker derail her lifelong dream. She hadn't worked this hard for this long to see it go by the wayside all because of some crazy hormonal reaction to a man who looked exactly like the one she'd promised to spend the rest of her life with.

And she and Keaton would have a great life together. She had no doubt of that. They were on the same page with everything from how many children they wanted to how they planned to continue to work together. Okay, so they were a little lacking in the passion stakes—she could live with that.

But could he?

She'd never truly asked herself that question before today. Was she forcing him to settle for less than he deserved? Was he happy looking forward to a tepid love life for the next fifty or sixty years? She hated that she was second-guessing herself all of a sudden and that she was second-guessing Keaton, too. It was patently evident that they needed to talk. She had to be certain he was happy. She did love him and she wanted happiness for him, and more. But was she the right person to give that to him?

"Are you coming up?" she asked as he pulled into one of the two parking spaces allocated to her apartment.

"I'll see you to your door, the way I always do," he said with a smile.

"I was hoping that maybe we could do a bit more than that."

"More than that?"

"Yes, like talk about our future."

He sighed a little. "Let's go upstairs."

He got out of the car, walked around to her door and opened it for her. Always the consummate gentleman. She loved that about him, she truly did, but manners didn't make a relationship, did they? They both needed more than that.

Upstairs in her apartment, Honor offered him coffee.

"No, thanks. What did you want to talk about, specifically?" he asked, not even taking a seat.

Honor drew in a deep breath. This would be so much easier if he'd just sit down instead of looking like he was ready to bolt for the door at the earliest opportunity.

"Us. I feel like there's a distance between us lately, and it's growing. Are you happy, Keaton?" she asked him, studying his expression carefully.

She'd always been able to tell if he was being truthful, but right now his eyes were shuttered and the set of his face made him look more distant than she'd ever seen him.

"There's a lot going on, not to mention I have to leave on the red eye for San Antonio in a few hours. Look, can't this wait until I get back?" he hedged.

Honor took a step toward him. "This is important, Keaton. I need to know. Are you happy?"

He closed his eyes briefly before looking straight back into hers, and in that moment Honor regretted pushing the issue and dreaded what she was about to hear.

"I think we should consider taking a break," he said, bluntly.

"A break away together?" she asked hopefully, even though she knew that wasn't what he meant.

"No, apart."

Honor made a small strangled sound. Suddenly, it felt as though everything she'd ever worked for and wanted was slipping out of her grasp.

"Look, I know this probably comes as a shock, but I feel like lately we're on different wavelengths. I've tried to ignore it. Even tried to blame it on the resurrection of my sainted, long-lost brother. But if I'm totally honest with myself, this sense of separation started before his arrival on the scene. You've felt it, too, haven't you?"

Honor found herself nodding. She knew exactly what he was talking about, even if she hadn't wanted to admit it.

Keaton took a step toward her and wrapped her in his

arms. "Look, let's take some time to think about what we really want."

"I thought we knew what we wanted," she said, her voice breaking on the last few words.

He sighed and shook his head slightly. "So did I. Look, I'm gone most of this week. Let's use the time apart to figure things out, and if we need more space when I get back, we'll take however long is necessary till we can agree on our paths for the future."

Paths? Did he mean separate paths? Honor couldn't bring herself to verbalize the question, because she was afraid of what he might say.

"Okay?" he prompted.

"It'll have to be okay, won't it?" she said carefully. "When we marry, it's going to be forever. Like you say, we need to be sure."

"I'm sorry, Honor. With everything going on with work and the family, this is just one more log on the fire, isn't it?"

"As a couple we should be supporting one another through this. I'm not certain that taking time out is the best idea."

She had to fight for this, for him, even if it felt as though she was a drowning woman grasping at straws.

"Trust me, Honor. Even if you don't need the space to think, I do. Everything that I took as a given in my life has been turned upside down with Logan's arrival. It's making me take a good long look at everything that's important to me, and I'm coming to realize that some of those things aren't as important as I thought."

"And I'm one of those things?" Sudden burning tears filled her eyes and began to track down her cheeks.

He made a sound of frustration and lifted his hand to wipe away her tears.

"Our relationship is important. I love you, Honor. Truly,

I do, but do I love you enough to marry you and spend the rest of our lives together? I'm not sure about that anymore."

The fact that he was verbalizing what she'd been feeling herself was no balm to her panicked mind. She pulled free of his arms and he stepped back immediately, as if grateful for the space. Fighting to hold on to her sanity, Honor forced a teary smile to her face.

"You'd better go. You have an early start, as you said."

"Are you going to be okay?"

She straightened her shoulders. "Sure."

He kissed her then, but it was not the kind of kiss lovers shared. Instead it felt more like a bittersweet expression of a regretful goodbye, and with that realization Honor knew the writing was on the wall. She walked him to the door of her apartment, twisting her engagement ring off her finger as she did so.

"Do you want this back while we're on this break?" she said, holding out her hand with the ring in her palm.

"No, of course not! And even if we—" He shook his head firmly and took the ring from her palm and slid it back on her finger. "The ring is yours, no matter what *we* decide."

After another night with next to no sleep, Honor had worked herself into quite a state of irritation by the time she arrived in the office. As usual, Logan Parker was already settled at the desk opposite hers. Did the man never rest? He was always first in and last home. Or maybe he was just trying to impress Douglas. No, she was being churlish. He didn't have to impress Douglas or Nancy. He wasn't after the family's money. He was a millionaire in his own right; she knew that because she'd done more research on him than any uninterested person had a right to do.

Which meant what, exactly? That she *was* interested? She shoved the thought away and fought to compose herself.

"Good morning," Logan said, looking up as she set her briefcase beside her desk.

"If you say so," she answered.

"Bad night?"

Since he'd arrived on the scene, every night had been a bad night—well, almost every night—but she wasn't about to give him the pleasure of knowing that.

"I always hate it when Keaton goes away. I miss him already."

There, that was exactly what a loving fiancée should say, wasn't it? But she was such a fraud.

A rustle of movement in the hall caught her attention. She turned to see Douglas Richmond moving swiftly toward their office, and the expression on his face was one of extreme excitement.

"Glad I caught the two of you together," he said without any preamble. "I just heard that the deal fell through on a riverfront development in Portland we bid on and lost. The owners didn't want the site cleared and rebuilt on. Mentioned a whole lot of sentimental claptrap when they turned us down, even though we offered more money. Now the buyers have backed out, saying the covenants put on the building are too restrictive. The sellers are offering it to us again if we're willing to redesign the existing structures and not do a teardown.

"I think this is a perfect opportunity for Logan to manage a project for us, and I want the two of you to head there today and do a site examination before I agree to terms. Don't let on we're too eager, but I have a feeling this could be the jewel in the crown."

"And the site we went to last week?" Logan asked.

"Figures aren't looking feasible for what you were suggesting. We can keep some of the buildings for retail and restaurant development, but Kristin says we need a better return on the residential side. I back her up on that. The girl knows money, and we're not just here to make friends."

Honor wondered how Logan would take the news, but if she expected him to argue with Douglas, she was disappointed. Instead, he merely shrugged.

"Got to agree with the bean counters," he said philosophically. "But I'm glad we can look to preserve some of the buildings at least."

Douglas nodded. "And this new project. I need you guys on the next flight to Portland." He stated the check-in time. "Can you pack and be ready on time? My assistant has already booked you on the flight and arranged accommodation."

"I have a bag in the trunk of my car," Honor said. "I'm always ready."

"That's one of the things I always know I can rely on with you, Honor. How about you?" Douglas asked, looking at Logan.

"If we can swing past my hotel on the way to the airport, it won't take me more than ten minutes to throw some things together. It's just for one night, right?"

"Possibly two. Depends on how long it takes you to get all the information you need."

Honor hid the shudder that ran down her spine. Two days pretty much alone with Logan Parker? It was a good thing she'd had that little pep talk with herself this morning.

"We'd better get going then. I'm assuming Stella has emailed the flight details to us already?" Honor checked her email app on her phone and nodded. "Yes, they're all here."

"Good. I look forward to your report when you return. It's vitally important that this is done right. I was pretty sore when we originally lost the bid, and I don't need to tell you how much it cost us in wasted man-hours. I don't want anything to screw it up this time. Got it?"

"Got it," Logan said firmly.

Douglas nodded at them both and left as quickly as he'd arrived. Honor looked at Logan.

"Well, don't just stand there. We need to move. When the man says hurry, he means it."

"Okay, I'm moving."

Logan bent to grab his camera from the bottom drawer of his desk. The fabric of his trousers stretched tight across his butt, and the sight made something clench hard deep inside her. *Nope, nope, nope.* She forced herself to avert her gaze. She had this under control. She wasn't about to do or say anything that put her precarious future in even more jeopardy. But she couldn't resist another peek, nor could she forget what his body had felt like as it moved against hers or what his skin had felt like beneath the palms of her hands.

Palms that were growing sweaty at the thought. She couldn't stay here in this room with him right now or she might do something irreparably stupid. She walked out into the hall. Honor felt him behind her, moving quickly to catch up as she reached the elevator.

"Does everyone around here jump this fast when Douglas says so?" he drawled as he stopped next to her.

"Usually they ask how high, but then they spring into action. You don't stay here long if you don't do what he says," she said, willing the elevator to come quickly. "That's not to say he's unreasonable. He's a fair employer. But he's fiercely results-driven."

There was a ping, and the doors slid open. She and Logan stepped inside. She moved directly to the opposite wall of the car from where he stood. She knew he noticed and saw the way his jaw clenched ever so slightly. So he was irritated by her putting distance between them? She didn't care. It was the only way she could keep her equilibrium right now.

Honor tried to convince herself it was only because he looked so much like Keaton that she was drawn to him, but she knew that it was more than that. So very much more. It was attraction on a fiercely instinctive level. The kind that kept humankind alive as a species.

And it terrified her.

Eight

"What do you mean, the hotel has only one room booked for us? Obviously we require two rooms. This is unacceptable," Honor ranted at the implacable hotel receptionist.

It had been an arduous day already, and this development was the icing on a rapidly sinking cake, as far as she was concerned.

"Ma'am, we explained it to the person making the booking and they said it would be all right as you and Mr. Richmond were a couple. We are fully booked with no rooms to spare, and with several major events here in the city over the next two days, none of our other hotels have rooms available, either."

"Well, can we get a room with twin beds? Or maybe a rollaway could be brought to the room?"

She wouldn't share a bed with him. There was no way on earth she was getting that cozy with Logan again. No, if they couldn't change their room, he could find his own accommodation elsewhere.

"No, ma'am. I'm afraid not, and safety regulations do not allow for a rollaway bed in this room. Do you wish to relinquish the booking? We do have a wait list of people asking for rooms. As I said, it's a busy time."

She wanted to scream at the receptionist, but she knew the woman was simply doing her job. The trip had been planned at short notice, and clearly Stella had misunderstood exactly which Richmond brother Honor was traveling with.

"No, look, I'm sorry I was rude. I'll take the booking." She looked over her shoulder at Logan. "Can you call around and see if you can find anywhere else?"

He raised one brow. "You don't think we can share a room?"

The challenge was barely there, but it sent alarm bells ringing in her head. Did he honestly think she was going to spend the night with him in such close proximity?

"After all," Logan continued, lowering his voice, "we're both adults, aren't we? I think we can remain true to our pact. Or are you afraid that once we're behind locked doors you won't be able to control yourself?"

"Of course I can control myself," she said, stiff with disapproval.

"So you're suggesting *I* can't? That I'll be so overwhelmed by your beauty, your scent, your very nearness, that I won't be able to control myself?"

Desire spread through her like wildfire. She pushed it down, refusing to be seduced by the tone of his voice or the reaction of her wayward hormones.

"Can you guarantee you won't?" she challenged him.

"Oh yeah, I can guarantee it. I've never had to force myself on anyone, Honor, and I'm not about to start now."

She'd made him angry, and for some reason that filled her with regret.

"Let me see if I can find you somewhere else first. If there's absolutely nothing available, then we'll share."

Logan stood back and crossed his arms, observing her with an air of boredom as she called the central reservation lines of every hotel chain Richmond Developments had an account with and several it didn't. Thirty minutes later she conceded defeat and passed Logan the second key card to their room.

"I'm tired, and I'm sure you are, too. It's been a busy day. We may as well go and see how bad it is," she said, accepting the inevitable.

The room itself was lovely. Spacious, with a large bathroom and wide windows overlooking a park on the edge of the Willamette River. The bed was exactly as advertised. Queen-size. Honor eyed the carpet and wondered whether she could bear a night sleeping on the floor. Perhaps with a blanket underneath her she could do it.

"Which side do you want?" Logan asked, setting his small suitcase on the floor.

"Side?"

"Of the bed."

"Um…" She stared at the bed and then at him. He wasn't small. Over six feet tall and with shoulders like an Olympic swimmer, he'd take up a fair bit of room. "Look, I can sleep on the floor. If I fold up the bedcover and make it into a mattress, I'm sure I'll be fine."

"Fine?" He cocked his eyebrow in that ridiculously sexy way of his again. "Don't be silly. We have another busy day tomorrow. If you don't get a good night's sleep, you won't be able to jump high enough when Douglas issues his next imperative."

She detected a note of distaste in his voice. "Not a fan of your newfound father?"

"Not all his business methods, no. My own management style is less confrontational. But I can live with having opinions that differ from his on a few things. And I can stick to my side of the bed, too. Since you don't seem to want to make a decision, I'll sleep on the window side, okay? You can take the side closest to the bathroom."

He made it sound so simple, Honor almost thought she could do this. In fact, she darn well could do this. Sleeping on the floor was for kids at a sleepover. She was an adult in command of herself in all things. And if she said it long enough and firmly enough, she might even begin to believe it.

"Maybe we can roll up the bedspread and put it down the middle between us," she suggested hopefully.

"Sure, whatever rocks your boat."

He rocked her boat. And that was the problem. No, *she* was the problem.

Keaton. She had to think of him. She had to keep the glimmer of hope that they might work things out in the forefront of her mind at all times. It wasn't such an impossible ask. Despite what he'd said last night about taking a break, she knew he'd be justifiably upset if he found out she and Logan were sharing a room, no matter how innocently it had come about. Would he understand it was a circumstance out of their control? Did he even need to know?

She hated that she was in turmoil like this, second-guessing every thought and feeling. Logan Parker unsettled her on every score.

"Did you want to head out somewhere for dinner to discuss what we looked at today and where we want to focus tomorrow?" Logan suggested, oblivious to the thoughts racing around in her crazy head.

"Sure," she quickly agreed.

It would certainly be better than having room service. The less time they spent together in the confines of this room, the better, no matter how perfectly it was appointed.

"You want to grab a shower first?" Logan asked.

"Thanks, I'll only be a minute."

"Take your time," he said, kicking off his shoes and stretching out on his side of the bed.

For some stupid reason she couldn't help the blush that rose to her cheeks as she watched him. Seeing him like that felt unbearably intimate, but then her stomach rumbled, reminding her that they'd skipped lunch today while touring the property and that it had been a very long time since breakfast. She riffled through her case and grabbed the long-sleeved designer T-shirt and jeans she always kept ready to go for situations like this. Casual enough for downtime on her own, yet smart enough—teamed with a pair of heels, some chunky jewelry and her warm coat—to wear to dinner at a restaurant.

When she emerged from the bathroom, fully dressed, with her face scrubbed free of makeup and her hair freshly washed and blow-dried, Logan appeared to be asleep on the bed. His breathing was slow and even and his features had relaxed from the slightly stern look he sometimes wore. While he was definitely more laid-back than Keaton, she had seen glimpses of the hard strength he would have needed to get where he was today. And, while it was easy to think of him as the underdog given the situation with his family, she'd learned he was a powerful player in New Zealand's business world.

"You all done?" he murmured.

She realized he'd been watching her stare at him.

"Yes, bathroom's all yours."

He moved off the bed and grabbed a couple of items from his case before shutting himself in the steamy confines of the bathroom she'd just vacated. Try as she might, she couldn't suppress the visions that plagued her as she imagined him under the hot spray of the shower. She didn't have to struggle with herself for too long, though, because within four minutes he was back out, dressed and smelling all too enticingly fresh.

"That was quick," she commented as she picked up her bag and headed toward the door.

"Yeah, well, y'know. Guys."

There was absolutely no answer to that, she thought, as they headed out for their meal. The pizza joint they settled on was noisy and busy and just the kind of thing she needed to avoid having to make too much conversation with Logan—even work conversation was difficult. Since they were hungry, they made short work of their dinner. Which meant they were left with time on their hands when they were done.

"Shall we have a drink back at the hotel?" Honor suggested as Logan picked up the tab. "Finish our discussion?"

"Sure, I could kill a beer," Logan said.

It was cold out, and the air around them misted on their breath. They walked side by side back to the hotel, their arms occasionally brushing as they continued along the sidewalk. Honor tried to ignore the sensations aroused in her and kept increasing the distance between them, but the world was full of lampposts, hydrants and other pedestrians that, to her eternal irritation, kept pushing them back together. Even the brightly lit holiday displays all around them couldn't soften her mood.

Man, if she couldn't even walk alongside him without touch being an issue, how on earth was she going to sleep tonight? It was a relief to enter the lobby of the hotel and to be able to put that necessary space between them again. In the bar, Logan ordered a pale ale and she ordered a glass of champagne. The waitress brought their drinks over to where they sat in a secluded corner.

Honor worked hard to keep their conversation focused on work and what they had to do tomorrow. They were both on the same page with their vision for the property, which made things a lot easier. She couldn't help wondering if Keaton would have been so easy to work with. He had a habit of wanting to take the opposing side of any argument, whether he personally supported it or not. She'd always put that down to his stint on the college debate team and had frequently teased him about it, but in this situation it was definitely a whole lot less stressful to easily reach agreement on their objectives.

"We're going to recommend Douglas make that offer, aren't we?" Logan said after finishing the last of his beer.

"It would be foolish not to. Especially if he's serious about expanding into repurposing versus demolition. To be honest, I'm surprised he was so open to the suggestion."

"He's a businessman. He can see that we can charge premium prices for both the commercial and the residential sides if we refurbish what's already there."

"That's what you do in New Zealand, is it? Aim for the premium market?"

"Absolutely. There's a huge demand for repurposing worldwide. Bigger and newer isn't always better, and if we can reconstruct in an ecologically sustainable way, then all the better. Obviously I'd like to see more affordable housing for lower-income families, too, and we're working on that back home."

Their conversation expanded to the potential of green building practices, and Honor felt excited to be able to share her ideas with someone of a like mind. But all of a sudden, she caught herself yawning widely.

"Oh, heavens. I'm sorry, that was rude of me."

"Not at all. You look tired, and I don't mean that in an unkind way. We've had a full day and have another ahead of us tomorrow. Why don't you go to the room? I'm going to sit back, have another beer and come up a bit later. Okay?"

She nodded and all but scurried from the bar. She'd wondered how they were going to manage the whole bedtime routine together, so his suggestion made everything much simpler. And, with any luck, she could even be fast asleep before he came back to the room.

Ten beers wouldn't have been enough to dull his hunger for the woman he was about to sleep with—in the literal sense only, he reminded himself. She'd been so skittish today it had been all he could do not to grab her by the shoulders and kiss her soundly, just to get this crackling tension that bristled between them out of the air. But he'd promised her and, even more importantly, he'd promised his brother that there was nothing to worry about between them. And nothing meant exactly that.

No sweet taste of her lips. No swallowing the sighs and moans she made as he touched her delectable body. And certainly no losing himself in the slick heat of her as he had when they'd made love.

Damn. And now he had a hard-on.

At least she'd be asleep when he got to the room. He'd waited in the bar long enough. Weariness pulled at every muscle in his body. He'd never understood how much strain it could put a person under to be with someone and yet try not to be with them at the same time. It was the kind of game he'd never wanted to play—never had to, to be honest. But he was a man of his word. He was not going to touch her, no matter how much he craved her.

It was dark in the room when he let himself in. Honor had left the bathroom light on and the door slightly ajar, though, so he wasn't entirely blind when he entered. He went to the bathroom and got ready for bed, realizing too late that he'd brought no pajamas. He'd have to sleep in his boxer briefs—and hopefully keep some measure of circumspection between him and Honor.

She moaned slightly as he slipped beneath the sheets. He stretched out one foot, tentatively seeking to discover if she'd put some kind of barrier between them and smiled as his foot touched what was very obviously a rolled-up towel down the middle of the bed. He pulled back, closed his eyes and lay on his back, willing himself to sleep.

Of course, it was impossible. Instead he lay there, listening to Honor's breathing, feeling the warmth that poured off her body as she slept. Slept, yes, but not peacefully. Every now and then she made a sound of distress, as if she was caught in a bad dream and couldn't verbalize what it was that she needed to say. The noises that came from her were indistinct but clearly unhappy. And then she twitched. An almighty jerk that yanked the covers from him as she burrowed deeper into her side of the bed, still making those noises.

"Honor?" he said gently.

He couldn't just lie here and do nothing. She was obviously upset. Maybe because he was here, but maybe because of something else. Whatever it was, he had the power to wake her and release her from the grip of whatever it was that distressed her. He reached a hand over to touch her lightly on the shoulder and called her name again.

"Honor!" he said more loudly. "Everything's okay. It's just a dream."

She mumbled something that sounded like "no." He could feel her thrashing her head from side to side. This obviously called for more direct contact. He reached out again, this time taking a firm hold on her shoulder, giving her a slight shake and repeating what he'd just said.

He knew the exact moment she was awake from the way her breathing went from rapid and shallow to a sharp gasp followed immediately by a deep sigh. She reached for him, burrowed in tight to his chest as if seeking comfort. Without thinking, Logan wrapped her in his arms and held her tight. Her shoulders shook and he could feel moisture on his bare chest. She was crying? Hell. What kind of dream had it been?

He stroked her hair, her shoulders, her back. Anything to try and soothe away whatever had driven her to this point. And she held on to him tighter than before. Even with that damned rolled-up towel there, he couldn't help his physical reaction. No matter which way he turned, he wanted her, but he knew that it was inappropriate now. Hell, it was inappropriate, period. She was engaged to his brother. He didn't care about the fact that she and Keaton hadn't been intimate in months. It was none of his business. *She* was none of his business. And yet, here she was, in his arms.

And then she kissed him.

Nine

Honor breathed in the scent of Logan's skin, telling herself it was purely to soothe her fractured senses, but somehow even her brain wouldn't accept that truth. Not when her blood pounded through her veins at the nearness of him. Not when his every breath made her breasts press against his chest with enough delicious pressure to make her nipples harden into tight points.

The dream had been a repeat of so many she'd had. Its roots were burrowed deep in her childhood memories and the sense of abandonment she'd always felt even though her mom had never physically left her. Well, not for more than three days at a time, anyway. But she wasn't going to go there again. It was beyond time to put the past to rest, but whenever she was stressed, the old loneliness and fear came surging back, forcing her to seek distraction.

She poured everything she had into that kiss. Everything she'd ever wanted to be. Everything she'd lost. And she had lost. She knew now there was no going back. Doing this, with Logan, meant she was closing a door forever on a future with Keaton.

It was a conscious choice and one she should have made after she'd discovered who Logan Parker was. Whether they went anywhere from here was something she wouldn't think about tonight.

Honor yanked the towel out from between them and slipped one hand over his hip, her palm skimming against the waistband of his briefs and lower to his thigh. No matter what she told herself, it all kept coming back to the same thing. She wanted him. Right here, right now. And more than that she wanted the escape that losing herself in him and the pleasure that she knew they'd find together would bring.

She let her hand slide upward to his chest, feeling his nipples tighten into hard discs before she skimmed her hand down over the taut muscles of his belly and back down to the waistband of his boxers. His hand caught hers, holding her firmly by the wrist and preventing her from reaching her goal as he pulled away from her kiss.

"Are you sure about this?" he asked, his voice thick with desire.

She answered without allowing herself to think. "Yes."

She kissed him again and felt his grip on her hand loosen, allowing her to continue to touch, to explore. He was hard and hot and so ready she couldn't help the groan of need that came from deep inside her as her fingers closed around him. They'd gone past the point of no return. She needed to be with him just as she needed to breathe. It was instinctual. It was necessary.

His lips and tongue met hers in a fierce duel. The ache at her core became an insistent thrum, demanding she possess him in the most literal sense humanly possible, but now that they'd embarked on this path, she wanted to make it last as long as possible. The first time they'd made love, he'd taken control. Now it was her turn, and she wanted to make the most of it.

Heat poured off his body and she straddled him, lifting off her nightgown and tossing it to the floor beside them. She wanted that heat, craved it, craved him. Inside her, around her, everywhere.

Honor couldn't get enough of the taste of him, let alone the feel of the texture of his skin against her fingertips, her palms. She tugged at his briefs, freed his straining erection and positioned herself to take him into her body. His hands clamped on her hips, holding her in place.

"Protection," he grunted.

"I'm covered," she said.

He groaned as she began to lower onto him, letting her take him inside her at her own pace—slow and steady and with a determination she'd never been so certain of in all her life.

This was what she wanted. No, *needed*. Sensation, pleasure, distraction. No more was she the frightened little girl, or the desperate teen, or the insecure young woman. This—taking power and using it—was what she needed more than anything. And as her body adjusted to his, the ripples of pleasure were already forming. She started to move, at first slowly and then with an increasing frenzy as she reached for completion. Beneath her Logan met her every thrust with one of his own as he reached up to cup her breasts, to tease her rigid nipples and squeeze and mold the soft, full flesh.

"Let go," he urged in a harsh whisper. "Take us both over."

His words were her undoing. She let out a small scream as she relinquished her control over the sensations that had built behind an invisible wall of restraint. There was no more holding back as her climax bloomed from deep inside her. She was vaguely aware of Logan reaching his own, felt his body stiffen and surge and surge again as he came deep inside her. She collapsed onto his chest, both of them slick with perspiration, their breathing heavy, their hearts hammering in their chests.

She lay there hardly believing what she'd just done, exhaustion pulling at every sated muscle. Logan's hand stroked her back, up and down and again, until she felt his body grow slack as he drifted off to sleep. She slid from him and back to her side of the bed, waiting until his breathing was deep and steady before she rose and went to the bathroom, collecting her discarded nightgown on the way.

In the harsh light of the bathroom, she stared at her reflection. Guilt sliced painfully through her. Her gaze dropped to the ring she still wore on her finger, and she tugged it off and slipped it in her toilet bag. She could never wear it again. She would return it to Keaton as soon as she saw him next, along with informing him of her decision that things between them were well and truly over. She'd known it, deep inside, when he'd requested the break, but it hadn't been until she'd woken and reached for Logan that she'd finally accepted it for the truth.

She lifted her eyes to study her face again in the mirror and saw much there to disappoint her. She had the same eyes as her mom, the same shape to her face. The same hair color, even. And the same morals, she thought with a sharp pain in her chest. She really was no different than her mother after all. Ready to throw everything away for a fling with another man and damn the consequences.

Honor quickly washed herself and yanked her nightgown back on before switching off the light and going back to bed. As soon as she was beneath the covers, Logan's arm curled around her waist and pulled her to him. He muttered something in his sleep before settling back into the deep, regular breathing of before. And Honor lay there, taking scant comfort from his presence, unable to sleep as she visualized her entire world disintegrating around her.

* * *

As soon as the gray light of dawn began to peep through the windows, Honor bolted from the bed and, grabbing her clothes, went to the bathroom to armor up. She must have had some sleep, she reasoned as she regarded herself in the mirror while brushing her teeth, but not enough to ensure she didn't have deep shadows under her eyes this morning. By the time she'd showered and dressed and returned to the bedroom, Logan was very much awake.

"That your version of the walk of shame?" he challenged, propped up on his pillows with his hands tucked behind his head.

"Bathroom's all yours," she said, ignoring the expanse of bare chest and the question in his eyes, and went to pack her toilet bag and nightgown into her case.

"You're going to ignore what happened between us last night?"

"Why not? Worked last time," she said with fake insouciance.

She saw anger flare in his eyes.

"So that's all I am. A convenient scratching post? We're just going to go back to Seattle today and pretend nothing has happened and you're going to carry on with my brother like last time?"

There was a note of something else in his voice that hadn't been there before. She sighed and turned to face him.

"Keaton and I are on a break, mutually agreed," she said, but before she could continue, he interrupted.

"So what the hell does that mean? You're both free to screw around?"

She flinched at his blunt turn of phrase. He had every right to be angry. She'd messed this up just like she'd messed everything else up along with it.

"No, it doesn't mean that at all. On Sunday night we agreed to take a break, but when he gets back from his current trip, I'm going to break off our engagement. Obviously, it can't continue. I should have done it immediately after our first night together. What Keaton and I have isn't what he deserves. *I'm* not what he deserves."

"Nor I, apparently. I'm still finding my way with my family. This is going to blow everything apart."

"Why? No one needs to know."

"Seriously? We have sex twice—mind-blowing, soul-searing sex—and you want to pretend it never happened?" He pushed aside the bedcovers and rose from the bed, taking two steps toward her before making a sound of self-disgust and heading for the bathroom.

"Logan, stop."

He stopped but didn't turn around.

Honor took a deep breath. "We can't see one another outside of work. I can't do that to Keaton on top of breaking things off between us."

"But sleeping with me is okay?"

"No, it's not okay." To her horror her eyes filled with tears. "Please, don't say anything about us."

He laughed, and it was a harsh sound. "Oh, don't worry. I got the message. Loud and clear. You're quite safe from me."

The bathroom door closed behind him with a loud snick. Honor took advantage of his absence to finish her packing and, after scrawling a short note to say she'd wait downstairs, she all but ran from the room.

All the way downstairs to the lobby she castigated herself. Why couldn't she have felt the same way about Keaton as she did for Logan? She'd had her life mapped out. Her future secured. Everything she'd ever wanted had been right there, within her grasp. And she'd messed it up. Two years she'd invested in her relationship with Keaton. Two years of planning together for the life they'd lead. Two years irrevocably down the drain. Her thumb went to the ring finger of her left hand and she felt a jolt of loss when she remembered her engagement ring wasn't there and why.

She was her mother's daughter, no matter which way she looked at it, and the painful truth cut deep.

Honor counted the days until Keaton's return. They'd spoken on the phone a couple of times, but the impending breakup discussion was not the kind of thing you did on the phone. They'd made promises to each other. He deserved her honesty face-to-face. She'd mentioned the trip she and Logan had taken to Portland, mainly because she had a suspicion that Douglas's assistant might let that little gem slip if she was talking to Keaton. The woman was super-efficient but garrulous.

Keaton had expressed some shock that she and Logan had been put up in one room after a mix-up, but Honor had impressed on him that it had been a genuine error on Stella's part and that Logan had been a complete gentleman. What she didn't tell him was that she hadn't been a lady. That discussion would have to wait until Keaton's return, and thinking about it had her tied up in knots.

Keaton was due back in the office today, and she'd hoped to see him in private before they came face-to-face in the latest family meeting called by Douglas, but she hadn't been able to catch him. Their talk would clearly have to wait, she thought as she walked to Douglas's office for the urgently called meeting.

While Douglas and Nancy hadn't arrived yet, Logan was already there. Not surprising, she thought, as the man was nothing if not punctual. No, she was being unkind. He was everything *and* punctual with it. She felt the all-too-familiar shock of awareness ripple through her as she saw him standing by one of the large picture windows looking out over the water. And yet again, she wondered why she had never felt this way about Keaton. They were essentially peas in a pod to look at, with the minor exception of Logan having a small chicken pox scar above his right eyebrow. The fact that she'd been close enough to notice and remembered that small detail was another black mark against her.

Honor nodded at Logan, who lifted his chin in acknowledgment of her presence. He'd been scarce in the office these past few days, locked in meetings with Douglas and the architectural team and spending time in the Richmond Developments library studying up on building statutes and related paperwork. He was either being very efficient or he was avoiding her, and she couldn't help but feel it was mostly the latter.

Keaton and Kristin arrived together, their joint laughter a scar on her soul. When was the last time she'd made Keaton laugh? She couldn't even remember. She stepped forward to greet him.

"Welcome home, traveler," she said, giving him a quick hug and a kiss.

Keaton turned his face so her lips landed on his cheek. She knew he wasn't a fan of overt public displays of affection, especially here in the office, but Honor couldn't help but feel perversely slighted by his reaction until she acknowledged the only reason she'd done it was likely to irritate Logan. Which raised the question of why she wanted to irritate him anyway. He'd made it blatantly clear that he wasn't going to pick up his brother's leavings again. When push came to shove, blood was thicker than any attraction they shared and she was good with that, wasn't she?

Douglas and Nancy arrived, and Honor could feel her boss's excitement like a palpable force in the room.

"Good, good. Glad you're all here," Douglas said, rubbing his hands together with obvious glee. "Shame it's too early in the day for champagne, because I have excellent news to share."

"Please, everyone, sit down," Nancy urged them all.

Once they were seated, Douglas turned to Nancy. "You first," he said with a beatific smile on his face.

She gave him a nod then fixed her attention on Logan.

"Logan, we are very pleased and proud to officially welcome you into the family. Your test results are back and you are, without any doubt, our son and Keaton's older twin. I can't begin to tell you how thrilled we are to have you back in the fold." She crossed to Logan, who stood as she enveloped him in her arms. Her voice broke on her next words. "My lost boy, home again. Back where you've always belonged."

Honor watched the tableau before her, her gaze running between mother and son and Keaton and Kristin. Neither of Logan's siblings looked overly thrilled to hear the news. Keaton, in particular, remained stony faced, and when Nancy finally pulled away from Logan, Keaton looked directly at his father.

"So what does that mean going forward, Dad?"

Honor noticed that Keaton's hands had tightened into fists resting on the tops of his thighs. Frustration? Anger? Keaton had a tendency to let irritation and anger take the upper hand from time to time. It was part and parcel of his self-imposed quest to be all and do all to win favor from his father, no doubt. Couldn't he see he was everything Douglas wanted him to be without even trying? He was darn good at his job and would make a great CEO when Douglas stepped down, just as he'd always been groomed to be. But she knew that Keaton had never felt like he was enough.

"I'm glad you asked that, son," Douglas said, rising from his desk. "With Logan coming back to the family and fitting so smoothly into the business dynamic we have running here, I've made some changes in my succession planning."

"What kind of changes?" Kristin demanded.

"Now, now, don't get all worked up. You both know it

was always my intention to hand the yoke of control to Keaton. Now, with Logan's return, and given his expertise in the field, it's my wish that he also be considered for contention when I step down."

"What? You have to be kidding!" Keaton shot to his feet and all but shouted at his father. He cast Logan a quick glance. "No disrespect to you, Logan, but you've been here all of five minutes. There's no way you can step in and run the company when Dad steps down. Our corporation is much larger than what you're used to and you haven't spent your entire life being groomed to do this like I have. Dad, this decision is not only grossly unfair to me, it makes very poor business sense. The board of directors are bound to object. Seriously, I beg you to reconsider."

"My mind is made up. You know I plan to retire in two years. That's ample time for Logan to be brought up to speed. Many CEOs have far less when they take on a new role. I know this must be disappointing to you, Keaton, but it is what it is."

"And what about Logan?" Kristin asked, her face now as pale as the white blouse she was wearing under her conservative navy blue suit. "What do you think of all this?"

"I'm shocked, obviously. I hadn't even decided to stay in the States."

"*Hadn't?*" Kristin said, leaping instantly on the most telling word in his statement.

"Yes, hadn't. Until now."

She made a derisive sound. "So, now that you're proven to be one of us, you think you can just romp straight home to the finish line and take over? Just like that?" Kristin turned to her father. Her fury was clearly painted on her face. "How could you? As if it wasn't bad enough that you never even considered me as your replacement, when I have more business acumen in my little finger than Keaton has, period. Now you go and stomp all over him. After all these years of his dogged loyalty to you, this is how you treat him? Frankly, right now, I'm ashamed to be your daughter."

She rose from her seat and stalked out of the room, letting the door bang closed behind her.

Keaton turned his attention back to his father. "I'm going to ask you to reconsider this preposterous idea. Hopefully in a day or two you'll come to your senses. If you don't, I'm going to make a recommendation to the board that you be let go from your position here."

High color flooded Douglas's cheeks. "On what grounds?" he challenged.

"Diminished mental capacity," Keaton said succinctly before following in his sister out of the room.

Ten

Honor was exhausted when she let herself into her apartment that evening. The atmosphere at work had been incredibly strained for the balance of the day after Douglas's announcement. And it hadn't taken long for it to filter out to the rest of the staff, many of whom were shocked that a newcomer could be in line to become their new CEO. To make things worse, she hadn't been able to track Keaton down anywhere. Even his executive assistant had no idea where he'd gone, and he wasn't answering his phone. Honor was beginning to become seriously worried, as she tried for the umpteenth time to reach him, when her doorbell buzzed repeatedly.

She rushed to open the door, knowing it had to be him, and was shocked when he lurched across the threshold, reeking of cigarette smoke and booze. His dark blond hair, normally so tidy, was in complete disarray. His tie was loosened and askew, and there were stains on his suit jacket that hadn't been there this morning.

"You shtill love me, doncha?" he slurred as he slung one arm over Honor's shoulder and hugged her to him.

"Of course I love you," she said.

"At least shomebuddy does," he said, sounding slightly reassured.

But even as the words had fallen from her lips, she knew them to be a lie. Well, not an entire lie. She loved Keaton as she'd love a very good friend. But not the way she ought to have loved him. Not the way he deserved to be loved by someone he'd asked to marry.

She guided him to the couch, where he lay down almost immediately. Honor swiftly removed his shoes and went to the kitchen to grab him a glass of water. She stood at the kitchen counter for a full two minutes, wondering how she was ever going to tell him the truth that he'd been a part of her ticket to a respectable and successful life. That she'd been prepared to accept second best and to force him to do the same. Not for the first time, she wished Logan Parker had never discovered his true identity. Life had been so much simpler before he turned up.

But even so, she couldn't blame him. Her planned future with Keaton had been a hopeless cause, destined to failure, right from the start. Cracks would have formed eventually. At least this way they'd found out before more damage was done. She poured his glass of water and walked back to her sitting room. Keaton was already fast asleep and snoring lightly. Honor looked at him, feeling nothing but compassion fill her heart as she watched him sleep off what she was certain was his very first drunken episode since college.

A man as buttoned up as Keaton never let himself go like this. That his father's announcement today had driven him to this, well, it just made her mad all over again. At Logan Parker for existing. At Douglas Richmond for being such an idiot and so careless with his children's aspirations. And at herself for not loving Keaton better. And somehow she was going to have to find the courage to tell this broken man that she couldn't be engaged to him anymore.

She'd failed in her quest to create the life she'd always wanted, and she knew she certainly could not continue to work at Richmond Developments with Logan Parker eventually at the helm. She'd have to start over again, somewhere else. But as soon as the thought formed in her mind, she felt a corresponding pain in her chest over walking away from the man she now realized she was falling in love with.

Shock drove her to sit down before her legs gave way completely. Love Logan Parker? That was madness. Madness doomed to ultimate failure. So what if she felt an inexorable pull toward him every time she saw him? In fact, right from the very first time she'd laid eyes on him? It was just animal attraction. A primeval itch that needed scratching. And they'd scratched it. Not once, but twice. Each time instigated by her. Each time equally as intense and sexually fulfilling.

That didn't mean she loved him. She couldn't love him. She barely knew him. But the deeper she looked into her heart, the more she knew the truth. It didn't make sense. In fact, it was the most awful realization to reach. But she was in love with Logan. And she could never, ever have him.

Logan was thoroughly pissed off. How could Douglas have made such an announcement without at least running it past him privately first? Sure, he could understand the DNA results being shared with the entire family, but Douglas's harebrained scheme to install him at the head of Richmond Developments?

He paced his hotel room for the hundredth time and threw himself down on the bed when he realized that all this pacing only served to wind him up even more. He needed to run or swim or do something—anything—that would burn up this restless energy and frustration that had clawed at him all day long.

Sex would work, the contrary voice at the back of his mind suggested, but Logan slammed that thought right back where it belonged. There was only one person he wanted sex with, and look how that had turned out so far. No, Honor Gould was so far off-limits she was virtually in another galaxy.

Or just across town, the voice said again.

With a growl of irritation, Logan quickly changed into a pair of shorts, a T-shirt and running shoes and took the elevator to the hotel gym. An hour or ten on the treadmill ought to do it, he thought to himself as he programmed the machine to the highest incline and started to run. But the running didn't help. Even though it wore him out physically, his mind continued to return to Honor. To how she felt, how she tasted, to the little sounds she made when they made love. Made love? No, it was just sex, pure and simple.

Nothing pure about it, came that wretched voice again. Under any other circumstance, he would have enjoyed pursuing the idea of building something with Honor, however, under this circumstance he wasn't going near her again. He'd waited his entire life to be a part of his rightful family. Sleeping with Honor had been a stupid thing to do the first time, but the second confirmed that he was a real fool. He hadn't wanted to do anything that would jeopardize his chances for acceptance within the Richmonds' tight familial group, but his relationship with Honor, along with his father's blasted announcement today, had thrown everything to the wind.

Logan set the treadmill to a cool-down pace, reached for the towel he'd slung over the rail and swiped at the perspiration that beaded his face and throat. His sweaty T-shirt clung to his body. Maybe this was all his fault after all. He had a good life back in New Zealand. He had a family that loved and accepted him there, even if they weren't his blood. He had a thriving company, friends and interests that kept his life full. But for all that he loved those things, none of it filled the hole in his heart where his true family should be.

And now, even though he'd found them and his parents had accepted him wholeheartedly into the family, there was a yawning chasm separating him and his siblings. His twin, whom he should be closest to, now probably wanted nothing to do with him, and his sister, well, the waters ran deep with her. Clearly she'd always felt she was the better candidate to take over their father's role at the company, and equally as clearly, his father had never considered her for the position. Because she was female? Or because he truly had believed Keaton better suited to the role?

When Logan returned to his hotel room, he stripped and stepped into the shower. Keeping the water on a stinging cold temperature, he lathered up, rinsed off and then turned the water up a little. He could turn down Douglas's position, he thought as the water streamed over his body. Or find some way to extend an olive branch to his brother and sister. Maybe find some kind of way to generate a three-way split of the company leadership. Surely they'd be on board with that? He could only try, right?

Wrong.

Logan looked from Kristin to Keaton and back again. His brother looked somewhat the worse for wear; Logan recognized his pallor as that of someone who'd had a few too many drinks and then slept poorly into the bargain. He recognized it because he also had looked like that a time or two. Kristin, well, she was about as buttoned up and tense as a person could be without shattering into tiny splinters all over the meeting room where he'd called them this morning.

"We need to learn to work together," Logan said firmly.

"Or you could just go back to New Zealand and stay there," Kristin said with viperish scorn.

"Oh, he's here to stay, and good luck to him. He'll soon find out that no matter how hard you work, how often you break your back to please, or how many years of your life you give up doing it, Dad will never be satisfied. And, by the way, *bro*, don't think that when he steps down he'll actually be stepping down. He'll be there at your shoulder like the Ghost of Christmas Past. Criticizing, analyzing and interfering, because that's what he does best."

"Rethinking your desire to find your family?" Kristin sneered when Logan didn't immediately respond.

"Look, I can see why my arrival has upset both your lives. It hasn't exactly been a walk in the park for me, either. But I do have just as much right to be here as you do."

"Except you haven't earned your stripes here the way we have," Kristin responded sharply.

"And if I had? What then? Would you hate me any less?" Logan replied with equal sharpness.

Kristin held his gaze for a few seconds then flushed and looked away. "We don't hate you, Logan. How can we? We barely know you."

"And maybe that's the problem here," Logan offered. "We could try harder to get to know one another, don't you think?"

"I guess," Kristin agreed. "What do you think, Keaton? You want to get to know this guy before he becomes our boss?"

Keaton focused his gaze on his brother. "Whatever. I still don't think he's got what it takes to run this place. It's what I was raised to do. Every choice and every decision I've faced was with that role in mind. I can't believe he chose you."

"I agree," Kristin said, rising from her chair. "And I've

always thought I was the better person for the job, because let's face it, I run the money side of things and my grades were always better than yours, plus I'm more of a people person than you are. But better the devil we know, right?"

"I am actually still here in the room," Logan reminded them. "And, to be totally honest with you both, I'm fully capable of running this company as CEO on my own, but—" he raised his hand as they both looked set to argue that point with him "—I would prefer to come to some agreement with you both whereby we work together instead of trying to tear each other down. If you guys can't be on the same page as me with that, then I will work alone. Do you understand me?"

"Do you hear that?" Kristin said, looking at Keaton with a hint of a grin tugging at her lips. "He's got that big brother thing down pat."

"Yeah, I guess we'd better toe the line, huh?" Keaton said with a glimmer of a smile on his face, too.

Logan felt a slight sense of relief until he looked at his brother and felt the dreaded guilt that always filled him whenever he thought about what he'd done with Honor. Sure, the first time had been innocent enough, but the second? No, he couldn't go there. He was surprised, though, that he hadn't heard any news about their engagement being off. He was certain Honor would have followed through on that when they returned from Portland. But then again, he rationalized, would she have had the opportunity with Keaton's travel and then the bombshell yesterday?

He only hoped that when she did finally break that connection with his brother, that she didn't tell Keaton the full reason why. Because if she did, he doubted he'd ever be able to build the kind of relationship with his brother that he wanted. Goodness only knew it was the kind of thing he'd never forgive if the tables were turned. And didn't that just make him feel like he was the lowest of the low.

"So, what do you two say? How about dinner tonight? Just the three of us. Somewhere casual where we can start to really get to know one another."

"Are you paying?" Kristin asked with a raised brow.

"Sure," Logan answered with a smile. "If that's what it takes."

"Then I can make myself available," she answered.

"Me too. But this better not give me indigestion," Keaton said reluctantly.

"A few beers together and you'll be right," Logan said, slapping his brother on the back and earning a sharp glare in return.

"I won't be drinking," Keaton said firmly, before adding under his breath, "ever again."

Logan laughed. "I know what that feels like."

Kristin rolled her eyes as the two of them began to discuss hangover remedies.

"While you two good ol' boys do your reminiscing together, I have work to do. What time tonight, Logan?"

"How about seven?" he suggested. "I saw a place over by Lake Union the other day." He mentioned the name of the restaurant. "I'll make a reservation and see you there."

After they'd gone back to their offices, he felt a glimmer of hope that he might be able to build something of a friendship with his brother and sister after all. Which left one more problem on his horizon. Honor. Sharing an office with her was no longer an option. Yes, they may have to liaise with one another on a regular basis, but there was no real need for them to be within the same workspace, day in and day out, was there? He'd check if that office refit on the architectural design team's floor was complete.

But a week later, he discovered it wasn't as easy to relocate as he'd hoped. Plus, he began to see a different side to Honor here in the office. She was intensely focused and had some very strong and worthwhile opinions on his vision for the Portland contract.

"Look, I see where you're going with this," she said to him on the Friday morning the week before Christmas. "And while I applaud what you're trying to do here, I think we'd be better if we went for a more industrial look for the interiors of the stores and restaurants. Not only would it shave costs, but it would add to the overall aesthetic of the entire courtyard precinct we'll be developing."

He nodded and leaned in a little closer to the concept drawings she had spread out on the table in front of them. It was dangerous ground. The nearer he got to Honor, the more tantalizing was her scent. He had to school himself not to want to nuzzle against the side of her neck and breathe in deep. Easier said than done, he acknowledged as she shifted slightly, giving him an all-too-enticing view of the lace of her bra peeking out from just inside the neckline of her top. Red. The color of passion.

Logan forced himself to train his eyes on the sketches and studied them as though his life depended on it. But it was no use. Her nearness, the warmth of her body as she leaned over the table and scribbled something on the drawing in front of them—all of it conspired to fry his brain and heat up other parts of his body that had no business getting heated in the workplace.

"Logan?"

He started a little and realized she'd been talking to him.

"Sorry, could you repeat that?"

She sighed a little, the action making the fabric of her top shift a little, and darn it if he didn't catch another little peek of ruby-red lace.

"Look, maybe it'd be easier if I just took you out to a place about half an hour away that illustrates what I'm talking about."

He stifled a groan. A half hour in a car with her there and then another back? It would be sheer torture.

"Sounds good to me," he heard himself saying.

"Are you free to go now?"

"Sure."

"You know, when you first came here and started espousing your ideas about preserving the history of a lot of these old buildings, I thought you were mad. I'd always adhered to Douglas's policy of making a fresh start, especially when it came to housing. But I really love your ideas of creating homes for families and space for small businesses out of these old industrial buildings. You're creating new community hubs and giving people an opportunity to connect on a personal level with family and friends that we don't tend to see very often these days."

She actually sounded really excited about what they were doing, and Logan felt a burst of pride that she'd come around to his way of thinking and without too much effort on his part. But underneath the excitement he heard a wistful note in her voice that made him curious. As if she had some hidden pain stuffed down deep inside. It was unusual for her to show a chink in her armor, and it made him all the more curious to know exactly what made her tick.

"Are you close to yours?" he asked.

"My what?"

"Your family."

She stiffened and pulled a slight face. "Not at all. My father left us when I was about six or seven. And my mom is in a care facility now. Alcohol-related dementia."

She said the words as if she was reciting a shopping list but Logan could hear the wealth of hurt behind them.

"I'm sorry."

She shrugged as if it didn't matter. "It is what it is. Shall we go?"

Subject firmly closed, he acknowledged silently as he

followed her. With all she'd left unsaid, he knew her childhood couldn't have been easy. But maybe it explained why
he'd heard nothing yet about her breaking off her engagement. Had she changed her mind about that? Was her own
past the reason why she was clinging to the security a future with Keaton would offer? After all, it wasn't as if he
could offer her the same. Or could he?

Eleven

Honor drooped with weariness when she let herself into her apartment that evening. She usually felt drained by Friday evening because she put so much into her work week. But this week had been especially taxing. Spending time with Logan challenged her on every level and left her feeling like a wound-up spring of tension by the end of each day. He was so…everything. It irritated her that he was really good at his job, even though Douglas hadn't bestowed an official title on him yet. And he was always open to ideas, as today's trip had proven. He'd been really impressed with the site she'd taken him to, and when they got back to the office he'd been excited about working her suggestions into the concepts for the Portland project. His enthusiasm had been infectious, and she'd even found herself enjoying his company in a way she'd never believed she'd be capable of with all that lay between them.

And what lay between them was just as strong as it had

ever been. He was like a magnet for her, and she was little more than a metal filing inexorably drawn to him at every turn. She could only hope that in time she'd inure herself to the crazy way her body reacted to him. Surely frequent contact would eventually desensitize her, right?

She'd struggled to find the right time to have that talk with Keaton. And it wasn't just because she was reluctant to have it. Pinning him down for the discussion had proven more difficult than she'd anticipated. He'd been away at a golfing tournament the previous weekend and then involved in negotiations with overseas suppliers all this week, which had, in turn, required him to wine and dine the suppliers' representatives every night.

Honor kicked off her shoes and sank down onto her couch. She remembered just how vulnerable Keaton had appeared last week after Douglas's announcement appointing Logan as his successor. It had been as though Keaton's entire reason for being had been stripped from him. It would have been cruel of her to end their engagement on top of all of that. But now that he seemed to be coming to terms with Logan's permanent place in the family, the time to discuss this with him had to be now and tonight he'd agreed to call in.

She had to release him from their engagement. She got up from the couch, went to her kitchen and poured herself a glass of wine.

She was just about to take a sip when her apartment door buzzed. Keaton. She felt a sudden sense of trepidation. Honor put down her glass and after pasting a smile on her face, swung open the door.

"Keaton, I was literally just thinking about you."

"Thinking about me? Are you sure you didn't confuse me with my brother? You two can't seem to stop looking at one another. I thought it was just him, but you're just as bad."

She felt as shocked as if he'd slapped her. His voice was sharp with an edge of something cruel lingering under the surface that she'd never heard from him before.

"You'd better come in," she said, stepping aside for him to enter.

"You don't deny it, I see."

"Please, sit down."

She sat opposite him. Despite the fact his features were so very familiar to her, he had the air of a complete and utter stranger. His mouth was set in an implacable line, and his eyes were icy and unforgiving.

"Am I right?" he asked coldly. "Is there something between you and my brother?"

Her mouth went dry, and she felt nauseous that Keaton had guessed the truth. She'd wanted to spare him that. She'd wanted to end their engagement in as civilized a fashion as possible, without imparting just how foolish she'd been.

"I'm sorry, Keaton, I—"

"I'll take that as a yes," he ground out through clenched teeth.

Keaton closed his eyes briefly, and she saw his chest rise and fall as he drew in a deep breath, as if he was trying to steady himself. Twin spots of color stained his cheeks red, a sure sign it was one of those rare moments when his temper truly got away with him.

"I can explain," she started, but Keaton put up one hand.

"Don't insult me with your explanations. They're too little, too late as far as I'm concerned. I can't believe it took me this long to see you for what you really are."

"What am I?"

Honor's voice sounded thick and strained, even to her ears.

"I knew you were ambitious. I liked that about you, more fool me. But I never realized that you'd be prepared to play my brother and me. I imagine now that Logan's set to take over from our father, you'll shift your allegiance to him as he has by far the most to gain."

"That's not true. Not at all!" she protested. "Keaton, honestly, the first time—"

"There's been more than one?" he asked, sounding shocked.

Honor swallowed the bitter taste in her mouth. He deserved the whole truth.

"Please, Keaton, hear me out. You need to know everything."

"I'm not sure I do."

"Look, the night of the awards dinner I was in the hotel bar and I was just about to go up to my room when I saw a man I believed was you come into the bar and take a seat."

"But I told you I couldn't make it to your award presentation. Why would you have thought he was me?"

"You're identical twins. Honestly, I really thought that maybe you'd come into town to surprise me with some role play."

"Role play," he repeated, his voice now devoid of any emotion.

"You know we'd had a discussion about spicing things up. I thought maybe you'd taken that on board. Anyway—" she waved a hand in the air in front of her "—I thought he was you. I went over to him. Kissed him. Gave him my room number and key card and asked him to join me."

"And he did." Keaton's face was stony.

Retelling the story just made it sound all the more sordid.

"So you slept with him that night, too? And Portland? The shared room? Was that something the two of you engineered?"

"No!" she cried. "Stella made the reservation thinking I was traveling with you, and when the hotel only had the one room left, we had no choice but to share it."

"Even so, you didn't have to have sex with him."

She hung her head in shame. "I know. I couldn't help it."

Keaton made a sound halfway between grief and disgust and then rose abruptly.

"Well, I wish you luck. Obviously, I have no further interest in continuing our engagement."

"I'll get your ring."

"You haven't been wearing it?"

"I couldn't. Not after Portland. It…it wasn't right."

"No, it wasn't. None of this was."

"Are you going to tell your parents and Kristin?"

"About you screwing my brother? I don't think so. Life's bad enough without them knowing that, too."

Her chest felt as if it was being compressed in a vise. "Thank you," she whispered.

Honor left him waiting in the sitting room while she went to retrieve the diamond solitaire she'd been so proud to accept. When she came back and handed it to him, she felt as if she was returning everything she'd ever strived for. Stability. Security. Structure. Acceptance. And with her own ridiculous carelessness, she'd thrown it all away.

Keaton took the ring, pocketed it and turned and left without saying another word. The moment the door closed behind him, Honor crumpled to the floor and began to cry. Great wrenching sobs shook her entire body and, when they eventually subsided, left her feeling broken and empty in a way she'd never felt before. She staggered to her feet and grabbed the glass of wine from her coffee table. She lifted it to her mouth with a shaking hand but then stopped herself.

How many times had she seen her mother turn to alcohol for comfort when life went wrong? She would not be like that. Honor walked to the kitchen and tipped the wine out in the sink before heading to her bedroom and lying down on her bed, in the dark and fully clothed.

She waited for sleep to come, but it was impossible. Her mind was full of all the things she and Keaton had done and planned together. All the times his family had included her as though she was one of them and had value and importance. She couldn't expect to experience that again. She was a cheater. The worst kind. Just like her father and just like her mom.

Honor curled up on her side and let the tears fall again. This time she wept silently, feeling her heart break into a million pieces as she cried for all she'd destroyed. She cried for the little girl who'd had hopes and dreams of a better life and who'd wanted to be loved and accepted for herself. Who'd wanted to make a difference for others. Who'd wanted to be a part of something greater than who she was and where she'd been and what she'd done.

The girl who'd ruined everything.

By Monday morning, Honor still wasn't certain she could face the others. She'd be a pariah once the news came out. There'd be no one in her corner, especially not Logan. He'd already made it clear that he wanted nothing to do with her on a personal level. And that was as it should be, too. His family situation was too fragile and new and precious. If she'd been in the same situation, she'd do the same.

Family was everything. If you had it.

She felt another wave of pain, and she gripped the edges of her vanity table so tightly her fingers began to hurt. She couldn't face going in to work today. She'd just call in sick. And how long could she continue to do that, she silently asked her reflection. No, she had to go in and face the music.

How long would it be, she wondered, until she was asked to leave Richmond Developments? It was bound to happen eventually. The family was tight, even with their infighting, and eventually they'd discover that she'd overstepped the invisible boundaries that held a family together. She'd do the right thing and resign. Maybe then she might still be able to expect a reference. She'd been good at her job, had

helped lift the company profile. Surely she'd have no difficulty finding work elsewhere. Her portfolio was impressive.

But her financial commitments were extensive, and she
couldn't take a hit right now. Not only was she still paying down her student loans, but the care facility where
her mother now lived consumed most of her financial re-
sources. Job security was vital for her to be able to make
those payments for her mom. Sure, Honor could maybe
move to a cheaper apartment, sell her car and take public
transit. But that wouldn't make much difference for long.

She was going to have to take stock of her life, her new
life, and make contingency plans like tightening her budget, creating a new résumé and registering with some em-
ployment agencies. Then she would have to wait and see
what happened next.

Over the next two days at work, Honor felt as though
she was perpetually walking on eggshells. It was the Tuesday before Christmas, and the atmosphere in the office
should have been festive and joyful. Maybe for the rest
of the staff it was, but between the Richmond siblings,
and between herself and Logan, you could cut the tension with a knife.

Keaton barely spoke to anyone, and Kristin was so
tightly wound she was like a bomb waiting to go off. And
Logan? Well, he was very creative at finding ways not to
be anywhere near her, until now as they exited the conference room after attending a department heads meeting.
When he went to speak with Keaton, she was horrified to
see his brother cut him dead in the hallway and turn and
walk away without acknowledging him.

"What was that about?" Logan asked as he and Honor
walked along the corridor.

"He hasn't spoken to you?"

Logan made a helpless gesture with his hands. "As you

can see, he isn't talking to me. Not even to say good morning. Not sure what bug has crawled up his ass, but I thought we were making inroads into getting to know one another. Now this. Has he always been so moody?"

Honor shook her head. "It's my fault. Well, *our* fault."

"Ours?"

She watched as understanding dawned on his face.

"You told him?"

"I did." Even as she said the words, she felt the now-familiar nausea from knowing she'd inflicted such humiliating pain on Keaton.

"He didn't take it well, did he?" Logan cursed under his breath. "I'm so sorry you bore that alone. We should have told him together."

She looked at him in surprise. "No, it was my responsibility."

"Honor, we were both involved. I should have been there for you. I'm sorry."

The reality that she'd been the instrument of her own demise hit home all over again, crushing the air from her lungs and making her stumble a little as she walked. Logan instantly put out a hand to steady her, and the warmth of his touch filtered through her blouse to her arm. She pulled away, when all she wanted to do was revel in his touch. To take the comfort he offered and let it heal the darkness inside her.

"Still can't keep your hands off each other I see," Kristin sniped as she passed them in the hallway.

Kristin flung Logan a look laced with disgust and continued on her way. Honor closed her eyes briefly and groaned. This was impossible. Obviously Keaton had talked to Kristin. And if he'd told her, who else knew? This was turning into a disaster. The strife she'd caused with her careless and reckless behavior, and her inability to keep a sensible distance between herself and the temptation that was Logan Parker, was causing a rift between the reunited siblings that was wider and deeper than anything she could ever have imagined.

Simply by remaining here at Richmond Developments, she was making everything so much worse than it needed to be. She had no doubt they'd forgive Logan in time, but no one would ever forgive her. And, as much as that hurt, she had to admit that if the situation was reversed and this was her family that was being ripped apart, she'd be reacting exactly the same way.

But there was something she could do to make it right. She could step away. By doing so it would clear the path to allow the siblings to find their way back to each other without her presence being a constant reminder of the wedge she'd driven between Logan and Keaton. She had to at least try to make something right here.

Honor stopped in her tracks.

"What's wrong?" Logan asked.

"There's something I need to do. You go on. I'll be in touch later about the cost analysis for the local waterfront restaurant and boutique complex."

Before he could say anything else, she turned around and went back the way she'd come, heading directly for Douglas's office. She nodded to Stella as she entered the inner sanctum.

"The boss man free?" she asked.

"He doesn't have anyone with him right now, but—"

"Good," Honor said firmly and continued to his office door.

She rapped her knuckles on the wood, and without waiting for him to answer, she let herself in. Douglas was sitting at his desk. He didn't look too good as he lifted his head and acknowledged her.

"Honor, to what do I owe the pleasure? I hope everything is okay?"

"I've come to give you my resignation," she said without preamble.

Douglas rose from his chair and walked around his desk. He took her hands in his.

"Now, which one of my boys has upset you? I'll deal with it. There's no need for you to resign over some petty argument."

"The thing is, Douglas, this isn't a petty argument. I've done something really stupid, and I'm the only person who can do anything to fix it."

Then, to her absolute horror, she burst into tears. Douglas led her over to the sofas that faced one another on one side of his office.

"There, there," he said, looking more uncomfortable by the minute. "I'm sure it can't be that bad."

"It's worse. I slept with Logan. I thought he was Keaton but he wasn't and now Keaton knows and our engagement is off and they're not talking and Kristin thinks I'm evil and I just can't stay here anymore."

Douglas listened to her crazy run of words and reached into his pocket. He withdrew a clean white handkerchief, shook it open and passed it to her. She blindly took the square of cotton, wiped her eyes and unceremoniously blew her nose.

"I'm sorry," she said through tears. "I didn't mean to dump all that on you that way, but it's the truth. I did a stupid thing, and the only way I can make it right is by leaving."

Douglas looked at her, his expression serious. "We can work this out. People make mistakes. Some of us more than others," he said with a somewhat wistful look in his eyes.

"I can't stay here and be a constant reminder to them both. I need to move on. I'm sorry I was unfaithful to Keaton. You know how much I was looking forward to marrying him and being a true part of your family, but I had to admit that I didn't love him enough to do that. I didn't love him enough to recognize that it wasn't him that I slept with three weeks ago."

And she hadn't loved him enough not to repeat the experience in Portland less than a week later.

"Let me talk to him," Douglas offered.

"No, it won't make any difference, and nor should it. I betrayed him, Douglas. I betrayed his trust with the brother he has spent his whole life trying to make up for."

"Make up for? Why? Keaton has always been a source of great pride to Nancy and me."

Douglas looked affronted. No, not affronted exactly, but not right, either. Something was bothering him deeply, and Honor felt even guiltier that she was the one heaping additional stress on him.

"I know he has, but he's always felt he had to be more because of the one you lost. He never felt like he was enough."

Douglas got up and began to pace the room. "That's ridiculous. He never said anything to—" He put his hand to his head and grimaced. "This damn headache just won't go away."

"I'll get you something. Look, I'm sorry to have offloaded on you like that, but I mean it about resigning. I'll give you my written letter this afternoon, and I'd like to finish up as quickly as possible."

He looked at her, and to her horror, his gaze went completely blank before his eyes closed and he dropped to the carpet in a crumpled heap. Honor rocketed to her feet and ran to him, kneeling at his side. He wasn't breathing. She put her fingers to his neck, desperate to feel his pulse, but there wasn't even so much as a flutter.

"Stella, help!" Honor yelled. "I need help. Call for a paramedic!"

When Stella opened the office door, Honor was already doing chest compressions, but somehow she knew, in her heart, that it was a waste of time. She'd watched the man die right in front of her. She'd seen the life dull then disappear from his eyes. Worse, she'd been the one to ensure his last moments were filled with worry and regret.

Twelve

Logan stood in the outer office together with his brother, sister and Nancy, as Douglas's covered body was wheeled away. Kristin began to sob quietly, and Logan put an arm around her, offering her solace. Stella was quietly crying at her desk. Honor stood, leaning against the wall, her face pale and drawn, and her arms wrapped around her middle as if she'd fall apart if she let go.

He ached to comfort Honor but his sister needed him too, which left him feeling utterly torn. Honor looked shattered and so desperately alone in this moment and he knew she had to be grieving too. That, combined with the shock of being with Douglas when he died so suddenly must have been really tough to deal with. He'd heard she'd worked tirelessly, performing CPR until the paramedics had arrived.

He felt cold and numb inside. And cheated. He was only just beginning to know his father, and now the man had been taken from him. Keaton was holding their mother in a tight hug, and Logan could see how she shook as grief racked her body.

The paramedics who'd attended Douglas came through from the office—all their equipment packed up, somber expressions on their faces. One of the men stopped by Nancy and Keaton.

"We're sorry for your loss, ma'am."

"Thank you. I know you all did everything you could," she said on a choked sob that cut right through Logan's heart.

The silence in the room was near deafening once the medical professionals had departed. One of the police officers who'd attended the 9-1-1 call talked briefly to Keaton and Nancy, explaining the procedure with the coroner's office.

"Since we've spoken with Mr. Richmond's doctor and his vascular neurologist and they've confirmed his medical situation, it should be a fairly straightforward procedure with the autopsy. They'll be in touch with you regarding the release of his body."

"Thank you, Officer. So, we are free to leave now?" Keaton asked.

"Of course, and my condolences on your loss."

"Thank you. C'mon, Mom, I'll see you home. There's nothing we can do here."

"We'll have to start making arrangements, letting people know," Nancy said, a note of hysteria coloring her voice.

"Not yet, Mom," Kristin said, pulling free of Logan's embrace and crossing to her mother. "Soon, but not yet. I'll come with you two."

"And Honor?" Nancy asked, reaching out a hand in Honor's direction.

"No, Mom, not Honor," Keaton said firmly.

Keaton's dismissal of Honor's right to be a part of the family at this time cut Logan like a jagged knife. Honor deserved compassion, too. Logan wanted nothing more than to say he'd join them as well, but something in the set of Keaton's shoulders and the expression on his face made it abundantly clear he was not welcome, either.

Kristin met Logan's gaze. "Are you coming with us?" she asked, ignoring how Keaton stiffened beside her in silent protest.

"I'll see that Stella and Honor are taken care of and try to join you later, okay?"

Kristin nodded, and Logan watched as his brother and sister shepherded Nancy from the office toward the elevators, and his heart ached for the man they had all lost so abruptly. He'd spent his whole life feeling as though he didn't quite belong and he'd thought it would be different with his own blood relatives. How wrong could he have been? He'd never felt more of an outsider in his own family than he did right now. The others had drawn together in a way that had excluded him. They shared memories with the man who'd been such a powerful force in their lives— the person who had knitted them all together. Logan was no more than the new guy on the block, no matter what the DNA results had said.

He looked at Honor. "You okay?" he asked.

"I…he…he just dropped right in front of me. There was nothing I could do."

Silent tears began to streak down her face, and her entire body shook. He couldn't help but draw her against him in an all-encompassing hug of compassion. When she began to calm again, he reluctantly let her go.

"Let me see that Stella has a support person and then I'll take you home. You can't drive yourself in this state."

He called HR and asked for someone to come and stay with Stella until a family member could be reached to collect her, and he asked that Honor's coat and bag be collected from her office so she wouldn't have to face anyone else just yet. She wasn't in any state to field questions.

As soon as the HR staffer arrived with Honor's things and to attend to Stella, he tucked Honor's arm in his and began to lead her away. She immediately tugged clear of him.

"I'll be fine," she said.

But there was a tone in her voice that said she was anything but. The need to care for her overtook everything else and Logan quickly fell into step beside her. She was so brittle right now he was concerned she'd fracture into a tiny million pieces. Several other staff members looked up as they passed, a mix of shock and sympathy on their faces. It hadn't taken long for the news of Douglas's death to spread through the office.

"Give me your keys," he commanded as they headed for the elevators.

She did so without another murmur of objection, and that worried him more than anything. As they waited for the car to get to their floor, he looked around. The decorations festooning the office had never looked more garish and overdone than they did at this moment. Christmas. A time for joy and sharing, but for the Richmond family, it would forever be a time marked by loss as well.

When they reached the parking garage, they walked to Honor's car. He hit the unlock on the remote and opened her door for her. She settled into the seat with a softly murmured thank-you.

Once he was behind the wheel, with the seat and mirror adjusted for his far greater height, he turned to her. "I'll need you to give me directions."

In answer, she tapped on the navigation app on the dashboard screen and hit a location. Taking that as a very strong hint that she wasn't up to talking, Logan put the car in gear and followed the directions issued by the disembodied voice through the speakers.

Traffic was heavy as he negotiated through the streets. People everywhere scurried around wrapped in hats, scarves and coats, obviously eager to get out of the elements. The sky, as usual, was thick with heavy, gray, low clouds, and drifts of rain kept the roads slick with moisture. At four o'clock in the afternoon, it was getting dark already.

He'd never felt so far from home as at this moment. Back in New Zealand it was sunny, warm and humid and people were in shorts, T-shirts and flip-flops already. This flip side of his reality felt more foreign than he'd ever realized. Did he even really belong here?

He'd thought he did, but the way things were turning out, maybe he ought to just cut his losses and head home to New Zealand. To the heat of summer, to the family where he'd never quite fit in, to his business and new opportunities there. But even as he considered all those things as he drove through the busy streets, he knew he wouldn't—no, *couldn't*—quit on his family here or on Honor. His feelings for her were complicated but he thrived on that. He'd find a way to make it work—to make *them* work. Somehow.

After parking Honor's car in her underground parking garage and escorting her to her door, he was feeling about as wrecked as she looked. He'd get a cab back to his hotel, lock himself in his room and take a long, hot shower to try to chase away the chill that had invaded his body right to the marrow.

"Will you be okay?" he asked as Honor opened her apartment door.

"I guess," she answered in a voice that was little more than a whisper. "How about you?"

He shrugged. Words defeated him right now, and a solid lump of emotion had taken up residence in his throat.

"Logan? Do you want to come in for a while? I can make some coffee, or something stronger, if you'd like?"

She sounded lost, alone and desperate for the company. Much how he felt, too. And despite thinking he was ready to leave her and dwell alone on his loss, he found that he wasn't quite ready to do that yet. He nodded and stepped inside behind her. Her apartment wasn't quite what he'd expected. In fact, it barely looked as if she lived here at all. For a woman whose workday was all about decor and color and design, very little of that was reflected in her home. There wasn't even so much as a colored throw rug or cushion on the sofa to reflect her personality, he realized as he looked around. No photos or anything beyond generic art prints on the wall, either. It was about as soulless as his hotel room.

He followed her to the kitchen.

"So? Which is it? Coffee or something stronger."

"Coffee will do, thanks."

"Black with one sugar, right?"

He nodded, surprised she'd even noticed how he took it. Honor methodically made their coffees and handed him his steaming mug. He wrapped his hands around the ceramic cup, letting the warmth seep through his skin, but it didn't touch the ice that had taken up residence around his heart.

"Come through and sit down," she said, taking her cup as she returned to the sitting room.

She perched on the edge of a chair, resting her elbows on her knees and holding her mug between both hands. Logan lowered himself onto the sofa and tried to relax. Honor's eyes still held a shocked, bruised look, and he imagined she was reliving everything she'd done and questioning whether she could have done more. He knew he would, in the same situation.

"You did everything you could, Honor. Even the paramedics couldn't bring him back."

"Did I? Did I really do enough? I'll never know."

"The autopsy will give us the answers we need."

"I didn't even know he had health issues."

"Judging by the looks on Kristin's and Keaton's faces, they didn't, either. Maybe that's why he was so happy to welcome me back into the family. Maybe he knew he didn't have a lot of time left."

"Logan, I'm so sorry. You must feel dreadful. You've only just got him back and now he's gone."

Logan took a sip of his coffee and let the hot liquid burn a trail down his throat to his stomach before answering.

"They say you can't miss something you never had, but it's not true. You can." His voice broke on the last two words, and he bowed his head and closed his eyes against the stinging burn of tears.

He heard Honor's mug clunk onto the wooden coffee table, then the rustle of her clothing as she moved from her chair to the couch. She wrapped one arm around his shoulders and with her other hand she took his mug from him, set it on the table and clasped his hand.

"He was so glad you came back into his life. You can take strength from that."

"I know. I mean, I could've arrived here tomorrow instead of three weeks ago." He shook his head. "But I should've been here all my life. That's the thing that makes me the most angry at the mother who raised me. How dare she have stolen me from my true family? How dare she have kept the truth from me? If I hadn't found that box, if I'd let someone else clear the house out when she died, I might never have known any of this. I've lost two people this year. Alison Parker and Douglas Richmond—and both of them, right or wrong, were my parents."

"I can't imagine how you must be feeling right now," Honor said with genuine sympathy. "My own relationship with my mom isn't great, but I don't know how I'll react when she's gone. All I know is the person she was when I was growing up, shaped the woman I am today, for better and—" her breath hitched "—for worse. Alison Parker may have committed a terrible crime against the Richmonds and you by taking you as she did but even so, she loved you and she raised you as a good man. Your drive to succeed may not come from her, but what's in here—" She let go of his hand and tapped his chest lightly. "That's from her and the rest of the extended family you grew up as a part of. In fact, when you think about it, you're doubly lucky. You have your family in New Zealand and your family here."

"Lucky? Keaton hates me and Kristin is totally on his side. My birth mother has just lost the man she's been in love with for more than thirty-six years and barely knows me. She didn't even try to include me today—instead she reached for you." He shook his head again. "I'm an outsider here. And I'm afraid I always will be."

"Logan, no. It's still early, and you've all suffered a terrible shock. Nancy is a compassionate woman and I know she loves you—has always loved you. She'll be wondering where you are right now. It wouldn't have occurred to her to ask you to join them at the house, she would have expected it. But Keaton—" She winced. "With how he's feeling at the moment, I would guess it's best not to bait the bear in his den. I'm persona non grata, too. I feel like there's a massive void in my body. Like I don't belong anywhere, either."

"Which leaves us where?"

"Together, Logan. It leaves us together. For now, anyway."

Together sounded mighty good to him right now. More than anything else he wished they could embrace and simply find comfort in one another. He would have moved toward her, offered her comfort in his arms, but she had looked away and he could see she was struggling to hold onto her composure. As intimate as they'd been, she obviously wasn't ready to let him in and share her true emotions and, as much as that hurt him, too, he could understand it.

"We're a fine pair, aren't we?" he commented wryly.

She attempted a smile, but it was little more than a grimace. It was then that he realized she had tears slowly rolling down her cheeks. Logan pushed a strand of hair from the side of her face.

"Douglas meant a lot to you, didn't he?"

She nodded, and when she spoke her voice was thick and choked. "He taught me so much. I started at Richmond Developments straight out of college in the lowest-paid administrative role they had, and I worked my way up. He was the one who pushed me to always strive to reach further and work harder. And when he saw I was worthy, he didn't hesitate to put his weight behind me as I applied for better roles within the company.

"My dad left us when I was young. Cut off all ties to my mom and me. Douglas Richmond was more of a father figure to me than my dad ever was. I know Douglas's style didn't suit everyone, but it suited me and I owe him a lot."

"I'd say that was true of a lot of people at Richmond Developments. I didn't have the opportunity to work with him for long, but I could see how his focus brought out the best in many of the teams he had working for him."

"Keaton wouldn't agree with you there. He felt his father's methods were draconian and autocratic. They were often at loggerheads."

Logan thought about that for a moment. In the short time he'd known his brother, the only times he'd seen Keaton blow up in anger or frustration were when they were with their father. Even his anger toward Logan over Honor was a quiet seething thing. Kristin, too, had always had an air of suppressed irritation around their father at work.

"How about Kristin? She seemed really annoyed that he'd never considered her for the CEO role within the company."

"She'd make a great CEO. But that was never Douglas's plan."

"And what about you? If I'd never turned up, where would you be?"

"Where I am now, I guess, except probably still engaged to Keaton and planning a wedding."

There was a note of bitterness in her voice that he couldn't ignore.

"I'm sorry. I've really stuffed things up for you, haven't I?"

"No, I can't blame anyone but myself for whcrc I am right now. In fact, I was in the middle of giving Douglas my notice when he collapsed." Her eyes filled with tears all over again. "I can't help but feeling that his stroke was my fault. He was arguing with me, telling me he didn't want me to leave the company."

Logan felt his gut clench in a knot at her words. She'd resigned? It was obvious that their relationship had brought her to this and knowing that filled him with frustration and regret. He hated that he'd been instrumental in making her want to leave a job that she clearly loved.

"Honor, you can't honestly believe you're responsible for him having a stroke. He was under the care of several doctors. I overheard the conversation between the police and the vascular neurologist. Douglas had been cautioned to take his condition more seriously and to make changes to his lifestyle. From what I understand, he just asked the doctor to fill his prescriptions and carried on in his inimitable way. He made his own choices, Honor. The way we all do."

She went still as she processed his words. He was surprised when she abruptly stood.

"I don't know about you, but I need something to eat. Frozen pizza and soup work for you?"

He looked at her in surprise. She wanted to eat? He suspected she just wanted to be busy, doing something that might distract her from her thoughts.

"Sure," he replied. "Let me help."

"Not much to reheating a pizza and opening a can of soup," she said dismissively.

"Hey, I've opened a lot of cans in my time. I'm expert at it," he said, rising from the sofa.

He followed her into the kitchen, where they heated the food then sat at the breakfast bar to eat it. For all her profession of hunger a few minutes ago, Honor was doing a good job of pushing her food around without eating it.

"This is going to destroy Nancy," she said abruptly. "She lived for Douglas."

"They certainly seemed close," Logan commented. "Do you think she'll keep working?"

"I don't know. Nancy is old-school. She always deferred to Douglas's wishes, barely expressed an idea of her own that he hadn't preapproved. She's going to be lost without him."

Logan considered Honor's words. It didn't sound like a terribly great way to live your life, but who was he to judge?

He wondered how Nancy was doing now, so he slid his phone from his pocket and dialed her home number before he could change his mind.

"What are you doing?" Honor asked.

"Calling to see how she is. They might have shut me out at the office, but I need my mother to know I'm thinking about her."

The phone rang several times before Keaton answered. "Richmond residence."

"Keaton, it's Logan," he said awkwardly. "I just wanted to check on you all, especially Nancy. How's she holding up?"

"As well as can be expected. Is there anything else?"

Logan tried not to be angered by his brother's tone. The man was grieving. Hell, they were all grieving.

"I would like to be there, to help support Nancy, if you'll let me," he said carefully.

"That won't be necessary. Mom's been sedated and she's in bed. Kristin and I are here."

We don't need you hung silently in the air between them. Logan had to accept what Keaton said. The last thing he wanted to do was create more strife by inserting himself into their grief.

"Okay, when she wakes, would you please pass on a message from me? Please tell her I'm thinking of her."

"Anything else?"

Logan closed his eyes and counted to three. His brother's tone was so dismissive. Could he not even put his anger with Logan over Honor aside for one moment and allow them to be brothers united in the loss of their father? It seemed not. Logan sucked in a deep breath.

"When do you expect to meet with the funeral director? I'd like to be a part of that meeting."

"I imagine that would be acceptable. He's coming to the house at ten thirty tomorrow morning. Is that all?"

Keaton obviously couldn't wait to be rid of him and, if the circumstances had been any different, Logan would have thought up something else just to tick him off in true brotherly fashion. But this was not the time.

"Thank you, no, there's nothing else. I'll see you tomorrow. And, Keaton?"

"Hmm?"

"I'm so deeply sorry for your loss."

There was silence on the other end before his brother replied.

"Yours too. See you tomorrow. Come alone."

The message was loud and clear this time. Honor was

persona non grata. It was unfair. She'd been a part of the
Richmond family longer than him. Before his involvement,
she would have been a natural part of their family group and
she deserved to be a part of it now. A fierce need to stand
up for her right bloomed from deep inside him. Could he
push it? Honor caught his attention and shook her head, as
if she knew what he was thinking.

"Sure," he said succinctly. "See you in the morning."

Logan disconnected the call and felt his shoulders relax.
At least he wasn't going to have to force his way into planning his father's farewell. But he still felt it was wrong that
Honor be excluded as well. Maybe he could speak on her
behalf tomorrow.

Honor looked at him as he put his phone back in his
pocket.

"You okay?"

"As well as can be expected. I'm going over to the house
tomorrow to meet with the funeral director."

"They don't want me there, do they?"

"I'm sorry, Honor. I'll talk to them tomorrow and—"

"No, I understand. Please don't feel bad on my account
and please, don't say anything."

He saw her eyes film with tears again, but she stoi-
cally blinked them back. His being here was making things
worse for her than they needed to be. Hell, his coming to
Seattle had turned her life upside down. Maybe he should
just go.

He pushed his plate away, all appetite now gone.

"Look, thanks for the meal. Sorry I couldn't do it justice. Let me help you clear this up and I'll be on my way."

"No need. I can do it. It's hardly a lot of cleaning up
to do."

She bit her lip as if she was considering saying something else.

"What is it?" he asked.

"Nothing, I... I just wondered if you'd stay tonight. I don't really want to be alone."

Her words tumbled over one another in a rush and he couldn't help but feel a spark of relief that she still wanted him here.

"Are you sure?" he asked.

She put a hand on his arm and looked directly into his eyes.

"Please, stay. We don't have to...you know. I just think we could both benefit from the comfort of company."

"Thank you," he answered solemnly. "I'd like that."

The thought of leaving her right now was torture. She was right. They were all each other had and they needed each other right now.

They tidied the kitchen together and Honor showed him where to find the bathroom.

"There's a new toothbrush in the drawer, and you'll find fresh towels on the shelf there," she said.

When he was done, Logan walked into the bedroom and lay down on top of the covers while Honor used the bathroom. It was all so civilized, he thought. And unlike their stay in Portland, at least it wasn't fraught with the sexual tension that had driven them into one another's arms. Honor came through from the bathroom and saw Logan on top of the bed.

"You can get under the covers. I won't attack you this time."

"I know," he answered.

But even so, he remained exactly where he was.

Unable to trust himself.

Thirteen

Logan woke the next morning, curled around Honor's form beneath the sheets. Surprisingly, they'd both slept well. It felt so right to wake with her in his arms, but at the same time it brought a lot of conflicting feelings and life didn't look as though it would be getting any less complicated soon.

Honor stirred and turned to face him.

"Thank you for staying."

"It was what we both needed," he said with a smile before untangling himself from her and rising from the bed. "Don't get up. I'll let myself out."

"You don't want breakfast, or at least a coffee before you go?"

"I might get something at the hotel, but thanks. I'll see you later, okay?"

"Sure."

Back at the hotel he showered and changed, then asked the concierge for directions to a florist where he chose cut flowers for Nancy. Then he hailed a cab and headed to the Richmond home. The cab let him off outside the gates. The firmly closed gates, Logan noted as he walked toward the pillar with the intercom.

"Yes?"

Logan recognized his brother's voice immediately. "Keaton, good morning. Can you let me in?"

"You're early."

Logan bit back the response he was itching to make. Now was not the time to enter into a pissing contest with his brother.

"Yes, I am," he said quietly. "And I'd like to speak with Nancy."

There was a long pause before the gates hummed and began to smoothly open. Logan shivered in the damp, cold morning air and wished he'd thought to grab a scarf as he started down the long driveway toward the house. The gates clanged shut behind him. Keaton was waiting at the door when he reached the house.

"Nice flowers. Mom's favorites," he commented as Logan stamped his feet on the mat at the front door.

"That's just good luck," Logan admitted. "But I liked them, so it's nice to know she'll like them, too."

He looked his brother straight in the eyes. Keaton's gaze had the weary strain of someone who was still shell-shocked and yet needed to be the one everyone could turn to. More than anything, Logan wanted to share the load, but would his brother let him?

"You're looking rough, man," Logan said as he entered the house and passed Keaton the flowers so he could remove his jacket. "What can I do to help?"

Tension filled his brother's shoulders for a moment, then bit by bit, Logan saw Keaton begin to relax.

"You want to help?"

"That's what family is for, right?"

"I guess," Keaton admitted and passed the blooms back to Logan. "Mom's in the breakfast room. She's holding up pretty well today, so far at least."

"That's good to hear. And Kristin?"

"Distraught but hanging in there. She wanted to go in to the office today, but I told her we needed her here more."

"Good move. I can understand why she'd want to lose herself in work, though. It's a constant. Something you can rely on to stay mostly the same day in, day out. When you've had a big shock like this, you crave everything that's the old normal."

Keaton looked at him with a deeper understanding reflected in his gaze. "I keep forgetting you've been through this already this year. Are *you* okay?"

"I'm all right. Shocked like the rest of you. Sad I didn't have the chance to know Douglas as well as you and Kristin. I feel cheated, to be totally honest."

"Understandable. Logan, I should have included you in our family circle last night, too. It must have been shitty to have to go back to the hotel on your own."

"Actually, I stayed with Honor last night. She was pretty upset."

"Honor?" Keaton's face set in implacable lines and Logan realized that the slight softening of his brother's manner a second ago had now set into solid ice. "You know she's looking out for herself, don't you?"

"What do you mean?"

"By attaching herself to you, she's ensuring her position. I never really saw it before, but she's a corporate climber. She's solely focused on getting up that ladder, no matter what, and she'll do whatever it takes to get there."

"That's pretty harsh."

"It's the truth. You may have slept with her a couple of times, but remember I have known her for years. Looking back, I don't know why I didn't recognize it sooner.

The drive that pushes her to constantly make something of herself."

Logan fought to keep the flash of anger that Keaton's words had initiated out of his voice. "Isn't that an attribute to be commended? After all, if no one wanted to better themselves, how would anyone or any corporation ever get ahead?"

"Just be wary, Logan. That's all I can say."

"With all due respect, I think you've got her wrong. Whatever bitterness you may feel over what happened the night I arrived in Seattle—and yes, you're entitled to that bitterness—it's misplaced. She thought I was you."

"And when she knew you weren't? In Portland?"

"Yeah, well in that instance, we were equally to blame. Look, I know you, and we might never be as close as we could have been if we'd been raised together, but I really want to apologize for allowing Honor to become a wedge between us."

"And yet you spent last night with her?" Keaton looked at him incredulously.

"She needed someone. She watched our father die right in front of her and she worked damn hard to try to bring him back. You know why she was in his office, don't you?"

"I assume she was having a meeting with him."

"She was. To give him her resignation."

"What?" Keaton sounded shocked.

"And you want to know why?"

"I'm sure you're about to tell me."

"Because she felt guilty about what she'd done and how it was making it impossible for *us* to get along. Does that sound like the kind of thing a corporate climber would do?"

Logan heard light footsteps on the parquet flooring, and Nancy came into the front entrance.

"Keaton? Who's at the do—" She stopped in her tracks

when she saw the two men standing together in the foyer. "Oh, Logan, you've come. I'm so glad."

"Nancy, I brought you these," Logan said, stepping toward his mother and offering her the flowers.

She ignored them at first and stepped in close to give him a hug. "Thank you. It wasn't right not having you here last night. I need you all more than you could ever know. We need each other at this horrible, horrible time."

In her tight embrace, Logan had to fight back the sting of tears. He swallowed against the emotion that swelled up from deep inside him, choking him. She had no idea how much he needed them, too.

In typical motherly fashion, Nancy asked, "Have you eaten yet? Come through to the breakfast room. Our housekeeper does great French toast, and now that you're here I feel a little appetite returning. Are you coming, Keaton?"

She took the flowers from Logan, making approving noises over the blooms, and headed toward the back of the house. Logan and Keaton made eye contact.

"We'll continue our discussion another time," Keaton said.

"Yes, we most definitely will," Logan answered.

The rest of the week passed in a blur with Christmas Day being the quietest Logan had ever known as they waited and prepared for Douglas's funeral. At Nancy's request, he'd moved out of the hotel and into a guest suite at her home. With Kristin and Keaton in their own places, Logan felt it was the least he could do to support his mom. She'd also asked that he call her Mom, and while it had felt a little awkward to begin with, now it felt right.

Unfortunately, at the same time, that discussion with Keaton never stood a chance of happening, and the tension that simmered between the brothers only seemed to get stronger. And, at the office, Honor seemed hell bent on keeping clear of him on the few times he'd called in. She'd avoided his phone calls to check in on her, too. She was never far from his thoughts and it worried him, wondering how she was coping.

On the morning of the funeral, the siblings met with Nancy in the foyer of the house as the driver and car from the funeral home pulled up to take them to the service. Logan had finally managed to get hold of Honor and offered her a ride to the cemetery, but she'd said she'd make her own way. Nancy, who'd been stoic and surprisingly strong in the preceding days, today appeared fragile and absolutely lost. Douglas's wish had been for a short graveside service only, and despite the frigid weather they'd agreed to observe his request. Even so, Nancy had insisted on a catered gathering at the house immediately afterward for all those who'd wanted to pay their respects and remember him.

When the car pulled up at the cemetery, Logan felt as if a giant weight had settled in his chest. The four of them, dressed in heavy coats, hats, scarves and gloves, made their way toward the people who were already assembling at the graveside. Puffs of air filled the spaces between them all as people talked and milled about in small groups, the sea of bodies separating slightly as Nancy and her children joined the throng.

Logan's eyes searched out Honor, who excused herself from a group she was talking with and walked over to Nancy, giving the woman a huge hug and sharing some quiet words. Nancy clung to her a moment before reaching in her pocket for a tissue.

"You'll sit with us, won't you? And you'll come back to the house, too?" Nancy said. "I know you and Keaton aren't engaged anymore, but I feel like you're one of my own and I know Douglas felt the same."

Honor's eyes flicked to Keaton for a moment. Whatever

she saw reflected in his face made her shoulders relax a little as she nodded and smiled back at Nancy.

"If everyone else is okay with that?"

Honor looked from Keaton to Kristin and finally to Logan. He stared back at her, taking in the shadows beneath her eyes and the slight frown on her forehead. He wanted nothing more than to gather her in his arms and offer her comfort, as Nancy had done, but she took a step back.

"You can sit by me," he offered when his siblings remained silent.

"Thank you," she said on a tightly issued breath. It was almost time for the service to begin when a last-minute group consisting of two men and two women, related judging by their resemblance to each other, arrived and made their way toward the graveside.

"Do you know them?" Logan asked his sister.

"Never seen them before," she replied. "Maybe they're business associates of Dad's."

To Logan's surprise, they assumed seats in the first row in front of the waiting casket. Seats that had been reserved for Nancy, Keaton, Kristin and Logan. The eldest woman, in her fifties by the look of her, appeared quiet and composed but pale. Her children, too, had similar expressions, and Logan couldn't help but feel there was something familiar about them. He watched as the funeral director approached them.

"Excuse me, ma'am. Could you move to the next row back, please? These seats are reserved for the widow and children of Mr. Richmond," Logan heard the man say discreetly.

They were all surprised when the woman vehemently shook her head.

"Ma'am, please," the funeral director urged again, a little less gently this time.

Logan stepped up to the newcomers and put a hand on the funeral director's shoulder.

"Let me," he said firmly before turning to the newcomers. "Perhaps you could move back a row, please? These seats were reserved for my family."

The woman looked at him, and for a moment her eyes blazed with suppressed fury.

"*Your* family? I have *every* right to be at the graveside of my husband's burial and so do our children!"

"Logan?" Nancy drew closer. "What is that woman saying?"

The woman in question stood, her children following suit, almost as if they formed an honor guard flanking her. Nancy's children did the same.

"I'm saying I have every right to be right here," the other woman shouted as she pointed to the seat she'd just vacated. "I am Douglas Richmond's wife and I can prove it."

"Ma'am... Mrs. Richmond, perhaps now is not the time." The funeral director tried to insert himself between the families.

"Really?" said the second Mrs. Richmond. "If not now, when? My husband has died and this woman has organized his burial without my permission."

She turned to face Nancy, who looked incapable of speech. "I was prepared to let this go, to let you go ahead and bury my husband before stating my claim, but now I'm not feeling so inclined. In fact, I want Douglas's body brought back to Virginia where he belongs."

"What are you talking about? He's my husband and he's being buried in accordance with his wishes." Nancy's voice shook with the emotion evident in her strained features.

"Well, they're not my wishes and as his wife, I'm telling you this is not going ahead."

"I'm his wife," Nancy countered.

Logan looked from one woman to the next and back

again as their voices rose in anger. Then Keaton and Kristin entered the fray together with the other Mrs. Richmond's children. This had to stop before it became some sordid story in the news. Logan tugged on the funeral director's arm. The poor man looked as though he was paralyzed in shock.

"Obviously this can't go ahead until we've sorted this mess out," Logan said firmly. "Let's clear everyone away and take this elsewhere."

The man looked relieved to be given a clear instruction, and he and his staff moved to shepherd the gathered mourners well away from the verbal fracas taking place at the graveside. Logan stepped back up to the melee and held up a hand.

"People, can we please stop for a minute. Obviously, there is some discussion to be had and proof to be given before we can go any further. Might I suggest we take this back to the house?" he said in a voice that brooked no discussion.

"Good idea," said Keaton. "This is preposterous. This woman is saying she and Dad were married two years before him and Mom. It can't be true. That would make him a bigamist."

The daughter of the other Mrs. Richmond cast a scornful glance at the highly polished, flower-bedecked coffin poised over the grave. "If the shoe fits," she said succinctly.

Nancy and Kristin both looked as though they were about to launch themselves at her. Honor, who'd been standing nearby, stepped between them. Grateful to avoid a full-on physical confrontation, Logan suggested everyone get back to their cars and reconvene at Nancy's house.

"I'm not setting foot inside that woman's house," the other Mrs. Richmond stated firmly.

"Then perhaps you'd prefer to leave and allow us to continue with my father's farewell," Logan said darkly, his eyes flicking from her to her children and back again.

"I most certainly would not," she spluttered indignantly.

"Then I would respectfully ask you to put your emotions aside for a few hours while we discuss this in a reasonable and rational way," Logan suggested. "Mom? Are you okay with that?"

Nancy wavered slightly where she stood, prompting Kristin to take her arm to steady her.

"I don't understand this, but I guess it will be okay. Where's Hector?" Nancy asked, scanning the crowd for the family's lawyer. "I saw him here before. He should be there, too, shouldn't he?"

She looked to Logan, who nodded and said, "Yes, he should."

"He's heading to his car," Honor said. "I'll go stop him."

Logan murmured his thanks and watched as she briskly walked toward the roadside, where groups of people continued to linger despite being asked to move on. He saw Honor catch up with Hector Ramirez and watched as the two of them spoke before Hector nodded and waited by his car. Gratitude mixed with pride for her filled him—even given how she was being treated by Keaton and Kristin, she was willing to step up and help.

"I'll speak with him now if we're all agreed?" Logan asked.

He looked at each person in turn, not moving onto the next until they'd all nodded their consent. The funeral director scurried toward them.

"I've never had this happen in forty years of business. What am I to do with Mr. Richmond?" he asked.

"Perhaps you could take him back to the funeral home until we clear this up."

"Yes, yes. That's what I'll do."

Muttering to himself, the man gestured to his staff, and

they began to assemble their equipment to return the coffin to the hearse parked by the curb. Turning his back to the activity, Logan followed his family, and the other family, back to the waiting cars by the sidewalk. He gave Nancy's address to the driver who'd brought the other family and suggested the man follow behind Nancy's car.

"Look after Mom," Logan directed Keaton and Kristin, who appeared to be equal parts stricken and furious right now. "And don't allow any discussion until I get there with Hector."

"You're coming with him?"

"I am."

"And Honor?"

"I think Nancy would want her there. Besides, you'll need someone to deal with the caterers and staff while we're all dealing with that lot," Logan said firmly. He wasn't about to cut Honor out now.

To his relief Keaton nodded. "Okay. We'll see you back at the house. Thanks for stepping up and taking charge there."

"Hey, what else is a big brother for?" Logan said in an attempt to defuse the tension that now gripped everyone.

Keaton snorted a laugh. "You're not so big I couldn't take you."

Logan smiled back, feeling something ease deep within his chest. They might not be the perfect family and he might not be close to his siblings, but he had the feeling that right now they needed him more than they'd ever dreamed possible—and he would be there for them, one hundred percent.

Fourteen

Hector and Logan spoke in undertones up front as Hector drove them to the Richmond family home. Honor listened but didn't contribute to the conversation. In fact, she had no idea what to say or think about any of this aside from agreeing it was almost farcical to have a whole other family arrive at Douglas's funeral claiming to be his.

She looked out the window and tried to figure out how Douglas could have possibly maintained two completely separate lives and families for so long without being caught. Why on earth would a man do something like that? Surely he knew that eventually his deceit would be discovered. Was that what he'd been talking about the day he died when he mentioned people making mistakes—some more than others? Had he been thinking of his own decisions? Either way, if these people's claims were true, what he'd done was immoral, not to mention illegal.

And speaking about the legality of it, where did this leave everyone in terms of succession at Richmond De-

velopments? Had Logan and Keaton even thought about
that yet? Douglas had never made any secret of the fact
that his firstborn heir would be appointed to head up the
company on his death. What if his son from his first wife
was older than Logan and Keaton? And were Logan, Keaton and Kristin now illegitimate?

Her mind spun on the possibilities until she felt dizzy.
One thing was absolutely certain, however, and that was
the effect this betrayal by their father would have on his
children. All of them. Honor knew a lot about betrayal.
The scars ran deep and had lifelong ramifications. From
what Honor could tell, for all their privilege, Kristin and
Keaton had spent their whole lives trying to please their
father. Finding out he might have had another family had
to be doing a number on both of them.

She looked at the back of Logan's head and wondered
how he felt about it all. He had barely had a chance to
get to know Douglas, so was he even surprised about today's events? He certainly had stepped up and taken control pretty quickly. Even Keaton hadn't pushed back when
Logan had done that. She was relieved to see the brothers working together and it firmed her resolve to create as
much distance between herself and Logan as she possibly
could. He deserved his family, unfettered by the complications she brought to everything, no matter how deeply
she felt for him.

The lawyer pulled into the driveway at the Richmond
house and parked outside the front door. They alighted and
the men went inside, but Honor paused to ensure the gate
at the end of the driveway was closed first. The last thing
they needed now was rubberneckers joining the party; she
had no doubt that the gossip mill was already churning
away over what had happened at the graveside. She then
went out to the kitchen and advised the caterers to contact
a local homeless shelter to see if they'd accept the food that

had been prepared for the guests who would now no longer be coming. She suggested to Nancy's housekeeper that she keep some platters aside for the family, who were now assembled in the parlor at the front of the house.

When she joined the family in the formal parlor, you could just about cut the seething, silent atmosphere with a knife. Her eyes sought out Logan, who remained standing as everyone else took their seats. The families lined up facing one another on Nancy's favorite chairs, all bearing very similar expressions. This wasn't going to be pleasant but she felt a swell of respect for Logan, who looked as if he'd more than capably chair this awkward meeting. Her instincts urged her to stand by him and offer him the support he was due but she knew she couldn't, and that just about crushed the air from her lungs. She'd thought she would cope with being near him again today, but it was proving more difficult than she'd imagined. Even so, she couldn't just desert him, or Nancy for that matter. Not when they might need her help.

"I think we can agree that today's developments have come as a shock," Logan started.

"I am not a development," the other Mrs. Richmond stated firmly. "I am Douglas's first and legal wife. She and her spawn are the *development*, and a very unwelcome one, I can tell you."

"Mom, don't. We are all shocked. There's no need to be unkind. None of this is anyone's fault except for Dad's," her daughter said firmly.

"You're right," Logan said in agreement. "First, I think we need to introduce ourselves, then, if you have no objections, we can ask Hector for his legal opinion on the situation."

The woman snorted. "As if his opinion will be unbiased. You can rest assured, my lawyers will be all over this no matter what your man says."

Logan said nothing but fixed his gaze on her and raised a brow.

"Fine," she said on another outraged huff of breath. "My name is Eleanor Richmond. I married Douglas on the first of July, thirty-six years ago, in our hometown in Virginia. We were high school sweethearts. These are our children— Fletcher, Mathias and Lisa."

"And I am Nancy Richmond. I, too, married Douglas thirty-six years ago, on the second of September, here in Seattle. We had a whirlwind courtship. He told me he couldn't live without me and begged me to marry him. And these are my children—Logan, Keaton and Kristin."

"And this is Hector Ramirez, our family lawyer," Logan introduced the attorney, who was sitting quietly to one side of the room observing the proceedings. "Hector, would you like to say a few words?"

"Thank you, Logan. I knew Douglas for many years, and I have to say this development has shocked me as much as it has clearly shocked you all. The first step I believe we need to take is to ascertain whose marriage has legal standing. Once that is done, the way forward will be clearer."

"The way forward?" Nancy asked.

"In terms of the execution of Douglas's final wishes. Aside from his personal effects, which he has been quite explicit in naming the recipients of, there's the matter of his business."

"My husband maintained a well-respected construction company in Virginia," Eleanor interjected. "Don't for one minute think that her children will be entitled to any of that or my home or financial portfolios."

Honor watched as Hector blinked in surprise at the barely suppressed vitriol in the other woman's voice. She herself was shocked, too. The woman hardly acted like a grieving widow. More like an avenging one. Her son Fletcher leaned forward and began to speak.

"Mom, this is going to be complicated enough as it is without you stirring the pot. If you have nothing positive to add, then, under the circumstances, it would be best if you kept your thoughts to yourself."

"Fletcher, that's unfair. I am your father's legal widow. You are his legitimate children. I'm making a stand for what's ours. For what's right."

"Then let's allow the lawyers to determine this quickly. The longer we take over this, the longer both our businesses and all our lives will be in limbo." Fletcher looked up at everyone assembled. "Are we agreed on that?"

There were murmurs of assent all round.

Fletcher slid out a business card and passed it to Hector. "If you could let us know exactly what you need from us to prove my mother's claim, we will advise our lawyers to provide that information accordingly. We will be staying in town tonight before flying back home tomorrow."

"And we'll be demanding that Douglas's body be returned to Virginia when this is all settled," Eleanor snapped at Nancy.

Honor couldn't believe the other woman's unpleasant attitude. Nancy had done no wrong. To her credit, Nancy didn't lower herself to respond; she merely turned to Hector and thanked him before proving herself the consummate hostess by offering everyone assembled something to eat and drink. Eleanor's second son, Mathias, refused on behalf of his family.

"If you don't mind, we'll make our way back to the hotel. I think you'll agree this is hardly a social situation that we'd like to prolong."

"Of course," Keaton said, standing and offering his hand to each of his purported half brothers and sister. "We all have a lot to process."

"You can say that again," Kristin muttered as she rose to her feet as well.

Eleanor merely sniffed as she stood up and led the way to the front door, her children following behind. Honor moved quickly to open the door and show them out. Eleanor didn't even acknowledge her, but Lisa smiled her thanks as she walked past. Once they were settled in their car, Honor activated the gate and waited until she caught the flicker of taillights at the end of the driveway before closing it again. Only then did she begin to feel her body start to relax.

"We sure weren't expecting that," Logan said from behind her.

She turned around slowly, forcing herself to ignore the way her heartrate kicked up a beat at his nearness. "No, we certainly weren't. Don't you think it odd that Douglas maintained mirror lives on each side of the country? If what they're saying is true."

"Odd isn't the word I'd choose." Logan wiped a hand across his face. "What a mess."

Her heart ached for him. Now that the confrontation was over, for now at least, the strain Logan was feeling was clear on his face. Honor hastened to choose words that might be of some encouragement.

"I can't help but feel that something isn't right about it all. Eleanor was so…aggressive, for want of a better word. It almost made me feel as if she was hiding something."

"You got that, too, huh?"

Honor sighed and reminded herself that while they were on the same wavelength, she could offer him no more than words right now. "This situation is going to make a whole bunch of lawyers very rich, isn't it?"

"Yeah," he agreed, his expression grim. "We're all going to be on tenterhooks until we know exactly where we stand."

Honor nodded. "Look, you all have a lot to discuss. I'll call a cab and head off and leave you to your privacy."

"Are you sure you won't stay? Nancy wouldn't object."

And you? she wanted to ask even though she knew the answer. It was clear in his expression that he was torn. She knew he wanted to include her, but was mindful of what her presence would do to his siblings. No, it was better she went, no matter how much it tore her apart to leave him at a time like this.

"I know," she said softly. "But it's better this way. Trust me."

He took her hand and she instantly felt awareness tingle through her at his touch.

"Thank you for all you've done today. I mean it. You gave me strength when I needed it."

Her throat choked on all the words she wished she could say in reply. She swallowed hard and said, "Give Nancy my regards."

Then she let herself out the door and closed it firmly behind her.

Fifteen

Two weeks later and they were no closer to a resolution. And, worse, Douglas continued to remain unburied, which was a deep source of distress to Nancy. Hector had advised the family that, based on the information provided by Eleanor's lawyer, including notarized copies of documents, her marriage to Douglas had indeed taken place prior to Nancy's, which made Nancy's claim the invalid one. The shame and sorrow at discovering she'd been deceived for so long had had a huge impact on her health, and she'd been unable to work since Douglas's death.

"How was Mom this morning?" Kristin asked as she popped into the office that had been her dad's and which was now, temporarily at least, Logan's.

"Still the same. I can't seem to get her interested in anything, and believe me, I've tried."

"Yeah, Keaton said she won't even leave the house. She's terrified she'll bump into someone she knows and she can't stand to face the questions, or worse, the pity."

The only bright side of this whole debacle was that it had drawn the siblings closer together. Not only were they dedicated to providing a united front of support to their mom, but also to the staff. So far, they'd managed to continue with business as usual and the three had worked together on major decisions and planning.

Honor had insisted she was working out the notice she'd given to Douglas on the day he died and had proven intractable on the subject. Not even a plea from Keaton had swayed her. And she'd gone back to avoiding Logan as much as possible. When they did cross paths, she kept herself apart and kept their conversations short. It was driving him crazy.

Logan leaned back in his chair and swiveled it around to look out the window. He still couldn't believe his father had managed to maintain two families for most of his life without anyone discovering his deception until now. What kind of man did that?

"You okay?" Kristin asked as she moved over toward the window and stared out at the view with him.

"I guess. I just can't get my head around what he did and how he did it."

Kristin shook her head. "I know what you mean. To us, he and Mom were always a tight unit. Totally devoted to one another. Yes, he traveled a lot with work, but no one would have suspected that he lived a double life. I feel so betrayed—I can't even begin to imagine how this is messing with Mom. He was her entire life and that life was a complete and utter lie."

"Not a complete lie," Logan said, trying to reassure her. "He loved Nancy deeply. Anyone could see that."

"But he loved Eleanor, too. And how he could love that woman is totally beyond me."

"I think it's probably fair to say we didn't see her at her best."

Kristin snorted. "That's true. How did she find out about Dad's death, anyway? Why didn't she or her lawyers make contact before the funeral?"

Logan sighed. "From what I have gleaned from Fletcher, she saw the notice in the paper and pretty much ordered the kids to book the flights and come with her. I'm not sure she had a plan—she just wanted to stake her claim."

"Well, she certainly did that. And how're things with our big brother from the East Coast? Is he champing at the bit to take over here?"

"For now he's like us. Waiting for the appropriate confirmation before any further decisions are made. In the meantime, he's focusing on business over there, and we need to keep doing what we do here."

"I hate waiting."

"We're agreed on that one. Keaton's frustrated, too."

"And Honor? She's still adamant she's leaving?"

Logan felt that all-too-familiar twist in his chest when he heard her name. They'd barely seen one another. She'd been busy ensuring her work was fully up-to-date and ready to hand over to her replacement as well as training her assistant and his colleagues on holding the reins in her department until an appointment was made. On top of that, she'd sent her assistant to attend any department meetings in her stead.

"Yeah," he answered dully.

He really missed her. Not just physically, but he missed her quick wit, her intelligent observations about work—everything. He kept telling himself it was ridiculous. They'd only met at the beginning of December and here they were, halfway into January and he couldn't get her to budge from his mind. Even in sleep she invaded his dreams, making him wake aching and frustrated and wishing she was there. He'd never experienced anything like it before.

"You know, I think Keaton would be okay now if you and Honor—" Kristin started.

"No. I can't go there."

"But, seriously. He isn't acting like a spurned lovelorn idiot. If you ask me, he got over her far more quickly than a man engaged to a woman should. Dad always said they were a good match but not a perfect one."

"Like he was an expert on relationships," Logan commented wryly.

"Yeah," Kristin laughed. "You're probably right. But it's a shame. Honor is a really awesome person. We've all enjoyed her friendship and her talents here at the office."

"Has HR advertised her position yet?"

"Yes, and they've had applicants, but none of them are of her caliber."

Logan closed his eyes briefly. And that was the problem, he thought. No one else was Honor Gould. And no one else had ever affected him quite as deeply as she had, either.

Honor couldn't help it. Waiting around had never been a particularly strong suit of hers, and the suspense surrounding the Richmond family situation was beginning to take its toll on everyone around her. Several of her team had expressed concern at the stability of the company with no officially appointed CEO, while others were more concerned about the idea of a total stranger coming from the East Coast to run the place. One or two had even handed in their notice already. While Honor had done her best to try and dissuade them, with her own last day fast approaching, no matter how she phrased things, it came across as hypocritical to try to talk people into staying.

On the few occasions her path had crossed with the Richmond siblings, she'd seen the obvious strain on their faces, and it upset her that Nancy had yet to return to work. She understood they were all grieving, but the complexity of Douglas's family relationships had created an added burden. The only bright side to any of this was seeing how Logan, Keaton and Kristin had begun to work together as a tight unit. And that made her choice to go worthwhile.

She loved Logan. And loving him meant she was prepared to do whatever it took to ensure he was happy. She understood his need for family, for identity, and she respected that was paramount for him right now. She was the last person who'd expect him to give up everything he'd just gotten back for her. And she knew that it would be a her-or-them situation. That much had been made clear when Kristin, who'd been her closest female confidante, had closed ranks with Keaton against her.

There had to be something she could do to make things right for them before she left. She'd thought long and hard about the whole situation with Douglas's second family, and no matter how she'd looked at it, it simply didn't feel right with her. There'd been something about Eleanor's behavior—not merely defensive, but aggressive—that made Honor want to look deeper into her claims. Yes, she knew that Hector Ramirez had received the information that Eleanor's lawyers had sent through. On the surface everything appeared to be legitimate, so far. But a feeling still niggled at Honor that she was missing something.

Growing up where Honor had, she'd seen and studied at close quarters what happened when people got caught in a lie, and in her experience, they behaved in one of three ways—they capitulated and admitted guilt, they acted like it didn't matter, or they went head-on at the challenge and their aggression would make the other person back off. Her gut told her that Eleanor's behavior fell into the latter category.

Judging by the information provided by Eleanor so far, she and Douglas were married on July first, as she'd said. Fletcher's birth had come seven months later, so Honor was pretty sure that Eleanor had been expecting him already when she and Douglas had married. Not that there was any scandal to that even if they'd just been fresh out of high school. And Fletcher's date of birth definitely made him around eighteen months older than Logan and Keaton, which threw Douglas's succession plans for Richmond Developments well and truly into the fire.

Not for the first time, Honor wondered what the heck he'd been thinking. Surely he'd known that when he died his sordid truths would come creeping out of the woodwork, hadn't he? Had he had such a God complex that he thought he'd be able to keep all his plates spinning and that no one would ever discover the truth? Had he no idea how hurtful and cruel his choices had been?

Honor reached her decision. Even if it meant she had to eat canned soup for the rest of the month, she was going to hire a private investigator to dig up the dirt she just knew to the soles of her feet hung around Douglas and Eleanor's marriage. She owed it to the Richmonds. To Douglas for always encouraging her, to Keaton to right the wrongs she'd done him and to Logan especially because after all he'd been through he deserved the very best. She might have jeopardized his position in his family, but if she could help to put things right, she would.

A week later she received the report from the Norfolk-based investigator she'd hired. The woman had set out the information she'd gleaned with crisp clarity and as Honor read through the data, she began to wonder if she'd been wasting both her time and money. Until she reached the last couple of pages, whereupon she felt a sudden spike in adrenaline and a tremor of excitement shook her body. Without waiting another moment, she grabbed the report and headed for Douglas's office.

"Stella, is Logan in?" she asked the assistant as she all but skidded to a halt on the carpet.

"He is, but he's in a meeting with Keaton, Kristin and Hector Ramirez right now."

"That's good. I need to see them, too."

Without waiting for Stella to announce her, she pushed open the office door and walked straight in. All four heads swiveled to see who had interrupted and Stella followed hard on Honor's heels, muttering apologies for the intrusion.

"That's okay, Stella. Obviously it's important. Perhaps you could organize someone to bring some coffee in for us?" Logan said.

"Certainly. It will be here right away."

Honor waited for Stella to close the door behind her before speaking.

"Look, I'm sorry to barge in on you all like this, but I just found out something really important and you need to know."

"What kind of important?" Kristin asked.

"Important to all of you, and your half brothers and sister. But most of all, it's going to be very important to Nancy."

"Well, spit it out," Keaton said impatiently.

"Hang on. First of all, take a seat, Honor," Logan suggested and gestured to the only vacant seat in the office, right in front of him.

Honor sat down but could still feel the tension that had driven her to the office in such a hurry holding her in its grip. Logan reached for the water carafe on the tray on his desk and poured her a glass of water and pushed it in her direction.

"Here, you look like you could do with this," he said.

"Thanks," she said with a grateful smile.

Her hand shook slightly as she lifted the glass to her lips and drank half of it in one gulp.

"Right, would you like to share your information with us?" Logan prodded gently.

"From the beginning I felt like there was something not quite right about Eleanor's claim. I had a feeling she was trying to hide the full truth."

"What's she trying to hide? Everything Hector has presented to us here today stacks up as the truth," Keaton said in a tone that would have stopped her under any other circumstances.

"That's what she wants you to see. But what she doesn't want you to see is this." Honor put the report from her investigator on the desk in front of them. She flipped through to the last page and stabbed at it with her finger. "This is what Eleanor didn't want anyone to know. She was underage when she and Douglas married."

Hector leaned forward and read the document. "Yes, that's true. But in the state of Virginia if you're under the age of eighteen and have the permission of your parents, you can legally marry."

"Yes, but Eleanor didn't have her parents' permission," Honor insisted.

"According to the data we've gleaned from the circuit court clerk, she did. It states her mother signed the necessary permissions."

Honor shook her head vehemently. "But her mother couldn't have done that. She was in Monte Carlo at the time, with her husband, Eleanor's father. They were on a six-month tour of Europe. Neither of them could have given permission because they weren't there when the license application was completed."

"So you're saying the license is invalid?" Kristin said, leaning forward in excitement.

Honor nodded and waited for Hector to finish reading the report summary she'd put in front of them.

"So it would seem," he said in agreement. "According

to this report, Eleanor bribed her parents' housekeeper to pretend to be her mother when the application was made for the license. A handwriting expert has verified that the signature on the application is not the same as that on record for Eleanor's mother."

"Why would she do such a thing?" Keaton asked, looking totally stunned by the revelation.

"I don't know for sure, but from what the investigator was able to find out, Honor was only seventeen when she found out she was pregnant with Fletcher. The housekeeper has since passed away, but the investigator talked to her daughter. Apparently the poor woman lived her life in fear of being found out for impersonating her boss. She had a habit of helping herself to Eleanor's father's good brandy. Eleanor knew this and threatened to tell her father if the housekeeper didn't help Eleanor with her plan to marry Douglas before her parents returned from Europe.

"Eleanor believed that if she was already married to Douglas, her parents couldn't do anything about it, and since she was pregnant they'd have to accept Douglas, too. Seems they'd had greater aspirations for their daughter up until then, which included a Swiss finishing school and the likelihood of a marriage to the son of a family friend, who was a diplomat."

"Wow, you kind of have to feel sorry for her. She must have been terribly desperate to go to those lengths," Kristin said with a liberal dose of sympathy.

"According to the housekeeper's daughter, Eleanor's parents disowned her on their return from Europe. Her father was a high-ranking naval officer and her mother was from a very wealthy family. On their deaths, their entire estate went to a naval charity. Eleanor got nothing."

"And from the looks of her claim on Dad's estate, she's still trying to make up for that," Keaton said.

Hector cleared his throat noisily before speaking. "I

think the key thing here is that Douglas and Nancy's marriage is the one that's valid."

"Which means that Logan is Dad's chosen CEO for Richmond Developments," Kristin added.

"Yes, and that woman and her children have no claim on our company," Keaton said vehemently.

Logan leaned back in his chair, and Honor was relieved to see the lines of tension that had scored his face over these past few weeks begin to ease.

"So, it's business as usual?" he asked Hector directly.

"I believe so. I'll head back to my office and prepare a letter for Eleanor Richmond's lawyers requesting that she drop all claims to Douglas's body, and to his business interests here on the West Coast based on the information that Ms. Gould has brought to us. They will no doubt need to verify the information uncovered in the private investigator's report. The question now arises as to whether you wish to state a claim on your father's business interests in Virginia."

"We could do that?" Keaton asked.

Hector shrugged slightly. "Under the terms of your father's will, you probably could."

"But more important is, would we want to," Logan said, playing devil's advocate. "Do we really want to subject Fletcher, Mathias and Lisa to what we've been going through?"

"Absolutely not," Keaton said vehemently. "When all's said and done, we're all family, whether we like it or not."

Honor watched as Logan looked to his sister.

"I don't see why we should allow Dad's actions to victimize us any further, do you?" she asked.

"Then we three are agreed," he said and directed his attention back to Hector. "Please make it clear to Eleanor and her family that, provided she drops her claims, we will not make any counterclaims against our father's interests in Virginia. Also inform her that we will proceed with honoring our father's wishes regarding his interment here in Seattle."

They all stood, and Hector shook hands with each of the siblings before turning to Honor. "I trust that I can take this copy of the report?"

"Of course," she said fervently.

Hector nodded and made his goodbyes. Once he was gone, Logan looked at Honor.

"Thank you," he said, his voice laden with relief. "Without your hard work things could have turned out very different, for all of us. We owe you for that."

Honor met his gaze and her voice shook as she answered him. "No, I owed you all. I had to do something."

Logan looked as if he wanted to object but she shook her head slightly and he got the message. He turned to his brother and sister.

"So, now we know this is ours, are you two ready to help me run it?"

"Aren't we doing that already?" Kristin asked.

"Not the way I was thinking," Logan continued. "How about we take a good hard look at the company structure? I think it's time we assumed joint control of Richmond Developments."

"Are you serious? How on earth will that work?" Keaton asked skeptically.

Logan shrugged. "We'll figure it out, but most importantly, are you guys on board?"

Both Keaton and Kristin nodded.

"I think we should head over to Mom's and let her know the news face-to-face. What do you think?" Keaton said.

"That's a great idea," Kristin said. "Are you coming, too, Honor? After all, if not for your hard work, we'd still be waiting for the next ax to fall."

Honor smiled and shook her head. "No, I need to finalize a few things here this afternoon, but I have to say I'm really glad you guys will be working together. I'm sure you'll have your differences—you're all such strong-minded individuals—but if you could pull together the way you have since Douglas died, I'm sure you can work through anything. Good luck."

"Are you sure, Honor? You could come later," Kristin pressed.

"No, really. I'm really busy, and this is a special time for you all as a family," Honor insisted.

"Are you coming with us now, Logan?" Keaton asked.

"I just want to say a few words to Honor first. You guys go ahead. I'll be there soon."

After they'd gone, Logan looked at Honor. She ached to move forward into his arms. To lay her head on his chest and feel his warmth and hear the strength of his heartbeat. To maybe lift her face to his and kiss him, even if it was just one last time. Because she'd reached a decision today. After delivering the information from the private investigator to the family, she planned to leave, immediately. Staying here was slowly tearing her apart. They might not give her a reference for not working out her full two weeks, but she didn't care anymore. She just needed to remove herself from a situation that was becoming more painful every day.

She fought back the urge to cry and lifted her chin slightly as she asked, "What was it you wanted to talk to me about?"

"I can't begin to tell you how much I appreciate you bringing that information to us."

"I had to. I owe all of you—your parents, too."

"You don't owe me anything," Logan said.

"Maybe not now, but I did. I nearly ruined your chance to build the family you always wanted. I hope we're clear now."

"Hardly. We all owe you."

She shook her head. "No, it's my gift to you."

She started to leave.

"Honor, wait. Don't go. Please. Let's work this out."

"We can't work it out, Logan. Every time I'm in the same space as you and Keaton I'm driving a wedge between you. I won't do that to you. You deserve so much more than that."

And then, using every ounce of control she had in her, she turned on her heels and walked out of his office and out of his life, forever.

Sixteen

The biting cold of January had eased up in February, but it was still darned cold. Back in New Zealand, temperatures were at sweltering levels with hot, sticky nights and high levels of humidity. Logan had Skyped with his grandmother, whose fluffy white hair had been blown sideways by the large fan oscillating next to her. He'd offered to put air-conditioning in her house on more than one occasion, but she'd insisted she was fine. He missed her. He missed all of them, and he'd scheduled a trip home in April.

But there was one person he missed more than everyone else altogether.

Honor.

He'd been shocked when he'd discovered she'd cleared out her office after delivering the report that had seen Eleanor Richmond pull back on her claims against Douglas's estate. Fletcher, Mathias and Lisa had traveled to Douglas's interment ceremony, and all six of his children were working toward establishing a stronger connection. So, instead of discovering his lost family, Logan had discovered two. But that side of things apart, there was still a yawning hole in Logan's life where Honor belonged.

"You're daydreaming again, Logan," Keaton said from across the meeting room table. "Care to share your thoughts?"

The two men had been discussing their roles and responsibilities under the new regime that had been approved by the board. And so far at least, there'd been no head-to-head disagreements.

"Sorry, Keaton. Look, maybe we can take a break for ten minutes."

Keaton pushed his chair back from the table. "Good idea. Let's go grab a coffee at the place downstairs. We could both do with the change in scenery."

After ordering their identical coffees, one of many things they'd discovered they had in common, Keaton led the way to a small table by the window. Once they were seated, he pinned Logan with a stare.

"What?" Logan said. "You're starting to creep me out, brother."

"Something's wrong. You're different."

"I thought we were still getting to know one another. How can I be different?"

Keaton shook his head. "No, don't try to hedge with me. You're as on point in the office as you've been right from the start, but something's missing inside you. It's Honor, isn't it?"

Logan felt his defenses shoot up. "I'm not seeing her, if that's what you're getting at."

The girl at the counter called out his name, and he rose to collect their order before sitting back down again.

"Actually, no. That wasn't what I was getting at," Keaton said as they put sugar in their black coffees and stirred in synchronization. "Do you love her?"

"Keaton, don't do this. You know I wouldn't do anything to destroy our relationship as brothers."

The bond between them was growing stronger but Logan doubted that it would survive him striking up again with Keaton's ex-fiancée. That definitely went against the guy code, and he'd already overstepped that mark. As much as he wanted to, he wasn't about to put his feelings for Honor ahead of the fragile bond that was growing between him and Keaton.

"We're doing okay," Keaton admitted. "I have to say I didn't want to like you, but I do. Although it still feels weird seeing myself every time I look at you."

"Same." Logan took a sip of his coffee. "Shall we head back and finish our business?"

"Hang on. I'm not done. I'm worried about you."

Logan spread his hands and shrugged. "Nothing to worry about."

"You're not happy," Keaton pressed. "If Honor will make you happy, I think you need to pursue that."

Logan just looked at his brother. A part of him wanted to agree, but navigating this new family was a minefield, and he wasn't about to have anything blow up in his face.

"You'd be okay with that? You two were engaged to be married, remember?"

Keaton pushed a hand through his hair and sighed. "Yeah, yeah. I know. It was the right thing to do, y'know? Get engaged. Plan for the future. But when I look back on it, there was no fire, no real spark. Sure, she's a fine-looking woman with a sharp mind and a depth of compassion you don't see in everyone. But we fell into our engagement because of proximity and a brief mutual attraction. We couldn't maintain that spark. If we had, she'd have known instantly when she saw you that you weren't me.

"And yeah, we probably would have made marriage work because we're equally stubborn and focused on success, and we would have continued to put Richmond Developments' needs before our own. But you know what? There's more to life than that and I'm only just beginning to understand that now. I think that if you still have feelings for Honor, you should do something about them. Bring her back and love her as she deserves to be loved."

Logan looked at his brother and could see the sincerity in his eyes. And inch by inch, Logan felt the ice encasing his heart slowly begin to thaw.

"You're sure about that?"

"Look, if you can handle that I saw her first, then we can get through this. It's what true family is about, right? Being there for one another. Supporting each other. Living in truth."

"Living in truth. Yeah, I like the sound of that."

Logan looked at his watch. Meeting be damned. He was going to find Honor right now. He downed his coffee and rose from his seat.

"Hey, I'm not finished yet," Keaton protested. "And we have a meeting to wind up, remember?"

"Later," Logan said. "Some things can't wait."

He was never as grateful for his perfect resemblance to Keaton as he was when the concierge waved him through to the elevators in Honor's apartment building. She was quick to open the door but wasn't looking as she spoke.

"Hi, Marcus, if you could put those cartons over there, that would be great. Thanks." And then she looked at Logan. "Oh."

Logan looked past her to the chaos of her living room. It was half-full of packing boxes, and all her furniture was pushed to one side.

"Moving?" Logan asked as he stepped inside without waiting for her invitation.

"I'd offer you a place to sit, but as you can see I'm a little busy right now."

"You're leaving?" he repeated.

"Yes." She pushed her hair off her face and left a smudge of dust on her cheek. "I haven't found a job yet and I can't continue to stay here. I need to get farther out of the city to where I can afford the rent."

Logan was surprised. She'd been earning a high salary at Richmond Developments, and if her surroundings were any indicator, she lived well within her budget. Surely she had money socked away for a rainy day?

"You got a gambling problem I don't know about?" he asked, half joking.

"What? Oh—" She gave a short laugh. "No. But I pay for my mother's care. There's not a lot left over at the end of month."

"That's hard."

"Yes, it is."

Her short and simple response gave Logan the tiniest insight into what it might have been like for Honor growing up.

"Anyway," Honor continued. "What are you doing here?"

There was another knock at the door.

"That'll be Marcus with my boxes. You may as well make yourself useful and tape them for me while you're here. If you're staying awhile, that is."

"Sure." Logan opened the apartment door and took the new stack of boxes being delivered. "Where do you want these?"

She gestured down the hall. "My bedroom. I'm about to start in there."

He went into her room and sat on the bed.

"Hey, no slacking," she chided softly as she followed him.

"Honor, don't go."

"Um, did you not get the memo? I can't afford to stay here."

"No, I mean, don't go. Don't leave Seattle—don't leave me. Please."

She looked shocked. "You know why I can't stay, and it's not just the money."

Logan stood up and clasped her hands in his. "But what about this?" he said. "You feel it, don't you? This burning awareness. The thing you didn't know you needed until we met, until we touched? That's what I feel every time we make contact, whether deliberately, like this, or just brushing your arm in a corridor. Honor, Please. Don't go."

"Keaton—"

"Has nothing to do with this. This is about us. You and me and what we mean to each other. I know it's only been a couple of months, but I feel you inside me like I've never felt anyone else ever before. I can't start my day without thinking about you, and you're the last thought on my mind when I fall asleep at night, too. I want you. Not just sexually, although that was bloody great." He gave her a bittersweet half smile. "But I want you in my life. I want to know what makes you tick. What makes you mad. What makes you laugh until you cry."

"You know we can't do anything. Your family—"

"Will be thrilled to have you among us. We missed you at Douglas's interment."

"I couldn't… I just couldn't bear to say goodbye. To him or to any of you all over again."

"Sneaking away from the office the way you did was kind of cruel. You didn't give anyone the chance to say goodbye to you, either. And not returning calls? Harsh. But most of all, you didn't give me the chance to tell you how much you mean to me."

"Don't, please." She pulled free, and tears filled her eyes.

"Just go. I can't do this with you. We can't be together. You stand to lose everything that means so much to you."

"You're not listening to me. *You* mean everything to me. Keaton and I have talked, properly, like actual brothers. He admitted to me that you two fell into your engagement, that there was no grand passion. He told me you deserve better than that. He told me to come after you if I loved you. And I do. I love you, Honor Gould. I want to build a future with you. A family with you, if you'll let me."

Honor sank down onto the bed. "You say that, but you don't know me. You don't know where I've come from. Who I really am. I've never had much, y'know? When I was little, my father cheated on my mom, and then she cheated on him in retaliation. They fought about it all the time, and then one day he left us and never came back. But even through all the fights and the cheating, she loved him. So much that she couldn't function without him. I didn't want to be like that. I didn't want to be so weak that I couldn't live without the person I thought I loved. She couldn't even look after me. Most of the time we had no food in the house and lived on handouts. She turned to men and booze and then drugs, in that order, just to get through a day.

"So I learned from an early age to take every opportunity that came my way. To work hard at school despite being teased for wearing dumpster couture, for never having lunch or bright new coloring pens or the latest calculator. I had to be better than my mom was. I had to be more. To have more. And I was getting there. I earned my degree and I got an entry-level position at Richmond Developments. Douglas gave me the opportunity to continue to upskill and be better at every turn. He saw the hunger in me. The desire to be the best.

"And I was doing great, until I got a call from a social worker to say my mom had been found in a derelict building. She was starving, covered in sores and in a complete state of delirium. And I'm all she has. I had to look after her. To make sure she had the right care so her final days aren't as awful as the life she chose to allow to happen to her. You see, while I climbed my ladder, I stopped checking on her, even though I knew she needed to be checked on. She kept telling me she didn't want me. That her latest boyfriend would look after her. I knew better, but I chose to accept what she said. I just wanted to get a step up. But one step leads to another, and you keep going. That's the kind of person I am. Selfish. Self-absorbed. I abandoned my mom. I never fit in anywhere, so I created a persona that would fit in. That didn't have my horrible past. See? You don't know me at all. I'm a fake."

Logan sat down next to her and turned her face to his, swiping away at her tears with his thumb.

"You know what I'm hearing? I'm hearing about a determined little girl who did what she had to do to survive, despite the people who should have cared for her letting her down in every way a parent can let down a child. Your mom made her choices, Honor, and you've done your best for her. Even now, you're still doing it. You're putting her needs ahead of your own. That's not selfish or self-absorbed or fake. You have nothing to feel guilty about. Let me help you shoulder that burden. Let me be there for you."

"You have no idea how much I want to do that. How much I want to lean on someone else. But it doesn't come easily to me to trust people like that."

"I know. And we can work on that together. But, Honor, you can trust me and I want to spend the rest of my life proving that to you. Letting you be the real you. You fit, with me."

She lifted a hand to his face and stared into his eyes. "You really mean that, don't you?"

"I do. With all my heart. Stay. With me. Come back to Richmond Developments. You know you belong there, with all of us, but especially because you're the best at what you do and we deserve the best. You deserve the best."

"I can have my job back? I don't know if I could do that. Return to what I already walked away from."

"You don't have to, but the option is there for you if you want it. But most importantly, stay because it's what you want and need. I love you. I'll help you be whatever you want to be, and I'll be there for you, always."

She hesitated and firmed her shaking lips a moment before speaking in a voice that trembled with emotion.

"Yes, I accept. You and our future together. I love you, too, Logan. I don't deserve you, but I'll take it all. Thank you. I won't let you down."

"We won't let each other down. We're going to do this together."

"Yes, together."

Logan pulled her into his arms and kissed her and felt something ease inside him. A sense of rightness filled him to the depths of his soul. Coming to Seattle had been a gamble, but he'd gained so much. A family and a future he hadn't expected and, best of all, this woman in his arms.

* * * * *

TAKING ON THE BILLIONAIRE

ROBIN COVINGTON

To my editor, Charles Griemsman, and my agent,
Nalini Akolekar: thank you for making my dreams
of becoming a Harlequin author a reality.

Patrick, Rory and Fiona—the best family in the world.
I'm so lucky that you're mine.

One

Tess Lynch was a distraction.

A sexy, smart, competent, mouth-wateringly tempting distraction.

For the millionth time since he'd first met her, Adam Redhawk regretted his decision to take the office that was glass on three sides. Everyone had told him that this office, with its commanding prize of place in the corporate headquarters of Redhawk/Ling, was the best way to announce to the world that he was the CEO of a billion-dollar tech company.

Now he'd give at least a million to get one damn solid wall.

His luxury corporate fishbowl gave him zero opportunity to get his act together before his favorite redheaded private investigator sauntered into his space and plopped a thick file on the center of his desk. And God knew that Adam needed every second to get his act together when it came to Tess Lynch. He spared a glance at the pile of papers she'd tossed down, the sprawl of folders out of place on the immaculate desktop, but he couldn't resist the compulsion to return his gaze back to her face and the sparkling flash of her golden-jade eyes.

She was laughing at him, dammit.

Of course she was.

"Good afternoon, Ms. Lynch." He glanced at his watch, knowing full well what time it was but taking the extra few seconds to school his expression before looking at her again. Her auburn curls were loose today and she wore a body-skimming dark pink dress that ended just above the knee. The entire outfit looked like it was specifically made to showcase her full, voluptuous figure. Tess reminded him of the classic film star Rita Hayworth, a favorite of his adoptive mother. Bold and self-assured, Tess was…breathtaking. "You're late."

She laughed, tossing off her jacket and his censure at the same time. "Only fifteen minutes."

"That is *still* late."

He wanted to keep the steel in his voice, wanted to keep the necessary distance between them, *needed* to keep believing that he didn't want her. But it was impossible when she slinked around the edge of his desk until there was barely an arm's length between them. This close he could see the splash of freckles across her nose and smell the scent of her, soft and citrus sharp. Everything in his body went on high alert and he marveled that she didn't feel the heat wafting off him in pulse-pounding waves.

Temptation. If he looked the word up in the dictionary, she'd be there, complete with red-gold hair, freckles and a sly, kissable grin.

"You're right," she agreed, surprising him with her quick acquiescence. Usually they sparred a bit longer before one of them begrudgingly conceded temporary defeat and they proceeded to take care of business. "But I knew you had a meeting with Justin right before this and he *always* starts fifteen minutes late and goes over by the same amount." Tess leaned against his desk, her body language communicating just how much she didn't care if he was irritated with her being late to the meeting. He watched as she picked up the pair of drumsticks on his desk and lazily twirled them between her slim fingers, the look in her eyes daring him to stop her. "So, Mr. Redhawk, I'm not late. I'm right on time."

Adam couldn't argue with her. Her position was logical and fact based, two things that always made sense to him. And her lips twisting in a sexy "you know I'm right" smile crumbled any argument he was going to make.

He grinned and nodded in concession while he reached out and took his sticks out of her hands and placed them back on the desk. "One day I'm going to take Justin's watch and reset it so that he'll be on time for once."

"That won't work. You'd have better luck trying to change the tide."

That was true. His best friend and business partner marched to his own internal clock. He was never going to change.

"How did the two of you ever become friends?" Tess asked, shifting over toward the grouping of personal photos on the low table behind his desk. She leaned over, focusing on one of Justin and him at Stanford. Two smiling idiots, stupid enough to think they could quit academia and make their dream come true.

The idiots had done all right.

"It was in the campus security lockup. Justin talked them into letting us go with just a warning." Adam shook his head at the memory. What a pair of dumbass, know-it-all jerks they'd been back then.

"I bet he did." Tess laughed, shifting to peek up at him between glossy auburn curls. "What did you guys do to get busted by the cops?"

"I'll never tell."

"I can find out, you know." She murmured, "It *is* my job."

Tess touched the photo and Adam watched her. The way she moved so confidently in his space was mesmer-izing. Tess was gorgeous, her body curvy and sexy, but it was the way she owned her place in the world that kept him awake at night. It was her take-no-prisoners bra-vado that kept him hard and wanting anytime she was near. When she straightened and looked at him over his shoulder, he almost forgot that they were in an office ex-posed to all of his employees. The office where he was supposed to be running his billion-dollar company and not yearning to kiss this woman, to taste this woman, to possess this woman.

What was this thing between them? Tess Lynch was not the kind of woman who usually caught his eye. She was secretive and elusive, mouthy and brash, and owned her blatant brand of sexuality. She was also decisively stubborn but also changed her moods and mind as quickly as a hummingbird flew. Tess Lynch was a walking dan-ger sign that he should heed but spent way too much time figuring out ways to ignore. She did not fit in the way he wanted his world to function, but he found himself caring less and less.

A few months ago he'd taken the referral from a friend

of his and hired Tess to find his younger brother and sister. They'd all been taken from their parents and separated in an illegal adoption twenty-four years ago, and now he'd finally made good on the promise that six-year-old Adam had made to himself and his ancestors. Tess had been successful and located both Sarina and Roan and now she was here to deliver the final report.

But while the job he initially hired her to do was over, he was glad to have another reason to keep her around a little while longer. Which was insane because if he was right, the problem he needed her to help solve could take down his company and everything he'd fought to achieve.

Adam needed to focus. He'd asked for this meeting because he needed to take quick action if he was going to save the company he created. Adam turned away from her, needing to break the connection and regroup.

He spied the folders on the desk and tapped a finger on the papers. "What's this?"

"The final report..." she paused, tilting her head to the side, watching him closely "...and copies of everything I found while I was searching for your family. Court records. Newspaper clippings. Educational, job and criminal records. The last twenty years condensed on paper and a USB drive." He raised an eyebrow in question and Tess shrugged. "I know you didn't ask for all of that extra stuff but I thought you might like to have it. It might connect some dots."

Damn. Well, he'd asked. And wasn't this just like jumping from the corporate frying pan into the fire of messy family relations?

His hand hovered over the top folder while he played chicken with his past. He'd spent a ton of money and a lot of time to find his lost brother and sister and the answers to all of the questions that had tormented him for the last twenty-four years were sitting on his desk reduced to words and pixels.

Finally forcing himself to open it, he was greeted by his own face looking back at him in two pictures. The first was his current headshot and the other was when he was six years old, the photo his adoptive parents had first seen when they were picking out a kid to give a better life to. Hardened brown eyes that knew way too much about the shit life could throw at you stared back at him from the page. Adam shut the folder. He knew the rest of his story.

The other two packets contained similar but completely different histories. His brother and sister, Sarina and Roan, flashed across his line of vision in a stream of photos and facts and data about what had happened to them after they'd been separated and sent to different families. Different states. Different lives. Different trauma but the same hard expression stared back at him in the photographs. He was anxious to read every word and sickened by the sensation that he was prying into things he had no business knowing.

Things he had paid Tess to find out when he'd hired her to find them.

Things he'd know firsthand if their lives had turned out differently.

Adam slammed the folder shut and tossed it with more force than he intended, causing a couple of pens to shoot off the other side of the desk onto the hardwood floor. He cursed under his breath and took a step to pick them up but the firm press of Tess's hand on his arm stopped him cold. He glanced down at where she touched him, her warmth raising goose bumps on his own skin, and then lifted his eyes to meet her gaze. He'd expected pity so the open, clear expression of understanding on her face surprised him.

"Adam, I gave them both the same information. You're all starting at the same place, with the same facts about each other."

He shifted his arm and Tess's grip slid until their hands fit together. The touch of their palms was electric, sharp but totally right. They stared at each other, his eyes drifting down to her lips as they parted on a stutter as she temporarily lost her train of thought.

"Family is hard," she whispered, voice catching on the last part with whatever baggage she brought along with her.

Oh hell. Adam squeezed his eyes shut to the gut punch her words delivered. He'd never been good with the family who'd raised him and now he had a long-lost sister and brother to make some kind of future with. What the hell had he been thinking?

"If it helps, the three of you are more alike than you'd think," she continued, her voice stronger, soothing and laced with humor. "You all ride motorcycles. Fast ones. Loud ones. And no European crotch rockets, either. You people are a Harley family. It's like it's imprinted on your DNA or something."

This surprised a laugh out of him and something tight in his throat broke loose. Tess's eyes widened as she tilted her head to the side with the unspoken question.

"Our dad had a crappy Harley. I remember riding around with him on the Qualla Boundary." The memory was one of the few he still had that felt real. Most of that time felt like he made it up or that it had happened to someone else. Twenty-four years was a long time. "I guess it is in our DNA."

Adam released her hand, breaking their connection, and walked over to the windows looking out over the wooded tech campus. This part of California was beautiful, nothing like what he could remember of the lush, blue-tinged mystery of the mountains of his boyhood home. But it was gorgeous in its own way. He'd built something here with Justin, a company that employed a lot of people and had the potential to help many, many more.

He'd created a really good life for himself. It would only be better with his brother and sister in it.

But while he wanted to sit down and devour every bit of the information about his family, now was not the time. The future of his company was on the line and he needed Tess and her skills to save it.

Redhawk/Ling had a launch in eight weeks, the app that would make or break this company, and they had a problem. A very big problem and he needed her help.

He turned to Tess and finally got to the main reason he'd asked her to meet him today.

"Tess, I didn't ask you here just to get the final report. I need to hire you for another job. Somebody from inside Redhawk/Ling is trying to take us down and I want to hire you to find out who it is."

Two

It was as if the universe was finally on her side.

Tess tried not to do a happy dance at the revelation that Adam Redhawk was keeping her on for another job. Just when she was wondering what excuse she was going to use to continue their contact, he invited her right in.

And ensured that she would get her revenge.

She couldn't afford to give anything away; this development was too crucial. So, Tess got her excitement under control and focused on the business at hand.

"I'm flattered that you think I can do the job but I don't know much about corporate espionage."

She let the silence spread out between them. Adam was a thoughtful man and he wasn't going to speak in haste. It had served him well throughout his life, keeping him insulated and beyond the hurt and pain life wanted to inflict. Tess had admired it from the first moment she'd met him although it had made him a very difficult mark.

It also made him intriguing, mesmerizing, completely intoxicating. Adam Redhawk was a constant temptation to her. He made her want things, made her want him. In her bed, inside her body but also in her life. He was sexy, whip-smart, strong and honorable. He was the kind of man every woman hoped they would find but he was also the one that none of them could capture.

Adam never had a lack of women in his bed. Not that he bragged about it; she'd had to do her own digging on that point. And by all accounts from those who knew, his still waters ran deep and dirty in the bedroom. A staple on the "top ten sexiest bachelors" lists, Mr. Redhawk was a definite catch, but he refused to take the bait. Nobody stayed over. Nobody lingered in his life for long.

He was a challenge and Tess thrived on a challenge. She knew how to use her looks, her body and sexuality to get what she wanted. But she'd not pursued him, not taken that tack in her plan to get closer to him. He wanted her; she knew it. She wanted him; they both knew it. But she *liked* him and that feeling would not help her do what she needed to do. Those feelings would only lead to complications that she didn't want or need.

So, the fantasy of Adam taking her, rough and tumble on his immaculate desk, had never become a reality.

A regret that had kept her up more than one night.

Adam continued his pitch, oblivious to where her mind had wandered. "You can find people. You blew apart the maze of bureaucratic bullshit and found my sister and brother so I think you can find out who is trying to ruin this company."

Tess nodded toward the long leather sofa in his office. "This feels like a long story. Mind if I sit?"

"Of course."

Tess took a seat, watching Adam prowl the perimeter of his office, pacing back and forth in front of the window as if he was imprisoned here in his high-end Silicon Valley prison. Maybe he was. Adam Redhawk had grown up with high expectations imposed on him and now he'd shouldered ones of his own making. When he spoke, it was controlled and even but she could hear the undercurrent of fury.

"In eight weeks we are launching an app that will revolutionize the world." Adam glanced at her, his eyebrows raised in question. "All of this is confidential in accordance with your previously signed agreement. You understand?"

"Of course. You can count on my discretion," she answered, not taking any offense at his question. Redhawk/Ling was a company that made dreams an actual reality and it was only natural that they would protect them like children.

"This app will make it possible for any device to communicate and work together with any other device. You can interchange apps, programs, music, documents…the operating system will no longer matter."

Tess sat up a little straighter, her brain trying to wrap around this information. "This is going to make you rich." She shook her head, laughing at the stupidity of her statement. "It is going to make you richer. Ridiculously rich."

"Justin says that that there is 'fuck you money' and that this will be 'I can pay someone to fuck you money.'"

"Justin would say that." Tess chuckled, her mind turning the situation over in her mind. "So, someone is trying to steal information about the app?"

Adam nodded, coming over to sit next to her on the couch. He had his sleeves rolled up and when he leaned on his knees, his forearms flexed in that sexy way that got her attention every time. He was in great shape. His muscles shifting underneath his impeccably tailored suits made her mind wander to speculation about what he looked like under all that fabric.

Not that she had to leave it all up to her imagination. He'd been photographed when he'd raced in a triathlon last year. Miles and miles of taut, bronzed skin over muscles formed through years of running and hiking and competition. Her heart rate sped up and her palms itched to reach out and touch him again like she had just a few moments ago. That had been unexpected since she made it a point to avoid physical contact with Adam. But he'd looked so vulnerable, so lost that all the rules flew out the big floor-to-ceiling windows.

Adam answered her question. "Someone is trying to ruin the launch. Not sure if they want to try and reverse engineer it or just steal our thunder. Either way, we cannot afford for that to happen. Justin and I have reinvested a significant portion of the company's money into this app, so it has to work."

"Or you lose everything?"

"Everything that counts. Besides our investment, we'd have to lay off people. These folks stood by us when we were just two crazy college dropouts working out of the back of a warehouse. I don't want to let people down." Adam shifted next to her, their knees brushing as he faced her head-on. His eyes were dark with the intensity of his emotions and he leaned in close enough for her to smell the exotic woodsy scent of his aftershave. "I need someone on this that I can trust, Tess. You're smart and I know you can do this."

Tess tried not to cringe every time he mentioned the

word *trust*. He really shouldn't. He had no idea how much he shouldn't. "I'm just a P.I. I'm a great P.I. but I don't know anything about corporate espionage."

"I'm not worried about it. You're a quick study and I don't need you to know my business. You know people and what would make someone steal from me. That's what I need." Adam paused, before adding with a wink, "Besides, I know you, which means I don't have to get to know anyone else."

"I forgot—you don't like people."

"Not as a rule, no." Adam shrugged, pulled a piece of paper out of his shirt pocket and held it out to her. "Justin and I wrote down a list of people who we think are worth looking into. It should get you started."

Tess ignored the way he assumed she would be taking the case and took the paper, opening it to read the names written down. Her heart kicked up a beat when she read the first one, convinced that the universe was sending her a signal.

"Franklin Thornton? He's at the top of your list?"

Adam nodded, his eyes narrowed in suspicion and anger. It was no secret that there was no love lost between Adam and his adoptive father.

"Franklin would love to see Redhawk/Ling crash like the Hindenburg. He also has the juice to make it worth someone's time to sell our asses out." Adam reached out and grabbed a cup of coffee, took a sip and grimaced before putting down the mug. "Franklin is always at the top of the list. That's not paranoia. It's just business to him and it is what he does. Putting me in my place is the cherry on top of the goddamn sundae."

Tess was very much aware of how Franklin Thornton ate people up and spit them out. She knew the way that

he trashed people's dreams, destroyed their hope and
betrayed their trust. She knew what happened to people
who ended up on the shit end of Franklin Thornton; they
ended up broken, insane with grief and oblivious to the
two daughters that needed them to be their dad.

Franklin Thornton ruined people but he also created
enemies.

He'd created Tess Lynch and she'd spent the last ten
years looking for the perfect chance to get close to him
and bring him down. And it didn't matter if she had to
go through the man sitting next to her to get to him; she
was going to get him.

There was only one answer to Adam's question.

"I'll need an office here, access to security files and
IT support."

Three

The files were everywhere.

Adam tried not to twitch at the absolute shitshow his office had become. Stacks of folders were scattered across the table, three laptops were open with spreadsheets covering all of the screens. And coffee cups and empty food containers littered the coffee table and piled up in the trashcan.

Adam didn't want to be the guy who was bothered by the disorder and chaos but he was one hundred percent *that* guy.

Justin was not.

"How did we end up with so many weirdos working here?" Justin asked, lounging back with his size twelve Converse Chucks kicked up on the coffee table. He held a folder in his hands, reading over the reports Tess had compiled on the most likely employees of Redhawk/Ling. "What the hell is LARP-ing? Is that the costume thing? The Comic-Con stuff?"

"It's live-action-role-playing." Tess strolled by him and nudged his feet to the floor, shooting Adam a secret smile. "It's what you would have been doing if you'd actually had the guts to get out from behind the computer screen in your parents' basement and go out and meet real girls."

Justin sat up straight and looked absolutely offended. "I was not in my parents' basement. I had a computer in my room." He motioned to Adam. "Do I have to put up with this?"

Tess scoffed. "If you yuck on somebody else's yum, you get what you get."

Adam snorted and grabbed the file from Justin. "Yeah, Justin, stop yucking on—" he read the name off the folder "—Bryan Lane's yum."

"He's not our guy anyway," Tess interjected, plucking the file from Adam's hand.

Their fingers brushed; their eyes locked on each other and everything else in the room disappeared. He stared at her, zeroing in on the way her body swayed into his. He knew how it was; gravity had nothing on the pull of Tess Lynch.

"How do you know?" Justin inquired, sifting through the stack of files and trying to pretend like he wasn't staring at the two of them. "What are you looking for? What does a traitor look like?"

Tess's gaze lingered on his for a moment longer and then she transferred all her attention to Justin. Adam felt the loss as a physical pang, deep in his gut. And if he zoomed in closely on his emotions, he'd acknowledge that jealousy was in the mix too. But he wasn't zooming in on anything except the task at hand, right now.

"They look like you and me and Estelle," she said,

mentioning Adam's long-time and highly beloved personal assistant. "Or that beautiful boy at the corner coffee shop with all of the tattoos."

"Felix. His name is Felix." Adam spoke without thinking, waving off the extended, curious looks from Tess and Justin. "He takes the time to remember my name and my order. I remember his."

"Okay, yes, Felix," Tess agreed. "It would be great if they walked around with a big *T* on their chest or a mustache to twirl like a villain. But, they don't. So, you have to look for an area of exploitation, usually debt, sex or family. It will be a miracle if the IT guys found evidence on the company computers. I'd be shocked if someone was so dumb or brazen. So, I need to look deeper."

"File by file," Adam observed.

"Person by person," Tess answered, pointing to the stacks on the table. "But I'll find them, whoever they are."

Estelle Conway appeared in the doorway, her expression wary. She glanced back over her shoulder, angling her wheelchair across the opening and effectively blocking whoever was behind her. "Mr. Thornton is here to see you, Mr. Redhawk."

Adam went rigid while Justin shot into movement. There was a flurry of arms and legs and thunderous muttering as he rose from the couch in a cascade of paper and folders and advanced toward Estelle.

"What the fuck does he want?" Justin asked, his typically smooth voice ragged with anger.

"I *want* to fucking talk to Adam." Franklin Thornton answered as he pushed past Estelle and barreled through the door, jamming Estelle's chair into the door frame with a metallic thud and bang. His voice was calm and even, in contrast to his physical aggression and demanding movements.

He was a handsome man, his tall frame still broad in the shoulders with a power that hinted at his college football player past. But one look in his eyes told you the truth behind his money and power. It wasn't that he was fouled by hatred or rage. Franklin Thornton was dead inside. He didn't care enough about the people around him to worry about hurting them; you couldn't harm a thing, an object. Adam had learned early that his adoption had had its reasons and none of them involved him or his welfare. He was around because he was useful to Franklin and nothing more. Everything was that complicated and that simple with his adoptive father.

"Mr. Redhawk, I'm sorry," Estelle began to apologize for what she clearly thought was her failure for this man barging his way into the office.

Adam wasn't having it.

He stepped forward and stood in front of Franklin, using his own bulk to block any further progress into the office, any progress toward the work they were doing in here. Adam didn't raise his voice; he'd learned early and often to keep complete control of his reactions, to deny his opponent the opposing show of force they tried to incite.

"Franklin, you need to apologize to Estelle."

He was ignored as he expected, the other man's lips curling into a grin. "Hello, Adam. You've been ignoring my calls."

"If I'd known that answering would have prevented you from showing up here today, I would have..." He considered his options. "I still wouldn't have answered."

Adam crossed his arms over his chest and dug in. "Apologize to Estelle. Now. I'm not asking."

Franklin considered him, his gaze never leaving Adam's face. "I apologize."

It was as good as he was going to get. Adam nodded at Estelle, his smile communicating his own apology. He waited until she'd left before he turned back towards Franklin, dropping the smile entirely.

"Whatever you're here for, the answer is 'no,' 'none of your business,' and 'get out.'"

"All of the above," Justin added.

"That too," Adam agreed.

"Cute." Franklin sneered. "I'm here to find out why you have a redhead with big tits asking questions about me."

Franklin's tone was ambivalent but the words hit Adam like a sledgehammer and it took most of his will to not react physically to his words. However, the spark of interest in his adoptive father's eyes told him that he wasn't holding his poker face as well as he usually did. A guttural sound of outrage behind him communicated that Tess wasn't maintaining her cool either. Franklin's eyes slid from Adam's face to look beyond him, to where Tess was standing.

His eyes raked over her before he spoke. "Well, they weren't wrong about the tits."

"Shut your mouth," Adam warned, facing off with Franklin with a shove to his chest before Adam turned and walked toward the fuming Tess.

Now he knew what she looked like when she was pissed and it was so not the right time for him to linger on the fact that she was gorgeous. Anger raised the pink in her cheeks and made her eyes flash a poisonous green.

He never wanted to kiss her more than he did right this instant.

He never wanted to keep Franklin away from someone more than he did in this instant.

"Tess," he murmured as he reached out and grabbed her hand. She tensed, attempting to get him to let her go as she peered over his shoulder, the venom shooting out of her glare like a laser. If it had been leveled at anyone other than Franklin Thornton her opponent would be cowering in a corner, but Adam guessed that Franklin was giving as good as he got. Letting these two at each other would be a very bad idea. He tugged her in closer and leaned down to murmur, his voice pitched low and edged with a warning that he wasn't going to argue about this. "Don't."

At his demand, she stopped resisting him, her eyes snapping to meet his with the sizzling impact of a lightning bolt hitting too close to the mark. Tess wanted to fight. Her reaction was visceral, a tremble of tension that ran up and down her body and hitched her breath with every inhale. Adam slid his hand around her wrist, letting his fingers soothe her with the gentlest touch against her rapidly fluttering pulse point. Franklin got him riled too, pushed buttons he didn't even know he had, but her reaction was strange, more than just anger over his words, and prompted a million questions in his mind. Questions that would wait until later. Right now, he wanted to put as much distance between Franklin and Tess as he could manage.

"Tess, go make sure that Estelle is okay," he asked. She hesitated, her refusal poised on the edge of the tensed hard line of her lips. "Please, baby, just do this."

The unexpected endearment shocked him as it slid

past his lips and she was now utterly focused on him. He would have bet money that the world had ground to a damn halt except for the electric current running between the two of them. Tess didn't look angry, didn't look like she objected, her expression was more shocked pleasure and sharp interest than anything else and he wondered what her reaction would be if he tugged her even closer and tasted her mouth. Only the knowledge that Franklin was watching, a viper in his house, kept him from acting on the impulse.

"Please."

His one-word plea broke the spell and spurred her into action. He took in the stiffening of her muscles and the quizzical, lingering glance aimed at him. Then she was gone with a nod and a determined stride past Franklin and out the door. She didn't even spare his adoptive father a glance, but she didn't shrink away, either. Proud and defiant. The Tess he knew and wanted way too much.

"So, who is she, Adam? You're not screwing your help now these days, are you?" Franklin tsked and shook his head. "That doesn't seem like you at all."

Adam took two long strides and then he was toe-to-toe with the man who'd given him a roof and an education but never any affection or acceptance. "Don't ever talk about her like that again."

"So, who is she? What is she doing for you? Why is she asking questions about me?"

"Are you worried about what she'll find out?" Adam replied.

"That's not an answer to my question," Franklin insisted.

"That's all you're going to get so you can leave. I'll

have a member of my security staff walk you out," Adam said, nodding toward the burly man in a dark suit now standing in his office doorway.

Franklin followed the path of his attention and glanced over his shoulder, the smirk on his mouth more amused than angry when he turned back.

"No need. I got the answers I wanted anyway." Franklin swept his eyes over the rest of the office, his gaze taking in all of the papers and files. "This office is a mess. No wonder your company is in trouble."

Adam didn't flinch at the icy coldness in Franklin's tone. He was used to him bashing his business, his skill, his ambition, and he was well versed in not giving him the satisfaction of knowing that it pissed him off.

And it infuriated him that the rejection by this man still hurt a little.

Not enough to get him to become the man Franklin wanted him to be but enough to keep him from giving up from his dreams. From giving up and letting down the people who believed in him. He had a lot of people depending on him and he wasn't going to let them down.

Adam waited until Franklin had exited his office and Justin had secured the door behind him before grabbing the nearest object and hurling it across the room. The mug hit the wall, created a significant crater in the dry wall and shattered and scattered across his hardwood floors.

"Man, you just broke the wall," Justin said, walking toward Adam with his hands raised in a placating gesture that made Adam roll his eyes.

"Yeah. Yeah, I'm sorry. I just…"

"You lost your shit." Justin pointed at the mess. "I

mean, you're the CEO so you can break the wall if you want to break the wall…"

Adam ground his teeth and searched for words that could shatter the rage haze induced by Franklin.

All he could manage was another lame apology. "I think I threw your mug. I'm sorry."

Justin waved him off, crossing the room while making a show of sidestepping the large shards of ceramic on the floor. "Adam, just shut up already. I'm glad to see you lose your cool for once."

"Losing my cool is unproductive."

"It's also human and a relief to see that you're not actually a robot. I just can't believe that you haven't punched Franklin by now."

Adam knelt down, casting a glance up at his best friend as he picked up the larger pieces of ceramic. They'd known each for a long time and Justin was one of the few people who knew everything that Adam could remember about his life before coming to California and what he couldn't forget about what had happened once he'd arrived.

"It's not like I haven't thought about it," Adam admitted, rising up to toss the pieces into the trash. "Helene would lose her mind if we ended up in the ER and on the front page of the papers."

"Or she could have told her husband not to be a dick," Justin said, shrugging in an apology that didn't look like he meant it at all. His best friend wasn't a fan of anyone in the Franklin family.

If Adam's adoptive mother, Helene, were a color, she'd be beige. All she really cared about anymore was her charity work, keeping her roots from showing, and not ending up in any of the tabloids. She hadn't always been like that, or so Adam had been told. Years with Franklin had made her into the kind of woman who kept quiet and looked pretty and ignored every bad act by her husband.

She'd been distantly kind to Adam, never motherly, but she'd never tried to cause him harm. For that, he would try not to cause her pain if it could be avoided.

"Helene hasn't had it easy either," Adam said, not wanting to cover this old ground again.

Justin shrugged, his expression morphing into the closest thing Justin ever got to serious and Adam braced for what he knew was coming. It was a well-worn topic between them—as familiar as the focus on women, sex, money and poker was in their frequent late-night cigar-smoking sessions after long days making a company run. "It's not your job to take care of everyone, Adam. Redhawk/Ling isn't going to rise and fall on you alone."

"Justin, I know that but this is important. If we don't figure this out, I'm going to let a lot of people down. People who have banked their futures on Redhawk/Ling surviving."

"You mean 'we,' not 'I.'" Justin moved even closer to shove against his chest, his glare echoing the anger and frustration in his voice.

"I know," Adam replied, avoiding making direct eye contact. But Justin wasn't letting him off the hook that easily.

"No, I don't think you do." Justin grunted out the last of his frustration and scrubbed a hand against the stubble on his cheek. "Look, I'm done trying to change you but you've gotta start letting some of this shit go. Rely on other people. Now you've got a brother and sister to help you work on that life skill."

Oh yeah, the one subject sure to make him stress even more than usual. Now he had a family to worry about when he knew nothing about family.

"I'll be sure to call you out of your next weekend-long poker tournament to help out at the office. *That* will work," Adam grumbled, immediately feeling a pang of guilt at the jab that he knew would strike the soft under-belly of his oldest friend.

"Okay, now you're being an *asshole* and that's my cue to give you some space to brood and fixate on all the things you can't control." Justin paced over to the couch, grabbed his phone off the table and headed toward the door. "While you're pondering all the shit in the universe during your ninety-mile run tonight, don't forget to fig-ure out what the hell was happening between you and Tess a little while ago."

And there it was. Payback for the poker comment. He deserved it.

"I'm not talking to you about that," he answered, not bothering to deny that he knew exactly what Justin was talking about.

He had to figure out how to navigate the fact that he'd called her *baby* and how hard it was to stay away from Tess. He'd failed miserably at not fantasizing about her or dreaming about her—why did he think that actual physical contact would be easier to navigate? There was no easy answer, but he had to make a decision to give in to temptation or cut Tess loose. And he knew in his gut that letting her go wasn't the answer.

"You were leaving, right?" Adam prompted, needing time to process the day's events.

"I was. I am. I'll be back here tomorrow morning and we'll find out who is trying to destroy our company."

Justin pointed at him, his grin telling Adam that all was forgiven. "And we'll also discuss why you can't seem to understand the difference between asking Tess out and hiring her." He shook his head. "No wonder you're still single."

Four

"One day I'm going to show up and you'll be wearing an aluminum foil hat."

Tess put a Post-it on the file she was reviewing and looked up to find her baby sister leaning on the door frame swinging her set of house keys back and forth in front of her. Well, Mia wasn't a baby anymore. She was twenty-one years old, a junior in college and a testament to the fact that Tess had done something right.

Except for the part where Mia was such a smartass. That part was *all* Mia.

Okay, maybe that was all Tess.

"Is that how I taught you to speak to your elders?" Tess asked, surprised at the stiffness in her back and the tingly sensation running up and down one of her legs. She glanced down at her watch; she'd been head down for hours. She pushed back her desk chair and shook out her sleepy leg, smacking her sister's hand when she flipped open a file on the desk. "No peeking at stuff on my desk. I can't believe I still have to tell you this."

"I still can't believe that *you're* such a broken record," Mia grumbled, tapping her finger on the file in question. "I was just checking to see if this was about your favorite subject. I rang the bell twice and called out and you still didn't hear me."

Tess groaned, stretching out her leg as she headed toward the kitchen for the strongest, biggest cup of coffee on the planet. She still had a dozen files to read through before she could even think about hitting the sack. It had been a long week and it looked like it was about to get longer. Somebody was definitely trying to sabotage Redhawk/Ling and she'd been hired to do a job.

Adam was depending on her.

And she was lying to him.

Tess shook her head to clear the cobwebs and the memory of him and the way he'd called her *baby* in his office earlier. It had been unexpected and clearly, if the flare of surprise in his eyes was any indication, something he hadn't planned on saying. But the endearment had been uttered with a sexy rumble and a protective ferocity that sent a shiver of anticipation down her spine. Factor in how he'd been immediately concerned with the well-being of Estelle, his sweet assistant, and Tess added another item to the long list of reasons why she wanted to jump Adam Redhawk.

Okay, she really needed that caffeine.

"I was working, Mia. Why aren't you at school?" Tess shuffled behind the counter and flipped the switch on her coffee maker, grabbed a pod and slipped it into the machine. She turned around to lean on the countertop while the machine worked its magic and created the elixir that would keep her from making bad man-oriented decisions. "Not that I don't love seeing you but don't you have a paper to write or a class to attend? A study session with coeds in your pj's?"

"It's college, not an Anna Kendrick movie," Mia mumbled from where her head was stuck inside the fridge.

She emerged, her auburn pixie cut sticking up at odd angles due to the static electricity, a string cheese in her hand. For a minute, it was ten years ago and Mia was the pain-in-the-butt little sister who tried to listen in on Tess's phone calls with boys and who also crawled into bed with Tess when their father was having a rough spell. Those days solidified their relationship; they'd learned the hard way that in the end they really only had each other.

Tess had worked her ass off, juggling several jobs for a number of years and cases she would have loved to turn down to secure this little house. It was only two bedrooms and one bath and a backyard that was barely big enough for a grill but it was their home. Tess used the space in what was intended to be the dining room to work from home on the days she didn't need to go to the tiny office she leased from a local insurance company on a barter basis. She always kept Mia's room open for her and tried not to let on just how much she missed her since she'd gone to college.

"Fair enough but please don't join an a cappella group. That still doesn't explain why you're here." Tess held up a hand in defense at the site of her sister's glare. "Not that I don't love it when you come and see me but…"

Mia rolled her eyes and opened the string cheese. "I need to do my laundry."

"Of course, you do."

"*Whatever.* I also haven't heard from you in a couple of weeks and I wanted to make sure it was a case and not a serial killer home invasion that had removed you from your usual place of up my butt and all in my business."

Tess's machine gurgled and sputtered the signal that it was done and she turned to grab the mug of hot coffee. "I'm going to drink this and pretend that you're not here."

Mia sidled up beside her, chuckling as she nudged Tess to the side to start her own brew. "You love me and we both know it." Her sister nudged her again and leaned down to peek up at Tess. "Seriously though, are you okay? I haven't heard from you in a while."

Tess huffed out a sound that was part sigh and part laugh. "Define *okay.*"

Mia frowned, tossing the cheese wrapper into the trash with a dunk shot that would have made their dad proud. Clearly, hours spent in the driveway shooting hoops had paid off. "Tess, I love you and I respect your dedication to the cause but you have got to let this vendetta go. Franklin Thornton is untouchable and always will be. He got away with it. End of story."

"No, that is not the end of the story," Tess fumed, sloshing coffee out of her mug when she picked it up with a little too much force.

"No, you're right. It's not the end of the story because the actual ending will read, 'Daughter ruins her life just like her father. Franklin Thornton wins twice.'" Mia emphasized her harsh words with a flourish of her hands in the air like she was highlighting a movie marquee. "Let it go, Tess. Get laid. Read a book. Go to a movie. Get a fucking life."

She didn't need the caffeine because her sister's words woke her up like an injection of epinephrine straight to the heart. Where fatigue and lethargy had weighed her down just moments before, she was now fueled by anger and a betrayal that cut to the quick.

"Fuck you, Mia." Tess squared off with her sister, her voice bouncing off the hardwood floors and cabinets. "If I don't have a life it's because I'm doing this for you and for Dad."

"Bullshit, Tess. I didn't ask you to do this and Dad has been dead for years and he doesn't care anymore. If you want to do something for me, then stop all this avenging angel crap and let me have some peace instead of carrying around all this guilt for everything you've done for me. If you can't let yourself off the hook, then get it off my back. Please."

Whoa. Tess blinked hard, trying to clear the roaring in her head and the hot tears stinging her eyes and blurring her vision. Mia's words pierced her deeply and Tess reached for her coffee, taking a too-hot sip to fill the heavy silence that polluted the air between them. It wasn't easy to hear that her efforts weren't recognized for what they were, that her sister didn't see the value in making the past right.

Mia had been so little—she didn't always remember just how bad it had been after Franklin Thornton had cheated their father and sent him spiraling into depression and self-destruction. But Tess remembered it all because she had been the one who had stepped in and shielded Mia from the worst of it. In a way, Tess had made it possible for Mia to not understand how she couldn't just let this go.

Tess wouldn't tell Mia that she'd met the man today, that he was as awful up close and personal as he was on paper and the internet. She wouldn't tell her because it

wouldn't change anything for her sister. This was a conversation that they'd had in some form or other a million
times before and she wasn't going to change her path so
it was best to let it drop.

Tess cleared her throat, testing her voice a little before she changed the subject. "I wasn't working on the
Thornton case, anyway. Adam Redhawk hired me to help
him find someone."

"I thought you wrapped that case up," Mia said and
Tess let out a grateful breath that she was going to let their
fight over their dad and Franklin Thornton go.

"I did. This is a new one."

"That guy sure does lose a lot of people," Mia mused,
her eyebrow raised in self-congratulatory amusement at
her very bad joke.

"It's not that kind of case. Nobody is actually missing."
Tess considered how much she could talk about and not
violate her confidentiality agreement. "It's like a bunch
of background checks on steroids."

"And he doesn't have anyone at that huge company he
owns who could possibly do that for him? Not. At. All?"
Mia shook her head on beat with her words, her grin wide
and a little bit lascivious.

"Mia," Tess said, amused warning coating her response. She knew exactly where this was going and if
it was possible, she wanted to talk about this topic even
less than she wanted to argue over their father.

"Tess." Mia hopped up on the counter and kicked out
to poke Tess with a purple sparkle–painted toe. "I saw
you and Adam Redhawk together and let's just say that
they can see the sparks zipping between you two from the
space station. I felt like I needed to get you guys a room

with a horizontal surface as soon as possible or risk the entire building going up in flames."

"I don't know what you're talking about." Tess shuffled over to the dishwasher, opening it to see if the load was clean and needed to be put away. She peered into the dim interior and found only a couple of plates and mugs on the racks; a clear reminder that she was a single woman living alone. She shut the door with a thud and desperately looked around the tidy space for anything that could distract her sister or at least give Tess a refuge from the turn this conversation was taking. She spied a stack of catalogs strewn across the coffee table in the family room that needed her immediate attention.

"The house is spotless, you neat freak. Stop avoiding the discussion," Mia yelled at her back from the kitchen.

"This isn't a discussion, it is you letting your imagination run on that little squirrel wheel in your head. Adam Redhawk and I have a professional relationship only. He had a job that needed discretion and I had done good work for him already and so he asked me to stay on. As a small business owner, I'm not going to turn down a good job."

Behind her she heard Mia jump down from the counter and she could feel the distance closing between them. Images of unsuspecting gazelles being stalked by cheetahs on the Nature Channel crossed her mind and Tess knew exactly who was the gazelle in this situation. She turned and faced her tenacious younger sister and decided to put this to rest once and for all.

Maybe she'd believe it herself this time.

"Mia, Adan Redhawk is a good guy…"

"And smokin' hot."

"Mia, please focus."

"I *did* focus. I focused on those pictures of him in the *L.A. Style* weekly the last time he competed in a triathlon. I focused on his six-pack and I focused on his biceps and I focused on his bounce-a-quarter-off-it ass. Believe me. I was *f-o-c-u-s-e-d*."

Mia grinned as she sat on the arm of the sofa, grabbing Tess by the arm and dragging them both down onto the seat in a tumble of cushions, arms and legs. It brought back memories of the many nights they'd cuddled up like this together on shabbier furniture, heads bent together as they shared secrets. Tess missed those days when things had been simpler and her crush on a boy had been something she could indulge in. Before sex was a weapon and trust was a fiction.

"You're ridiculous," she murmured, wrapping a strand of her sister's hair around her finger. "Mia, I can't get involved with Adam."

"Because you might have to use him when you make your move to take down his father?" Mia asked, her expression ridiculously coy.

"Franklin Thornton *is not* Adam's father." Tess surprised herself at the visceral reaction Mia's words triggered in her gut. And her rapier tone shocked her sister as well, if the raised eyebrow and gaping mouth were any indication.

"Wow. Protective much?"

And that was exactly what she was feeling: protective. Protective of a man who'd had very little of that in his life but who offered it to so many people around him. His employees. His best friend. His long-lost siblings.

She was neck-deep in background files because he needed to protect Redhawk/Ling from an unknown enemy. He had stood toe-to-toe with Franklin, demanding an apology for Estelle, and had put his body between her and the man, physically trying to shield her from his words. Adam had come into her life because he needed to find his brother and sister, determined to ensure that they were okay.

Adam had a hero complex. In only the best way.

It wasn't the first time she wondered who protected Adam Redhawk. If he ever let anyone close enough to take care of him.

As far as she could tell, the answer to that question was a decided no.

"Yeah, I guess I am a little protective of him." Tess remembered the moment this afternoon in his office and the jolt of connection that had leaped between them and seared her skin and down deeper in a place she didn't want to acknowledge. "Franklin came into Redhawk/Ling today and Adam physically stepped in between the two of us. He actually used his body to shield me from the venom of Franklin Thornton." She paused, remembering the shiver-induced goose bumps that ran up and down her spine during the moments when they'd been so close and she'd had all of his focus on her. "It was intense."

"That's good. I'm glad. I think it's been a while since somebody looked out for you," Mia murmured, her voice low and tentative, as if she didn't want to scare Tess away from this conversation. "You must mean a lot to him."

Tess shook her head, confused about a lot of things but pretty clear on this situation. "Mia, he takes care of everybody. It's what he does. It's why his employees stick it out even if the risks they take at Redhawk/Ling aren't guaranteed. It's why he had me look for his brother and sister after so long. It was killing him not to know where they were or how they were doing. He is so confident in his ability to change the world that he couldn't imagine a world where he didn't find them and guarantee that they would never want for anything."

"And today he stood up for *you*."

"He did."

And he'd called her *baby*.

What would he call her when he learned about her deception? Not that she didn't have the best reason to walk that line between lie and truth. Franklin had irrevocably destroyed her family and she had to make him pay. Had to avenge her dad and restore his good name and reputation.

As much as Adam carried the burden of restoring his own family, he would understand why she had to do what she was doing.

They were really two sides of the same coin. Doing what they had to do to make things right for the people in their lives who mattered most.

At least that's what she'd tell herself every time Adam called her "baby."

Five

Adam was going to ignore the light on in Tess's office.

It was late at Redhawk/Ling. Not night-before-an-app-release late but there weren't many people in the building on this Tuesday night. All the ones who had lives had left long ago and Adam didn't want to dwell too long on what that meant about him and Tess. They'd been working from Robin Roberts to Conan O'Brian time with very little off-duty opportunity to do much but grab a run and hit the sheets. Alone.

Not that he hadn't thought about being in his king-size bed with somebody—somebody who looked a lot like Tess—but sleep deprivation and long hours hadn't diminished his belief that getting involved with the sexy redhead would be a very bad idea.

Tess was reading a file, taking notes on her laptop as she flipped between the pages. Her hair was piled on top of her head, curls sneaking loose and tumbling around her shoulders like a titian waterfall. Emerald green reading glasses were perched on her nose, the old-fashioned chain that helped her keep track of them looped around her neck. Dressed today in a black pinstriped double-breasted suit with high heels, she looked like his bossy librarian wet dream fantasy suddenly live and in person.

And it was ridiculously cliché and predictable but he barely resisted the compulsion to cover the distance between them and bend her over the desk—glasses intact—and explore every inch of her until this inconvenient and all-consuming need for her was nothing but embers and ash. Tess was driving him crazy, and in his sleep-deprived state he knew that being alone with her was a really bad life choice. What he wouldn't give to have just an iota of the poker-faced talent that Justin used at the card tables right now. Because he knew that nothing about his desire and need for Tess Lynch was hidden from anyone who was looking.

And Tess was looking. Whenever they were in each other's orbit it was as if their bodies and minds synced into perfect rhythm. They completed each other's sentences, reached for the same files at the same time, and jumped to the same conclusions. Justin said it was creepy but to Adam it was mesmerizing and enticing; for a man who'd been uprooted so early and had never found his balance it was the closest thing to equilibrium he had ever experienced. And Adam knew that it was dangerous in the best and worst ways as only the most visceral of need fulfillment could be.

He should leave; turn on his heels, walk down to his bike, go home and work out this insanity in the gym or in the bed of a woman who didn't make him want things he wouldn't do justice to.

But he knocked on Tess's door anyway.

"I order you to go home and do whatever it is you do when you're not working," he said, trying for an I-don't-really-care-what-you-do-when-you-go-home tone only to be undone when Tess lifted her head and smiled at him with a hazy focus that whispered of slow and easy mornings in bed. She was sexy as hell and his body thrummed in response, his dick getting hard under the well-worn denim of his jeans. Adam shifted slightly to try and hide his reaction.

Tess laughed, shaking her head as she leaned back in her chair and gave him the once-over. "I know you know me better than that. You don't really think that I'd allow anyone to 'order' me to do anything." She flashed him a grin and a raised eyebrow that said she had his number. "Even though I hear that you're really good at it."

Her words sucked all the oxygen out of the room, heat flashing like a wildfire along his skin as he struggled to catch his breath and steady his racing heart. Adam knew what she was referring to; he was discreet about his bedroom practices but he knew his partners were not and the stories about him were all true. Not that he kept a dungeon or anything in his basement but he often liked to be in control of the moment and his partner when he was having sex and it was in stark contrast to his usually reserved demeanor. It wasn't what people expected and that made it hot gossip in Silicon Valley.

Tess's grin faded and her cheeks flushed with a blush, something he'd never witnessed on her before. Her stammering would have been almost cute if he hadn't been so turned on.

"Adam, that was…holy hell, I can't believe I said that."

He waved off her apology as he moved into the office, feeling just how small it was with the sweet-hot tension building between them. He wasn't embarrassed by her comment—he was intrigued. Because Tess had sounded interested and that was something he had no choice but to explore.

"Well, I *am* really good at it." Adam kept his eyes locked on hers as he rounded her desk, stopping just shy of her personal space but close enough to feel the heat generated by their proximity and chemistry. Pure chemical reaction. Spontaneous combustion.

He crossed his arms over his chest as he leaned against the edge of her desk, his last-ditch effort to keep his hands off Tess Lynch. Adam locked on her gaze, now defiant and smoldering with any hint of embarrassment long gone. His stare flicked away long enough to note the white-knuckle grip she maintained on the arms of her chair, a welcome reminder that he wasn't the only one struggling with what was brewing between them.

He ended the standoff. It was time.

"I'm a decisive man, Tess."

"Yes. I am aware." She rose from the chair and he tracked her movements, soaking in the way she moved in closer, but not close enough to touch. With her heels on, they were almost eye to eye, mouth to mouth, chest to breast. "You are also private, loyal, harsh, fair and intense." Her voice lowered and he leaned in closer to catch every word. "And you're very sexy."

Adam let his gaze drop to her mouth, giving himself one last chance to not do the thing that would complicate an already complicated situation. His gaze traveled higher and he locked eyes with Tess, the arching of her right brow in question and invitation cutting through the last, fragile threads of his common sense.

Her mouth was soft, lips warm, and she tasted like the sweetest fruit: like all things forbidden. Tess took a moment to react, her breath caught on a swift intake of surprise that quickly gave way to her leaning into the kiss and opening to his tongue. Her fingers ghosted over his chest, his hands skimming over her arms and along the curve of her hips, their only firm connection the warm, wet tangle of their tongues and the hungry press of their lips.

Adam ended it first, needing to attempt a small grip on his sanity. "Damn. Tess, that—"

With that one sexy eyebrow raised again and a grin teasing at her swollen lips, Tess skated her hand down his torso, letting it hover over his aching hard-on. "If you say it was a mistake and apologize, you'll regret it."

If Adam didn't think that he could be in serious trouble with this woman, that moment sealed it. Smart and ballsy, Tess was a puzzle he was compelled to decipher, an indulgence that he would allow himself for once. For tonight.

"I'll never regret that kiss. The question is what we do next." Adam snaked his hands around her waist, pulling her lush body against his for the first time outside of his fantasies. Tess fit against him perfectly, her full breasts pressing against his chest, her long legs entwined with his, her hips cradling his hard length with heat that tempted him to strip her down and move on from kisses to something more. "I'll make it clear what I want."

"I'll add that you are direct to that list of things I know about you," Tess said, her fingers warm against his chest, her hips bucking against his own as she gave him a mischievous smirk. "But I think I know what you want."

Adam chuckled, his grip tightening on her hips to keep her from moving. If she kept that up, he'd bend her over the desk and make a mess of her and the files strewn across the surface. But he had somewhere to go and something to do.

He leaned in and pressed a kiss against her temple, groaning again when she wiggled against him. "I just want to be clear because we are working together. It could get complicated."

"Adam, it won't get complicated," Tess said with conviction as she unwound herself from his grip, her hands moving to fix her hair and straighten her suit as she rounded to the other side of the desk. He wanted to pull her back into his arms but this was a conversation they probably needed to have with some acreage between them. "You don't do complicated. You do sex. Great sex. You do clear rules and parameters with your bed partners and nothing that lasts over a couple of months. They don't leave happy but they do leave knowing that you were honest with them."

Tess held her hands out in a "how did I do?" gesture and Adam let out a harsh breath of shock. He wasn't sure why he was surprised at her information. He'd hired her because she was good at what she did and his sex life wasn't something he spoke about but it wasn't a secret in the small community of Silicon Valley. In the end, it was relief that settled low in his belly, relief that whatever they decided tonight, they would be on the same page.

But he didn't have to have a full dossier on her to understand her.

"I could say the same thing about you, Tess. No long-term relationships for you. No strings." When she raised an eyebrow and put her hand on her cocked hip, he bit back a laugh. Bull's-eye for him. Adam strode around the desk, moving slowly toward the very kissable and very tempting woman he desperately hoped would accept what he could offer. "So, are we on? No strings? Nothing serious? I have enough serious in my life. Hundreds of employees that depend on me and a new family that I have no clue how to navigate."

"And when the job is over?"

He nodded, reaching out to wrap an arm around her waist to pull her close. "When the job is over, it's over. Can you live with that, Tess Lynch?"

Tess stared at him, her green-gold eyes shrewd but lit with heat that gave away what her answer was going to be. She wasn't a woman to back down from what she desired and she wanted him as much as he wanted her.

"I can live with that, Adam Redhawk."

Adam laughed, leaning in to brush a swift kiss against her mouth before checking his watch.

Tess glared, glancing down at his watch. "Do you have somewhere to be?"

"Yeah." Until tonight, he'd never regretted his second Tuesday of the month plans in his life. But he didn't want to let Tess go. Not yet. She was clearly up for propositions tonight and maybe she'd go for another. "Have you ever been a groupie?"

Six

Tess added "owning a motorcycle" to her bucket list.

She loved the hum of an engine and hot metal in between her legs as she sped down the road with nothing between her and high-speed danger. It was a thrill that couldn't be rivaled by many things. Sex, great sex, was one of those things but the instances of *that* kind of sex she'd had in her lifetime didn't outnumber the fingers on her right hand.

The hand currently settled over Adam's heart and gripping his tight, black T-shirt as they sped down the road, chasing the city lights and dodging cars filled with people looking for a good time. Tess took advantage of the ride requiring her to hold on tight to the hard-bodied man nestled between her legs, and indulged in the anticipation of this night and their new arrangement.

Adam's black Heritage Classic Harley-Davidson was a

sweet ride, powerful and loud and everything you wanted a motorcycle to be. It was an odd choice for such a quiet man who did nothing to grab for attention. But it suited him when you really got to know him.

This bike was outward evidence of the part of Adam he buried down deep inside of him: reckless, intense and rebellious. Adam was a man of a million layers and she wanted to unpeel every single one.

So, it was a no-brainer to change her clothes and jump on the back of his bike to find out what the hell he did the second Tuesday of every month. Tess knew where he went, she'd discovered it during her background check of him, but something had held her back from following him inside the bar located on the seedier side of the Valley and finding out exactly what it was that brought him there every month, come rain or come shine.

Before she knew it and before she wanted the ride to end, they pulled up in front of Duke's, passing by the entrance to enter a parking lot and head to an empty space. Duke's had seen better days, the front of the building a dirty brick and the sign faded, but it had a loyal clientele and was packed almost every night. Live music and a generous pour were the hallmarks of this local institution.

Adam motioned to a guy sitting in a booth in the parking lot, giving him a thumbs-up of thanks and acknowledgment when the guy waved him in. Adam cut the engine, slipped off his helmet and twisted to look at Tess. She bit back a grin, unwilling to let him see just how adorably sexy he was with his dark hair mussed and an excited smile on his face. He reached into a side bag and pulled out a black baseball cap with Stanford embroidered on it, placing it low on his head so that the bill hid part of his face.

"You ready?" he asked, turning and reaching up to help her remove her helmet. His grin was genuine, a little bit shy and all kinds of sexy. "I'm running a little late."

"A little late for what? You never did tell me exactly what is happening here." Tess watched him hop off the seat and she accepted his outstretched hand to help her do the same. She'd changed into a jade-green T-shirt-style mini-dress and ankle boots and the length of her skirt required her to maneuver a bit to not land on her face on the pavement or flash the patrons of Duke's milling about the parking lot.

Adam held on to her hand, lacing their fingers together, his eyes mischievous but narrowed a bit with skepticism. "Are you telling me that you *really* don't know why I come here?"

She shook her head, allowing him to tug her along to a side entrance as she waited for him to clue her in. "It wasn't necessary for the job."

Adam paused at the door. "That never stopped you before."

She shrugged, opting to go for honesty on this one, even if it was embarrassing. "I wanted to leave some things for you to tell me."

Her reward for her candor was a quick, hard kiss and a flash of his dimple before he pulled the door open and she was hit by a wall of sound from the crowd of people inside Duke's. The space was dim but not dark, the long bar visible where it ran the length of the room on one side. There was a stage at the end of the room and on it a band was setting up for the show. As if on cue, the two men and one woman on stage turned and waved at Adam.

It was too noisy to hear what they were saying but

their gestures were the universal symbol for "where the fuck have you been?" and suddenly Tess had a pretty good idea about what Adam did here once a month on the second Tuesday.

Adam turned back to her, gesturing toward the stage. "I've got a tab here. Order whatever you want and there's a table up front for our guests."

Tess gripped his arm, tugging him back to get a little more info. "Whose guests? Who are those people?"

Adam grinned, his smile contagious and de-aging him about a decade. Tess caught her breath, grateful to have saved this revelation for now, this time and this place. He was so damn cute, sexy, so excessively fuckable. Agreeing to indulge in this thing between them was looking like one of the best mistakes she ever made. Now she only wondered how long this gig would go before she and Adam could get back to one of their places and a horizontal surface.

"It's my band, The Double E's!"

"Your *what*?"

"My band." He winked at her. "Didn't you ever wonder why I have drumsticks all over my office?"

Tess had wondered but had figured that they were his version of those fidget widgets, something for him to mess with as he let his mind solve all the problems at Redhawk/Ling. And even though she'd purposefully left some things in his life unrevealed, once again Adam Redhawk had surprised her more than she'd considered possible. The drumsticks constantly lying around in his office weren't props.

It looked like Adam Redhawk was a secret rock star. Sweet Lord, this was a sexy tidbit she really didn't need to know.

"Why the Double E's?" she asked, tugging on his arm as he moved to head to the stage.

"We started playing together at Stanford. It seemed like a good name for a bunch of electrical engineering majors."

She watched him stride across the room with palpable excitement, and up onto the stage where he traded high fives and back slaps with the very-average-looking-not-a-rock-star-among-them group. They looked like a group of electrical engineers. Engineers who played in a rock band the second Tuesday of every month.

Adam eased behind the drum kit, reaching down to grab a set of sticks and twirling them between his fingers. Tess laughed, startled by the tap on her shoulder.

"I *knew* I should have bet on it." Justin Ling was smiling, waggling his eyebrows up and down like the idiot he pretended he was. "I would have cleaned up."

Tess wasn't fooled by his usual court jester act but she was thirsty. "I have no idea what that means but I know you don't need the money from that bet to buy me a drink."

"True enough. But let me get one for you. I'm just going to put it on Adam's tab anyway," Justin answered with a grin, motioning for her to follow him over to the bar. He was slim, tall with an athletic build and possessed a presence that made the crowd part like the Red Sea. Once more she was thrown by the difference between Adam and Justin: one made every effort to fade into the shadows and the other was disappointed if the spotlight wasn't bright enough.

It was starting to get crowded; what looked like students piling in to fill the bar, all yelling drink orders and staking out claims to tables. It wasn't a dive but it wasn't a trendy Silicon Valley bar either. This had more of a local vibe; a neighborhood place where regular people came to meet friends and hook up. And from the snippets of conversations she was picking up, they were excited to see the band.

Justin traded high-fives with the bartender and shouted their order, only waiting a minute to have their drinks served. He grabbed the two bottles, nodding toward a table in front of the stage marked with a reserved sign on it. They settled on the stools, both taking sips of their beer as they watched the band warm up.

"Thanks for the drink." Tess saluted Justin across the table. "Now tell me more about this bet you didn't take."

He waggled his finger at her. "I'm not sure I should tell you. That might be breaking the 'wingman code.'"

"What the hell is the 'wingman code'?" Tess asked, glancing over when the band started a short sound check. "They aren't bad."

Justin threw a look over his shoulder at them and shrugged. "They don't suck."

"And you're his best friend? High praise." Tess poked him in the arm to get his attention back to answering her question. "What is the 'wingman code'?"

"It means that I shouldn't tell you that I *almost* bet Adam that he would eventually bring you here. You see, if I told you that I told him he was interested in you as more than an independent contractor *and* that I told him he would bring you here to try to impress you…well, *that* would be breaking the 'wingman code.'" Justin saluted her with his drink and grinned from ear to ear. "But I wouldn't do that."

"Of course not." Tess laughed at him, shaking her head at his absurdity. Justin Ling was the very loose yin to Adam's tightly wound yang and it was easy to see why they were such good friends and even better business partners.

"Do you like him?" Justin surprised her with his question and shocked her even more with his attempt to look like it didn't matter. But it clearly did matter and it should when you were just trying to look out for your best friend. It was sweet and it deserved a straight answer, so she gave him the most honest one she could.

"I do like him." She swirled her finger in the condensation formed on the glass of the beer bottle, mulling over how much she wanted to share about her situation with Adam. She couldn't try to convince Justin that there was nothing going on; he'd never believe it. "But this isn't anything to get excited about. It has a shelf life."

Justin leveled a look at her that gave away nothing. No surprise that he was so successful at the poker table. "That's a real shame, Tess. Total bullshit but also a real shame."

She sputtered and spilled beer on the table, preparing to argue with him about the bullshit comment but the band started playing a really loud song and any chance for argument was lost. Tess glared at him, noted that Justin was no longer paying any attention to her, and then focused on the happenings on the stage.

The band was tight, with a driving sound and excellent vocalist, but they really lacked stage presence. Not one of them really engaged with the audience, even though the crowd was completely riveted on them. Her attention was riveted on Adam.

Adam was seated behind the drum kit, baseball cap pulled down low over his face while he wailed away in a rhythm guaranteed to get people on their feet. And it was working. The crowd was dancing, the energy enough to raise the roof, and Adam looked sexy-as-hell with his arm muscles flexing with every beat.

Tess couldn't take her eyes off him. Adam was a commanding man, quietly owning a room with his brilliant mind and determined focus but this was a wholly new outlet for all of that intensity. One song ran into the next, and the crowd got bigger and rowdier with every one.

And then the set was over and she was on her feet cheering for the band as they took their bows. Without any fanfare, Adam jumped down from the stage and bounded over to her, sweaty and boyishly sexy with the baseball cap now turned backward. His grin was wide and contagious and she offered no resistance when he pulled her against him with a hand around her waist and took her mouth in a kiss.

They broke apart, still laughing, and he looked down at the table and grabbed her beer, chugging down half of it in a few long swallows.

"Hey! That's my drink," she protested, shoving against his chest. "Is this how you treat a groupie, rock star?"

"If you were any good at being a groupie, you'd have my own cold beer waiting for me."

"Well, if you were Mick Jagger, I would."

"Ha! I knew I liked her," Justin interjected, handing off a beer to both of them as he returned from the bar. "She won't take any of your shit and she's completely unimpressed by this 'I'm in a rock band' crap."

"You're just jealous," Adam shot back.

"Well, of course I am," Justin said with a comical roll of his eyes. "Women love rock stars."

Adam waved him off, looking down at her with curiosity. "So, what did you think?"

"I think I'm pissed that I didn't come to hear you

sooner. You guys are really good." Tess ran her hand over his chest, ending with a poke in his side. "And it really explains all of the drumsticks lying around your office."

Adam grinned at her, his gaze slipping down to her mouth, and her heart pounded, her mouth going dry at the heat in his intense focus. Tess wasn't one to hesitate once she'd made up her mind and she'd made up her mind about this fling with Adam.

He was smiling when their lips met, the pressure soft and teasing. Tess ran her tongue along his bottom lip and she felt rather than heard his groan at the touch. Adam tugged her around to face him, his large hands on her hips as he pulled them flush against each other. He slanted his mouth over hers, tongue now invading as he deepened the connection between them.

The noise around them faded into a blur of music and voices as they sank into each other. He tasted of beer and heat and the promise of something darker. Her hands wandered over his chest, the softness of the T-shirt fabric covering the hard muscles underneath. Tess was dying to lift his shirt and find out what was hiding under the clothes but this was not the place, although they had decided that it was their time.

Adam broke the kiss, his hands lifting to frame her face, fingers tangling in her hair. "I've got something I want to show you."

"I'm pretty sure I want to see it," she answered, allowing the leer to coat every word.

Adam took a step back and held out his hand, the dimple showing when she slipped her hand in it. "Well, then, let's go."

Seven

"This is *not* what I expected you to show me."

Adam hooked the helmets on the back of the bike, turning to watch Tess as she paced the length of the long patio behind the Lick Observatory. It was clear tonight, the stars brilliant against the dark sky, so bright that you didn't even need the huge telescope housed in the observatory building just to the right of where they stood to see them.

"Well, one of us needs to get their mind out of the gutter," he said, sputtering out a laugh when she whirled around, green eyes wide and hands on her hips in indignation.

"Oh really?" Tess sauntered toward him, her stride half dangerous swagger and half sensual invitation. "If you haven't noticed, this place is closed. Are the cops going to show up and arrest us for trespassing?"

Now it was his time to swagger, and it was easy when

being with Tess made him feel ten feet tall. He moved toward her, meeting her in the middle of the patio, reaching out to pull her flush against him. Adam loved her curves, her breasts, hips and ass reminiscent of the pin-up girls of the 1940s. But what made her absolutely mouthwatering was the way she owned her body, the utter confidence she had in her power as a woman.

Women in his family's wealthy circles lived as though their money or connections gave them what Tess had naturally. They hid behind designer labels and expensive vacations that were handed over to them on a platter and never had to fight or scrape for their place in this world.

But Tess was a self-made woman, independent and strong, and he didn't even have to know all of her story to know that she'd had a rough time of it. She was everything he wanted and even more than he was sure he could handle.

But he'd be damned if he wouldn't give it his best try.

"We don't have to worry about the cops."

"Sure about that?" Tess asked, running her hands up his chest and over his shoulders, her fingers tangling in his hair. Her touch was electric, lighting him up from the inside out, brighter than any star in the sky.

"I'm as sure as a half-million-dollar donation to the observatory foundation last year."

"And I thought my twenty-five-dollar donation to the fire department was living large."

"Did I tell you that this is one of my favorite places?" Adam asked, taking her hand and leading her over the stone wall running along the edge of the overlook that led to the wooded valley below. He stood behind her, one arm wrapped around her waist and the other gesturing toward the broad swath of sky surrounding them.

"I used to come here and stare at the stars. We came here on a field trip in school and I fell in love with the way this sits so high above everything. It reminded me of the mountains where I lived when I was little and how you could hike to the top of the ridge and the stars seemed like they were so close you could reach out and touch them." He pointed to a different area as he named each constellation in turn. "The Big and Little Dipper. Orion's Belt. The North Star. I could come here and I knew that the stars I saw here were shining down on my family… wherever they were." Adam kissed her neck, noticing her little shiver at his touch and ramping back his surge of anticipation. Tess was here and there was no hurry. He buried his face in the soft fall of her hair, pressing kisses and tiny love bites over the exposed skin of her throat. "Pretty sappy, I know."

"Not sappy," she replied, nuzzling back. "Have you talked to your brother and sister?"

He nodded, resting his chin on her shoulder and his cheek against the silk of her hair as he recalled the phone calls it had taken him three hours of psyching himself up to make.

"Yeah. Roan was cool, running off to some gallery thing so he couldn't talk long. We set up another time later this week." Adam had been relieved to hear the genuine interest in his brother's voice. "He sounded really glad to hear from me."

"And Sarina?" Tess asked, the tentative edge to her voice betraying her worry.

"Sarina wasn't an easy call." He sighed, voicing the concerns that had almost kept him from hiring Tess to find his siblings. "When I first started looking for them, I was worried that they were dead, that I was too late. But, since I heard that you found them, I've been up nights worried that they wouldn't want anything to do with me."

Tess's fingers wove together with his own, a squeeze that let him know he wasn't alone. "Did Sarina say that to you?"

"No. No." Adam replayed the very brief phone call with his sister. "She was just…flat. I've had more interest from Siri."

"Keep trying. Sarina has had a hard life, built ways to protect herself." Tess leaned back and pressed a kiss to his jaw. "She's worth the extra work."

"Have you met me? I'm never giving up on her. She's my sister." He paused, wondering how they'd swerved onto this topic. This wasn't what he'd had planned and it wasn't a place he wanted to be right now. Not when he had Tess in his arms under the stars. "Sorry. Pretty sappy."

"You're not sappy," she repeated, her ass pressing against his rapidly hardening dick. "Pretty sweet and crazy sexy."

"Sexier than being a rock star?" he teased, ghosting a kiss over her lips and relieved to be back on track for tonight's planned events.

Tess chuckled at that, the laugh evolving into a moan as his lips grazed her earlobe and his hand traveled up her stomach, cupping her breast at its final destination. Her nipple was hard, jutting against the soft material of her dress, and he could not resist rubbing the pad of his thumb over it, softly pinching it and grinding his erection against her when she gasped and dug her fingernails into his thighs. The pinch of pain was electric, sending the aftershock of pleasure racing along his nerve endings, emphasizing every rub of his own hard nipples against the softness of his T-shirt, the press of his zipper against his long, stiff length.

This moment was the manifestation of a fantasy he'd lived on for months. His need for Tess had been there since the first meeting and he'd worked so hard not to give in and so had she; both were aware of the high-tension wire attraction that sizzled and snapped between them at every interaction. And here they were, on the verge of a moment that would destroy all of the carefully created walls that kept them apart for very good reasons. And while they'd agreed earlier, agreed to set everything on fire and contain the blaze, he wanted to be sure. They needed to be sure.

"Tess, I've got to know if this is still what you want," he growled against the curve of her jaw, surrounded by the sweet scent of her citrus perfume and the arousal-fueled aroma of her skin. She was writhing against him, falling with him into the enticing bliss of their pleasure, and he needed to hear her say yes just one more time before he let them both fall over the edge. "We can stop if you want to. No repercussions, no fallout."

Tess turned in his arms, backing up against the stone half wall as she met his gaze head-on. Her eyes were sharp with their intensity, clear even in the midst of the haze of sex they were currently stirring to life between them. He watched in fascination as she inched up the miniscule skirt of her dress, each tangle of her fingers in the fabric exposing another sliver of the soft pale skin of her thighs.

Her panties were black, a lace pattern that covered the place he longed to touch and taste, and with slow, deliberate movements they were sliding down her long legs and then lying in a puddle on the patio. Tess's curls were dark red and neatly trimmed; his attention was riveted there for a few moments by the sensual weaving of her fingers in their springy tangle. He forced his gaze to return to her face, needing to see that she was one hundred percent in this with him. If she backed out, it wouldn't be the first time he'd gone home horny and hungry for Tess; it hadn't impacted their working relationship in the past and if the brakes went on now, it wouldn't be a problem in the future.

Tess's voice was clear. "Adam, I know what I want and it is you. Like we agreed—no strings and we both walk away when we're done."

Adam took two steps forward, taking her mouth and inhaling her words as if they were the very life force he needed to keep breathing from one minute to the next. Tess opened to him immediately, her surrender echoing his own demand, and the heat between them rose with every rub of tongue and slide of lips.

She wasn't sweet, but Tess's brand of need was addictive and he already knew he'd have to tread carefully on this path or he'd find himself on the wrong side of what this was supposed to be about. He didn't have time for a relationship and he really didn't have time to be nursing a yearning for a woman he couldn't have.

Adam leaned her against the half wall, pressing kisses along her jawline, and down the pale column of her throat. The V-neck of her dress allowed him access to the delicate line of her collarbone and the shadowy top of the sweet cleft between her breasts, and he tasted, licked, nipped as much as he could reach. Tess writhed against him, bracing herself against the edge of the wall as she wrapped her legs around his waist.

Adam slid his hands down her body, cupping her bare

ass and lifting her up in the air so that he bore all of her weight. From this position, Tess gazed down at him and he could see every detail of her expression. He observed the way her lids fluttered halfway closed when he grazed the folds of her sex. Observed the way she tried to bite back her moan when he found her slick and hot and spread it over her clit. Groaned out his own desire when he dipped a finger inside her heat and she lifted herself up and down on the digit, taking her own pleasure. He was absolutely at her service.

"Jesus, Tess, you feel better than I dreamed. Go ahead, take what you need, baby."

He used his thumb to massage her clit, adding another finger as she anchored her hands on his shoulders, grinding down on his fingers. Adam loved this look on Tess, debauched and hungry, powerful and honest. She leaned down, claiming his mouth in a fierce kiss of teeth and tongues, tasting of the months they denied themselves the sating of this primal need.

They broke off the kiss, Tess's cheeks flushed and her lips swollen and red. She threw her head back, her passion-coated shout of laughter ringing out into the night.

"You look like a queen with the stars making up your crown," he whispered, letting the awe in his voice shine through. "And every true sovereign deserves to be worshipped."

Adam slid her down his body, ending with her sitting on the half wall. He dropped to his knees at her feet, running his hands along her inner thighs, pushing the hem of her dress to expose the soft curls hidden beneath. He took his time, tracing the blue veins lying just under the skin, following with soft kisses and tender nips that made her gasp.

"I've never known anyone like you, Adam Redhawk," she whispered, her nails digging into his shoulders in an attempt to drag him closer. He resisted with a smile; he was going to take his time.

"Well, that just means that you never had a man who appreciated what an incredible woman you are." He placed a kiss next to her right knee. "Stupid men not knowing what they had." A kiss on the left leg. "You're smart." A lick on the right inner thigh. "Beautiful." A bite on a tender spot on the left. "Strong." Another kiss. "Powerful." Another lick. "Sexy as hell."

"Lean back," he said, watching as she leaned back slowly until she was resting on her elbows, looking down at him with eyes heavy lidded and dark with her desire. Her breasts rose and fell rapidly, her chest expanding with each ragged, panting breath.

"Tess, you are so damn perfect," he confessed, his own heart beating like the rhythm he'd pounded out on the drum kit earlier in the evening. He leaned forward, taking the first long, thirsty look at her sex in the full moonlight.

With his hands trembling with excitement, Adam ran his thumbs over her lips, making sure to give special attention to the places that made her gasp and squirm. He didn't want this to end too soon, needed to take his time to savor every second since he'd been dreaming of it for so long. So, he kept it slow, light, a gentle graze along the flesh designed to awaken every nerve and every pleasure.

Slick and wet, he couldn't wait any longer to taste what was on offer. He slid his hands under her thighs, under the sweet, round globes of her ass and lifted her, gently tugging her toward the edge of the half wall. Tess was level with his mouth, her sexy, sweet body just waiting for his touch, and he wavered between teasing her a little longer or indulging the pleasure he craved. He was hard, throbbing in his jeans, but he pushed it to the back of his mind. His only thought was doing everything he could to make Tess come apart.

Her first taste was heaven, so sweet and edged with the spice of her need. It was a first kiss, a first taste, his first step toward total addiction. Adam lapped at her, long licks, slow kisses, all calculated to push her over the edge. Tess's hands roamed over his shoulder, nails digging into his muscles and then traveling upward to tangle in his hair. He let her guide him, reading her pulls and presses and letting her control where she wanted his touch as he drove her desire higher and higher.

Adam watched her face when he finally—finally— grazed her clit. Tess moaned and grasped his hair tighter in her fist as she thrust her hips forward, greedy and begging. Delicious. It wouldn't take much more to get her to the end but he wanted to stretch it out a little while longer. A trip to heaven shouldn't be over too soon. Tess was very wet, so his finger slid into her easily, her body tight and hot on his skin. She cried out again, loud enough for it to echo in the ravine and Adam angled his tongue against her bundle of nerves, willing to do anything to hear that sound again.

Gently, he pressed his finger deeper inside, thrusting it slowly in and out, adding a second when she pressed down hard against it, seeking more and more friction, more sensual invasion. Tess rode his hand, her nails now grazing his scalp, and the pinpricks of pain shot straight to his cock, bringing him to the very point of the intersection of pain and pleasure.

Tess was writhing against his face, one of her hands

now running over her breasts, her belly, fingers pinching the hard, tight peaks of her nipples through the fabric of her dress. Her eyes were closed tightly, lips parted on every sigh and pant of breath. She was a feast for his eyes and mouth and he rewarded her with intense focus on her clit.

Tess trembled, her thighs clenching around his head as frustrated and desperate moans passed over her lips. Her orgasm was *right there*, and he could not wait to see her fall apart around him, on him. With an addition of a third finger, Tess seized up, her body frozen as her pleasure hit her like a star shooting across the sky.

Adam rode out the pleasure with her, continuing to lick and suck and kiss her flesh until she pushed him away, her body limp and boneless above him. He rose up over her, kissing along her jaw and neck, claiming her mouth in a sweet tangle of lips and tongues as she came back down to earth.

Tess rose up, sliding to the ground in front of him on her knees. Her eyes were open as their tongues slid against each other, her hands trailing down his chest, fingers fumbling to undo his jeans. He broke off the kiss with a moan that rattled up from his gut when her fingers wrapped around his shaft. Her first touch was tentative, exploratory, her fingers tightening around him when he thrust up into her grip.

He groaned and Tess smiled, causing a shiver of lust to race through him. She stroked him, her grip firm and hot and slicker with each pass. It was hot, sexy as hell, but the connection that kept his eyes locked on hers was visceral, elemental. He moved against her, snapping his hips up into her grip in a rhythm calculated to drive him closer and closer to the endgame.

"Come on, Adam. I'm your queen. I demand it."

Her tone was all it took. He was already on edge, tuned up to one hundred times his usual level of endurance. The tingling started in his spine, racing through his veins and under his skin and then spilling out of him with a shout and a deep, greedy kiss.

Long moments stretched into minutes as they leaned against each other, heartbeats slowing down to a normal pace, sweat cooling on their skin in the chilly evening air. Adam leaned back against the half wall, pulling Tess against him and tucking her against his chest as they both looked up at the stars.

The silence wasn't awkward, sex hadn't changed that between them, and Adam breathed out a sigh of relief. He'd wanted Tess but he'd wanted her body and her mind and the way he and she worked together, the way they'd moved in sync. This way when their affair was over, they could still be friends, still be in each other's lives. That prospect made the sex even sweeter, hotter.

"That was amazing, Tess," he murmured, brushing a kiss against her temple.

"Of course it was," she murmured. "It's why we avoided it for so long."

Adam felt the truth of that statement, knowing in his gut that was why he'd steered clear of giving in to his obsession with Tess until now.

Lights moved on the long drive that led to the observatory and they both sat up a little straighter. It could be another pair of lovers ready to do some star-gazing of their own or it could be the police. Either way, it was time for them to leave. Adam rose to his feet, helping Tess as they searched for her underwear in the shadows.

Laughing, they snatched them up from the ground and Tess shoved them in her pocket.

"How much did you say your donation was again?" Tess asked as they strode over to the bike, grabbed the helmets on the back and slipped them on. "Enough to get us out of this?"

Adam glanced quickly at the approaching car. "Let's not stay around to find out. Run for it?"

"Like Bonnie and Clyde?"

Adam considered this option, willing to go with it... to a point. "As long as it's the version with more sex and no murders or bank robberies, I'm in."

Tess jumped onto the bike, blowing him a kiss. "Well, hop on, Clyde. Let's go chase some stars."

It was the best offer he'd had in a very long time.

Eight

"A woman cannot live by takeout Chinese alone," Tess declared as she dug into her Szechuan chicken with a pair of chopsticks.

The food was delicious, delivered hot and fresh from her favorite restaurant, and normally she would have loved it except that tonight was the most recent of too many nights eating out of cartons or pizza boxes in the offices of Redhawk/Ling, trying to find the mole. They were racing against the clock and Adam and Justin and Tess were killing themselves to win that race. Adam and Justin had the business to run so most of the time it was just Tess and the IT guys they'd put at her disposal. Tonight, Justin had a family thing to attend so it was Tess and Adam in his office digging over piles and piles of information.

And the piles of information—physical and digital— kept growing. Tess was skilled at searching databases and sites to uncover people and their secrets but the volume that had to be processed during this short time was more than one person could tackle. So, the gift of the IT guys meant more eyes on more data and a quicker elimination of dead leads and people who could not be their mole. The last piece of the puzzle was out there, she just needed to find it.

"We could always order something different," Adam offered from his place at the table across from her, his carton of shrimp with pea pods in brown sauce sitting by his stack of documents. He cocked his head to one side, observing her, a slow grin taking over his face and showing off the dimple that made her want to kiss it and then him—all over. He picked up his food, scooping up chopstickfuls to eat. "Or we could always go out."

It was past midnight and the building was dark, empty except for the two of them and the guards settled in down at the entrance. She was exhausted and so was Adam, the dark circles under his eyes testifying to how little sleep he'd been getting these days. But Tess couldn't claim being the cause of his fatigue. They'd yet to spend an entire night together, opting to have sex at the office or in a car. But the encounter always saw them sated and separately in their own beds at the end of the night.

Though they couldn't keep away from each other, neither of them wanted to take this fling to their homes, content to exist in this half state in between work and their personal lives where nothing mattered except that they wanted each other. Tess squirmed in her seat, her body still aching a little from the last time they'd been together—hot and fast on her desk in her office. It had been fun, the need to be quiet only ramping up the pleasure and making it hotter.

But they'd never suggested adding any activity other than sex to their time together.

"Go out?" She knew what he meant but she was stalling for time, trying to figure out how she felt about his suggestion. Did she *want* to take this out of the shadows?

Hell. It didn't matter what she wanted. No strings. Nothing serious. Adding anything that resembled dating was something she should not do. It was something she might not be able to live with later.

As long as it was just sex she was comfortable walking in the gray area of her real reason for staying close to Adam. He got her one step closer to Franklin and avenging her father.

And *that* was why she was here. Not to date Adam Redhawk. Not to fall for Adam Redhawk.

It didn't matter that she wanted him. That she liked him. None of that mattered, even if she wanted it to.

Adam nodded, still picking at his food. His movements were jerky, nervous, but he plowed ahead anyway. "Yeah, like a date."

"Ummm…this had a shelf life…we agreed."

"And having a meal together in an actual restaurant and not surrounded by a stack of papers covered with ridiculously private information about my employees is a deal breaker?" he asked, giving her an innocent look banked in an otherwise unreadable expression.

She couldn't tell if he was kidding or not but if she couldn't be honest about the real reason she was here, she could be honest about the sexual relationship between them.

"It might be. I think it should be."

"I'm not talking about what it *should* be," he answered. "I'm talking about what we want, which I think is really all that matters." Adam set his carton down, grabbed his beer from the table and took a sip. "And I'm not asking for us to go steady or to even change our Facebook status. I just thought we could have a meal at a restaurant before we do wicked things to each other."

Tess shook her head, letting her laugh bubble past her lips as she put down the carton and reached for a spring roll. Now *she* was stalling, attempting to parse through the butterflies doing somersaults in her stomach. But one sensation came through loud and clear: she wanted to go to that restaurant with him. Adam was the real deal. A good man, smart and ambitious and so incredibly determined. When he set his sights on you—when he set them on her—she felt like she was the only woman in the world, like she mattered beyond taking care of other people and righting old wrongs. It felt like she might matter to someone, to him, just because she made him happy. And that was a feeling no one had ever given her.

Damn. This was getting complicated. Sex she could handle. Amazing, off-the-charts sex, leaving-her-limp-and-wrung-out sex, ruin-her-for-other-men sex; she could handle all of that but this was new territory. Scary. Enticing. Not a good idea at all.

But she still couldn't say no.

"Can I think about it?" she asked, inwardly rolling her eyes at her own cowardice at not being able to say what she knew she should. She should just say no.

She was lying to Adam. She was lying when she pored over the all-access files on Franklin he'd given her. She was lying when she tucked away in a private file tidbits about Franklin that she would use later to connect the dots between Franklin's greed and the destruction of her father. Everyone said to follow the money, and she now had unprecedented access to just how his deep pockets had been filled with dirty money. It wasn't a complete picture yet and it wasn't pretty, but she was close. Very close.

This wasn't going to end well. Not for her and certainly not for Adam when he realized that she was only here, was only helping him because she was looking for any inroad to take down Franklin. There was no love lost between the two men and he might applaud her exposure of Franklin but Adam would never forgive the deceit that made it happen.

"Yeah, sure. You let me know."

Tess needed to fill the next few moments with some other conversation so that she didn't say something she knew she would regret.

"How does it go with your brother and sister?" It was a cheap move to change the subject to his newly found family, but she wanted to focus on the one good thing they'd done together. She selfishly needed to be reminded that she'd done something right for Adam.

"Nothing much has changed on that front. We've talked on the phone every few days, video called. I'm trying get them to come out here. Roan is on board but Sarina sends me to voicemail most of the time." Adam wiped his hands on his napkin, picked up his beer and settled back in his chair. He rubbed his face with his free hand, running his fingers through his hair in a mixed move of frustration and concern that told all the tales on how he was handling the extraordinary situation. "Let's just say that I'm much better at figuring out data analytics and computer coding than I am at being a good brother."

"No, I don't believe that." She interrupted him, not wanting him to put that on himself for one second longer. She moved over next to him, pushing his tousled hair out of his eyes, the black strands sliding silkily against her fingers. "You found them. You never stopped looking for them. That's being a *great* brother in my eyes."

"I'm not so sure that disrupting their lives is the act of a great anything. They were living...doing fine on their own and I sent you to find them, dig up all their secrets and drop a bomb right in the middle of all of it." He sighed, shaking his head. "I feel like I'm driving this reunion, doing all of this just to make myself feel better. I never had a chance to stay connected to my community, my traditions and my culture. I never had anyone ask about my life before coming to California, never had anyone try to help me remember. So...this feels...selfish. I wonder if I should just leave them alone. Let them live the lives they've made for themselves."

He looked at Tess, scanning her face for an answer she didn't even know the question for, and her heart pulled tightly for him. This man carried so much on his shoulders, she couldn't help but reach out and cover the broad expanse with her hand, giving him a squeeze in an attempt to absorb some of the tension coiled there under his skin.

"Adam," she ventured, breaking off when it was clear he had more to say.

"I found them out of guilt, you know. You never asked and I was glad you didn't because I didn't want to explain that it was all my fault. I didn't want to admit that I was the reason we were taken away."

This time she wouldn't be stopped. There was no way she letting him take the rap for what had happened. "Adam, no. Your family was blown apart because some overzealous white social workers decided that you would be better off completely ripped away from your family, your tribe, your history and your culture." He opened his mouth to speak and she placed a finger on his lips, asking him with a smile to let her finish. "These people, everyone from the social workers, to the police, to the judge, violated the Indian Child Welfare Act. *They* did this to the three of you. I did the research and I know this. Trust me."

His returning smile was dim, watered down with the regret and guilt he wouldn't release.

"I knew something bad was going to happen but I didn't tell anyone." Adam huffed out a laugh, brittle with judgment. "When I came home the night before they showed up there were owls in the trees around our house. All in the trees and it wasn't even twilight."

"I'm sorry," she asked. "I don't think I understand the importance of the owls."

"Yeah, you wouldn't. Naturally." Adam shifted in his seat, reaching out and taking a sip from his beer. His voice was low, quiet and reverent. "In the Cherokee legend—superstition I guess some people would say—the owl is a bad omen. Precursor to death or something bad that is going to happen. I should have said something and I didn't. Social Services showed up the next day and I don't remember ever seeing my family again."

She thought she understood a little bit better now. Adam thought that his not telling anyone about the owls somehow led to what happened, the destruction of his family. It sounded ridiculous, was impossible, but it would have been very real to a six-year-old boy. It would have been very real to someone whose life was based upon such tradition, such legends. It wasn't her background but she respected that it was Adam's and it was as much a part of him as her ingrained culture was a part of her own makeup.

But she couldn't let him carry this guilt. She'd read the reports and the local social workers had wrecked so many families with their blatant disregard for the sanctity of their culture and their lives. There had been countless numbers of children ripped away from their homes, and people who were sworn to protect and ensure that the laws were followed looked in the other direction at the least and abetted the tragedy at the worst. And it wasn't just in his community where this happened. All you had to do was a cursory internet search and it would spit out thousands of similar stories across the United States and Canada.

But the pain of that day and every day since then was real to Adam. The who, what, why and how were secondary to the fact that his life was never the same.

Tess reached out to him, cupping his jaw and drawing him close enough for their noses to brush in the most tender of touches. His eyes were dark and heavy with his sad memories and she wished she had the power to take some of this from him, to bear it herself.

"Adam, I'm not going to tell you that you shouldn't feel that way or try to ease your pain with a saying from a really crappy greeting card. But I'm going to tell you what I *know*. Okay?" She waited for his nod, given jerkily in between the ragged intake of deep gulping breaths. "There was nothing you could have done to stop it. And not because you were just a child, only six years old. Your parents couldn't have done anything. They weren't connected, educated, powerful. They were poor and doing their best just like every other family. They went through a rough patch and had to reach out to social services for help and got on the radar of an overzealous case worker. The people who should have done better, who should have been better, decided that your family wasn't good enough for you and your siblings. They also decided that they were above the law and the people who could have stopped them didn't. So, yes, the owl was the sign of the terrible things that were coming for your family but they were going to happen whether you told anyone or not. And *that* is the truth."

The moments slid one into the other. Adam stayed where he was, leaning on her for strength that she was ready and willing to give. It wasn't a permanent thing, wasn't a shift of what they were. This was what they were to each other, both strong people who'd had to bear more on their shoulders than what was normally required from a very young age. What they recognized was a kindred spirit, someone who understood a lot without being told.

This moment didn't change what they could and couldn't be for each other. It didn't absolve her from her lies or the guilt and it wouldn't shield her from his anger when he found out. It was just a moment. A really special moment. A few seconds of mutual understanding in the middle of a tangled mess of secrets.

"It's the truth," Adam agreed, his voice deeply etched by the remaining shards of glass that had cut him for so long. "But I don't know if I did my brother and sister a favor by finding them. I sure as hell don't know what to do with them now that they are back in my life. Family is a mystery to me."

"Well, you all have that motorcycle obsession. Maybe you do a road trip?"

He huffed out a weak laugh. "Roan would probably say yes. Sarina would take the first exit and ditch us both."

Tess sat back, taking the opportunity to push his hair back from his forehead, needing to maintain the physical connection between them. She loved touching Adam, craved the electric thrill that went through her whenever they connected. He made her feel…seen…wanted.

"Family is very hard." She gave him a sidelong glance, nervous about giving away too much of herself. Afraid to let him get too close. "I think I told you that once."

"You did." He reached up, running a finger along her brow, down her cheekbone. "Sounded like you knew what you were talking about."

Tess started shaking her head, her grin twisted with her reluctance to share. "You don't want to hear about it."

Adam leaned forward, pressing a sweet kiss to her mouth, barely a brush of lips, an exchange of breaths. "I showed you mine…come on, show me yours."

Nine

It wasn't right to push Tess.

Adam knew what it was like to have a secret you needed to keep close, parts of yourself that you didn't want to share. He'd spent his entire life after his adoption guarding his real self from the world he'd been dropped into. Adam had never fit in, he'd always been on the outside. At school. In his new home. Nobody made any effort to ask him about his past, his family, his community. He'd given up after a while; it was easier just to bury himself in the books or sports. Easier to forget the memories that crept back in at night. Easier to forget the family he'd lost.

Justin had been the first person he let in. But he'd also been the first to give Adam the space to keep the secrets he needed to keep in order to survive.

So, he also knew how important it was to have people who respected the distance you needed to function under the weight of the secrets and the pain that went with them. But it didn't stop him from wanting to know more about this woman who occupied his thoughts and made his body hard with need with just a glance.

But he wanted to know all of her secrets, all the things she hid behind her sexy smiles and bravado. Unlike Tess's deep dive into his past, he hadn't done a full background check on her when he'd hired her. Yes, he'd asked his security to check on her and they'd run a criminal scan, verified that her business and license were in order and legitimate, and that her references checked out. He had not had them give him a full dossier on her life, her background. It had felt sordid and unnecessary and overly intrusive. But now when every part of him screamed to get closer to this woman, he wished he'd received that file.

No, that was not the way he wanted to learn all the unique and special things that made Tess Lynch a woman who kept him awake at night.

He wanted her to tell him. Willingly. Because she wanted to make this connection with him too. It wasn't keeping within their rules, just like the dinner out that he'd suggested earlier before he'd had a minute to think about it. The question had popped out, something that never happened. He wasn't someone who made a habit of speaking without thinking long and hard about it. It was his strength or his weakness, depending on who you were. His business partners loved it. The women in his life, not so much.

But as soon as he'd said it, he wanted it. More time with Tess, no matter how he could get it.

But not this way.

"You know what? Don't answer that." He tucked a

curl of hair behind her ear. "You don't owe me that. Not just for listening to my story."

Tess considered him, her green eyes taking him apart inch by inch. He didn't shy away from it, he was man enough to take it. Her armor didn't scare him.

"I have a sister too," Tess began, her smile chagrined as she shook her head in an I-can't-believe-I'm-doing-this way. "Her name is Mia and she's making me prematurely gray."

"Your parents? Is it just the two of you?"

Tess nodded, breaking eye contact to pull fluff she could not see off her skirt. "My mother was gone when Mia was a year old, I was five. My father passed when I was twenty. I raised Mia."

"You got the teenage years," he noted, relieved to see a smile twist up her full lips. "Not the best luck."

"And she gave me fits. Sneaking out of the house, terrible boyfriends, even worse clothing and hairstyle choices. It's a miracle we both survived."

"And now?"

"She's at college. Whip smart but still has horrible taste in men and clothes." Tess shrugged, her grin more genuine this time, and his stomach flipped with the impact of it. "We didn't have an easy time of it. My father was ill, mentally ill, and it made life hard at times. Mia's success is a happy ending to all of that."

"I'm so sorry. What did he do? Is Mia following in his footsteps? Did you?"

"What? No." She waved him off, weaving her fingers with his as she avoided his eyes. This was where she buried the worst of it and he'd let her keep her skeletons where they were. "He was a scientist. An inventor."

"All scientists are the kissing cousins of poets."

Tess considered that, nodding her agreement in the end. "That must be true. He was as tortured as a poet. Broken dreams haunted him, things that had been taken from him chased him to the end."

The pain in her voice was palpable, the words weaving a scent of bitterness in the air that he could almost smell and taste. There were also traces of anger in her tone. Understandable under the circumstances. Anger was something he understood very well.

"So, you see, I know firsthand that family can be hell."

Tess rose from the chair and Adam took her hand, turning it over to kiss her palm, nipping the most tender part and making her squirm. Tess giggled and he wanted more of it, standing and leaning over to press kisses along her neck, her shoulder.

He pulled back and looked down at her, pleased to see the flush in her cheeks and the sparkle in her eyes. No more heavy talk tonight. They'd lived it once, they didn't need to go through it again.

"So, dinner... Are you still thinking about? Can we be seen together in public now that I know you have a sister?" he teased, feeling the mood in the room lighten as her eyes lit up with shrewd humor.

"We just ate. How can you be hungry enough to talk about our next meal?"

"That's not what I'm hungry for right now," he said, the truth slipping out easily as the mood shifted again, sliding deeply and completely into something darker and needier.

Tess moved in closer to him, her hands sliding up his chest and around his neck, ensuring that every part of her body was flush against his.

"I love your body," he growled, running his hands

up and down every part of her he could reach. Her fine, full ass. Heavy, soft breasts. The curve of her hip. The soft velvet of her skin. "It should be illegal for anyone to look like you, Tess."

"I could say the same about you, Adam Redhawk. You're tempting enough to make me break all of my rules."

"Really? You always seem to be in perfect control around me."

"Then you're not paying attention." She considered Adam, a wicked gleam darkening her eyes to the deepest emerald as she stepped in even closer. If that was possible. As it was, he wasn't sure where he began and she ended. "I think you're hot."

"Good to know, but I don't think my looks rock your control."

Tess let loose with the tiniest hint of a smile, transforming her expression into the epitome of pure sin. "Your taste. I can't get it off my tongue. I'm always craving more."

He groaned as she leaned in closer, her lips just a breath away from his own. Adam leaned in to close the distance but Tess inched back. He moved in again and she shifted back a hair's breadth, dragging another groan out of him, this one of frustration. He lifted his hands to her face, anchoring her in place as he took his turn to play the game, coming close but not sealing their mouths together.

Now it was Tess's turn to moan, her breath coming fast on a pant that heaved her breasts into his chest with every inhale. Her pulse was visibly hammering under the delicate, pale skin of her throat. Adam dipped his head, unable to resist licking that spot, savoring her salty-sweet flavor.

"I want you to fuck me, Adam."

Damn, that was exactly what he wanted too. The only thing that would satisfy this ache building deep inside him.

"Hell, yes. I want that too. Your legs wrapped around me, your nails digging into my back. Your screams passing over these lips." Adam reached out with his tongue, tracing the full plumpness of her lips, capturing her own moan on the tip and savoring the taste of her surrender.

He glanced up at the glass walls of his office and was reminded of the reason he'd never had sex with her here. Security wouldn't be making rounds at this time of night but anybody who decided to walk by would see them.

"I should take you down to your office," he said.

"Too far. I don't care about anyone seeing us. I just want you, Adam." Tess reached down between them and ran a hand up and down the length of his erection. "I've always wanted to have you fuck me in your office."

"Damn it, Tess," he whispered, the only warning she was going to get about how this was going to go down. Hot. Intense. Passionate. The way it always was between them, but every time they touched it burned hotter the next time. Her breath caught just before he angled his head and took her mouth.

The kiss was hard and hungry, lips bruising and teeth clashing as they devoured each other. After weeks of total access to each other's bodies and mouths nothing between them had cooled down. Tess moaned into the kiss, wrapping her hands around his neck and pulling him in closer, as if her next breath depended on his being as close to her as possible. Adam echoed her movement, hands cupping her ass to drag her closer as he sought to dominate her, possess her.

With them it would never be easy, only complete and total surrender would satisfy this craving and neither of them would give in to that. They'd both been burned too much and too often.

But they'd get as close as they could, feeding off each other's need until this fire between them died.

Tess broke off the kiss first, her breasts rising and falling as she struggled to catch her breath. She licked her lips, pink and kiss swollen, and he wanted nothing more than to see them wrapped around his cock.

"I want that too. So much," Tess answered and he realized that he had spoken the words aloud.

He groaned again as her hands traveled over his body, stopping to wrap around his neck and pull him down to her. This time Tess took over the kiss, slanting her lips over his and sliding her tongue into his mouth. This time it was slower, softer, Tess exerting her power in this thing between them, controlling the gradual buildup of passion and possession. It turned him on, compelling him to slide his hands over her ass, angling their hips forward, finding the perfect position to grind his erection into her body.

It was bewitching. Intoxicating. Addictive. He explored the curves of her body with his hands, cupping her breasts in his palms, thumbs rubbing against the hard nipples straining against the soft fabric of her dress.

Tess released his mouth, her palms pressed firmly against his chest as she eased him backward toward the sofa. When his knees hit the edge of the seat cushion, she gave him a firmer push, forcing him to sprawl on the sofa, legs spread open in blatant invitation.

He wanted Tess. No hiding it.

Tess leaned over him, her lips close enough to his own that they were exchanging sharp, shallow pants of breath. Adam raised his hand, stroking up the side of her bare leg, under her skirt, under the silky material of her panties.

The first touch of his fingers against the wet, slick heat of her body had them both gasping, teeth biting into lower lips in anticipation of what was to come. The second slide of skin upon skin had Tess's eyes easing shut, her body swaying into his caress, silently begging for more. Adam kept his focus on her face, soaking in every erotic turn of her expression, burning them all into his memory.

"Ohhhhh noooo." Tess opened her eyes, stepping back and out of his reach, her head shaking back and forth. "Naughty boy. You're not going to distract me. Hands down. Stay put."

Adam chuckled at her tone, contemplating whether to let her run this show but realizing that he was never in control of any situation with Tess.

Tess walked back a few paces, staring down at him, her eyes dark emerald with need but assessing, full of all the wicked plans she had on her mind. He clenched his hands at his sides, determined to sit back and see what she would do to him.

"I feel like I'm overdressed for this activity," Tess murmured, her fingers drifting over the edge of the V-neck of her dress, between her breasts, and down to where her dress tied at the side. A quick movement and her dress opened, sliding to the floor at her feet in a swoosh of fabric and leaving her standing before him in nothing but a gorgeous black bra and panty set, a gold necklace, high heels and a sinful grin. "Much better."

Adam groaned, digging his heels into the carpet as he resisted every urge to reach out and take.

"Having that dress on would have made it so difficult to do this," Tess said, dropping to her knees in front of him, shifting onto all fours as she slowly crawled across the floor toward him.

Adam moaned, ending on what suspiciously sounded like a whimper, the dirty twist of her lips making his heart thunder in his chest and his ears. He stared at her as she covered the short distance between them, back arched like a cat and eyes locked on his own. He held his breath when she was right in front of him, releasing it on a shudder when her hands slowly slid up both of his calves to his thighs, finally ending on the swollen bulge making his pants very tight.

"Remember. My rules," Tess warned him again, her fingers hovering over his zipper until he gave a terse nod of agreement.

She undid his belt, then the button, sliding down the zipper with a metallic sound that was as loud as thunder rumbling in this office, the whole world vectored down to just the two of them. Tess's hand wrapped around him and his eyes shut hard, his groan of pleasure reverberating behind his clenched teeth, his hands tightening into fists at his sides. He willed himself to not break the rules and risk Tess stopping.

Up and down her hand glided along his length, her voice a deeper, huskier version of her typical tone. "Adam, I want this in my mouth. Can I?"

"Oh my God, yes. Please."

Adam stared down as she leaned back in and took his erection deep into her mouth. Lips clamped tight around his flesh, Tess bobbed her head up and down, the rhythm leading to a slow burn in his groin, his belly. Unable to resist the urge to touch, to thrust into her wet heat, his fingers slid into the auburn silk of her hair, his body throbbing at the sound of her whimper.

"Damn, Tess, you're so beautiful." His words cut off but the lust in her eyes, the electricity of their attraction, snapped across the distance between their bodies. And like the images burned on the back of his eyelids after a lightning strike, he knew this sight would be branded on his brain. The burn of her touch intensified until he was almost there, way too soon for how he needed this to end. "Stop. Stop, baby, I need to be inside you."

Tess moved up and over his body, kissing him hard and fierce. "All you had to do was ask."

There was nothing better than Adam Redhawk wanting her.

Tess had known enough men in her life, spent enough time in their beds to know who would forget her the minute the sheets cooled, but Adam was different. The rules were that this was going to be temporary, and she wouldn't contemplate a change to that, but she knew that he would remember this time together long after they were over. And that…that was really sexy.

And Adam was letting her push his buttons. He was known to be a control freak in the bedroom but this game of give and take between them was hot, intriguing—it kept her running hot all the time.

Adam dragged her down to part her lips with a brutal kiss before pulling her onto his lap, her legs straddling each side of his thighs. Tess gave as good as she got, digging her nails into his shoulders as he broke off the kiss, his lips wet and red and pulled back in a grin.

"I want to taste you now, Tess. My turn." He growled as he tugged down the straps of her bra, exposing her breasts to his gaze and his touch. He wasted no time, cupping them both in his palms, dragging his thumbs across the tips.

Tess let her head fall back, body thrusting forward to offer them up to him, wordlessly begging Adam to taste them. He was taking too long, teasing her nipples into hard, tight points that ached under his attention. She wasn't above begging. Not when she knew how good he could make her feel.

"Adam, please. Put them in your mouth."

He rubbed his lips against her skin, just above where she really wanted him to be. He skimmed the curve of her breast, leaving a trail of hot, moist breath as he made his way to her neck. She felt a long lick along the column of her neck, tantalizing nibbles over the places that made her jump in his arms, writhe against his body in a desperate search for more of him, more pleasure.

But even Tess had her breaking point. She growled, weaving her fingers in his hair and leading his face down to her breasts. It should have been relief, getting what she wanted, but Adam was overwhelming, licking, teasing, sucking the hard nubs of flesh into his mouth. Lightning. Fire. An ache threaded its way under her skin, running along every nerve ending in her body and setting her mind on a whirling spiral of pleasure that rose higher and higher.

Adam ran his hands down her body as the cool air of the office washed across her thighs and goose bumps added that tingle of sensation to everything else she was feeling. It was almost too much and it wasn't enough. She needed him. Needed him inside her; the lazy circles his fingertips were tracing over the sex-slick core of her body were not enough. Tess ground her body down on his touch, legs shaking, muscles flexing, seeking the orgasm she knew he could give her.

She keened, leaning heavily on him as the pleasure made her weak. "Adam, I'm going to come."

As if those weren't the magic words that would open the door to all of her desires, Adam pulled away, releasing her flesh and removing his hands from between her legs. Tess gasped, thumping against his chest with her palms in protest.

"Damn you. I was *so* close."

"I want you to be all around me when you come, Tess," Adams growled against her lips, his kisses soft and tender, designed to soothe and tempt. "Don't you dare come right now. It's mine and that's how I want it."

She wouldn't deny that it was his. Hell, when they were together like this, she was his. Body and soul. But not her heart. She wouldn't go that far.

Tess was ready to risk the great sex and the fun they had together, the connection that always kept them tethered to each other. But she couldn't risk her heart. Her father had broken her heart. Life had shattered it over and over. She never wanted to feel that kind of helplessness ever again. Her heart was hers and it would never belong to another ever again.

But she could give Adam her pleasure.

"Then take it. Don't make me wait."

Adam shifted under her, maneuvering their bodies until she was facing the back of the sofa, legs spread with her body open to him. Tess leaned forward, resting the weight of her body on the sofa back, her ass up in invitation.

Adam leaned over body, his fingers snagging in the sides of her panties and sliding them down her legs, tossing them to the floor behind them. He trailed kisses over her skin, sweet presses of his mouth raising goose bumps all along her spine.

"You're beautiful, Tess. Can I have you? Anything I want?"

"Anything you want," Tess said, spreading her legs wider, smiling at the groan that erupted from Adam behind her.

She looked over her shoulder, taking in Adam leaning in behind her, his large hands spreading her wider. And then his tongue was on her, stroking over her core. She jumped, the first lick electric and the second causing her to push back against him, begging him for more. She closed her eyes, knowing that if she kept watching, she would come apart. Too soon. Much too soon.

Adam found her clit, his tongue executing a rhythm that was calculated to bring her to the edge. And just when she was almost there, hips mimicking his movements, he pulled back and brought her down again. Only to do it all over a few seconds later. He had her on the edge so many times that she was only need and desire and incapable of thinking of anything beyond what he was doing to her.

And just when she thought she would have to kill him for denying her what she needed so desperately, his mouth was back on her clit and she was rising and then falling down and down into a spiral of pleasure that spun out like a car spinning out of control. Tess's body went rigid, every muscle taut with her orgasm. As the pleasure released her, she went boneless, her heart racing in a body that couldn't have moved for love nor money.

Adam made it easy on her, turning her over and laying her out on the couch. The chill of the room threatened to make her shiver but he was over her, his body keeping her warm and raising her desire again, along with her temperature.

"So beautiful," Adam whispered, his words tracing along the damp skin of her neck. His kisses covered her skin, claiming every inch of her and then taking her mouth in a tangle of tongues so sweet that it made her bones ache. "Can I still have you?"

His question was so sincere. Adam was always so intent on making sure that this was what she wanted, she could never deny him. She wanted nothing more than to give him what he asked for because he made it so good for her. Every single time.

"Yes. Adam. Please."

Adam nodded, leaning back and pulling a condom out of his pocket before pushing his pants down to his thighs. He shivered a little, the office air also raising goose bumps on his skin. Tess reached out, tugging on the hem of his shirt, unbuttoning the shirt buttons she could reach, relieved when he unfastened the rest. She sighed, raking her nails across his chest, trailing them over the hard, taut muscles, the flat brown nipples. Adam sucked in a breath and she smiled, relishing the sight of the usually quiet and collected Adam Redhawk flushed and debauched, half-dressed and fully aroused.

"I need you Adam. Hurry."

Adam ripped open the packet and slid the condom over his length, leaning in until his tip pressed against her core.

"You ready?" he asked, waiting the moment necessary for her to nod, and then sliding inside her, her slickness making it an easy glide forward.

Tess wrapped her legs around his waist, drawing him

as deep as he could go, indulging in the feel of him inside her and his weight on top of her. She loved this part, the time when she was surrounded by him, filled by him. It was as if there was no way to know where she ended and he began. Perfection. For one brief second.

And then Adam pulled out of her body, almost all the way, and then slid back inside. Tess clung to his back, her nails digging in, anchoring herself to him with every hard thrust. She lifted her hips, angling her body so that he could be deeper inside her, hitting all the best spots.

And then the tingle forming at the base of her spine, in the space deep inside her belly, grew with each slide of his body inside her own and suddenly she didn't want to try to control this ride. She wanted to surrender to it. She wanted it to make her come apart with no hope of being put back together.

Tess let go of her grip on Adam, raising her arms over her head and hanging onto the sofa arm behind her. Her position was deliberately submissive, offering up all of her body to Adam. She trusted him to take her where she needed to go and to be there to catch her when she came down from the high. It was in his nature to protect. Tess would be risking nothing to let this happen between them.

"Yes. Adam. Yes."

"Jesus, Tess," Adam ground out, leaning down to take her lips in a hard, wet kiss. "You make me want. I can't get enough of you."

"Good," Tess panted out, reaching back now, her fingers digging into his hip. "I can't get enough of you."

"Good. Glad I'm not alone…in this."

Tess couldn't process the meaning of his words, not now when he was filling her body and scrambling her mind.

"I need to come," she panted, her words slurred with lust and desire. "I need…"

"I know what you need," Adam growled as he wedged his hand between them, stroking her clit with every thrust. "Come on, Tess. You know what I need."

"What?"

"You," he groaned against her lips. "You."

His words flipped all her switches and she fell over the edge, her orgasm causing her entire body to shudder and buck beneath him. The pleasure was white-hot, searingly intense, and imprinted on every cell of her body.

Adam cried out above her, his body, all sleek muscle and rigid bone, going taut with his own pleasure. He collapsed against her and Tess wrapped her arms around him, ignoring the cooling of the sweat on their bodies and the knowledge that they really weren't alone in this building. She just wanted to indulge in this moment, knowing that it would end soon enough.

That was the deal they had agreed to, after all.

But maybe some of the rules could be broken.

"So…" she ventured, trailing her nails lightly up and down his back.

"Yeah?"

"About that dinner out…"

Adam lifted his head, propped himself up on an elbow to gaze down and her, and raised an eyebrow in humor. "What? All it took was a mind-blowing orgasm to get a meal out of you?"

"A girl has got to have her standards."

Ten

Tess was probably going to kill him.

Adam pulled up in front of the small bungalow tucked into the end of a small street in the solidly middle-class neighborhood. Nearby yards and driveways were littered with abandoned bikes and skateboards, anchored with basketball nets, and dotted with "Please slow down— children at play" signs. It wasn't anything like the one he'd grown up in, with locked gates and housekeepers answering the door. This was a neighborhood where the streets filled with costumed kids on Halloween and wagon parades on the Fourth of July. Adam didn't remember ever having that.

He shook off the dark cloud that always accompanied his dwelling on the ghosts of shitty childhoods past and cut the engine of his car, pausing to consider just how weird this was. Adam hadn't heard from Tess in almost two days; no response to his texts and voicemails and she'd failed to show at Redhawk/Ling. None of that sounded at all like the Tess he knew. They'd spent every waking moment together or in constant contact in the past few weeks, either searching for the mole or finding chances to work off steam in a way that left him aching for more. So, he was down to two schools of thought about what he was currently doing: it was restraining order level of stalker activity or the action of a normal, noncreepy friend/fuckbuddy.

The jury was still out on which way the "Jury of Tess" would fall on the issue.

But he kept coming back to the fact that failing to show up for work or answer his inquiries was nothing like Tess Lynch. If she didn't want to talk to you, she'd tell you to your face in unequivocal language and then freeze you out like a blizzard at the North Pole.

Screw it. If she murdered him, so be it.

Adam opened the door on his Audi R8 Spyder and glanced around the neighborhood as he shut the door. Three doors down a young woman was pretending to pull weeds as she watched him and her toddler out of the corner of her eye. She paused when she got the full look of him and her wide-eyed reaction was either because he was a stranger in her neighborhood, he was a brown stranger in her neighborhood or she was ogling his car. He nodded, giving her his best "I'm a billionaire business owner so please don't call the cops" smile and walked up the short concrete walk lined with pretty flowers to the teal-painted front door and raised his hand to push the doorbell. He hesitated a brief moment, giving himself one more chance to back out before pressing the button.

He could hear the perky tone of the bell chime behind

the closed door but that was it. Not the sound of footsteps, no voice yelling at him to hang on. Nothing. He waited a few moments longer, shifting to try to peek through the large bay window in the front of the house but noting that the privacy blinds were shut tight. He reached out to the doorbell again, pressing on it an extra few seconds. It was irritating enough to wake the dead.

It worked because within a couple of seconds he heard the distinctive sound of Tess Lynch cursing whoever was at her door to one of the seven layers of hell. Relief loosened the knot that had settled in the bottom of his belly, only to be replaced by confusion about why Tess had decided to drop off the earth and out of his life. And out of his bed…well, his couch.

"Who is it?" Tess asked through the door and even with the solid wood barrier between them, Adam could tell that her voice was rough and scratchy.

"It's Adam. Are you all right?"

There was a brief pause and then the sound of the locks releasing followed by the door sliding open. He was greeted by a disheveled Tess, eyes red rimmed and cheeks flushed, glaring at him across the threshold. Her hair was a tangled mass of red curls and her pajamas looked like she'd been wearing them a few days. Of course, the absolute wrong thing fell out of his mouth.

"Tess, you look terrible."

The door slammed in his face with a ferocity that rattled the glass in the side lights.

"Tess, wait." He twisted the knob, grateful when it gave way and the door swung open. She hadn't locked him out. He stepped inside and spotted her retreating back as she shuffled down a hallway, rushing forward when she swayed and reached for the wall in a move to steady herself. He slid his hands around her waist, murmuring against her temple, "I've got you."

Tess was burning up, her skin hot and clammy to the touch. She leaned on him, accepting his support as he guided her around the corner into an open plan kitchen and family room. Adam picked up Tess and carried her over to the sofa, ignoring her indignant protest and attempts to wriggle out of his arms before he lowered her onto the bright yellow cushions.

"*Stay there.* I'll go get you some water." He strode over to the refrigerator, noting the sleek lines and warm colors of her home as he searched the cabinets until he located a glass and filled it with cold water. He moved back toward the sofa, relieved to see that Tess hadn't wandered off. He eased down next to her and placed the glass in her hands. "Take a drink. You need to stay hydrated with a fever."

"I'm fine," she insisted, taking a few large swallows before handing the glass back to him. She was pale, and her voice was scratchy when she gave him as much hell as she could muster. "What are you doing here, Adam?"

"You haven't been seen or heard from in a couple of days. I was worried. You could have been taken by a serial killer." He shrugged, feeling heat settle in his own cheeks at her piercing stare. "I wanted to make sure you were okay."

"How did you find out where I live?" she asked, taking another sip of water when he nudged the glass back toward her mouth.

"I employ a lot of people who are good with computers."

She narrowed her eyes at him. "That's pretty shady shit for you, Adam Redhawk. Illegal even."

"Well, the only other option was to call the police and ask for a wellness check and I figured that would get me murdered by you at the first opportunity."

"You're right." Tess set down the water glass on the coffee table and wiped her face with a shaking hand. "But, I'm fine. I just need to rest and I can't do that with you here."

Tess stood and swayed again, her body tensing when he gathered her against his body. She wasn't going to make this easy.

"Look, let me help you take your meds and fix you something to eat." She opened her mouth to argue with him but he cut her off with a shake of his head. She wasn't going to win this argument because he was pulling out the big guns. "No. I'm not leaving until I know you're okay or I'm going to call your sister."

"Oh, you suck." Tess glared at him but she sagged against him in defeat. Whether that was just from the illness or the threat, he didn't know and he didn't care.

"Well, get over it." He scanned the kitchen island for signs of any pill bottles or medicines. "When are you due for another dose of meds?"

Tess groaned and leaned her forehead against his chest, her already-scratchy voice muffled against the fabric of his shirt. "My doctor called in an antibiotic but I fell asleep and haven't gone to pick it up yet."

"Tess, you're running a fever. You need the meds." Adam bit back asking her why she didn't call him but he knew the answer: they were just sleeping together. You didn't call the current fling and ask them to pick up medication at the pharmacy. And with her sister at school, Tess wasn't going to reach out to anyone else. It wasn't in her nature to ask for help. Adam tucked her close to him again as he reached for his phone. "I'll call some-one to bring it here."

Her head whipped up. "Not Estelle."

"No, I wouldn't ask anyone from the company to come over here. Trust me." He looked around, trying to gauge where her bedroom was located. "Why don't you grab a shower while I fix you something to eat?"

"I'm not hungry," she mumbled as she moved toward the hallway.

"You'll need to eat with the antibiotic. Go shower and leave the rest to me." Adam pointed toward the hall-way, while thumbing across the screen of his phone and hitting the number for the person he knew would help him out.

"You're so bossy," Tess grumbled once more before she turned the corner. He smiled a little at her stubborn-ness and decided that he'd let her have the last word. She was sick after all.

A short phone call later and he was following Tess's path down the hallway, listening for the sound of run-ning water. The second door to the right was open, which led to her bedroom. He went in, turning on the overhead light and taking his first look around the space where Tess slept.

It was small for a master bedroom but in proportion to the scale of the cottage. But what it lacked in size, it more than made up for in comfort and style. Three walls were painted a warm honey color with the fourth decked out in a Mediterranean blue, giving the room the feel-ing of warm days on a beach in Greece. The comforter was a deep oceanic blue and pillows in white, silver and lighter shades of blue were scattered over the bed around the Tess-shaped spot on the left side of the mattress.

Ducking back out into the hallway, Adam grabbed a new set of sheets and proceeded to strip down the bed and remake it, stacking the decorative pillows on a large armchair in the corner next to the large window that faced the small fenced backyard. Adam could just spy a small patio filled with a table and chairs and a grill.

Hearing the water turn off on the shower, he moved toward the open door to the adjoining bathroom, leaning against the door frame as Tess finished wrapping a large towel around her long, lush body. Her hair was wet and darkened to the deepest shade of auburn, the strands sticking to the damp, heat-pinkened skin of her shoulders. Adam remembered the silk of her flesh, the sweet taste of her sighs as he kissed her all over.

Now she had no makeup. No hairstyle. No sexy outfit.

Tess Lynch was still the most beautiful woman he'd ever seen.

She looked over her shoulder at him and he could see the bone-deep fatigue in the lines around her mouth and the lack of brilliance in her eyes. And just like that the pull was back in his chest, the one that made it difficult to take a deep breath. Adam leaned against the door frame, willing his heart to revert to its normal rhythm and his tongue to form the right words.

"Your medicine is on the way. I'll be in the kitchen making you something to eat."

"Adam." Tess sighed in exasperation, the hoarse whisper barely traveling across the room to where he stood. She shuffled forward a couple of paces, closing the distance between them to less than arm's length. "Why are you doing this?"

She was tired but the suspicion etched into the rigid lines of her body and the doubt clouding her gaze were unmistakable. He reached out, lightly brushing wet curls off her forehead. "Don't get too worked up—I'm not that great a cook."

Tess shook her head and he knew she wasn't going to make this easy. "This is not what we agreed to. This is not something you do for a fuckbu—"

Adam stopped her with his thumb pressed gently to her lips. Yeah, he'd thought the same thing just a few moments before but he didn't want to hear it from her. He didn't want to think too hard on why he didn't like being shoved into a category he'd initially suggested either. Not today.

"Hey, we've got a friends with benefits thing going on…" He pushed off the door frame and turned to head back toward the kitchen. "Today I'm doing the friend thing. Don't overthink it, Tess. Get dressed and come get something to eat."

Adam searched her kitchen for something that he could prepare and not make Tess feel worse. He wasn't a terrible cook but he did only a certain number of dishes well enough to serve to anybody else and those consisted of things you could grill and an omelet. A quick check of the fridge yielded eggs and cheese. Good. He wouldn't have to order takeout.

Her kitchen was small but well organized and he found a skillet and all the utensils he needed. He cracked the eggs, shredded the cheese and concentrated on cooking and not on the real reason he was there in Tess's kitchen breaking all the rules.

"Now, that's something I never thought I'd see," Tess said as she entered the kitchen. She walked slowly, clearly not feeling well but looking fresh and beautiful in a set of emerald green pajamas. He nodded toward one of the bar stools pulled up to the island, smiling when she didn't argue with him.

"What's that?"

"A billionaire in my kitchen, cooking for me."

He chuckled, using the spatula to do the perfect flip over of the cooked eggs. "No, it's just me. Adam."

"Just Adam," she said, her eyes tracking his every move. "Who is that guy?"

Tess was trying to figure him out and he hoped she was successful and then explained it all to him. He hadn't known who he was since she'd walked into his office, since he'd found his family.

"When you figure it out, let me know." Adam avoided her gaze, it was too piercing, too knowing. Not today. He offered up another topic to take the spotlight off of him. "Roan agreed to come out here and spend some time together."

"That's good, Adam. Really good."

"He's wrapping up a commission and then he has to go to some party in Monaco or some other place with a palace." He smiled, remembering how his little brother acted like hanging out with celebrities was no big deal. "He's going to come out here after that is all wrapped up."

"And Sarina?"

He paused, gathering his thoughts as he checked underneath the egg, cheese and veggie mixture. Almost done. "I don't know if that's going to happen. I can't…" Adam swallowed hard, clearing his throat and trying to relax the ball of anxiety lodged in his gut. "I can't seem to reach her."

"Out of the three of you, she's been alone most of her life. She got lost in the system, fell through the cracks.

She had to be there for herself because there was nobody else." Tess tapped the countertop to get him to look at her. "She's worth it. Trust me. She's not rejecting you... it's how she survives."

And somehow Adam knew that Tess was also talking about herself. Whether she intended to or not.

"I won't give up. I'm not built that way." He plated the omelet and scooted it across the island toward Tess just as the doorbell rang. "I already poured some orange juice for you. That's your meds. Eat."

"You're so bossy today."

Adam hustled down the hallway and grabbed the medication from the courier, giving him a huge tip before shutting the door. He was already reading the directions on the side of the bottle when he turned the corner.

"Take this huge horse pill every eight hours for the next five days and you'll be back to kicking my ass before you know it." He placed one in front of her on the counter, pleased to see that she'd eaten most of the omelet. "And then it's back to bed for you."

"Bossy." Tess took the pill, glaring at him as he disposed of the food and put the dirty dishes in the dishwasher.

"Bed." He held out his hand, shocked that she took it so quickly but going with it. He led her down the hallway and to her bed, then pulled back the comforter and helped her slide between the sheets. Adam tucked the covers around her, smiling down at the goofy, sleepy grin on her face.

"You changed my sheets."

"Uh-huh. Nobody likes to get into a bed with dirty sheets when they're sick."

"Adam." She started to argue with him but the yawn

that racked her body took out any of the sting in the tone of that one word. "Don't get used to this. You're not the boss of me."

"Yeah, well, I think you need someone to boss you around sometimes."

"Adam, don't psychoanalyze me." Tess reached out and pushed the hair off his forehead, letting her finger trail down his nose, across his lips. He reached up and grabbed her hand, kissing the tips of her fingers.

"I've got you figured out a little, Tess. Neither one of us likes to let people take care of us but we spend most of our time taking care of everybody else." He kissed her fingers again, then gently tucked her hand underneath the covers, taking a moment to press a kiss to her forehead and then the tip of her nose. "Let me do this. I promise we'll never speak of it again. It will be our secret."

She nodded, her lids already heavy with fatigue as she snuggled down under the covers.

Adam leaned down one more time, pressing a kiss to her hair, breathing in the unique and completely addictive scent of Tess. She was argumentative, stubborn, difficult and the most frustrating woman he'd ever met but he couldn't shake her. He wanted to know all of her secrets and to create a million more that were just between them.

And for some reason, those thoughts didn't scare him as much as he thought they should.

Eleven

"Tess, why is there a strange, hot dude in your chair?"

Tess struggled against the weight of sleep and weariness and medication to get to the surface and answer the voice that accompanied the hand currently shaking her shoulder. She wiped a hand across her eyes, clearing away the gritty layer on her lashes and blinking into the pale light sneaking through the slats in her blinds. She stretched a little, testing out her body, and assessed that she didn't feel one hundred percent but she did feel much better than yesterday.

"Tess, are you okay? Is that Adam Redhawk?" Mia's face came into focus, her expression filled with equal doses of concern and curiosity.

"Mia, what are you doing here?" It was the middle of the semester and it was uncommon for her sister to make a trip home so close to midterms.

"I came home to get some quiet to study and found an expensive-as-shit-car in the driveway, you out cold in bed and him over there." Mia pointed to the over-sized chair across from her bed and to the man currently sprawled out on it.

Adam's large frame made the chair look small and very uncomfortable. He was slumped down onto the cushions, his long legs spread out before him, a too-small throw blanket tucked up under his chin. His hair was a mess, falling over into his face and obscuring his eyes but leaving visible the five o'clock shadow darkening his jaw. He looked different in his sleep as everyone did but his vulnerability and rugged handsomeness struck her as if she'd never seen him before.

And she'd never seen him like this. When they were together it was never in a bed, never overnight. She'd never woken up with him wrapped around her, never had the chance to watch him when all of his defenses were down and it was just the man.

What a mistake. She'd missed one of the best parts.

"Sis, are you okay? I saw a prescription on the kitchen counter. Are you sick?" Mia intruded into her thoughts, stopping her from going down a path that she knew led to nowhere she belonged.

Tess circled back over the last day, recalling Adam showing up at her door, cooking the omelet, taking care of her. He'd stayed while she slept, waking her in the night to give her a second dose of the antibiotic and tucking her back into bed. And he must have stayed all night.

"I am… I was sick. Caught something and got an infection." She shoved off the covers, sitting up in bed to facilitate her coming back to the land of the living. She waved in the general direction of the man currently the topic of discussion. "Adam stopped by to make sure I was okay. He…helped me out…must have stayed overnight."

"Uh, okay." Mia's face showed the considerable effort it took for her to digest everything she'd just heard. She sputtered with words, not bothering to disguise her confusion. "Wow. That's really nice." And then her eyes flew open, brows shooting halfway to her hairline. "Whoa, are you two…? I mean that's something you only do for close friends and people you're fu—"

Tess's hand whipped out almost on autopilot and covered Mia's mouth. They were not going to have this discussion with Adam only a few feet away.

"I think this might be the best time for me to let you know that I'm awake."

Adam's deep voice rumbled out from the direction of the chair and both she and Mia jumped and spun around to watch him as he stretched, arms and legs flexing with the effort of waking. His shirt lifted up and they both caught a good, long look at his gorgeous skin and cut abs. Tess knew that body, knew that he'd be warm and silky and she knew exactly what was at the end of the delicious treasure trail of dark hair.

"Good morning," Mia said, her smirk indicating that her thoughts were walking the same path. Tess jabbed her with a finger, fuming when she was ignored and all Mia's attention stayed on their guest. "I'm Mia."

Adam let out a sleepy chuckle and shook the hand her sister offered. "I'm Adam and I knew who you were."

"Oh yeah? Tess show you a picture of me?" Tess rolled her eyes at the antics of her soon-to-be-dead little sister. She remained braced to tackle her to the ground if this conversation took a turn for the worse.

"No. You two are identical. I'd know you anywhere."
Adam rose, his hands busy with folding the blanket and
draping it over the arm of the chair.

"Because we're both so gorgeous?" Mia asked, her
eyes flashing with humor and mischief.

"Mia!" Tess was only going to put up with this one
more minute and then she was going to become an only
child.

Adam laughed, shuffling over to press the back of his
hand on her forehead, assessing her with an allover gaze
that had her leaning into his touch before she could remind her treacherous body that her sister was present. It
wasn't as if Mia hadn't seen Tess with a guy before but
she wasn't positive that all of the emotions, the feelings
she had for Adam tumbling around inside her wouldn't
be evident to anyone looking. And Mia was looking.

"Definitely gorgeous." Adam smoothed her hair back
from her face, tangling his fingers in her curls and tucking one behind her ear. It was such a cheesy move but
the flutter in her stomach told her that it was working.
Damn him. "How are you feeling? I think your fever finally broke."

Tess reached up to touch her own cheek, her fingers
brushing against and then intertwining with his before
she realized what she was doing. Hell, make a meal and
change her sheets and she became a total sap for this guy.

"I'm better. You can go."

He smirked but didn't move.

"Thank you." Tess put some emphasis on it, sincerity
with a touch of "please go before my sister starts asking
too many questions."

"Okay. I get it. Just promise that you'll call me if you
need anything."

"Mia is here." She nodded toward her sister as a reminder to herself more than Adam. He nodded in return, making a move to let her hand go but she tightened her grip, giving it a squeeze. "Thank you, Adam. I'm sorry I was so much trouble—this isn't what you signed up for."

He glanced over his shoulder, his eyes full of humor and his voice lowered when he turned back. "I told you, I was just focusing on the friends part of the arrangement."

Tess sucked in a breath, loving the way his thumb rubbed along her wrist and the ripples of pleasure that raced under her skin. Adam Redhawk was dangerous. She needed to remember that but it was damn easy to forget when he was this close and was looking at her like she was Christmas and his birthday all wrapped up in one package.

He pressed a discreet kiss to the same place he'd just been caressing. She felt the heat rise in her cheeks and she knew it wasn't the fever returning, exhaling when he dropped her hand and took a step back.

"I'm going to go since you've got a very capable nurse." Adam turned to address Mia. "She needs to finish all of her antibiotics and is due for another dose in a half hour and she needs lots more rest. Don't let her tell you that she's better and can go back to work or anything."

"Now, wait a minute," Tess objected, not liking the teaming of these two for one second.

Mia held up a hand to shush her. "No to work. Yes to drugs. Got it."

Tess continued to object. She wasn't a child and she would know when she was ready to back to work. "He's not a doctor, you know."

"I got my degree at WebMD," Adam teased, backing toward the doorway like a man who was well versed in self-preservation. "Don't come to the office for a couple of days, Tess. Don't make me alert security to get you off the property. Call me."

"I owe you one," she answered, never wanting to be in anyone's debt but knowing when it was true.

"If you insist," he said, giving a salute as he disappeared around the corner.

Tess watched him leave, listening to his footfalls on the hallway floors and the sound of the door closing before she turned to her sister.

Mia beat her to the punch. "Don't even try to bully me into letting you go back to work or to stop taking your meds. I'm your little sister but not an idiot."

"I'm going to take my meds." Tess hustled by her sister, leaving the room in a huff that she didn't try to hide.

She was still sick, weak, flustered and confused by everything that had happened the last couple of days. And while she was glad Mia was here, she didn't want to have the conversation her sister was going to poke and prod to have with her. It wasn't that she wanted to hide stuff from Mia but there were lots of things that she hadn't figured out herself. Like how to keep Adam's trust and do what she needed to do to bring down Franklin Thornton. Like how Adam was quickly becoming important to her.

"Tess, you can take your meds and also tell me what the hell Adam Redhawk was doing in your room all night." Mia followed on her heels like one of those annoying yappy dogs who never gave up when they had a good bone on offer.

She made her way around the kitchen island, automatically going for the coffee maker but rethinking it when her stomach gave a little gurgle. Juice sounded way more appealing, and she busied herself grabbing it from the refrigerator along with bread for toast, and avoided the intense stare of her sister across the island. She popped the bread into the toaster oven and reached for the antibiotic, taking one as prescribed and washing it down with the orange juice.

"So…how long have you been sleeping with Adam Redhawk?"

"Wow. Way to go easy on the sick person." Tess flipped her the bird and grabbed the butter from the fridge. "He was just here to help me out. He knew you were at school." She shrugged as she spread some butter on the toast. "He's just a nice guy."

"And he's sleeping with you." Mia reached over and twisted a piece of bread off and popped it into her mouth. "It was obvious from the way you let him fuss all over you. You never let anyone do that."

"And you jumped to the sex conclusion?" Mia stared at her, her expression communicating that she could do this all day and Tess knew she could. Mia didn't fall far from the stubborn tree in this family. Tess slid into the seat next to her sister, crunching down on the toast to buy some time. "It's been a few weeks."

"A few weeks?" Mia threw her hands up and mimicked throttling her sister around the throat. "And I'm just hearing about this now? My sister is dating—"

"Oh no." Tess shook her head, nipping this misunderstanding in the bud. "We are *not* dating."

"So, you're a booty call? A one-and-done?"

Tess tossed down her toast onto the plate. "Holy crap, Mia. I know you're in college but I don't want to even think about the idea that you know what any of that means."

"Tess, I'm twenty-one and a sexually active woman.

So, wrap your head around that fact and tell me that *you* know what you're doing." Mia's hand covered hers and Tess wondered when that had happened. It was just yesterday when Mia's tiny, sticky fingers were engulfed by Tess's and life had been busier but a lot less complicated. "I don't want to see you get hurt."

Tess swallowed hard, Mia's words echoing the whispers that had already been circling in the back of her mind. But if she wasn't ready to deal with them in her own head, she wasn't ready to do it with her sister. The one she was supposed to be taking care of and not the other way around.

Tess patted Mia's hand, another gesture that brought back memories of earlier days. "It's just an arrangement." She leveled her with a stare that did nothing to wipe the all-knowing grin off her face. "Not a booty call. An arrangement between two consenting adults."

"Is one of those consenting adults still unaware of the vendetta the other consenting adult has aimed at his adopted father?"

Tess picked up her toast, taking a bite and grimacing at how the butter had congealed as the bread cooled. She chewed it anyway, forcing it down with juice and scrambling for an answer that would get her sister to drop it. With a sigh, she turned and faced off with Mia.

"Look, I know very well how this is likely to go. But it's what needs to be done and I promise you that I'm not taking anything on that I can't handle. Okay?"

Mia stared her down, her eyes scanning every inch of Tess's face for something she needed to see. But for once Tess didn't know how to give it to her.

Finally, Mia nodded and leaned over to press a kiss to her cheek. "You're not invincible Tess. I saw how you two looked at each other and you're headed for a whole lot of hurt if you insist on going after Franklin Thornton. I don't want to be right but you know I am."

And Tess did know. She just didn't have any choice.

Twelve

"Tess, I need to call in that favor."

The silence over the phone line did not bring Adam the comfort he was seeking. He was in a full-on panic and didn't even attempt to hide the fact. He was willing to grovel for what he needed. He'd faced down irate investors and the wrath of Franklin Thornton but this shit was scary.

"Tess, are you there?" He heard noises on the other end of the phone. A printer printing, a news program running in the background. What he didn't hear was the woman he'd called for help.

She was at home, where she'd been working since her illness a week ago. Adam still wanted her to rest. Tess wanted to go back to work. This was the compromise.

"I'm trying to remember when I agreed that I owed you a favor," Tess drawled into the line and he could picture her leaning back in her office chair, dressed in that sexy, green body-hugging dress he'd seen her in at Red-hawk/Ling. She'd stopped him in his tracks, completely well and in total control of her sultry, confident and stunning beauty. Justin had laughed at him but he couldn't have given less of a shit.

Tess was beautiful. She was his—temporarily. And he needed her help.

"Tess, don't mess with me here. Sarina and Roan are coming over for dinner and I don't know what the hell I'm doing." Adam took a deep breath and willed her to help him. He hoped she wouldn't make him beg but he wasn't above it for this situation. "I need your help, Tess. I don't think I can do this by myself."

The seconds passed by way too slowly for his heart or his mental health but eventually he heard the words he'd been dying to hear.

"I'm on my way."

Forty-five minutes later his knees almost gave out with relief when his doorbell rang. He sprinted down the short hallway into the foyer and ripped the door open.

Tess stood there, now dressed in a pretty green sun-dress with tiny yellow flowers embroidered all over it and flower-covered flip-flops. Her creamy pale shoulders were exposed by the way she wore her long red hair pulled up in a thingy that only let stray curls cascade down over her skin. She was delectable and enticing and his entire body went on high alert.

It had been over a week since they'd been together, her recuperation, work and his travel to Washington, DC, to vet some potential future business partners, putting up an insurmountable barrier to every need he had to taste her, touch her, make her sigh with her own pleasure around him. And now he had a bunch of family he'd not seen in fifteen years coming over and any private time reconnecting with Tess would have to wait.

"Jesus, Tess, thanks for coming over." He ushered her inside with hands *this close* to shaking. Once the door was shut behind her he clenched them into tight, almost painful fists to resist the urge to reach out and touch her.

"Hey, Adam. Come here." Tess took a step forward and suddenly her arms were around him and her lips were on his and the entire world stopped spinning at light speed. Her mouth was soft, lips parting under his, her breasts pressed against his chest, and he was surrounded by the sweet-sharp scent of her perfume. It was like the closest thing he had to coming home and immediately he was centered. Not calm but not ready to crawl out of his skin.

Too soon, way too soon, she broke the contact and smiled up at him, her grin sly enough to scare him but dirty enough to distract him from the nerves hanging out on the rough edge of his sanity. She was exactly what he needed.

"I've met both Sarina and Roan and I know they're sitting somewhere right now freaking out too. You know that, right?" Tess reassured him. "This is going to be a rough night for all of you but you'll be okay. Are you cooking?"

"Yes."

"An omelet?"

He laughed, brushing a kiss across her lips. "No, steak. The only other thing I can cook."

"It will be great." She turned in his arms, gaze traveling around the interior of his home. "Nice place. Give me a tour?"

"Sure." Adam slid his hand down her arm, enjoying the slide of their skin together and the intertwining of their fingers as he led her through his house.

Her bright dress and curls were a stark contrast to the various shades of gray and silver the designer had used all over the house and for the first time he understood why Justin said that it was cold. It was like the rest of his life, only a place to pass though in between work and more work. Tess's presence made it all feel drab somehow.

The foyer spilled over into the great room, detours leading to a home office for him just off to the left, and three bedrooms upstairs. Tess peeked inside all the rooms but he didn't let her linger, tugging her toward the back of the house and his favorite part. The main reason why he'd bought the house in the first place.

"You've got to see the best part."

"Oh my God, Adam. This is incredible." Tess let go of his hand, dropping her purse on the dining table as she sprinted over to the three-story, floor-to-ceiling windows that spanned the entire width of the house.

The El Sereno Open Space Preserve sprawled out in front of them in every possible direction. Rolling hills of green, dissected by nature trails, and flowers blooming everywhere was the view that had convinced him to buy this house. But the woman standing in front of the window eclipsed all of it.

"Can I go outside?" Tess was looking at him over her shoulder, her hand poised on the handle for the sliding glass door that led out to the wraparound deck.

"Of course."

He laughed when she gave a little hop of excitement

and pulled open the door. It wasn't a typical Tess-like re-action but he had a feeling that he'd seen the "real" Tess in that moment. The one who was buried under her loss and pain and well-earned cynicism. And if this were a real relationship, he'd look forward to coaxing out more of those moments from this fascinating woman.

And more and more he wanted this to be a real rela-tionship. There was a reason why he'd called Tess and it wasn't because she owed him one.

Adam followed her out onto the deck, past the large table and the outdoor kitchen to the railing that edged the space. Past the overly large couch and the comfort-able chairs. She smiled into the waning afternoon sun, her eyes darting everywhere as she soaked it all in.

"This is why I bought this house," he said, leaning against the railing but watching her. He'd seen that view a million times but this one was better.

"And you would have been crazy not to. This is just unbelievable." Tess looked over at him, glancing back toward the interior of the house and then waving at the view. "This is more 'Adam' than the inside. Interior dec-orator?"

"Yeah," he answered, guessing she had the same opin-ion as Justin about the inside of his house. "She really liked gray."

"Obviously."

The doorbell chime brought them both up short, his smile vanishing as fast as the sun was slipping behind the mountains.

"I got this," Tess murmured and he didn't even try to stop her as she headed back through his house and quickly returned into view with two strangers who should have been family all along.

Roan was first, his swagger already recognizable from the videos of him on YouTube. Adam's little brother was an up-and-coming name in *the* art circles and he was painting and sleeping his way through the male and female populations of the rich and glamorous. Adam had expected his confidence, cocky smile and open curiosity but what he wasn't prepared for was the doubt in his gaze and that immediately made Adam relax just a little.

He wasn't the only one feeling ill at ease about this meeting.

Sarina was a tougher character and everything about her posture kept everyone at arm's length. Newly separated from the army, she stood ramrod straight, her gaze remote and her expression aloof. Adam could imagine how intimidating she'd been as a military cop and how she'd been very good at her job. Why she'd left a successful career in the military was a question he had no idea how to answer. His more immediate concern was that nothing about her said she wanted to be here and that pierced him to the core.

"Thanks for coming to dinner." Adam gestured awkwardly around the space, feeling as clunky as his first day in every foster home and every new school. He looked toward Tess for help and she nodded, understanding everything in the briefest of glances, taking over the situation.

"It's so nice. Why don't you all sit out here? Tell me what you'd like and I'll bring out a round of drinks and Adam can throw the steaks on the grill."

Drink orders relayed to Tess, they all watched her leave, the only person they had in common at this point, and the silence that erupted between them was as heavy as the fog that often coated the preserve in the mornings. In unison, Sarina and Roan slid out their chairs and took a seat and Adam busied himself pulling the steaks out of the outdoor fridge and firing up the grill.

"I didn't realize that you and Ms. Lynch were together," Roan said, smooth as silk but edged with a little bit of suspicion.

"No, we're not together. We're…" Adam said, eyeing Tess's progress on the drinks through the window. It was the truth but he didn't want to hurt her, didn't want her to think that he was dismissing her impact in his life. "We're friends and I thought it might be good to have her here. She's the most recent thing we all have in common."

"She knows all of our secrets, you mean," Sarina stated, her tone flat but also disapproving.

Adam and Roan exchanged a look; whether it was one of solidarity or sympathy he wasn't sure but he was grateful for it.

Tess emerged from the house a couple of minutes later and handed out the drinks before settling into a chair at the table. She'd had the foresight to turn on the sound system so they had some background music to accompany the world's most painful dinner party.

"Is this your first time in California?" she asked them in an obvious attempt to start conversation. Sarina didn't answer, only shaking her head in the negative before bringing her glass to her lips and casting her gaze over the preserve. Adam wondered why she was here. Curiosity? Obligation? Of one thing he was certain: gone was the happy, smiling toddler who teased the edges of his fuzzy memories, and that made him unspeakably sad and angry.

Roan took a drink from his beer before replying, "I've been here a couple of times. Never to this area, though. I mostly end up in LA, visiting galleries." He gestured toward the preserve. "But I love to hike and this is gorgeous. I'll have to come back and check it out."

Adam ventured a suggestion, uneasily offering a tentative connection to this stranger. "Maybe we could go out together. I'm not much of a hiker but I think I can keep up."

"You're a runner, a triathlete. I'm sure you can keep up," Roan said, his grin genuine and startlingly like his own. He turned toward Sarina, his twin, obviously trying to bring her into the conversation. They'd been separated from each other, a cut that had to run deep but you'd never know it from his brother's demeanor. Adam envied his ease. Roan might be faking it but his charm was working on him. Not so much with their sister from the shuttered look on her face. "What about you, Sarina? Might be fun."

"I don't hike. We didn't have time for that when I was growing up and even less when I was in the army," she said. Her tone didn't say the conversation was closed but nothing about it kept the ball rolling.

He mentally flipped through the report Tess had given him about his sister. She'd had it the worst of all of them: bad adoptive family, every reason to the get the hell out as soon as she could. And she'd been lucky to get out. Been lucky to last long enough to get out. Adam's gut tightened again at the recollection of facts that he could not change and he turned back to the grill, flipping the steaks and controlling what he could.

Adam plated the New York strips and took them over to the table, placing one in front of each of his guests. He grabbed the salad out of the fridge and transferred it and the various dressings to the table as well. It wasn't a four-course meal but it would give them all something to do with their hands and mouths.

They ate in silence for a few moments only occasionally making noises about how good it was. Sarina was markedly silent, pushing her food around her plate in an unconvincing show of eating. Adam had known this wasn't going to be easy but this barely sheathed hostility was impossible to penetrate and frustrating as hell. He wasn't the enemy but her cold shoulder made him feel like he was.

Even with Roan and Tess carrying the conversational load, they were done quickly and left staring at each other across the table as the evening slid into twilight. Tess reached out under the table, the weight of her hand on his leg, and the smile she offered centered him and his thoughts.

"Tess tells me that we have a mutual love of motorcycles. Harleys in particular." Adam looked at his brother and sister, relieved to see Roan's enthusiastic agreement and resigned to Sarina's exasperated nod. She didn't roll her eyes but it was pretty close.

He hadn't come this far, hadn't invested this much blood, sweat, money and tears into finding his brother and sister to watch his dreams die a quick and dirty death at this table. It was his responsibility to bring this family back together and he'd do everything in his power to make it happen.

"Our father, he loved riding a motorcycle." Adam dug into his memories, hoping to find something they could build a future on. "We had this carport attached to the house and he would spend hours out there, restoring this old Harley he'd bartered off a guy passing through the Qualla Boundary. Dad was good with his hands, could fix almost anything, and I'd sit with him and hand off the tools he needed."

Adam shook his head, surprised at his own memories. It had been years since he'd recalled that moment and he could smell the scent of grease and sunshine and the neighbors cooking sausages on a grill in their yard. How had he forgotten it?

Without thinking, he reached down and took Tess's hand in his own, comforted by the way her warmth infused his entire body with peace and assurance that this was worth it. What was happening at this table was important. And he wasn't just thinking about his brother and sister.

Tess was important and he knew the real reason he wanted her here. He wanted her to be a part of this future, his future.

"I remember when he finally finished the work on his bike and it needed a paint job in the worst way but it wouldn't keep him from firing it up and taking it for a ride." He smiled wider as the memory came more sharply into focus. "Our mom came running out of the house and yelled at him to stop doing doughnuts in the yard and he blew her a kiss and took off down the road. The bike was a piece of shit and the dust was flying but I thought he looked like the coolest guy I'd ever seen. That was when I fell in love with motorcycles."

"I think I have a photograph of him on that bike back at my place. It was in a bunch of stuff that ended up in my bag when we were taken," Roan said, his hands waving around in excitement. "I'll dig it up and make a copy." His glance widened to include Sarina. "I'll make one for all of us."

The sharp scrape of metal chair legs against the desk

made them all jump and Adam swiveled to find Sarina standing, her expression stormy and her jaw set in an angry line. Adam rose to his feet, automatically reaching out to his sister, but her razor-sharp flinch from him kept him on his side of the table. Adam dropped his hand and braced for impact. If he knew anything about his sister, she wasn't going to come in slow and sweet.

"Sarina, are you okay?" Roan asked, his own chair tipping backward on two legs with his agitation. He reached back, catching it before it slammed to the ground and putting it right.

Sarina tossed her napkin on the table, empty hand slicing across the air in front of her body as if she was cutting all of the tenuous ties between them. Adam's heart dropped to the depths of the valley of the preserve. He knew what she was going to say and while he didn't want to hear it, he knew he needed to let her have it out. In reality, he didn't really have a choice. He might have brought them all together but that had ended any control he'd had over the situation and how it would end.

"Adam." She glanced at Roan, implicitly including him in her comments before sliding her gaze back to him. "You seem like a nice guy but I don't know you and I don't remember any of this happy family stuff you're spouting off like it's some movie of the week. I don't remember the motorcycle or the carport or our mom or the fucking house. None of it."

"Sarina."

She ignored him, the hand she'd raised to silence him slowly curving into a fist. "I only remember where I ended up and if I started sharing those tales we'd all need something stronger than what you've got." Sarina took a deep breath and pressed her hands against her stomach, as if she was keeping those memories inside her, physically preventing them from coming out. "I just can't do this. I *don't want* to do this."

The silence that descended between them now felt impenetrable, worse than it had before, but he couldn't just leave it like this. He took a step forward and a huge risk by reaching out to touch her arm. Sarina's eyes narrowed with wariness and she let it sit there for a couple of seconds before taking one step backward. He let his hand drop but maintained eye contact with this woman who had his mouth and Roan's eyes.

"I won't say that I understand exactly where you are but I think I get most of it. Something really shitty happened to us, *all of us*, something that should have never happened and none of our lives were ever the same. And I understand that you were so young that you don't remember but I do. I *remember*. I remember your long hair and how you used to braid flowers and follow me around begging for piggyback rides. Those memories, my memories, I'm not ready to give them up."

"But this isn't about you and your fucking memories. This is about how you decided that we all needed to get dragged into your therapy-induced experiment. Well, I didn't ask to be part of your 'closure' or whatever the hell you're doing here. I didn't ask to be part of any of this."

He couldn't have filled the silence that followed because he didn't have anything else to say. Adam didn't have the answers, didn't know how to fix this, and that made him want to howl at the rapidly rising moon.

But Sarina wasn't looking for answers. From the sharp concrete-hard set to her mouth, he knew she wasn't going to relent, wasn't going to end this in a way that didn't cut him to the quick.

"I'm sorry that you went to all this trouble. Like I said, you seem to be a really nice guy. But I've read the files that Tess gave me and all they proved is that you are both total strangers to me and I don't think that is ever going to change."

She nodded to them all, a brittle, brisk nod that spoke of years of military training and an even longer education at the school of hard knocks and bitter disappointment. And then she was gone, disappearing into the shadows of the interior of his home toward the front door.

Roan stepped into his rapidly narrowing field of vision, his expression concerned and apologetic.

"Adam, I'm going to make sure that she gets to the hotel. I think it's just going to take her a little time." He paused, obviously searching for the right thing to say. Roan hesitated and then reached out, clasping Adam's shoulder and giving it a squeeze. "Thanks for this and thanks for finding us."

He nodded to Tess and sauntered off, following Sarina's path. Adam stood there, rooted in place by disappointment, anger, sadness and a bone-deep helplessness that threatened to bring him to his knees.

He had failed them again.

And then Tess was there, her arms wrapped around his neck and her words of comfort spilling over him in a balm that soothed like a summer rain on thirsty ground.

"Adam, it's okay. You knew this wasn't going to be easy. It will be okay."

He leaned into her, briefly concerned that his weight, his need would be too much for her but this was Tess. His Tess. Strong. Smart. His.

And he needed her.

"Tess, tell me you need me. Even if it's a lie. Tell me,"

Adam rasped against the soft, sweet skin of her cheek, heading for her mouth and the sweet relief her kisses could bring. It was selfish and it was too much to ask but he asked it anyway.

The last thing he heard before he took her mouth was the four words that kept him from falling apart.

"Adam, I need you."

Thirteen

Adam needed her.

Everything that they were about, every rule they had established between them told her to leave, to tell him that he'd be okay and go home. Because if she stayed, this would all be different between them and they would never be able to go back.

But she could never leave him now. Not after seeing the complete devastation on his face, the loss of hope. Adam might be stoic and strong but his bone-deep need to take care of the people for whom he felt responsible made him vulnerable. He hid it well but if you got close enough to see what mattered to him, it was hard to miss.

Tess opened to his kiss, using her own response to calm him, to let him know that she wasn't going anywhere.

He broke it off, looking down at her, his eyes searching for answers that she didn't have.

"Are you scared?" she asked him before she could stop herself. There was only so much she could do to soothe him with her body. Other things needed to be faced head-on. He seemed to know that she wasn't talking about them.

"All the time," he answered, tucking a curl around his finger. "I can't fail, Tess."

"You're not going to fail, Adam." She shushed him with a finger laid across his lips. "I don't know if everything is going to work out exactly like you want it to but you won't fail. We'll find the mole and Sarina will come around."

He shook his head, his dark eyes miserable. "I think she's right. I was selfish to drag them both into this. They were doing just fine without me."

Tess didn't know much but she knew some things and they were going to get those straight right now.

"Adam, maybe Sarina isn't ready but she was wrong about your being selfish. I was the one you hired, remember? I know what motivated you from the start and that wasn't part of the equation."

Adam paused, closing his eyes and clearly rolling things over in his head. He opened his eyes, dark lashes making the amber stand out.

"Are *you* ever scared?"

Tess didn't hesitate with the truth. "All the damn time."

"I need you, Tess."

"Then take me. I'm yours, Adam. You know this." Tess was startled by the words that tumbled out of her mouth but she wouldn't take them back. They were true. They'd been heading toward this place and she guessed that the time was right for them to arrive and figure it out from here. It would probably require another change in the rules and she'd have to come clean about her father but that didn't need to happen right now.

Right now, they just needed to be here for each other.

She let him lead her over to the outside lounger. Built like a huge sectional, there was more than enough room for both of them to stretch out and enjoy each other's bodies under the stars. Tess loved the idea of having each other in the wide open. They had so many things between them most of the time, it was impossible for them to erect barriers when the sky stretched out above them like a never-ending story.

Before she could lie down he stopped her, his gaze traveling over her body in a slow, deliberate glide that made her squirm with anticipation. Adam, focused entirely on her, was something she would never get enough of. It made her feel cherished and beautiful and special. Heady stuff for anyone but since she'd never felt this way before, it dug under her skin and buried itself somewhere scarily close to her heart.

As if he could read her mind he said, "You're so beautiful, Tess."

"You make me feel beautiful, Adam."

He nodded, his gaze drifting down to where his fingers were undoing the tiny buttons on her sundress, his skin grazing the sides of her breasts. She wasn't wearing a bra and the sensation of his flesh, warm and rough against her, was intoxicating.

"I love the way we look together," he murmured, his fingers slipping under the fabric to stroke her right nipple. Tess arched into his touch, squirming under his attention as her belly grew warm and her sex grew wet with lust. She could barely think about the question with him touching her like that. "Let me see all of you, Tess."

He slid the dress off her shoulders, helping it along as it slid down her body and pooled at her feet.

"Are you cold?" he asked, a wicked smile twisting his lips as he put a finger in her mouth, taking it out when it was good and wet and circling her nipple with it, then leaning over to gently blow on it. She shook her head, biting on her lower lip when he angled his neck to look at her from his position. He was teasing her, eating up every reaction, every moan, every frantic pulse of her heartbeat. "I'll warm you up soon enough."

Adam took two steps back, maintaining eye contact as he toed off his shoes and socks, and quickly removed all of his clothes. Tess took the time to admire his body, strong and lean, his dark skin dusted by silky black hair across his pecs. If she was beautiful, he was…decadent, delicious, the cause of every angel's fall from grace.

"I need you." Adam stepped forward again, kneeling down to remove her sandals, reaching up to lower her panties down her legs, before standing and pressing his body against the length of her own. Tess reached out, a tentative touch to his cheek, needing the physical connection with him right now. "Do you know why?"

She shook her head.

"It's because when I look at you, none of this matters anymore. All the pressures at work, the mole, my family… None of it matters because I see you and I can breathe again."

Adam reached out to her, drawing her down to the lounge cushions, settling over her with his body, his face blocking out the sea of stars shining just over his shoulder.

"I asked you here because I need you to make it disappear. You're the only thing I want to see for a while and then I can do what I have to do." He reached down, his fingers toying with a curl, wrapping it around his finger. "Does that make sense?"

Tess understood all of it. When you were the one who always needed to be on, to have all of the answers you needed a refuge. They had become that to each other. Somehow in all this insanity and secrets and half-truths, they had become a safe place.

She sat up, pressing her lips to his, filling every soft glide of her tongue with what she was feeling but would not say. Could not say with the secrets she held between them.

"Just look at me. I'll make it all disappear. It will just be the two of us. We'll forget it all together."

Adam's eyes were hot and needy as he stared down at her, his erection lying hot and heavy against her abdomen. She was wide open, as vulnerable as she had ever been and pouring everything into this moment with him.

"Just keep looking at me."

Tess reached down between them, closing her hand around him, squeezing and stroking until he writhed under her touch. His breathing was ragged: rough, needy and raw.

"More. Please. More." He groaned, writhing under each stroke of his erection. His head dipped down, fingers clenching on cushions at the sides of her body, knuckles white and body shaking with his desire. He was gorgeous, skin smooth and damp with sweat, heavy on top of her. "Jesus, Tess. More."

Adam suddenly gathered her close to him, flipping them both over so that she now hovered over him. Tess threw her head back, letting the starshine rain down over her, coating them both with its power. When she looked down at Adam he was smiling, tracing up and down her sides with the back of his hands.

"You're a witch, Tess Lynch. You cast your spell and I've never gotten away from it."

"You're not the only one under a spell, Adam Redhawk. What did you do to me?"

"If you figure it out, let me know. I'll keep doing it."

He leaned up and kissed her, deeply and thoroughly, ramping up the tension between them with the twist and tangle of tongues. Adam released her mouth, lifting slightly to trail his lips down her neck, across her collarbone, and into the valley between her breasts. Tess braced herself over him, hands on each side of his shoulders as he took his time with each breast, suckling and licking at each hard nipple until she squirmed against him.

Tess straddled him wider, her slick center rubbing along the hard, hot length of him. It reminded her of evenings in the back seat of cars with boys, not willing to go all the way but enjoying the buildup and anticipation of how good two bodies could feel together. This was better. She knew how good it was going to be with Adam.

"Adam, I need *you*. Now."

She reached down between them, taking him in hand and dragging the head of his penis against the swollen folds of her sex. It felt so good, the tip sliding inside her, then the rest of him following inch by inch. She slid down his length, gasping with the fullness of him. He was so hard, so thick. Tess stroked her hands over his chest, enjoying his masculinity. The glide was so sweet, so easy as she rode him at a gentle pace, drawing out the pleasure as long as she could.

Adam fell back onto the cushions, his body arching, meeting every one of her downward slides with an answering upward thrust of his own. He pulled her down to him, kissing her deeply as they rode each wave together, their bodies undulating in a syncopation that dragged them higher and higher with each hot, slick, hungry ride.

"Tess, wait." Adam froze, his fingers digging into her hips, holding her in place. His face was strained, teeth grinding against each other. "I have to go get a condom."

"But you feel so good, Adam." She would kill Mia if her sister were to do what she was contemplating but here she was. "I'm on the pill. Nothing on my last blood test a couple of months ago. I've never gone without a condom and I'm not sleeping with anyone else."

He stared at her, the wheels spinning as he weighed the decision between them. When he spoke, it was direct, clear. "I tested negative for anything three months ago. I've not had anyone since then but you, and I'm not sleeping with anyone else."

She nodded, heart pounding with the weight of this decision. But she wouldn't go back. She didn't want to go back.

She was not safe with this man. She wanted to protect him, to comfort him, to be with him. He'd worked his way inside her heart and she'd done nothing to stop him. It was as if she was finally acknowledging why she was here now, why she'd agreed to this fling in the first place. It hadn't been just sex. It hadn't just been an itch to scratch.

Adam is it for me. He could be the one for me.

She traced the contours of his face, his cheekbones, his eyelids, his lips, and then ran her fingers back up to lightly caress the dark shadows underneath his eyes.

Adam reached up, grabbed her hand and pressed a kiss onto the palm. The sweetness of the gesture, combined with the fullness of his body deep inside her made her breath catch, her heart actually skip a couple of beats.

"I need you, Tess. I want you so much." His gaze caught her own in a stare of unflinching unapologetic need and desire. "I've wanted you since the beginning."

"Adam."

"I want you, baby. Come on, you know I can make it good for you."

Adam pulled her down again and kissed her, his tongue thrusting inside with a brutal, possessive hunger that overcame all of her senses. This was possession, ownership, laying claim. The point of no return. But she claimed him back, so glad to know that she wasn't alone in this. They needed to know that they weren't alone in this; they had each other.

Their bodies moved together, beginning a slow rise and fall, an easy rhythm that would get them both there eventually. No rush. Nowhere to be except here with each other.

She sat up, bracing herself on each side of his shoulders, eyes locked on each other as they gave and took from each other. Tess was so wet, her body gripping him on each stroke. The loss was acute every time he pulled out and built the hunger again with every thrust back in.

I want you.

I need you.

I love you.

Their bodies said everything that neither of them was willing to say tonight. It was enough that they were honest with each other about what this was, what it had become. It would be impossible for them to go backward.

Adam knew it. She knew it. But they'd jumped off that cliff together and would figure it out later. It might be something. It might be nothing. It might be forever. But none of that would be settled tonight.

Her orgasm was on her before she realized it. Sudden and powerful, it wrenched a long, deep moan from Tess that she shouted into the open air, hearing its faint echo as it bounced along the ravine below. Adam groaned beneath her, his fingers grasping her hips as he thrust upward, once and twice and then three times. He came then, deep inside her as she collapsed against him.

Their bodies were slick against each other, sticky with their efforts, boneless and heavy as they sank deeper into the cushions of the lounger. Tess couldn't move, didn't want to move as she came down from her high, happy to be where she was and with the man who made her feel safe and wanted. Adam clung to her, large arms wrapped around her body, the aftershocks of their pleasure causing him to shiver against her.

Tess shifted a little, moving her head so that she could look at him. He met her eyes, his sleepy but satisfied.

"Are you cold? Do you want to go inside?"

She shook her head. "Let's stay here a while. Under the stars." And then she remembered what he'd said to her that night at the Lick Observatory. He'd been talking about his lost family but for her this sky would hover over only two people: Mia and the man in her arms. "I just want to lie under the same stars that shine down on the people I love."

Fourteen

She found him.

She yelled in triumph, so glad to be in her home office and not the spaces at Redhawk/Ling. Her shout would have had the security guards running to see what the hell was going on.

Tess fumbled with the keyboard, her fingers trembling with excitement as she pressed the keys to print the information displayed on her screen. She didn't need to print it, everything she'd been searching for was right there on the screen but she was so panicked that it would all disappear that she needed to get it in her hands. On paper. Not just pixels on a screen.

She picked up the phone, hitting speed dial for a number she knew by heart anyway. The line rang and rang, the ringtone shrill in her ear, but there was no answer and the system eventually clicked over to Adam's voicemail.

She could have pressed the code to skip his message but she loved hearing his voice, a little awkward but very, very sexy in its directness.

This is Adam Redhawk, CEO of Redhawk/Ling. Leave a message. I'm not great at checking my message so if this is urgent, call my office and leave a message with Estelle. She always knows how to reach me.

She'd already called and left a message with Estelle and sent him a text with no reply so she'd have to wait to deliver the news that she'd found the mole and who he was working for. It was information that Adam would need to protect Redhawk/Ling and it would also be something she could use for her own purpose. She would see him tonight—they had a date to attend one of those fancy-schmancy fundraiser events at the Nestledown Retreat and she could tell him the news then if he didn't call back sooner.

She grabbed the paper from the printer, scanning the words and data, marking the most important parts with a highlighter. The mole had all of the skill sets necessary to hack into any system and undermine the launch of the app so finding him at this critical point was momentous. It had taken her until the eleventh hour, but it was still momentous.

And he was also someone who could help her. Adam and Justin were reluctant to discuss the act of pressing charges against the person who was trying to sabotage their company. Making those kinds of headlines so close to the launch would pull the focus off their business and place it all on the company. And exposing the fact that you had been susceptible to a hack was never a good look for a tech company.

But the guy would absolutely lose his job and an unemployed man would be a desperate man and a desperate man would be vulnerable to job offers that highlighted his particular skill. Tess needed a hacker to get the final information on Franklin Thornton to expose him as the thief and destroyer he really was. And now she had one.

Pushing back her chair, Tess strode across her office and pulled out the box where she kept everything she knew about Franklin Thornton and her father. Folders and files, papers yellowed with age, stained with late-night coffee, and likely some tears. Some shed in grief and many more shed in anger. Tess let out a huff of air as she flipped through the stacks and stacks of papers— some of which she'd memorized—as she searched for that fury, the blinding rage that usually asserted itself when she indulged in these walks down memory lane.

It was all here on the table: years of instances when Franklin had taken advantage of people a lot like her father. Franklin didn't just play games with men and women of his same stature and wealth and power; he played with those who were less than him, taking their dreams from them when he wanted what they had. And he never cared about what happened to them. He never gave them another thought when he'd taken from them everything they had of value.

Franklin hadn't cared when he'd destroyed her dad. And he hadn't even cared enough to see Michael Roberts's daughters when they'd gone to him to beg for help. Both she and Mia had been turned away, hadn't even got-ten past the administrative assistant.

So why was she hesitating now when she almost had him in the crosshairs?

Tess knew why. Adam Redhawk.

She pulled out the chair nearest the table and slumped

down into it. She was tired, exhausted and queasy and wanting desperately to go back to bed. Tess touched her forehead, wondering if the infection from three weeks ago hadn't fully cleared up but she had felt fine after a few days of rest and all of the antibiotics. In truth this was probably related to the long days and even longer nights she'd been spending with Adam since the night of the dinner with this family.

That night had transformed everything between them, turned the entirety of their arrangement completely upside down, and she'd never been so happy and so scared in her whole life.

That wasn't true. She'd been terrified, bone-deep cold with fear, when she'd suddenly had to face raising Mia all by herself.

But this fear was something different; this was risking it all. To do this with Adam, to give in to what she felt for Adam would mean giving up this vendetta against Franklin. Not because she was worried that Adam would be implicated in any of it but because it would hurt him.

There was no love lost between Adam and his adoptive father but that didn't matter when it came to Adam and his huge heart. He took responsibility for the people in his life, carried so much of their burden as his own and this would be a blow she couldn't bear to see him take.

Adam's strength, his need to take care of everyone, was what made him survive the childhood in Franklin Thornton's house. He had needed to get through it so that he could find his family someday. He had needed to succeed at school and in his company so that he could take care of his employees. He'd paid for her to do anything necessary to find his siblings because he carried the guilt of having let them down.

If she exposed Franklin, she would hurt this man.

A man she wanted to protect because of what he did for everyone else.

A man she was falling for.

In frustration she grabbed the files on the table and shoved them back into the box. She couldn't believe that she was seriously contemplating giving up on her father for the son of the man who destroyed him. But Adam was a decent, good man in spite of what had happened to him. He was sexy and funny and smart and he needed her. He wanted her.

And no one had ever made her feel like she was enough.

That just having her in their life would be enough.

Tess squirmed in her chair, her stomach clenching with nausea that made her gasp with the intensity of the feeling. She checked her watch and realized that it was midafternoon and it had been many hours since she'd eaten a bagel along with her coffee.

Heading to the kitchen, she took a mental inventory of the contents of her fridge: leftover Chinese, cold pizza, yogurt, eggs. The eggs made her smile, thinking of the omelet Adam had made her when she was sick. It had been surprisingly decent; nothing that was going to get him on the Food Network but it was good, filling when she'd needed it.

She opened the fridge and grabbed the carton of eggs, butter and cheese and placed them on the island counter. Tess shifted to the coffee maker, popping in a cup and turning it on to perk while she threw some bread in the toaster. Soon the smells of melting butter and coffee filled the air as she worked at the cooktop and her mouth watered at the thought of breakfast for supper. It was one of her favorite things to cook, remembering many meals with Mia where bacon and eggs filled their bellies.

Her mouth watered again and her stomach rolled with another wave of nausea. Tess leaned heavily on the counter, breathing in deeply through her nose and pressing a trembling palm against her stomach. A cold sweat broke out between her shoulder blades, streaking down her back and her arms and along her scalp.

Tess turned off the burner and bolted to the bathroom, flinging up the toilet seat as she fell to her knees in front of it and emptied everything out of her stomach. She heaved, every muscle straining as she wretched, her nails digging into the palms of her hands. Finally, minutes that felt like an hour later, she slumped back against the side of the tub, legs extended on the tile floor. The chill of the porcelain seeped through her leggings and made her shiver.

It had to be the sickness back again but even during the worst of it she hadn't felt this bad, hadn't thrown up like she drank too much of the grain alcohol fruit punch at a fraternity party.

Tess stood and moved towards the sink, splashing cold water on her face. She felt better but not completely settled so she dried off and opened up the medicine cabinet, reaching for the Tums when the box of tampons caught her eye. She paused, shaking her head at the random thought that skittered across her brain and reached for her phone. It was crazy. Impossible.

Tess tapped the app that tracked her cycle and the dates on the display made the ball of anxiety in her gut expand to rivers of ice running under her skin.

She closed the app, slid her finger across the screen and searched for Mia's number. She was visiting for a long weekend, out running errands, and Tess might be able catch her in time.

She pressed the number for her sister and when she answered, asked for what she needed and settled in to wait.

The quickness of Mia's footsteps on the floorboards gave away that she was running at a clip.

Tess couldn't help herself. "Mia, I've told you a million times not to run in the house."

Her sister's face was ruddy with excitement and concern as she skidded to a stop in the doorway of the bathroom. "Tess, if you call me and tell me to pick up a pregnancy test or two on my way home and you expect me not to run? You are out of your mind."

"Fine. Fine." Tess waved off her arguing and held her hand out for the test. "Just give it to me, please."

Mia paused a moment, eyes locked on hers, and Tess had to look away to avoid the pain and confusion swimming in them. She didn't see disappointment there, not yet; she wasn't sure she could handle that right now.

The drug store bag rustled, the box was placed in her hand, and the door shut behind Mia with a gentle click. With shaking hands, Tess opened the package and followed the directions. When she was done, she opened the door and went to find Mia, taking the stick with her.

Her sister was on the couch, huddled with her knees pulled up to her chest. She glanced down at the stick, eyebrows raised in question.

"I have to wait a couple of minutes," Tess replied, slipping down on the sofa and easing down to lean on Mia's shoulder. "I don't want to wait alone."

The moments slid into each other, feeling both forever long and speeding by at the same time. Tess refused to look at the stick, refused to stare it down in a feeble attempt to get it to reveal its secret sooner rather than right on time. Mia fidgeted beside her, her distress advertised with every crossing of her legs and deeply troubled sigh.

"Do you want a baby?" Mia asked, her fingers plowing through Tess's curls.

What a question. What a question she didn't have an answer for.

"I've never thought about a baby." She spoke with conviction but that was a lie. She'd thought about children but only in the context of something she'd never have—along with a marriage. She'd raised Mia and she had an all-consuming purpose to see her father done right, and none of that left room for fantasies about commitments and children she was never going to have. "This wasn't planned. Antibiotics and unprotected sex." She cut a stern glance at her sister. "I knew better. I should have done better."

The next question came in a small voice, a tentative inquiry mumbled into her shoulder. "Would you keep it?"

"Yes." She answered before she thought about it but the answer felt right, was right. It would be a complete rocking of her world and she doubted that she would be very good at it but the answer would be yes. "I didn't screw up too badly with you. I think I could do it."

"What would Adam do? Does he want a family?"

Now *that* was the question. And she had no idea of the answer. He was a natural family man, a loving and caring brother, even though he thought he was a failure.

And he had quickly become the one person she would take a chance with, the person she trusted to take a risk.

She glanced at her watch and it was past the time for the stick to tell her future, like the psychic woman at the carnival. But instead of getting a bunch of cryptic premonitions about meeting a dark-haired man, this wouldn't be hocus-pocus. It would be the definitive end result, the end game, the final score. No wiggle room. No multiple interpretations.

And if the result of the test told her that she was carrying Adam's child could she still use the information sitting in her office to take down his adoptive father?

Adam would be thrilled, vindicated, and relieved to be told about the mole. But she had no idea if he'd be as thrilled to be a father. For a woman who had spent so much of her life avoiding unnecessary complications, she'd created a Rubik's Cube mess of her life. Making up for lost time, she supposed.

Tess reached out, pausing to squeeze the shakes out of her fingers, finally grasping the long white plastic stick and looking at the answer.

"Well," she said, swallowing hard and reaching out to take Mia's hand. "Isn't that something?"

Fifteen

"I was right."

Adam leaned in close to whisper into Tess's ear, brushing a soft kiss against the sweetest spot on the back of her neck as they walked into the gala to benefit the children's hospital. Held at the exquisite Nestledown Retreat, it was one of his favorite venues if he was forced to attend a five-thousand-dollar per plate dinner and endure hours of small talk with people who'd never made him feel like he belonged. Surrounded by magnificent redwoods and twinkle lights, it felt like they were walking across the starlit sky.

But nothing compared to how stunning Tess looked tonight.

"*Of course* you were right. Exactly what were you right about *this* time?" She stopped and turned into his arms, the brush of her fingers against his skin a brand of the sweetest fire. Damn, this woman.

But her touch wasn't just flirtatious. She was nervous about something and looking to bolt. He contemplated trying to cajole it out of her but Tess was the keeper of secrets and she'd let him know what was going on when she was ready and not a minute sooner. He was sure it had something to do with the call he'd missed and the message she'd left with Estelle. When he'd tried to call her back, his calls had gone to voicemail. Getting here tonight had been a whirlwind to the extent that he'd had to send a car for her and meet her at the event. But now she was here and he was looking forward to the time when they could talk about whatever was on her mind. He tightened his grip on her and pulled her closer, dipping his head to make eye contact.

"You *are* the most beautiful one here tonight."

And she was. He'd never be able to adequately describe her dress—computer chips and algorithms were his preferred language—but the deep purple of the fabric dipped low in the front and back and exposed mouth-wateringly tempting expanses of her pale skin. Adam couldn't wait to take it off her later. Slowly, very slowly.

"Adam, you need to stop being so sweet," she murmured, the shadows of the evening doing nothing to hide her blush. "I'll get spoiled."

"I think you deserve to be spoiled. Don't you?"

That spooked her. Her eyes went wide and the nervous fidgeting was back. Hell, this whole situation had him waiting for the other shoe to drop so he didn't stop her when she moved out of his arms. They'd moved from virtual strangers to lovers in the span of a few weeks and neither of them had been looking for anything close to a relationship. But they sure as hell were in the middle of one now and he suspected the one time he took this chance was going to break him.

He'd never done anything halfway in his life and he wasn't going to start now.

Adam reached out, laced their fingers together and led her down one of the candlelit paths, deeper into the shelter of the redwoods and away from the burbling voices of rich people pretending to like each other. The time had come for honesty, for showing his cards and betting it all on Tess. On them.

They reached an alcove in the trees and he turned, cupping her face in his hands and kissing her. Slow and deep, pleading and demanding, ending on a whimper that erupted from somewhere deep inside of Tess. Adam leaned back, maintaining their physical contact, his heart kicking in his chest when she reached out and pulled him back in for a kiss. It was hotter, wetter, and he wondered if there was a back exit to this place. Forget talking, they communicated better when it was just skin on skin.

"Tess, come on." Adam wasn't clear what he was asking her. To leave this place right now or to finally let him in and share whatever secret she was carrying around and guarding like the *Mona Lisa*. She hesitated, biting her kiss-swollen lips in an effort to keep her own confidence. "Baby, tell me what's going on. You've got me tied in knots. I can't stop thinking about you. I haven't felt this crazy over a woman since I was a kid and I tell you I don't like it one bit. Throw me a bone. At least tell me I'm not the only fool here."

"Adam, I didn't want this." Tess pressed her fingers to her mouth in a gesture meant to erase what she'd just said. He waited, giving her time. "I know you didn't want this."

"I wasn't looking for it."

She nodded. "No. Neither was I."

"But we're in the middle of it now, aren't we?"

"Yes. We are. And I can't stop thinking about you, either."

Yes. Yes. Adam let out a long breath, feeling the relief all the way down to his marrow. He had no idea where this was going, what they were starting, but it felt good. So damn good. He kissed her again, pouring out all of the feelings he had inside of him but couldn't say right now. One step at a time. One step toward something spectacular with Tess.

His Tess. Somewhere along the way she'd become his.

"Adam." Tess broke off the kiss, and there was something else he couldn't decipher in her eyes. Another secret. She took a deep breath, her hand hovering between them with her indecision. And then she reached out and grabbed his hand and tugged it down until it rested against her belly. "Another something neither of us was looking for."

Adam's brain wasn't catching up. Numbers. Equations. Algorithms. That stuff came so easy to him but this was indecipherable. Like an equation where he didn't know if he was solving for X or Y. He struggled, scouring her face for a clue. Any hint at what he was supposed to understand.

And then it clicked into place and one plus one equaled…three.

"A baby?" he whispered, his fingers flexing against the slippery fabric of her dress.

"I know it's not what you wanted," Tess said, her tone apologetic, her expression wary but determined. Her hand splayed across her abdomen in a gesture that could only be read as protective.

No, this wasn't what he wanted. Family was a problem for him. He didn't have any luck with family; he had no idea how to be a father. But it wasn't fear that had settled in his belly. No, he wasn't afraid. He was confused and scared…and happy. And that made no sense at all but it was the truth.

"I didn't know that I wanted it," he answered, realizing that he was speaking in damn riddles when he needed to be clear. "Until now."

"Really? Are you sure?" Tess asked, her green-gold eyes warming with cautious optimism.

Was he? Wasn't the answer in the fact that he'd hired her to find Roan and Sarina in the first place? That he'd finally acted on the undeniable compulsion he'd had to find his brother and sister? That he'd lain awake at nights tossing and turning with frustration and an emptiness that he could not name? It was a family-shaped hole in his soul and he was ready to fill it.

"Yes. I'm sure." Adam linked their fingers together over her belly and kissed her, soft and full of promise. Laughter bubbled up between them and the heat rising from the tangle of lips and tongues transformed into warm, lazy presses of lips to cheeks, eyelids and mouths. "I'm going to be a father." He pulled back, gazing down on her, a million questions swirling in his mind. "How? When? How do you feel? What did the doctor say?"

"I'm guessing that it was the night on your deck. My birth control was no match for the antibiotics I had to take when I was sick," she said, her voice full of her own speculation. "We'll go next week and you can ask all of the questions, I promise." Tess answered, her smile dimming as her hands skimmed up the lapels of his jacket, her fingertips lightly brushing against his cheek, tangling in the hair at the nape of his neck. The wariness was back in her eyes, matching the deeper shadows along the edge of the alcove where they stood. "Right now I need to tell you some things. I need to tell you the truth."

Unease pooled low in his belly, subduing the joy of the moment and he knew that this was going to be a night of secrets revealed. But he was determined that they would survive whatever was coming. He had a future with Tess and a baby to protect, and he would save them and their future—he'd failed with his own brother and sister but he wouldn't let history repeat itself. Not with this new chance at a full life of his own.

"What is it, Tess? I have to know everything if I'm going to protect you. Protect us."

"Adam, you have to understand that I didn't know you before." Tess lightly pressed a finger against his lips when he tried to speak again. "Before I knew what kind of man you are. Before I knew that you're not Franklin Thornton's son in any way."

"He's my son. Don't you forget it." As if Tess had summoned him by just speaking his name, Franklin emerged out of the darker spaces on the path, his grin flashing white and feral in the dim lighting. "And you, Tess Roberts, are your father's daughter."

Sixteen

She flinched at the sound of her own name.

For so many years she'd been careful to only use and respond to the name she'd adopted after her father had died. A name borrowed from her grandmother, so not entirely a lie. Or so Tess had told herself.

But the cloud of confusion and suspicion on Adam's face shook her confidence in the deceit she'd been living for the past few years. But in spite of his doubt, Adam was the man he'd proven himself to be over and over. He faced his father, his body shielding her from the threat that now polluted the air. The gesture turned her veins to ice because when he found out the truth, he'd realize that she was the poison.

"Franklin, what do you want?"

"I don't want anything from you, son. I actually have something for you." Franklin smiled and the slight sundown chill in the air turned icy on Tess's skin. She shivered, and when Adam pulled her closer, her heart cracked a little.

"I really don't give a shit." Adam turned to her, his hand sliding against her own, giving her a squeeze and an encouraging smile. "Come on, baby. Let's go home."

"Adam." Tess tried to pull out some semblance of a smile but she didn't have it in her. The happiness of the last few moments still lingered and she used it to give her the strength to do what she needed to do. "My name *is* Tess Roberts...or it was. I did have it officially changed a few years ago."

"I'm really confused right now." Adam shook his head but he didn't let go of her hand and she took that as a good sign. A hopeful sign.

"After my father died, I changed my name. Our name... Mia did it too. We needed a change from...well, we just needed a change. To start over."

"I get that. You had been through so much," Adam tried to soothe her but it made her feel only worse, like the liar she'd been for the past few months. It was time to be honest with Adam and herself.

"My dad was Michael Roberts and he died of an alcohol-induced broken heart after your father took from him the only thing he ever really loved. I only got through it because I had to raise Mia and I was fueled by hate and revenge and the single-minded goal to destroy the man who'd taken my father from me."

"Franklin Thornton."

"Yes. Franklin. The man who raised you."

"And why didn't you tell me sooner?" Adam asked but she could already see that he knew the answer. He just wanted to hear it from her.

"Because she planned to destroy me through you, son. Don't you get it?" Franklin was enjoying this moment; his arms were crossed over his chest and the closest thing he had to a smile twisted his expression into something ugly. In that moment Tess saw her father's face; he'd often worn the same look of hatred but he'd ultimately aimed more of it at himself than at Franklin Thornton. "It was never about you. She was using you."

She focused her attention back on Adam. He was the only one who mattered right now. She'd already wasted too much time on Franklin and her dad.

"He's right, Adam. I was using you." Adam let go of her and she scrambled not to panic. This couldn't be the end. It couldn't. "I *was* using you. Until I fell in love with you."

"Love? You just told me that you were using me to destroy Franklin and you expect me to believe that any of this was about love?"

Tess jumped, the razor-sharp edge of Adam's voice making the first deep cut. But she kept talking because this was the most important thing she was ever going to say in her life.

"Yeah, it ended up being all about love. I fell in love with you and I'd given up on what had brought me to you. Given up on getting back at anyone. Given up the hate and the revenge and living in the past. I fell in love with you, Adam. You replaced *all of that* for me." Tess wiped her eyes, not even realizing until that moment that she was crying. "And I was going to tell you. I was just starting to tell you when…"

"When Franklin beat you to it." Adam was stoic, hard and chiseled under the twinkle lights. "How many chances did you have to tell me the truth? All the time we worked side by side in my office? Any of the times you had access to every goddam thing about me? The times you slept in my bed? You had a million chances Tess and *you* let me learn this from *him*."

Adam's voice cracked on the last word and his expression crumbled. The cold lump that had settled into her chest shattered into a million pieces, the sharp edges making her bleed on the inside. And just as quickly his face was steeled into his usual mask of control. All of the kindness she'd come to love was gone. And she'd seen this face on Adam before; it was the face of the six-year-old boy in his adoption folder.

She'd never forgive herself for being the reason for that expression on his face. To be one more name on the list of people who had betrayed the trust he guarded so fiercely.

"Adam, *you have* to believe me." She was begging. She'd do anything to make this right.

And she had the information to turn the tables on this entire situation at her disposal. She had the name of the mole and the person who was backing the traitor but she couldn't reveal that in front of Franklin. It might be the only chance Adam had to protect Redhawk/Ling and she couldn't take away his right to determine when and where he was going to use the information. She couldn't reveal that in front of Franklin.

That would be the ultimate betrayal.

So she just stared at him, begging him with her eyes to not turn away from her now.

But all the affection and connection they'd had was gone and all that was left was the cold, dark emptiness of the chasm she had created.

"I don't have to do anything for you right now." Adam

stared at her for a few seconds and then he turned to walk away.

And then he was gone, becoming one of the shadows surrounding the redwoods, and she was left alone with Franklin. The last two standing; it made sense that they were here together. They'd been bound by toxic tethers for more than a decade.

Franklin moved into her tear-blurred field of vision, triumph in his eyes.

"The next time you want take somebody down, Ms. Roberts, strike first."

Seventeen

"**Y**ou're pregnant. You need to take better care of yourself," Mia said.

Tess paused in the task of dismantling all of the material she'd been obsessively working on for as long as she could remember. Photographs, notes, printouts—everything was going in the trash.

"I just got up early. I always get up early." It was a lie. After arriving home from the gala, she'd taken off her beautiful dress and slid into the cocoon of her bed. She'd hoped for some comfort in the dark but sleep had been impossible and after hours of tossing and turning she'd given up the pipe dream of sliding into the oblivion of unconsciousness and come downstairs to her office. Tess glanced at Mia and then at the clock. "You're not usually up this early. Why are you here?"

"Oh, I don't know. My big sister is knocked up by the

son of the man she's been hell-bent on destroying for the past ten years and she's also fallen in love with the guy but he doesn't love her back and now her heart is broken."

"I never said anything about being in love or broken hearts."

"I'm not an idiot. I know what's been going on here even if you don't want to admit it to yourself." Mia snatched the papers from her hand, read them and tossed them into the shredder. "Are you impersonating Marie Kondo?"

"Mia, you are *not* bringing me joy right now."

"Well, then what will bring you joy? Huh? What are you going to do?"

A night of restless sleep was catching up with Tess and she slid into her chair, tossing the papers in her hand across the desk. Her office was a disaster—it matched the hellmouth her life had become.

"I thought that was obvious. I'm ending this vendetta. Absolutely nothing is going to happen. I'm busted. Franklin and Adam have me on their personal most wanted list."

"But you're pregnant."

Tess placed a hand on her abdomen, still amazed. "I am."

"And you love him."

"I really do." And God help her, she did. "Not that it matters now. I betrayed Adam. I lied to him and as far as he's concerned, I'm in the same exact category as Franklin now. I really fucked it up."

Mia was shaking her head like Tess was the dumbest human on the planet. "Then unfuck it." She leaned forward, chin resting on her hand as she scrutinized her sister and the mess surrounding her. "Do the job he hired you to do. Then work on the rest."

"I'm trying."

"Really? To me it looks like your shredding and wallowing."

"I've tried to call Adam. He sends me straight to voicemail and even Estelle is ignoring me. A couple of guys from Redhawk/Ling delivered the personal items I had in my office here to the house." She was frustrated and her raised voice echoed off the walls of the room. "I'm trying to do my fucking job."

"No. You're trying to get the guy back. That's not the job. And the Tess I know would never let voicemail and a cold shoulder keep her from doing the job."

"Do the job…" Tess considered what Mia was saying. She had all of the information, the stuff Adam had paid her to find out about the person who was threatening Redhawk/Ling. And that person was still out there. She needed to put aside her broken heart and do the work she was hired to do. That meant getting her client the information he needed to save his company. She stood, tucking the relevant file in her bag. "I'm going to do my job."

Mia clapped. "And get the guy back?"

Tess rolled her eyes. "One thing at a time, Mia. One thing at a time."

She wasn't here to get the guy back.

That's what she kept telling herself. It wasn't that she didn't want to get Adam back, to erase all the lies that she'd let keep them apart and get back to the place where he looked at her like she was the beginning and the end of his world. What she wouldn't give to once again hear the awe in his voice and the tenderness in his touch when he realized he was going to be a father. Her favorite pair of heels to whoever got her the chance to taste his kiss, to have his hands on her again.

But one look at his face and she knew that wasn't how it was going to go down today.

She'd taken advantage of the night guards and breezed past them with a wave and a determined stride to the elevators. Once she'd arrived on his floor, Tess marched past his secretary, ignoring the gobsmacked expression on Estelle's face and giving her no chance to call security or warn Adam. The only advantage she had was surprise and she used it to get into his office and shut the door behind her. The stupid glass walls ensured that everyone could see the show but Tess was beyond caring and she knew she was on borrowed time.

"Tess, what are you doing here?" Adam rose from his chair, his posture rigid, hands fisted at his sides. Dark shadows under his eyes testified that he hadn't slept last night and that gave her courage.

"You hired me to do a job and I finish what I start."

He was already shaking his head. "No. I'm pretty sure I fired you last night when I learned that you've been lying to me for months. We have nothing to say to each other."

That pissed her off. "Considering that we're going to have a baby together, I'd say we have a hell of lot to talk about in the future but that isn't what I'm here about." Tess moved toward him, ignoring the couch where not so long ago Adam had made love to her. She'd help save his company and then she'd save their future. "You hired me to find the mole and I did it."

That got his attention. He moved from behind the shield of his desk and met her in the middle. He kept her at more than arm's length but he was listening and that was good. "You did? When?"

"It all came together right before the fundraiser but I didn't want to tell you in front of Franklin," she answered, reaching into her bag to pull out the file with everything she'd found. Tess shifted toward the table, spreading out the papers, notes and screenshots. "The guy who tried to do all of the damage is a software engineer named Mitchell Weiss. He was an easy mark with school debt and a sick mom. Couldn't have been a more textbook case as far as finding your weak link. He needed the money, end of story."

"Well, it's certainly the end of his story here at Red-hawk/Ling. He's gone," Adam said, his voice low and tense as he moved closer, taking a good look at her file. She tried not to notice how careful he was not to touch her. Tess wasn't going to debate whether Adam should give this guy another chance with him, that wasn't the most important fact on the table.

"The part you don't know is who was paying him." Tess pulled out a series of unencrypted emails, pointing to the highlighted email address. "I think you'll recognize the name. It's Franklin."

Adam stilled, his focus zeroed in on the paper and Tess waited for the explosion. He had every right to lose his shit and if she knew him at all he'd be pissed at himself for not realizing who it was from the beginning.

But the detonation didn't happen. Adam was silent as he bowed his head, hands braced against the surface of the table, everything about his posture signaling defeat instead of defiance. She dipped her head, trying to catch his eye and get some clue as to what was going on in his head.

"Adam?"

"Am I going to have to fight him for everything for the rest of my goddam life?" When he lifted his head, his dark eyes were blazing with pain and anger and a million unanswered questions. "I don't understand his determination to destroy everything that is mine. Franklin never wanted me so I don't know why he fights so fucking hard to keep me under his control."

"He wants to keep you under his thumb, there's a difference. A huge difference," she said, reaching out to touch his shoulder before she could stop herself. His body was rigid, hot with his anger, but he leaned into her touch and she let the sensation sink in, saving it for later when he remembered that she'd been his enemy as much as Franklin and never wanted to see her again. "And he only fights so hard because he knows that you don't need him. That you are already more of a success than he can ever be. You're already so much more of a man than he will ever be. A really good man."

Adam's sharp intake of breath racked his frame and Tess moved in closer, their chests brushing, warm breaths mingling, bodies giving in to the pull of gravity and emotions strung tight between them. His dark gaze dropped down to her mouth and she held her breath, praying that he gave in to what was still between them. One kiss and she'd know that she had a chance.

Adam raised his hand, fingertips poised to caress her cheek, to draw her in closer. Tess waited, every part of her screaming for him to shatter this wall between them that she'd built with every lie she'd told to him over the last few months. But he just dropped his hand, eyes losing any tender edge and voice as caustic as acid.

"Being a good man has gotten me nowhere, Tess.

What did you call that guy? An easy mark?" He laughed, bitterness stripping it of any joy. "I know what that feels like. It's like I have a target on my back." He motioned toward the door, turning his back on her with a harsh finality. "Thanks for the info. I've got a lot to do to save this launch and my entire company."

"Wait, I've got more," Tess stammered, seeing her window of opportunity closing. "I've got everything you need to end this once and for all. To get the target off your back." Her hand hovered over her bag for the briefest moment but she wasn't sure where the hesitation was coming from. She had what Adam needed to finally break free from his toxic situation with Franklin; what was stopping her? She finally reached in and pulled out the thumb drive and held it out to him. "This is everything I have on Franklin. Every dirty deal, every screw job. There isn't a rule, law or regulation that he didn't feel it was his mission to break. I've got enough to make an investigation by the SEC a foregone conclusion and the downfall of his empire a given."

Adam leveled a look of suspicion at her that would make a nun confess. "If it's so good why didn't you use it?"

This was the hard question that had plagued her for years and it wasn't until last night that she'd gotten her answer. "Because this vendetta was all I had. My dad died and I was an eighteen-year-old suddenly tasked with raising a younger sister and my hatred and obsession kept the terror away. I think that I thought I had to completely step into my dad's shoes to honor his memory—including his failures and his obsession." Tess scrubbed her fingers through her hair, trying to put into words the early morning epiphany that had almost brought her to her knees. "I grew up with a man who loved his desire for revenge and self-loathing more than he loved me. And it hurt me, so much that I couldn't see any other way to survive except to live his life and hope that it made everything worth it. I got so used to living that way that I was terrified to pull the trigger. If I took down Franklin, I would have had nothing. And I couldn't face it."

"So, if you give this to me—what do you have now?"

Oh, that answer was easy. "I have my business, and Mia and this baby." She laid her hand on her stomach and thought of how his hand had been there only a few hours ago. "And I have a life that I want to build with the man I love. It will be more than enough."

"Tess…"

"Adam, let me say this: I'm so sorry. I got close to you for all the wrong reasons and I didn't care if I was going to hurt you in the process of getting the revenge I thought I needed to be happy. But I got to know you and I started to care about the man who was stuck in the middle of this mess and I fell in love. I fell for the guy who plays drums incognito, and the guy who gives Estelle a gift card to the spa and the afternoon off just because she's had a rough week. I fell for the guy who moved heaven, earth and a crap ton of bureaucrats to find the brother and sister he'd lost. And I fell in love with the man who is trying so hard to make a family with them even though he never got a chance to see what one looks like. I fell in love with you, Adam Redhawk. I love you and I'm happy about the baby and I want a future together but more than anything, I want you to be happy and safe and free from Franklin ever having the power to hurt you again. And I want that for you even if you can never forgive me. That will always be more than enough for me."

"Tess, I don't…" Adam was shaking his head, the resolute sadness on his face worse than the anger she'd witnessed last night.

But she wasn't ready to hear that he didn't want her anymore so she moved quickly, pressing the USB into his hand and a kiss to his mouth. She turned on her heel and left his office before he could end it. The fight for them, for their future, would wait for another day.

Eighteen

"I didn't have enough caffeine for this."

Adam tried to ignore Justin pacing in front of his desk drinking both of their coffees. Answering Estelle's SOS, Justin had arrived just as Tess was leaving. Adam had laid out the truth of his fucked-up life: the baby, Tess's betrayal, the information about the mole, and the key to ending Franklin once and for all.

And she'd been right. It was all here, more than enough to take the man down. Tess had done her job and so much more.

"I was *here* all night. I think I need the caffeine more than you do," Adam murmured, hitting the print command for several selected documents. The machine behind him whirred to life and shot out a treasure trove of career-ending data.

"You act like you're the only one who didn't get any

sleep last night." Justin shook his head and took another gulp of coffee.

"Spare me the details of the girl you screwed all night and look at this." Adam grabbed the printouts and thrust them at Justin. "Tess has all the goods on Franklin. It goes back years and years, before I was even adopted."

His partner scanned the sheets, eyes getting wider with each one that he read. He whistled, long and loud. "Daddy Franklin has been very, very busy being a very, very bad boy." Justin looked at Adam. "So, what are you going to do with this? Go to the authorities?"

Adam was already putting on his jacket, gathering documents and shoving them into his briefcase. "No. Some of it is so old they wouldn't touch it and he's got too many people in high places in his pocket to guarantee that it would have the desired result."

"Okay, so what are you going to do with this? The last time I checked, Franklin was still gunning for us and we are two weeks away from release or ruin. We haven't even fired that Mitch asshole!"

"Justin, this is insurance. Leverage." Adam fished his cellphone out of his pocket and swiped the screen. "And we're not going to fire Mitch and tip off Franklin. I'm going to see Franklin now. You get security and IT ready to shut down everything associated with Mitch the minute I send word."

"Wait. Wait." Justin moved with the speed of a man fueled by two large coffees and plucked the phone out of his hand. "Franklin isn't going anywhere. What are you going to do about Tess?"

Adam didn't want to have this conversation. Not right now and preferably not ever. "She lied to me, Justin. Got close to me to get back at Franklin. There is nothing *to do* about Tess. We're done."

"What about the baby?"

"We'll work out arrangements for the baby but the white picket fence and happy family dream you're always talking about isn't going to happen." Adam grabbed his phone back and headed for the door.

"My dream is a week on a yacht with two or three supermodels in my bed and a high-stakes poker game on the offer. I didn't say anything about happy families and fences. *You* were the one dreaming about those things, man." Justin's words hit him in the gut, no they hit higher, right behind his ribcage. "And I heard what she said—"

"You heard? What? How?"

"I picked up Estelle's line and hit the intercom/listen code." Justin shrugged like it was something he did all the time and Adam made a mental note to have that function disabled on Estelle's phone as soon as possible. "So, I heard everything and all I know is that she's got a lot of guts and she must really love you to give up everything for you."

He scoffed, clearly not having heard the same conversation that Justin did. "She didn't give up anything. Franklin will get what he deserves and she'll get exactly what she wants."

Justin was shaking his head. "You are the dumbest genius I know, so I'm going to say this slow and in as few words as possible." Adam flipped him the bird but he ignored him and kept moving on. "Tess doesn't get *anything* she wants. She doesn't get her father the recognition for his invention. She doesn't get you, the man she loves. She doesn't get to move on and have a little happiness after the crap life she's been dealt." He held up a finger to pause the response hovering on Adam's lips. "Wait, I was wrong, she gets lots of things. She gets *you* being a stubborn asshole and refusing to acknowledge that you love her. She gets *you* making her pay over and over again for trying to survive and make a life of the crap her father put her through. And, this is the best part, she gets to raise *your kid* and hope to God that he or she isn't as stubborn as you are." He made an elaborate play out of counting on his fingers and ended the show with an empty hand, just like a magician. "So, in the end, she really does end up with a whole lot of nothing because she gave you everything—her information, her only chance at vindication and her heart. And I didn't hear her ask you for *anything*."

Justin wasn't wrong. He could be reckless at the poker table, terrible with women and he drove Adam crazy but he was a man who noticed the details. It didn't matter if it was a million numbers on a spreadsheet or a single puzzle piece out of place, nothing got past Justin. And he'd listened to every word that Tess had said, really *heard* her.

"She said she loves me."

"Clearly, she's crazy. I should get her help."

"I'm in love with her," Adam said, knowing that he sounded like an idiot. He didn't care.

"Again, you are the dumbest genius I know," Justin teased, making himself comfortable on the couch. "But you get there eventually."

"She's going to have my baby." Adam couldn't stop the grin from tugging at the corner of his mouth. "I'm going to be a father."

"Yeah, you are." Justin's wide grin was contagious. "And I'm going to be an uncle."

Adam slipped off his jacket and headed back to his desk. "Well, Uncle Justin, I have a plan to save Redhawk/Ling, get Franklin out of our lives forever and to get Tess what she never asked for. You in?"

Nineteen

"Mia, why are we here?"

Tess paused at the double doors leading to the largest conference room at Redhawk/Ling and squinted at the couple dozen people milling about the room. She recognized a number of them, all reporters from local and national news outlets. A small stage and podium were set up on one end of the room, framed by the view of the gorgeous campus through the floor-to-ceiling windows. Adam had the same view in his office and she'd often caught him staring out the window, his mind a million miles away.

She'd heard nothing from Adam since last week when he'd let her walk out of his office. Tess had scoured the news for any word on the mole but all the news that was fit to print was about the launch of the app. Full steam ahead. No complications. No espionage.

And no invitations to meet up and talk about the baby. About them.

She snagged the back of her sister's jeans and hissed into her ear, "I don't think we're in the right place."

Mia pulled out the printed email invite and took another look. "Nope. This is the place."

"This can't be right." Tess couldn't imagine why Justin would have asked them to come to the office and have all these people here at the same time.

When they'd received the email, Tess had presumed that Adam was using Justin as a go-between to discuss the baby, and while that was never going to fly in the long-term, she was willing to take the meeting to get the conversation started. Adam had been radio silent for almost a week and Tess had resolved to give him some space. While the clock was obviously ticking where the baby was concerned, they had time and she didn't want to push. She hoped that Adam would come around and they could have a life together but with each day that passed, it was harder and harder to believe that she would get what she dreamed about. And now, seeing this large gathering made her doubt if Adam even knew she'd been invited today.

"Tess, Justin said that we both needed to be here. He said it was important." Mia wriggled free from her grasp and sauntered into the room with the carefree nonchalance that Tess had possessed just a few short weeks ago. "And it's not like we have somewhere else to be."

That was the truth. Tess had wrapped up a couple of small cases and she'd referred another one to a colleague. Because of the payment for services rendered to Redhawk/Ling, she could afford to turn down a couple of jobs and nurse her broken heart. It was crazy how much she could miss a man who'd been a stranger a couple of months ago.

Tess moved to slide into a seat toward the back, nodding at several reporters she knew from prior jobs just as Estelle approached the small podium and asked everyone to take their seats. The room was at that point where the A/C wasn't keeping up with the mass of body heat and the flush across her skin added to the anxious itch that kept her on the edge of her seat. The rustle and noise of everyone settling into position masked the sound of Adam's entrance but her body went on high alert the second he crossed the threshold.

He was wearing her favorite suit, as midnight black as his hair and slim cut on his athletic build, with a crisp white shirt underneath. He moved like a large cat, smooth and graceful in his individuality, and the beautifully cut suit emphasized every muscle of his body. Adam was a beautiful man, sexy as hell, and several of the reporters murmured their admiration while she bit back the urge to tell them to back away from her man.

Because he wasn't her man. Not anymore.

The sight of Justin and then Franklin Thornton following Adam onto the stage ripped her out of her thoughts. It roused the crowd into a groundswell of murmurs and the flash of cameras highlighted the screen that descended from the ceiling to span the width of the area. Tess tried to get a read off their expressions and while Justin was sedately smug and Franklin was furious, Adam was a cool customer. He was poised and calm as he approached the microphone, his charismatic smile capturing everyone's full attention. She wished that he would notice her but he didn't even look in her direction and she wondered if he even knew she was there.

"Good afternoon, my name is Adam Redhawk and I

am the co-owner and CEO of Redhawk/Ling. On behalf of my partner and CFO, Justin Ling, and the President of Trident Investments, Mr. Franklin Thornton, I want to welcome you all to the announcement of an exciting collaboration between our two companies. Since Justin and I started Redhawk/Ling ten years ago, we have been committed to developing and creating innovative products that change the way we live for the better. Trident has been a leader in recognizing and financing projects that started in somebody's garage and those created in a state-of-the-art facility. Together we want to be part of a future that encourages and supports new, fresh and talented inventors to take the risks that create positive change that will impact generations to come. To that end, we are announcing the creation of a program that will recognize the best of the best in new ideas and give them the space, opportunity and the funding to make their dreams a reality. Ladies and gentlemen, I am proud to present to you the Michael Roberts Research Foundation."

Tess gaped in shock as Adam pressed a button on a remote control and a photograph of her father appeared on the large screen behind him. As his words penetrated the confusion and connected with her brain, a slideshow began that featured her father throughout his career, his inventions and finally a photo of their little family, smiling and leaning on each other. Tess didn't bother to wipe at the tears streaking her cheeks, not wanting to miss one of the images on the screen. Mia made a choking sound beside her and reached out to grab her hand, her sister's fingers cold against the suddenly overheated temperature of her own skin. And while Mia's grasp kept her grounded the expression in Adam's eyes as he met her gaze made her heart fly.

Adam paused a beat and then continued, never breaking eye contact with her. "Mr. Roberts was a tireless and brilliant scientist and engineer who was integral to the development of what is now Silicon Valley. Unfortunately, his life was cut short but this foundation will ensure that his enthusiasm, dedication, brilliance and innovative spirit will live on. To that end, Redhawk/Ling and Trident have endowed the foundation with matching grants of ten million dollars each with future opportunities for other companies to join us." Adam gestured toward Justin. "I'm going to hand the Q&A over to Justin Ling."

Tess watched Adam step down from the stage and stride across the room directly to where she sat. His expression was intense, his stride powerful; everything about him telegraphed that he was coming for her. She rose from her seat, poised to meet him eye to eye. If they had any chance to work, it was how it had to be.

He stopped in front of her and held out his hand. "Walk with me, please."

It wasn't a question she had to consider. She would go anywhere with Adam Redhawk.

Tess ignored the murmurs and quizzical looks thrown in their direction but threw a quick look toward Mia. Her sister's thumbs-up and big smile contrasted with her tear-stained cheeks. Mia nodded, giving her blessing as Tess headed out of the room.

They said nothing as they progressed down the hallway from the conference room, up the large, center staircase and past Estelle's desk. Adam opened the door to his office and tugged her inside, shutting it firmly behind them. He turned, his eyes dark as night and filled with enough heat to make her shiver.

"Adam." She gestured toward the conference room full of people. "I don't know what to say. What you did out there—"

"What I did was make things right," Adam said, advancing forward one measured step at a time. Tess wasn't one to run and she stood her ground, her breath quickening when they stood close enough to exchange body heat. His warm, sharp scent surrounded her and she inhaled deeply, drinking him in like a woman dying of thirst after days spent in the desert. "What I did was try to make up for the wrongs committed by Franklin against your father."

"Those are things Franklin did. They are on him and only him. They were not your mistakes to fix."

"Yes, they were." The timbre of his voice, the earnest expression in his eyes told her that he believed it, that he thought what happened was his responsibility. She'd believed the same thing for so many years, convinced that the sins of the father could be levied against the son but she'd been so wrong.

"No. No." She shook her head. "Why would you think that?"

"Because I love you." Adam lifted his hand and cupped her cheek, holding her still so that their eyes remained locked together. It was unnecessary; she would never look away from him as long as he looked at her the way he was looking at her now. "It didn't matter who was at fault. You were hurting and I could make it right. I did it because I love you."

Damn. She'd thought about him saying the words to her more times than she could count and the reality was better than anything she could have imagined.

"And what exactly did you do, Adam?" she asked, reaching out to grasp his lapel and draw him down even closer. His gaze dropped to her mouth and back up to meet her eyes, his lips twisting into a sexy slip of a smile that made her shiver in anticipation. "The foundation. My father... Franklin. What did you do to make that happen?"

"It was very simple in the end. I took copies of the information to Franklin—the file you had on his years of illegal and unethical conduct, the evidence of the mole and his payment for industrial espionage—and told him that I would give it all to the authorities, the SEC, the press, if he didn't help make it right. I made him agree to give the money for the foundation in your father's name. I'm not naive. He doesn't give a shit about the pain he caused or what I think of him, but he lives in mortal fear of losing his power, his company, his reputation. He cares about that more than he's ever cared about anyone, including me." Adam shook his head, his left hand slipping around her hip, settling in the small of her back to drag her body against his. "And I don't care about why he did it. I only cared that this would make everything you've done worthwhile. I wanted to give you and Mia peace." He leaned in, his lips brushing over her eyelids, his large hand lowering to cover her stomach. "I wanted to give us a chance to be a family. A real family."

Tess reached up, grasping his face in her hands and pulling him down to her in a kiss. It was hot and wet and deep and left them both panting and clinging to each other. Adam had given her so much. Now it was up to her to find the words to ensure that he knew how she felt, what she really wanted.

"I love you. And from now on, I will be your family."

Adam's grin was sexy and predatory and the last thing she saw before he took her mouth again in a kiss that started a little sweet but quickly morphed into a deep, dark press of lips and tongues. He groaned, his hands roaming all over her back, her face, her arms, her ass. He lifted her up, walking them both backward until he placed her on the desk. Adam settled between her legs and she moaned when his erection pressed against her core.

Suddenly, there were too many clothes between them; too much space and air and distance. Tess wanted him inside her, needing them to be one in every way that counted. She had his heart, she needed his body, his strength.

She reached for his belt, remembering at the last moment that they were exposed in his office. Anybody who walked by would see them and there were several dozen reporters in the building at this very moment. This might be the time but it wasn't the place.

Tess reluctantly broke off the kiss. "Adam, we can't." He looked confused, lust drunk, and she nodded toward the floor-to-ceiling glass walls of his office. "I don't really want to give any of the press *this* kind of story."

"Oh. Let me show you some of the upgrades I had installed in the office."

She watched as his confusion morphed into the expression of someone who ate not one, but every single canary. He lifted his left arm, tapped on his smartwatch a few times and then blinds began to descend from a hidden place in the ceiling. In less than a minute, the office was enclosed, intimately private.

Tess laughed. "I love this kind of upgrade."

Adam leaned over her, his finger tracing down from her collarbone to the cleft between her breasts. His touch was electric on her skin and she shuddered when he deftly undid the first button on her blouse and grinned his wicked grin.

"So, where were we…?"

Epilogue

Five months later.

"Justin is acting really weird."

Adam wrapped his arms around Tess and pressed a kiss against the bare skin of her shoulder. Tess smiled and leaned back into him, humming contentedly when he covered the baby bump with his hand. At five months pregnant, the morning sickness was gone, her energy was back, and none of her old clothes fit anymore. She really was glowing and her voluptuous body was even more lush and beautiful. She was the sexiest woman he'd ever seen.

Normally she was a complete and total distraction for him, but not right now. His best friend and business partner was *really* acting weird.

"Well, Justin *is* weird," Tess commented, reaching out to snag a carrot stick from the buffet table. "So, isn't that normal for him?"

"I guess so," Adam agreed but he wasn't convinced. "Sarina is acting weird too."

From their position they could view the entire party. It was a family and close friend affair for the gender reveal; an odd mix of all of the people in their lives. Among a couple of dozen other people, Mia and Estelle were there, along with Roan, Sarina and Justin.

And Justin was definitely avoiding Sarina.

And Sarina was avoiding Justin.

"What the hell is *that* all about?" Tess asked, twisting to look at him. "You don't think Justin said something to her?"

"I don't think so. They just met and even Justin can't piss somebody off that fast. It could just as easily be Sarina being her usual grumpy self." Adam watched his sister closely, and while he didn't know her well yet, he knew the difference between her usual I'm-pissed-off-at-the-world-in-general personality and when her dislike was aimed at one particular person.

And Sarina looked like she wanted to murder Justin. Slowly. Painfully.

If Justin had pissed her off, Adam would kick his ass. Sarina had initially declined to attend today but ultimately the universe had intervened and busted the motor on Sarina's Harley. Unsurprisingly, Sarina had refused his offer to pay to have the bike fixed or to buy her a new one and so she was hanging around for a few weeks and working at Redhawk/Ling to get the funds.

He shook it off, turning Tess in his arms and kissing her softly, with a hint of heat and a whole lot of promise for a private celebration later. "But I don't want to talk about them. I want to talk about whether you want a boy or a girl."

"Yes." Tess grinned, refusing to tell him her preference. It was their private joke and now he wasn't sure if he wanted to know. He knew everything he needed to know. He knew that she loved him and that she wanted to create a family together.

It was more than enough. It was more than he'd ever thought he'd have. Adam was slowly making progress with his brother and sister. The years had made them into such different people but they were all in this together, tentatively making memories and reforging bonds. Becoming a family. And now he was going to have a family of his own.

Redhawk/Ling was still riding high after the success of the app launch. The investors and employees were still celebrating the success and the money in their pockets. The Michael Roberts Research Foundation had awarded the first round of grants to promising inventors, with Tess and Mia delivering the first checks in person. They were making a difference in the world.

He had a very, very good life.

"I love you, Tess," he said, nuzzling against her throat before whispering into her ear. "And I want to spend the rest of my life with you. You and me and our baby, forever."

When he pulled back to look down at her, Tess was smiling at him, her cheeks flushed with her happiness. "I love you too. Always."

"Break it up, you two!"

They were interrupted by Mia, bringing over to them the box rigged to reveal the gender of the baby. Adam had been told that they would both tug on the ribbons sprouting from the top of the box and confetti and balloons in either pink or blue would spring into the air. Both of them had thought that the idea was silly but now that the moment was here, Adam was surprised at the rush of excitement bubbling in his belly.

He was going to be a father.

They both reached for a ribbon and Adam leaned over and took Tess's mouth in a quick, hot kiss. He winked at her and gestured toward the ribbons. "On the count of three?"

She nodded.

"One."

"Two."

"Three."

* * * * *

COMING SOON!

We really hope you enjoyed reading this book.
If you're looking for more romance, be sure to
head to the shops when new books are
available on

Thursday 10th December

To see which titles are coming soon, please visit
millsandboon.co.uk/nextmonth

LET'S TALK
Romance

For exclusive extracts, competitions
and special offers, find us online:

f facebook.com/millsandboon

🐦 @MillsandBoon

📷 @MillsandBoonUK

Get in touch on 01413 063232

For all the latest titles coming soon, visit
millsandboon.co.uk/nextmonth

MILLS & BOON

THE HEART OF ROMANCE

A ROMANCE FOR EVERY KIND OF READER

MODERN

Prepare to be swept off your feet by sophisticated, sexy and seductive heroes, in some of the world's most glamourous and romantic locations, where power and passion collide.
8 stories per month.

HISTORICAL

Escape with historical heroes from time gone by. Whether your passion is for wicked Regency Rakes, muscled Vikings or rugged Highlanders, awaken the romance of the past.
6 stories per month.

MEDICAL

Set your pulse racing with dedicated, delectable doctors in the high-pressure world of medicine, where emotions run high and passion, comfort and love are the best medicine.
6 stories per month.

True Love

Celebrate true love with tender stories of heartfelt romance, from the rush of falling in love to the joy a new baby can bring, and a focus on the emotional heart of a relationship.
8 stories per month.

Desire

Indulge in secrets and scandal, intense drama and plenty of sizzling hot action with powerful and passionate heroes who have it all: wealth, status, good looks…everything but the right woman.
6 stories per month.

HEROES

Experience all the excitement of a gripping thriller, with an intense romance at its heart. Resourceful, true-to-life women and strong, fearless men face danger and desire - a killer combination!
8 stories per month.

DARE

Sensual love stories featuring smart, sassy heroines you'd want as a best friend, and compelling intense heroes who are worthy of them.
4 stories per month.

To see which titles are coming soon, please visit

millsandboon.co.uk/nextmonth

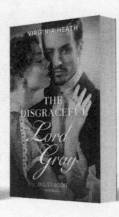

MILLS & BOON
MODERN
Power and Passion

Prepare to be swept off your feet by sophisticated, sexy and seductive heroes, in some of the world's most glamourous and romantic locations, where power and passion collide.

MILLS & BOON

HEROES

At Your Service

Experience all the excitement of a gripping thriller, with an intense romance at its heart. Resourceful, true-to-life women and strong, fearless men face danger and desire - a killer combination!

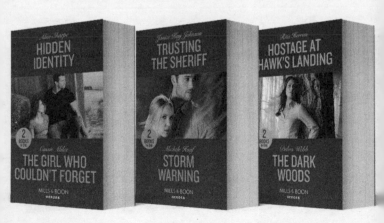

MILLS & BOON
True Love
Romance from the Heart

Celebrate true love with tender stories of heartfelt romance, from the rush of falling in love to the joy a new baby can bring, and a focus on the emotional heart of a relationship.